Why was she feeling such a strong attraction to Walker?

This wasn't usually how it worked with her and men. Most of the time she thought of them as a nuisance, not an attraction.

"You okay?"

The truck had slowed down for traffic again and she took a quick glance over at him, then wished she hadn't when she saw he was gazing at her with those gorgeous dark eyes. "Yes. Why would you think not?"

"You shivered just now."

He had to have been watching her mighty close to have known that. "Just felt a little chill."

"Then maybe I should turn up the heat."

Turn up the heat?

She was feeling hot enough already!

TEMPTING THE RANCHER

NEW YORK TIMES BESTSELLING AUTHOR

Brenda Jackson

&

Reese Ryan

Previously published as *Breaking Bailey's Rules*
and *His Until Midnight*

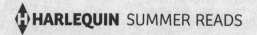

Special thanks and acknowledgment are given to Reese Ryan for her contribution to the Texas Cattleman's Club: Bachelor Auction miniseries.

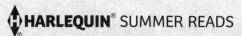

HARLEQUIN® SUMMER READS

Recycling programs for this product may not exist in your area.

ISBN-13: 978-1-335-45516-1
Tempting the Rancher
Copyright © 2021 by Harlequin Books S.A.

Breaking Bailey's Rules
First published in 2015. This edition published in 2021.
Copyright © 2015 by Brenda Streater Jackson

His Until Midnight
First published in 2018. This edition published in 2021.
Copyright © 2018 by Harlequin Books S.A.

This edition published by arrangement with Harlequin Books S.A.

For questions and comments about the quality of this book, please contact us at CustomerService@Harlequin.com.

Harlequin Enterprises ULC
22 Adelaide St. West, 40th Floor
Toronto, Ontario M5H 4E3, Canada
www.Harlequin.com

Printed in U.S.A.

CONTENTS

Brenda Jackson is a *New York Times* bestselling author of more than one hundred romance titles. Brenda lives in Jacksonville, Florida, and divides her time between family, writing and traveling. Email Brenda at authorbrendajackson@gmail.com or visit her on her website at brendajackson.net.

Books by Brenda Jackson

Harlequin Desire

The Westmoreland Legacy
The Rancher Returns
His Secret Son
An Honorable Seduction
His to Claim
Duty or Desire

Westmoreland Legacy: The Outlaws
The Wife He Needs
The Marriage He Demands

Visit the Author Profile page at
Harlequin.com for more titles.

BREAKING BAILEY'S RULES

Brenda Jackson

To the man who will always and forever be the love of my life, Gerald Jackson Sr.

Pleasant words are a honeycomb. Sweet to the soul and healing to the bones.

—*Proverbs* 16:24

Prologue

Hugh Coker closed his folder and looked up at the five pairs of eyes staring at him.

"So there you have it. I met with this private investigator, Rico Claiborne, and he's convinced that you are descendants of someone named Raphel Westmoreland. I read through his report and although his claims sound pretty far-fetched, I can't discount the photographs I've seen. Bart, every one of your sons could be a twin to one of those Westmorelands. The resemblance is that strong. I have the photographs here for you to look at."

"I don't want to see any photographs, Hugh," Bart Outlaw said gruffly, getting out of his chair. "Just because this family might look like us doesn't mean they are related to us. We are Outlaws, not Westmorelands. And I'm not buying that story about a train wreck over sixty years ago where some dying woman gave her baby to my grandmother. That's the craziest thing I've ever heard."

He turned to his four sons. "Outlaw Freight Lines is a multimillion-dollar company and people will claim a connection to us just to get what we've worked so hard to achieve."

Garth Outlaw leaned back in his chair. "Forgive me if I missed something, Dad, but didn't Hugh say the Westmorelands are pretty darn wealthy in their own right? I think all of us have heard of Blue Ridge Land Management. They are a Fortune 500 company. I don't know about the rest of you, but Thorn Westmoreland can claim me as a cousin anytime."

Bart frowned. "So what if they run a successful company and one of them is a celebrity?" he said in a cutting tone. "We don't have to go looking for any new relatives."

Maverick, the youngest of Bart's sons, chuckled. "I believe they came looking for us, Dad."

Bart's frown deepened. "Doesn't matter." He glanced at Hugh. "Send a nice letter letting them know we aren't buying their story and don't want to be bothered again. That should take care of it." Expecting his orders to be obeyed, Bart walked out of the conference room, closing the door behind him.

Sloan Outlaw stared at the closed door. "Are we going to do what he says?"

"Do we ever?" his brother Cash asked, grinning while watching Hugh put the papers back in his briefcase.

"Leave that folder, Hugh," Garth said, rubbing the back of his neck. "I think the old man forgot he's no longer running things. He retired a few months ago, or did I imagine it?"

Sloan stood. "No, you didn't imagine it. He retired but only after the board threatened to oust him. What's he's doing here anyway? Who invited him?"

"No one. It's Wednesday. He takes Charm to lunch on Wednesdays" was Maverick's response.

Garth's brow bunched. "And where is Charm? Why didn't she attend this meeting?"

"Said she had something more important to do," Sloan said of their sister.

"What?"

"Go shopping."

Cash chuckled. "Doesn't surprise me. So what are we going to do Garth? The decision is yours, not the old man's."

Garth threw a couple of paperclips on the table. "I never mentioned it, but I was mistaken for one of those Westmorelands once."

Maverick leaned across the table. "You were? When?"

"Last year, while I was in Rome. A young woman, a very beautiful young woman, called out to me. She thought I was someone named Riley Westmoreland."

"I can see why she thought that," Hugh said. "Take a look at this." He opened the folder he'd placed on the conference room table earlier and flipped through until he came to one photograph in particular. He pulled it out and placed it in the center of the table. "This is Riley Westmoreland."

"Damn," chorused around the table, before a shocked silence ensued.

"Take a look at the others. Pretty strong genes. Like

I told Bart, all of you have a twin somewhere in that family," Hugh said. "It's—"

"Weird," Cash said, shaking his head.

"Pretty damn uncanny," Sloan added. "Makes the Westmorelands' claims believable."

"So what if we are related to these Westmorelands? What's the big deal?" Maverick asked.

"None that I can see," Sloan said.

"Then, why does the old man have a problem with it?"

"Dad's just distrustful by nature," Cash answered Maverick, as he continued to stare at the photographs.

"He fathered five sons and a daughter from six different women. If you ask me, he was too damn trusting."

"Maybe he learned his lesson, considering that some of our mothers—not calling any names—turned out to be gold diggers," Sloan said, chuckling.

Hugh shook his head. It always amazed him how well Bart's offspring got along, considering they all had different mothers. Bart had managed to get full custody of each of them before their second birthdays and he'd raised them together.

Except for Charm. She hadn't shown up until the age of fifteen. Her mother was the one woman Bart hadn't married, but the only one he had truly loved.

"As your lawyer, what do you want me to do?" Hugh asked. "Send that letter like Bart suggested?"

Garth met Hugh's gaze. "No. I believe in using more diplomacy than that. I think what has Dad so suspicious is the timing, especially with Jess running for senator," he said of their brother. "And you all know how much Dad wants that to happen. His dream has been for one of us to enter politics. What if this is some sort of scheme to ruin that?"

Garth stood and stretched out the kinks from his body. "Just to be on the safe side, I'll send Walker to check out these Westmorelands. We can trust him, and he's a good judge of character."

"But will he go?" Sloan asked. "Other than visiting us here in Fairbanks, I doubt if Walker's been off his ranch in close to ten years."

Garth drew in a deep breath and said, "He'll go if I ask him."

Chapter 1

"Why are they sending their representative instead of meeting with us themselves?"

Dillon Westmoreland glanced across the room at his cousin Bailey. He'd figured she would be the one with questions. He had called a family meeting of his six brothers and eight cousins to apprise them of the phone call he'd received yesterday. The only person missing from this meeting was his youngest brother, Bane, who was on a special assignment somewhere with the navy SEALs. "I presume the reason they are sending someone outside their family is to play it safe, Bailey. In a way, I understand them doing so. They have no proof that what we're claiming is the truth."

"But why would we claim them as relatives if they

aren't?" Bailey persisted. "When our cousin James contacted you a few years ago about our relationship with them, I don't recall you questioning him."

Dillon chuckled. "Only because James didn't give me a chance to question anything. He showed up one day at our Blue Ridge office with his sons and nephews in tow and said that we were kin. I couldn't deny a thing when looking into Dare's face, which looked just like mine."

"Um, maybe we should have tried that approach." Bailey tapped a finger to her chin. "Just showed up and surprised them."

"Rico didn't think that was a good idea. From his research, it seems the Outlaws are a pretty close-knit family who don't invite outsiders into their fold," Megan Westmoreland Claiborne said. Rico, her husband, was the private investigator hired by the Westmorelands to find members of their extended family.

"And I agreed with Rico," Dillon said. "Claiming kinship is something some people don't do easily. We're dealing with relatives whose last name is Outlaw. They had no inkling of a Westmoreland connection until Rico dropped the bomb on them. If the shoe was on the other foot and someone showed up claiming they were related to me, I would be cautious, as well."

"Well, I don't like it," Bailey said, meeting the gazes of her siblings and cousins.

"We've picked up on that, Bay," Ramsey Westmoreland, her eldest brother said, pulling her ear. He then switched his gaze to Dillon. "So when is their representative coming?"

"His name is Walker Rafferty and he's arriving tomorrow. I thought that would be perfect since everyone is home for Aidan and Jillian's wedding this weekend. The Atlanta Westmorelands will be here as well, so he'll get to meet them, too."

"What does he intend to find out about us?" Bailey wanted to know.

"That you, Bane, Adrian and Aidan are no longer hellions," Stern Westmoreland said, grinning.

"Go to—" Bailey stopped and glanced at everyone staring at her. "Go wash your face, Stern."

"Stop trying to provoke her, Stern," Dillon said, shaking his head. "Rafferty probably wants to get to know us so he can report back to them that we're an okay group of people. Don't take things personally. Like I said, it's just a precaution on their part." He paused as if an idea had come to him. "And, Bailey?"

"Yes?"

"Since you're the most apprehensive about Mr. Rafferty's visit, I want you to pick him up from the airport."

"Me?"

"Yes, you. And I expect you to make a good impression. Remember, you'll be representing the entire family."

"Bailey representing the entire family? The thought of that doesn't bother you, Dil?" Canyon Westmoreland said, laughing. "We don't want to scare him off. Hell, she might go ballistic on him if he rubs her the wrong way."

"Cut it out, Canyon. Bailey knows how to handle herself and she will make a good impression," Dillon said, ignoring his family's skeptical looks. "She'll do fine."

"Thanks for the vote of confidence, Dillon."

"You got it, Bailey."

* * *

Bailey knows how to handle herself and she will make a good impression.

Dillon's words rang through Bailey's head as she rushed into the airport fifteen minutes late. And she couldn't blame her delay on traffic.

That morning she had been called into her boss's office to be told she'd been promoted to features editor. That called for a celebration and she'd rushed back to her desk to call her best friend, Josette Carter. Of course Josette had insisted they meet for lunch. And now Bailey was late doing the one thing Dillon had trusted her to do.

But she refused to accept that she was off to a bad start…even if she was. If Mr. Rafferty's plane was late it would not hurt her feelings one iota. In fact today she would consider it a blessing.

She headed toward baggage claim and paused to look at an overhead monitor. Mr. Rafferty's plane had been on time. Just her luck.

Upon reaching the luggage carousel for his plane, she glanced around. She had no idea what the man looked like. She had tried looking him up online last night and couldn't find him. Josette had suggested Bailey make a sign with his name, but Bailey had rolled her eyes at the idea. Now, considering how crowded the airport was, she acknowledged that might have been a good idea.

Bailey checked out the people retrieving their luggage. She figured the man was probably in his late forties or early fifties. The potbellied, fiftysomething-year-old man who kept glancing at his watch with an anxious expression must be her guy. She was moving in his direction when a deep husky rumble stopped her in her tracks.

"I believe you're looking for me, Miss Westmoreland."

Bailey turned and her gaze connected with a man who filled her vision. He was tall, but that wasn't the reason her brain cells had suddenly turned to mush; she was used to tall men. Her brothers and cousins were tall. It was the man's features. Too handsome for words. She quickly surmised it had to be his eyes that had made her speechless. They were so dark they appeared a midnight blue. Just staring into them made her pulse quicken to a degree that ignited shivers in her stomach.

And then there was his skin tone—a smooth mahogany. He had a firm jaw and a pair of luscious-looking lips. His hair was cut low and gave him a rugged, sexy look.

Gathering her wits, she said, "And you are?"

He held his hand out to her. "Walker Rafferty."

She accepted his handshake. It was firm, filled with authority. Those things she expected. What she didn't expect was the feeling of warmth combined with a jolt of energy that surged through her body. She quickly released his hand.

"Welcome to Denver, Mr. Rafferty."

"Thanks. Walker will do."

She tried to keep her pulse from being affected by the throaty sound of his voice. "All right, Walker. And I'm—"

"Bailey Westmoreland. I know. I recognized you from Facebook."

"Really? I looked you up but didn't find a page for you."

"You wouldn't. I'm probably one of the few who don't indulge."

She couldn't help wondering what else he didn't— or did—indulge in, but decided to keep her curiosity to herself. "If you have all your bags, we can go. I'm parked right outside the terminal."

"Just lead the way."

She did and he moved into step beside her. He was certainly not what she'd expected. And her attraction to him wasn't expected, either. She usually preferred men who were clean shaven, but there was something about Walker Rafferty's neatly trimmed beard that appealed to her.

"So you're friends with the Outlaws?" she asked as they continued walking.

"Yes. Garth Outlaw and I have been best friends for as long as I can remember. I'm told by my parents our friendship goes back to the time we were both in diapers."

"Really? And how long ago was that?"

"Close to thirty-five years ago."

She nodded. That meant he was eight years older than she was. Or seven, since she had a birthday coming up in a few months.

"You look just like your picture."

She glanced at him. "What picture?"

"The one on Facebook."

She changed it often enough to keep it current. "It's supposed to work that way," she said, leading him through the exit doors. And because she couldn't hold back her thoughts she said, "So you're here to spy on us."

He stopped walking, causing her to stop, as well. "No. I'm here to get to know you."

"Same thing."

He shook his head. "No, I don't think it is."

She frowned. "Either way, you plan to report back to the Outlaws about us? Isn't that right?"

"Yes, that's right."

Her frown deepened. "They certainly sound like a suspicious bunch."

"They are. But seeing you in person makes a believer out of me."

She lifted a brow. "Why?"

"You favor Charm, Garth's sister."

Bailey nodded. "How old is Charm?"

"Twenty-three."

"Then, you're mistaken. I'm three years older so that means she favors me." Bailey then resumed walking.

Walker Rafferty kept a tight grip on the handle of his luggage while following Bailey Westmoreland to the parking lot. She was a very attractive woman. He'd known Bailey was a beauty because of her picture. But he hadn't expected that beauty to affect him with such mind-boggling intensity. It had been a while—years— since he'd been so aware of a woman. And her scent didn't help. It had such an alluring effect.

"So do you live in Fairbanks?"

He looked at her as they continued walking. Her cocoa-colored face was perfect—all of her features, including a full pair of lips, were holding his attention. The long brown hair that hung around her shoulders made her eyes appear a dark chocolate. "No, I live on Kodiak Island. It's an hour away from Fairbanks by air."

She bunched her forehead. "Kodiak Island? Never heard of the place."

He smiled. "Most people haven't, although it's the second largest island in the United States. Anchorage and Fairbanks immediately come to mind when one thinks of Alaska. But Kodiak Island is way prettier than the two of them put together. Only thing is, we have more bears living there than people."

He could tell by her expression that she thought he was teasing. "Trust me, I'm serious," he added.

She nodded, but he had a feeling she didn't believe him. "How do people get off the island?"

"The majority of them use the ferry, but air is most convenient for me. I have a small plane."

She lifted a brow. "You do?"

"Yes." There was no need to tell her that he'd learned to fly in the marines. Or that Garth had learned right along with him. What he'd told her earlier was true. He and Garth Outlaw had been friends since their diaper days and had not only gone to school together but had also attended the University of Alaska before doing a stint in the marines. The one thing Garth hadn't done with Walker was remain with him in California after they left the military. And Garth had tried his hardest to talk Walker out of staying. Too bad he hadn't listened.

He'd been back in Alaska close to ten years now and he swore he would never leave again. Only Garth could get him off the island this close to November, his son's birthday month. Had his son lived he would be celebrating his eleventh birthday. Thinking of Connor sent a sharp pain through Walker, one he always endured this time of year.

He kept walking beside Bailey, tossing looks her way. Not only did she have striking features but she had a nice body, as well. She looked pretty damn good in her jeans, boots and short suede jacket.

Deciding to remove his focus from her, he switched it to the weather. Compared to Alaska this time of year, Denver was nice. Too damn nice. He hoped the week here didn't spoil him.

"Does it snow here often?" he asked, to keep the conversation going. It had gotten quiet. Too quiet. And he was afraid his mind would dwell on just how pretty she was.

"Yes, usually a lot this time of year but our worst days are in February. That's when practically everything shuts down. But I bet it doesn't snow here as much as in Alaska."

He chuckled. "You'd bet right. We have long, extremely cold days. You get used to being snowed in more so than not. If you're smart, you'll prepare for it because an abundance of snow is something you can count on."

"So what do you do on Kodiak Island?" she asked.

They had reached her truck. The vehicle suited her. Although she was definitely feminine, she didn't come across as the prissy type. He had a feeling Bailey Westmoreland could handle just about anything, including this powerful-looking full-size pickup. He was of the mind that there was something innately sensuous about a woman who drove a truck. Especially a woman who was strikingly sexy when she got out of it.

Knowing she was waiting for an answer to his question, he said, "I own a livestock ranch there. Hemlock Row."

"A cattle ranch?"

"No, I raise bison. They can hold their own against a bear."

"I've eaten buffalo a few times. It's good."

"Any bison from Hemlock Row is the best," he said, and didn't care if it sounded as if he was bragging. He had every right to. His family had been in the cattle business for years, but killer bears had almost made them lose everything they had. After his parents' deaths he'd refused to sell and allow Hemlock Row to become a hunting lodge or a commercial fishing farm.

"Well, you'll just have to send me some to try."

"Maybe you'll get to visit the area one day."

"Doubt it. I seldom leave Denver," she said, releasing the lock on the truck door for him.

"Why?"

"Everything I need is right here. I've visited relatives in North Carolina, Montana and Atlanta on occasion, and I've traveled to the Middle East to visit my cousin Delaney once."

"She's the one who's married to a sheikh, right?" he asked, opening the truck door.

"Jamal *was* a sheikh. Now he's king of Tehran. Evidently you've done research on the Westmorelands, so why the need to visit us?"

He held her gaze over the top of the truck. "You have a problem with me being here, Bailey?"

"Would it matter if I did?"

"Probably not, but I still want to know how you feel about it."

He watched her nibble her bottom lip as if considering what he'd said. He couldn't help studying the shape of her mouth and thinking she definitely had a luscious pair of lips.

"I guess it bothers me that the Outlaws think we'd claim them as relatives if they weren't," she said, her words breaking into his thoughts.

"You have to understand their position. To them, the story of some woman giving up her child before dying after a train wreck sounds pretty far out there."

"As far-out as it might sound, that's what happened. Besides, all it would take is a DNA test to prove whether or not we're related. That should be easy enough."

"Personally, I don't think that's the issue. I've seen photographs of your brothers and cousins and so have the Outlaws. The resemblance can't be denied. The Westmorelands and the Outlaws favor too much for you not to be kin."

"Then, what is the issue and why are you here? If the Outlaws want to acknowledge we're related but prefer not to have anything to do with us, that's fine."

Walker liked her knack for speaking what she thought. "Not all of them feel that way, Bailey. Only Bart."

"Who's Bart?" she asked, breaking eye contact with him to get into the truck.

"Bart's their father," he answered, getting into the truck, as well. "Bart's father would have been the baby that was supposedly given to his grandmother, Amelia Outlaw."

"And Amelia never told any of them the truth about what happened?" Bailey asked, snapping her seat belt around her waist. A waist he couldn't help notice was pretty small. He could probably wrap his arms around it twice.

He snapped his seat belt on, thinking the truck smelled like her. "Evidently she didn't tell anyone."

"I wonder why?"

"She wouldn't be the first person to keep an adoption a secret, if that's what actually happened. From what Rico Claiborne said, Clarice knew she was dying and gave her baby to Amelia, who had lost her husband in that same wreck. She probably wanted to put all that behind her and start fresh with her adopted son."

After she maneuvered out of the parking lot, he decided to change the subject. "So what do you do?"

She glanced over at him. "Don't you know?"

"It wasn't on Facebook."

She chuckled. "I don't put everything online. And to answer your question, I work for my sister-in-law's magazine, *Simply Irresistible*. Ever heard of it?"

"Can't say that I have. What kind of magazine is it?"

"One for today's up-and-coming woman. We have articles on health, beauty, fashion and, of course, men."

He held her gaze when the truck came to a stop. "Why 'of course' on men?"

"Because men are so interesting."

"Are we?"

"Not really. But since some women think so, we have numerous articles about your gender."

He figured she wanted him to ask what some of those articles were, but he didn't intend to get caught in that trap. Instead, he asked, "What do you do at the magazine?"

"As of today I'm a features editor. I got promoted."

"Congratulations."

"Thanks." An easy smile touched her lips, lips that were nice to look at and would probably taste just as nice.

"I find that odd," he said, deciding to stay focused on their conversation and not her lips.

The vehicle slowed due to traffic and she looked at him. "What do you find odd?"

"That your family owns a billion-dollar company yet you don't work there."

Bailey broke eye contact with Walker. Was he in probing mode? Were her answers going to be scrutinized and reported back to the Outlaws?

Walker's questions confirmed what she'd told Dillon. Those Outlaws were too paranoid for her taste. As far as she was concerned, kin or no kin, they had crossed the line by sending Walker Rafferty here.

But for now she would do as Dillon had asked and tolerate the man's presence…and his questions. "There's really nothing odd about it. There's no law that says I have to work at my family's corporation. Besides, I have rules."

"Rules?"

"Yes," she said, bringing the truck to a stop for a school bus. She looked over at him. "I'm the youngest in the family and while growing up, my brothers and cousins felt it was their God-given right to stick their noses in my business. A little too much to suit me. They only got worse the older I got. I put up with it at home and couldn't imagine being around them at the office, too."

"So you're not working at your family's company because you need space?"

"That's not the only reason," she informed him before he got any ideas about her and her family not getting along. "I'm not working at Blue Ridge Land Management because I chose a career that had nothing to do with real estate. Although I have my MBA, I also have a degree in journalism, so I work at *Simply Irresistible*."

She was getting a little annoyed that she felt the need to explain anything to him. "I'm sure you have a lot of questions about my family and I'm certain Dillon will be happy to answer them. We have nothing to hide."

"You're assuming that I think you do."

"I'm not assuming anything, Walker."

He didn't say anything while she resumed driving. Out of the corner of her eye, she saw he'd settled comfortably in the seat and was gazing out the window. "First time in Denver?" she asked.

"Yes. Nice-looking city."

"I think so." She wished he didn't smell so good. The scent of his aftershave was way too nice.

"Earlier you mentioned rules, Bailey."

"What about them?" She figured most people had some sort of rules they lived by. However, she would be the first to admit that others were probably not as strict about abiding by theirs as she was about abiding by hers. "I've discovered it's best to have rules about what I will do and not do. One of my rules is not to answer a lot of questions, no matter who's asking. I put that rule in place because of my brother Zane. He's always been too nosy when it came to me and he has the tendency to take being overprotective to another level."

"Sounds like a typical big brother."

"There's nothing typical about Zane, trust me. He just likes being a pain. Because of him, I had to adopt that rule."

"Name another rule."

"Never get serious about anyone who doesn't love Westmoreland Country as much as I do."

"Westmoreland Country?"

"It's the name the locals gave the area where my family lives. It's beautiful and I don't plan to leave. Ever."

"So in other words, the man you marry has to want to live there, too. In Westmoreland Country?"

"Yes, if such a man exists, which I doubt." Deciding to move the conversation off herself and back onto the Outlaws, she asked, "So how many Outlaws are there?"

"Their father is Bart and he was an only child. He has five sons—Garth, Jess, Cash, Sloan and Maverick—and one daughter, Charm."

"I understand they own a freight company."

"They do."

"All of them work there?"

"Yes. Bart wouldn't have it any other way. He retired last year and Garth is running things now."

"Well, you're in luck with my brother Aidan getting married this weekend. You'll see more Westmorelands than you probably counted on."

"I'm looking forward to it."

Bailey was tempted to look at him but she kept her eyes on the road. She had to add *sexy* to his list of attributes, no matter how much she preferred not to. Josette would be the first to say it was only fair to give a deserving man his just rewards. However, Bailey hated that she found him so attractive. But what woman wouldn't? Manly, handsome and sexy was a hot combination that could play havoc on any woman's brain.

"So were you born in Alaska or are you a transplant?" she asked him out of curiosity.

"I was born in Alaska on the same property I own. My grandfather arrived in Fairbanks as a military man in the late 1940s. When his time in the military ended he stayed and purchased over a hundred thousand acres for his bride, a woman who could trace her family back to Alaska when it was owned by Russia. What about your family?"

A smile touched Bailey's lips. "I know for certain I can't trace my grandmother's family back to when Alaska was owned by Russia, if that's what you're asking."

It wasn't and she knew it, but couldn't resist teasing him. It evidently amused him if the deep chuckle that rumbled from his throat was anything to go by. The sound made her nipples tingle and a shiver race through her stomach. If the sound of his chuckle could do this to her, what would his touch do?

She shook her head, forcing such thoughts from her mind. She had just met the man. Why was she feeling such a strong attraction to him? This wasn't usually how it worked with her and men. Most of the time she thought of them as a nuisance, not an attraction.

"You okay?"

The truck had slowed down for traffic again and she took a quick look over at him. She wished she hadn't when she met those gorgeous dark eyes. "Yes, why would you think I'm not?"

"You shivered just now."

He had to have been watching her mighty close to have known that. "Just a little chill."

"Then, maybe I should turn up the heat."

Turn up the heat? She immediately jumped to conclusions until he reached out toward her console and turned the knob. *Oh, he meant that heat.* Within seconds, a blast of warmth flowed through the truck's vents.

"Better?"

"Yes. Thanks," she said, barely able to think. She needed to get a grip. Deciding to go back to their conversation by answering his earlier question, she said, "As far as my family goes, we're still trying to find out everything we can about my great-grandfather Raphel. We didn't even know he had a twin brother until the Atlanta Westmorelands showed up to claim us. Then Dillon began digging into Raphel's past, which led him to Wyoming. Over the years we've put most of the puzzle pieces together, which is how we found out about the Outlaws."

Bailey was glad when she finally saw the huge marker ahead. She brought the truck to a stop and looked over at him. "Welcome to Westmoreland Country, Walker Rafferty."

Chapter 2

An hour later Walker stood at the windows in the guest bedroom he'd been given in Dillon Westmoreland's home. As far as Walker could see, there was land, land and more land. Then there were the mountains, a very large valley and a huge lake that ran through most of the property. From what he'd seen so far, Westmoreland Country was beautiful. Almost as beautiful as his spread in Kodiak. Almost, but not quite. As far as he was concerned, there was no place as breathtaking as Hemlock Row, his family home.

He'd heard the love and pride in Bailey's voice when she talked about her home. He fully understood because he felt the same way about his home. Thirteen years ago a woman had come between him and his love for Hemlock Row, but never again. Now he worked twice as hard every day on his ranch to make up for the years he'd lost. Years when he should have been there, working alongside his father instead of thinking he could fit into a world he had no business in.

But then no matter how much he wished it, he couldn't change the past. Wishing he'd never met Kalyn wouldn't do because if he hadn't met her, there never would have been Connor. And regardless of everything, especially all the lies and deceit, his son had been the one person who'd made Walker's life complete.

Bringing his thoughts back to the present, Walker moved away from the window to unpack. Earlier, he'd met Dillon and Ramsey, along with their wives, siblings and cousins. From his own research, Walker knew the Denver Westmorelands' story. It was heartbreaking yet heartwarming. They had experienced sorrows and successes. Both Dillon's and Ramsey's parents had been killed in a plane crash close to twenty years ago, leaving Dillon, who was the eldest, and Ramsey, the second eldest, to care for their thirteen siblings and cousins.

Dillon's parents had had seven sons—Dillon, Micah, Jason, Riley, Canyon, Stern and Brisbane. Ramsey's parents had eight children, of which there were five sons—Ramsey, Zane, Derringer and the twins, Aidan and Adrian—and three daughters—Megan, Gemma and Bailey. The satisfying ending to the story was that Dillon and Ramsey had somehow managed to keep all their siblings and cousins together and raise them to be respectable and law-abiding adults. Of course, that didn't mean there hadn't been any hiccups along the way. Walker's research had unveiled several. It seemed the twins—Adrian and Aidan—along with Bailey and

Bane, the youngest of the bunch, had been a handful while growing up. But they'd all made something of themselves.

There were definitely a lot of Westmorelands here in Denver, with more on the way to attend a wedding this weekend. The ones he'd met so far were friendly enough. The ease with which they'd welcomed him into their group was pretty amazing, considering they were well aware of the reason he was here. The only one who seemed bothered by his visit was Bailey.

Bailey.

Okay, he could admit he'd been attracted to her from the first. He'd seen her when she'd entered the baggage claim area, walking fast, that mass of curly brown hair slinging around her shoulders with every step she took. She'd had a determined look on her face, which had made her appear adorable. And the way the overhead lights hit her features had only highlighted what a gorgeous young woman she was.

He rubbed his hand down his face. The key word was *young.* But in this case, age didn't matter because Kalyn had taught him a lesson he would never forget when it came to women, of any age. So why had he suddenly begun feeling restless and edgy? And why was he remembering how long it had been since he'd been with a woman?

Trying to dismiss that question from his mind, Walker refocused on the reason he was here...as a favor to Garth. He would find out what his best friend needed to know and return to Kodiak. Already he'd concluded that the Westmorelands were more friendly and outgoing than their Alaskan cousins. The Outlaws tended to be on the reserved side, although Walker would be the first to say they had loosened up since Bart retired.

Walker knew Garth better than anyone else did, and although Garth wasn't as suspicious as Bart, Garth had an empire to protect. An empire that Garth's grandfather had worked hard to build and that the Outlaws had come close to losing last year because Bart had made a bad business decision.

Still, Walker had known the Outlaws long enough to know they didn't take anything at face value, which was why he was here. And so far the one thing he knew for certain was that the Westmorelands and the Outlaws were related. The physical resemblance was too astounding for them not to be. Whether or not the Westmorelands had an ulterior motive to claiming the Outlaws as relatives was yet to be seen.

Personally, he doubted it, especially after talking to Megan Westmoreland Claiborne. He'd heard the deep emotion in her voice when she'd told him of her family's quest to find as many family members as they could once they'd known Raphel Westmoreland hadn't been an only child as they'd assumed. She was certain there were even more Westmoreland relatives out there, other than the Outlaws, since they had recently discovered that Raphel and Reginald had an older brother by a different mother.

In Walker's estimation, the search initiated by the Westmorelands to find relatives had been a sincere and heartfelt effort to locate family. It had nothing to do with elbowing in on the Outlaws' wealth or sabotaging Jess's chances of becoming an Alaskan senator, as Bart assumed.

Walker moved away from the window the exact moment his cell phone rang. He frowned when he saw the caller was none other than Bart Outlaw. Why would the old man be calling him?

"Yes, Bart?"

"So what have you found out, son?"

Walker almost laughed out loud. *Son?* He shook his head. The only time Bart was extranice was when someone had something he wanted. And Walker knew Bart wanted information. Unfortunately, Bart wouldn't like what Walker had to say, since Bart hated being wrong.

"Found out about what, Bart?" Walker asked, deciding to be elusive. He definitely wouldn't tell Bart anything before talking to Garth.

He heard the grumble in Bart's voice when he said, "You know what, Walker. I'm well aware of the reason Garth sent you to Denver. I hope you've found out something to discredit them."

Walker lifted a brow. "Discredit them?"

"Yes. The last thing the Outlaws need are people popping up claiming to be relatives and accusing us of being who we aren't."

"By that you mean saying you're Westmorelands instead of Outlaws?"

"Yes. We *are* Outlaws. My grandfather was Noah Outlaw. It's his blood that's running through my veins and no other man's. I want you to remember that, Walker, and I want you to do whatever you have to do to make sure I'm right."

Walker shook his head at the absurdity of what Bart was saying. "How am I to do that, Bart?"

"Find a way and keep this between us. There's no reason to mention anything to Garth." Then he hung up.

Frowning, Walker held the cell phone in his hand for a minute. That was just like Bart. He gave an order and expected it to be followed. No questions asked. Shaking his head, Walker placed a call to Garth, who picked up on the second ring.

"Yes, Walker? How are things going?"

"Your father just called. We might have a problem."

"I heard Walker Rafferty is a looker."

Bailey lifted the coffee cup to her lips as Josette slid into the seat across from her. Sharing breakfast was something they did at least two to three times a week, their schedules permitting. Josette was a freelance auditor whose major client was the hospital where Bailey's sister Megan worked as a doctor of anesthesiology.

"I take it you saw Megan this morning," Bailey said, wishing she could refute what Josette had heard. Unfortunately, she couldn't because it was true. Walker was a looker. Sinfully so.

"Yes, I had an early appointment at the hospital this morning and ran into your sister. She was excited that the Outlaws had reached out to your family."

Bailey rolled her eyes. "Sending someone instead of coming yourself is not what I consider reaching out. One of the Outlaws should have come themselves. Sending someone else is so tacky."

"Yes, but they could have ignored the situation altogether. Some people get touchy when others claim them as family. You never know the reason behind it."

Since Bailey and Josette were pretty much regulars at McKays, the waitress slid a cup of coffee in front of Josette, who smiled up at the woman. "Thanks,

Amanda." After taking a sip, Josette turned her attention back to Bailey. "So tell me about him."

"Not much to tell. He looks okay. Seems nice enough."

"That's all you know about him, that he looks okay and seems nice enough?"

"Is there something else I should know?"

"Yes. Is he single? Married? Divorced? Have any children? What does he do for a living? Does he still live with his mother?"

Bailey smiled. "I didn't ask his marital status but can only assume he's single because he wasn't wearing a ring. As far as what he does for a living, he's a rancher. I do know that much. He raises bison."

"I take it he wasn't too talkative."

Bailey took another sip of coffee as she thought of the time she'd spent with Walker yesterday. "He was okay. We had a polite conversation."

"Polite?" Josette asked with a chuckle. "You?"

Bailey grinned. She could see why Josette found that amusing. Bailey wasn't known for being polite. "I promised Dillon I'd be on my best behavior even if it killed me." She glanced at her watch. "I've got to run. I'm meeting with the reporter taking my old job at nine."

"Okay, see you later."

After Bailey walked out of the restaurant, she couldn't help but think about Josette's questions. There was a lot Bailey didn't know about Walker.

She'd remedy that when she saw him later.

Walker was standing in front of Dillon's barn when Bailey's truck pulled up. Moments later he watched as she got out of the vehicle. Although he tried to ignore it, he felt a deep flutter in the pit of his stomach at seeing her again. Today, like yesterday, he was very much aware of how sensuous she looked. Being attracted to her shouldn't be anything he couldn't handle. So why was he having a hard time doing so?

Why had he awakened that morning looking for her at the breakfast table, assuming she lived with Dillon and his wife, since she didn't have her own place? Later, he'd found out from her brother Ramsey that Bailey floated, living with whichever of her brothers, sisters or cousins best fit her current situation. But now that most of her relatives had married, she stayed in her sister Gemma's house since Gemma and her husband, Callum, had their primary home in Australia.

He continued to watch her, somewhat surprised by his own actions. He wasn't usually the type to waste his time ogling a woman. But with Bailey it couldn't be helped. There was something about her that demanded a man's attention regardless of whether he wanted to give it or not. Her brothers and cousins would probably skin him alive if they knew just where his thoughts were going right now.

The cold weather didn't seem to bother her as she moved away from the truck without putting on her coat. Dressed in a long-sleeved shirt, a long pencil skirt that complimented her curves and a pair of black leather boots, she looked ready to walk the runway.

Squinting in the sun, he watched as she walked around the truck, checking out each tire. She flipped her hair away from her shoulders, and he imagined running his fingers through every strand before urging her body closer to his. There was no doubt in his mind he would love to sample the feel of their bodies pressed together. Then he would go for her mouth and—

"Walker? What are you doing here?"

Glad she had interrupted his thoughts, he replied, "I'm an invited guest, remember?"

She frowned as she approached him. "Invited? Not the way I remember it. But what I'm asking is why are you out here at the barn by yourself? In the cold? Where is everyone? And why didn't you say something when I got out of the truck to let me know you were over here?"

He leaned back against the barn's door. "Evening, Bailey. You sure do ask a lot of questions."

She glared at him. "Do I?"

"Yes, especially for someone who just told me yesterday that one of her rules is not answering a lot of questions, no matter who's asking. What if I told you that I happen to have that same rule?"

She lifted an angry chin. Was it his imagination or was she even prettier when she was mad? "I have a right to ask you anything I want," she said.

He shook his head. "I beg to differ. However, out of courtesy and since nothing you've asked has crossed any lines, I'll answer. The reason I'm outside by the barn is because I just returned from riding with Ramsey and Zane. They both left for home and I wasn't ready to go in just yet."

"Zane and Ramsey actually left you out here alone?"

"Yes, you sound surprised that they would. It seems there are some members of your family who trust me. I guess your brothers figure their horses and sheep are safe with me," he said, holding her gaze.

"I didn't insinuate—"

"Excuse me, but I didn't finish answering *all* your questions," he interrupted her, and had to keep from grinning when she shut her mouth tightly. That same mouth he'd envisioned kissing earlier. "The reason I didn't say anything when you got out of the truck just now was because you seemed preoccupied with checking out your tires. Is there a problem?"

"One needs air. But when I looked up from my tires you were staring at me. Why?"

She had to know he was attracted to her. What man in his right mind wouldn't be? She was beautiful, desirable—alluring. And he didn't think the attraction was one-sided. A man knew when a woman was interested.

But he didn't want her interest, nor did he want to be interested in her. He refused to tell her that the reason he hadn't said anything was because he'd been too mesmerized to do so.

"I was thinking again about how much you and Charm favor one another. You'll see for yourself when you meet her."

"*If* I meet her."

"Don't sound so doubtful. I'm sure the two of you will eventually meet."

"Don't sound so sure of that, Walker."

He liked the sound of his name from her lips. Refusing to go tit for tat with her, he changed the subject. "So how was your day at work, Bailey?"

Stubbornly, Bailey told herself he really didn't give a damn how her day went. So why was he asking? Why did she find him as annoying as he was handsome? And why, when she'd looked up to see him staring at her, had she felt something she'd never felt before?

There was something so startling about his eyes that her reaction had been physical. For a second, she'd imagined the stroke of his fingers in her hair, the whisper of his heated breath across her lips, the feel of his body pressed hard against hers.

Why was her imagination running wild? She barely knew this man. Her family barely knew him. Yet they had welcomed him to Westmoreland Country without thinking things through. At least, that was her opinion. Was her family so desperate to find more relatives that they had let their guard down? She recalled days when a stranger on their land meant an alarm went out to everyone. Back then, they'd never known when someone from social services would show up for one of their surprise visits.

Knowing Walker was waiting for her to answer, she finally said, "It went well. It was my first day as a features editor and I think I handled things okay. You might even say I did an outstanding job today."

He chuckled. "No lack of confidence on your part, I see."

"None whatsoever." It was dusk and being outside with him, standing by the barn in the shadows, seemed way too intimate for her peace of mind. But there was something she needed to know, something that had been on her mind ever since Josette had brought it up that morning.

Not being one to beat around the bush when it came to things she really wanted to know, she asked, "Are you married, Walker?"

Walker stared at her, trying to fight the feel of air being sucked from his lungs. Where the hell had that question come from? Regardless, the answer should have been easy enough to give, especially since he hadn't been truly married even when he'd thought he had been. How could there be a real marriage when one of the parties took betrayal to a whole new level?

Silence reigned. Bailey had to be wondering why he hadn't answered. He shook off the unpleasant memories. "No. I'm not married." And then he decided to add, "Nor do I have a girlfriend. Any reason you want to know?"

She shrugged those beautiful shoulders that should be wearing a coat. "No. Just curious. You aren't wearing a wedding ring."

"No, I'm not."

"But that doesn't mean anything these days."

"You're right. Wearing a wedding ring doesn't mean anything."

He could tell by her frown that she hadn't expected him to agree with her. "So you're one of those types."

"And what type is that?"

"A man who has no respect for marriage or what it stands for."

Walker couldn't force back the wave of anger that suddenly overtook him. If only she knew how wrong she was. "You don't know me. And since you don't, I suggest you keep your damn assumptions to yourself."

Then, with clenched teeth, he walked off.

Chapter 3

The next morning Bailey sat behind the huge desk in her new office and sipped a cup of her favorite coffee. Yesterday had been her move-in day and she had pretty much stayed out of the way while the maintenance crew had shifted all the electronic equipment from her old office into this one. Now everything was in order, including her new desk, on top of which sat a beautiful plant from Ramsey and Chloe.

She couldn't help thinking, *You've come a long way, baby.* And only she and her family truly knew just how far she'd come.

She'd had some rebellious years and she would be the first to admit a little revolutionary spirit still lived within her. She was better at containing it these days. But she still liked rousing her family every once in a while.

Growing up as the youngest Westmoreland had had its perks as well as its downfalls. Over the past few years, most of her family members had shifted their attention away from her and focused on their spouses and children. She adored the women and men her cousins, brothers and sisters had married. And when she was around her family she felt loved.

She thought of her cousin Riley's new baby, who had been born last year. And there were still more babies on the way. A whole new generation of Denver Westmorelands. That realization had hit her like a ton of bricks when she'd held Ramsey and Chloe's daughter in her arms. Her first niece, Susan, named after Bailey's mother.

Bailey had looked down at Susan and prayed that her niece never suffered the pain of losing both parents like Bailey had. The agony and grief were something no one should have to go through. Bailey hadn't handled the pain well. None of the Westmorelands had, but it had affected her, the twins—Adrian and Aidan—and Bane the worst because they'd been so young.

Bailey cringed when she thought of some of the things she'd done, all the filthy words that had come out of her mouth. She appreciated her family, especially Dillon and Ramsey, for not giving up on her. Dillon had even taken on the State of Colorado when social services had wanted to take her, Bane and the twins away and put them in foster care.

He had hired an attorney to fight to keep them even with all the trouble the four of them were causing around town. Because somehow he'd understood. Somehow he'd known their despicable behavior was driven by the pain of losing their parents and that deep down they weren't bad kids.

"Little hell-raisers" was what the good people of Denver used to call them. She knew it was a reputation the four of them were now trying to live down, although it wasn't always easy. Take last night, for instance.

Walker Rafferty had almost pushed her into reacting like her old self. She hated men who messed around after marriage. As far as she was concerned, the ones who messed around before marriage weren't any better but at least they didn't have a wedding ring on their finger.

Pushing away from her desk, she moved to the window. Downtown Denver was beautiful, especially today, seeing it from her new office. The buildings were tall, massive. As far as she was concerned, no other city had more magnificent skyscrapers. But even the breathtaking view couldn't make her forget Walker's callous remark.

Just like Bailey would never forget the pain and torment Josette had suffered while being married to Myles. Against their parents' wishes the two had married right out of high school, thinking love would conquer all as long as they were together. Within a year, Josette found out Myles was involved with another woman. To add insult to injury, he'd blamed Josette for his deceit, saying that it was because she'd decided to take night classes to get a college degree that she'd come home one night to find him in their bed with another woman. A woman who happened to be living in the apartment across the hall.

That was why Bailey had been so mad about Walker's insinuations that wearing a wedding ring meant nothing to a man. She'd been so angry that she'd only hung around Dillon's place long enough to hug his sons, Denver and Dade, before leaving.

It was obvious that Walker was just as mad at her as she was with him, but she didn't have a clue as to why. Yes, maybe her reaction had been a bit too strong, but seriously, she didn't give a royal damn. She called things the way she saw them. If he hadn't meant what he said, he should not have said it.

The beeping of the phone on her desk got her attention and she quickly crossed the room to answer it. It was an interoffice call from Lucia. Ramsey's wife, Chloe, was the magazine's founder and CEO but it was Chloe's best friend Lucia who ran things as editor in chief. Lucia was married to Bailey's brother Derringer. Although it was nice having her sisters-in-law as first and second in command at the magazine, it also put a lot of pressure on Bailey to prove that whatever accolades and achievements she received were earned and well deserved and not the result of favoritism. Just because Chloe and Lucia were Westmorelands, that didn't mean Bailey deserved preferential treatment of any kind. And she wouldn't have it any other way.

"Yes, Lucia?"

"Hi, Bailey. Chloe stopped by and wants to see you."

Bailey raised an arched brow. What could have brought Chloe out of Westmoreland Country so early today? It wasn't even nine in the morning yet. After marrying Ramsey, Chloe had pretty much decided to be a sheep rancher's wife and rarely came into the office these days.

Bailey slid into her jacket. "Okay. I'll be right there."

* * *

Deciding to take the longest route back to Dillon's place, Walker rode the horse and enjoyed the beauty of the countryside. There was a lot about Westmoreland Country that reminded him of Kodiak Island, minus the extremely cold weather, of course. Although the weather here was cold, it was nothing compared to the harsh winters he endured. It was the middle of October and back home the amount of snowfall was quadruple what they had here.

But the differences in the weather weren't what was bothering him today. What bothered him today had everything to do with the dreams he'd had last night. Dreams of Bailey. And that talk they'd had by the barn.

Even now the memory of their conversation made him angry. She'd had no right to assume anything about him. No right at all. She didn't know him. Had no idea the hell he'd been through or the pain he'd suffered, and was still suffering, after almost ten years. Nor did she have any idea what he'd lost.

By the lake, he slowed the horse and took a deep breath. The mountain air was cleansing; he wished it could cleanse his soul, as well. After bringing the horse to a stop he dismounted and stared at the valley below. *Awesome* was the only word he could use to describe what he saw.

And even though he was mad as hell with Bailey, a part of him thought she was pretty awesome, as well. What other way was there to describe a woman who could rile his anger and still star in his erotic dreams? He had awakened several times during the night with an erection. It had been years since that had happened. Not since he'd returned to Kodiak from California.

He had basically thrown himself into working the ranch, first out of guilt for not being there when his father had needed him, and then as a therapeutic way to deal with the loss of Connor. There were some days he'd worked from sunup to sundown. And on those nights when his body had needed a woman it had been for pleasure and nothing else. Passionate but emotionless sex had become his way of life when it came to relationships, but even that had been years ago.

Walker no longer yearned for the type of marriage his parents and grandparents had shared. He was convinced those kinds of unions didn't exist anymore. If they did, they were the exception and not the norm. He would, however, admit to noticing the ease with which the Westmoreland men openly adored their wives, wearing their hearts on their sleeves as if they were a band of honor. So, okay, Walker would include the Westmorelands in the exceptions.

He remounted the horse to head back. Thoughts of Bailey hadn't ended with his dreams. Even with the light of day, she'd invaded his thoughts. That wasn't good.

He had told Dillon he would leave the Monday after this weekend's wedding, but now he figured it would be best if he returned to Kodiak right after the wedding. The farther, and the sooner, he got away from Bailey, the better.

He'd learned enough about the Westmorelands and would tell Garth what he thought, regardless of Bart's feelings on the matter. If Bart thought he could pressure Walker to do otherwise, then he was mistaken.

Walker had nothing to lose since he'd lost it all already.

* * *

Bailey walked into Lucia's office to find her sisters-in-law chatting and enjoying cups of coffee. Not for the first time Bailey thought her brothers Ramsey and Derringer had truly lucked out when they'd married these two. Besides being beautiful, both were classy women who could be admired for their accomplishments. Real role models. The two had met at a college in Florida and had remained best friends since. The idea that they'd married brothers was remarkable, especially since the brothers were as different as day and night. Ramsey was older and had always been the responsible type. Derringer had earned a reputation as a womanizer of the third degree. Personally, Bailey had figured he would never settle down and marry. Now not only was he happily married but he was also the father of a precious little boy named Ringo. He had stepped into the role of family man as if he'd been made for it.

Chloe glanced up, saw Bailey standing in the doorway, smiled and crossed the room to give her a hug. "Bay, how are you? You rushed in and out of Dillon's place last night. We barely spoke, let alone held a conversation. How's day two in your new position?"

Bailey returned her sister-in-law's smile. "Great. I'm ready to roll my sleeves up and bring in those feature stories that will grow our readership."

Chloe beamed. "That's good to hear. I wanted to congratulate you on your promotion and let you know how proud I am of you."

"Thanks, Chloe." Bailey couldn't help but be touched by Chloe's words. She had begun working for the company as a part-timer in between her classes at the university. She had liked it so much that she'd changed her major to journalism and hadn't regretted doing so. It was Chloe, a proponent of higher education, who had encouraged her to also get her MBA.

"So what brings you out of Westmoreland Country so early?"

"I'm meeting Pam in a little while. She wants me to sit in on several interviews she's hosting today. She's hiring a director for her school."

Bailey nodded. Dillon's wife, Pam, was a former actress and had opened an acting school in her hometown of Gamble, Wyoming, a few years ago. The success of that school had led her to open a second one in Denver.

Taking her by the arm, Chloe said, "Come sit with us a minute. Share a cup of coffee and tell me how you like your office."

"I love it! Thanks to the both of you. The view is simply stunning."

"It is, isn't it?" Lucia said, smiling. "That used to be my office and I regretted giving it up. But I have to admit I have a fantastic view in here, as well."

"Yes, you certainly do," Bailey said, agreeing, glancing around the room that was double the size of her office. When her gaze landed on Lucia's computer screen, Bailey went still.

"Recognize him?" Lucia asked, adjusting the image of a face until it took up the full screen.

Bailey sucked in a deep breath as she felt the rapid thud of her pulse. Even if the clean-shaven face had thrown her for a quick second, the gorgeous eyes staring at her were a dead giveaway, not to mention that smile.

"It's Walker Rafferty," she said. He looked years

younger, yet his features, sharp and sculpted, were just as handsome.

Chloe nodded, coming to stand beside her. "Yes, that's him. At the time these photos were taken most people knew him as Ty Reklaw, an up-and-coming heartthrob in Hollywood."

Shocked, Bailey looked back at the computer screen. Walker used to be an actor? No way. The man barely said anything and seemed to keep to himself, although she knew he'd formed a pretty solid friendship with her brothers and male cousins.

What had Chloe just said? He'd been an up-and-coming heartthrob in Hollywood? Bailey studied his image. Yes, she could definitely believe that. His grin was irresistibly devastating, to the point where she felt goose bumps form on her arms.

She glanced back at Chloe and Lucia. "He's an actor?"

"He used to be, around ten years ago and he had quite a following. But then Ty Reklaw left Hollywood and never looked back," Chloe said, sitting back down in her chair.

A frown bunched Bailey's forehead. "Reklaw? As in Reklaw, Texas?"

Lucia chuckled as she poured Bailey a cup of coffee. "I doubt it. Probably Reklaw as in the name Walker spelled backward. You know how movie stars are when they don't want to use their real names."

Bailey's gaze narrowed as an idea popped into her head. "Are you sure Walker Rafferty is his real name?"

"Yes. I asked Dillon."

Bailey's brow raised. "Dillon knew who he was?"

"Only after Pam told him. She remembered Walker

from the time she was in Hollywood but she doubted he remembered her since their paths never crossed."

Bailey nodded. Yes, she could imagine any woman remembering Walker. "So he used to be an actor with a promising future. Why did he leave?"

Lucia took a sip of her coffee. "Pam said everyone assumed it was because of the death of his wife and son. They were killed in a car accident."

"Oh, my God," Bailey said. "How awful."

"Yes, and according to Pam it was quite obvious whenever he and his wife were seen together that he loved and adored her. His son had celebrated his first birthday just days before the accident occurred," Lucia said. "The loss was probably too great and he never recovered from it."

"I can understand that." Having lost both her parents in a tragic death a part of her could feel his pain. She reflected on their conversation last night when she'd asked if he was married. He'd said no and hadn't told her he was a widower.

She then remembered the rest of their conversation, the one that had left them both angry. From his comment one might have thought the sanctity of marriage didn't mean anything to him. Or had she only assumed that was what he'd meant? She shuddered at the thought.

"Bailey? Are you okay?"

She looked up at the two women staring at her. "Not sure. I might have offended Walker big-time last night."

"Why? What happened?" Lucia asked with a look that said she wished she didn't have to ask.

Bailey shrugged. "I might have jumped to conclusions about him and his attitude about marriage and said something based on my assumptions. How was I to know he'd lost his wife? I guess he said what he did because the thought of marrying again is painful for him."

"Probably since, according to Pam, he was a dedicated husband and father, even with his rising fame."

Bailey drew in a deep breath, feeling completely awful. When would she learn to stop jumping to conclusions about everything? Dillon and Ramsey had definitely warned her enough about doing that. For some reason she was quick to automatically assume the worst about people.

"Is that why you rushed in and out of Dillon and Pam's place last night? Because you and Walker had words?" Chloe asked.

"Yes. At the time I was equally mad with him. You know how I feel about men who mess around. Before marriage or after marriage."

Chloe nodded. "Yes, Bailey. I think we all know. You gave your poor brothers and cousins hell about the number of girlfriends they had."

"Well, I'm just glad they came to their senses and settled down and married." Bailey began pacing and nervously nibbled her bottom lip. Moments later she stopped and looked at the two women. "I need to apologize to him."

"Yes, you do," both Lucia and Chloe agreed simultaneously.

Bailey took a sip of her coffee as a question came to mind. "If Walker was so hot in Hollywood, then why don't I remember him?"

Lucia smiled. "If I recall, ten years ago you were too busy hanging with Bane and getting into all kinds

of trouble. So I'm not surprised you don't know who
was hot and who was not. I admit that although I remember him, he looks different now. Still handsome
but more mature and definitely a lot more rugged. The
beard he wears now makes him nearly unrecognizable.
I would not have recalled who he was if Pam hadn't
mentioned it. Of course when she did I couldn't wait
to look him up this morning."

"Was he in several movies?" Bailey asked. She intended to find any movies he'd appeared in as soon as
she left work.

"No, just two. One was a Matthew Birmingham
flick, where Walker played opposite actress Carmen
Atkins, as her brother. That was his very first. He was
hot and his acting was great," Chloe said, smiling.
"According to Pam, although he didn't get an award
nomination, there are those who thought he should
have. But what he did get was a lot of attention from
women and other directors in Hollywood. It didn't take
him long to land another role in a movie directed by
Clint Eastwood. A Western. He'd just finished film-
ing when his wife and son were killed. I don't think he
hung around for the premiere. He left for Alaska and
never returned."

Bailey didn't say anything. She was thinking about
how to get back in Walker's good graces. "I'll apologize when I see him tonight."

"Good luck," Chloe said, chuckling. "When I left
this morning, Thorn and his brothers and cousins
had arrived for the wedding and you know what that
means."

Yes, she knew. There would be a card game tonight.
Men only. And she had a feeling Walker would be in-

vited. Then she had an idea. For the past ten years Walker had lived on his ranch on that remote island. He'd indicated last night that he wasn't married and didn't have a steady girlfriend, which meant he was a loner. That made him just the type of man she needed to interview for one of the magazine's spring issues. She could see him being the feature story. She'd wait and share her idea with Chloe and Lucia until she had all the details worked out.

Bailey then recalled that Walker would be returning to Alaska on Monday after the wedding. That didn't give her much time. She looked back down at Walker's photo. Getting an exclusive interview with him would definitely mean big sales for the magazine.

She took another sip of her coffee. Now, if she could only get Walker to agree.

Chapter 4

Walker threw out a card before glancing at the closed door. How many times had he done that tonight? And why was he expecting Bailey to show up at a men-only card game? The main reason was because it was Bailey, and from what he'd heard from her brothers and cousins, Bailey did whatever Bailey wanted to do. But he'd heard more fondness than annoyance in their voices and figured they wouldn't want it any other way.

So here he was, at what had to be close to midnight, in what was known as Dillon's man cave, playing cards with a bunch of Westmorelands. He would admit that over the past three days he'd gotten to know the Denver Westmorelands pretty well, and today he'd met their cousins from Atlanta, which included those living in Montana.

Walker couldn't help but chuckle at Bart's accusation that the Westmorelands had targeted the Outlaws for monetary gain. Walker knew for a fact that wasn't true. Even if their land development company wasn't making them millions, from the talk around the table, the horse training business a few of the cousins owned was also doing extremely well.

"I hear you chuckling over there, Walker. Does that mean you have a good hand?"

He glanced over at Zane and smiled. "If I did you'd be the last person to know until it counted."

That got a laugh from the others. In a way, he was surprised at the ease he felt being around them, even those Westmorelands he'd only met that day. When he'd returned to Kodiak from his stint in Hollywood, he'd shut himself off from everyone except the Outlaws and those members of the community he'd considered family. As an only child, he wasn't used to a huge family, but he was being educated about how one operated, Westmoreland-style.

Thorn was telling everyone about the bike he'd just built for a celebrity. Walker just continued to study his hand. He could have added to the conversation, since he happened to know the man personally. But he stayed silent. That was a life he'd rather not remember.

Walker heard the knock on the door and all it took was the tingle that moved up his arm to let him know it was Bailey. The mere thought that he could want her with such intensity should have frozen him cold, especially after what she'd accused him of last night. Instead, the opposite was happening. He had dreamed of her, allowed her to invade his mind all day, and now his body was responding in a way it did whenever a man wanted a woman.

"Come in," Dillon yelled out. "And whoever you are, you better be a male."

Bailey stuck her head in the door. "Sorry to disappoint you, Dil. I decided to check and make sure all of you are still alive and in one piece. I can just imagine how much money has been lost about now," she said with a grin as she stepped into the room.

Walker was the only one who bothered to look up at her. She was gorgeous. Her hair hung like soft waves across her shoulders and her outfit, a pair of jeans and a blue pullover sweater, emphasized her curves, making her look feminine and sexy as hell.

All he could do was stare at her, and then she met his eyes. Bam! The moment their gazes connected he felt something slam into him. He was sure it had the same effect on her. It was as if they were the only two people in the room, and he was glad her family was more interested in studying their cards than studying them.

One of the things he noticed was the absence of that spark of anger in her eyes. It had definitely been there last night. Instead, he saw something else, something that had heat drumming through every inch of his body. Had frissons of fire racing up his spine. Was he imagining it?

"Go away, Bay. You'll bring me bad luck," wailed her cousin Durango, who'd flown in from Montana. He held his gaze steady on the cards in his hand.

"You're probably losing big-time anyway," she said, chuckling, breaking eye contact with Walker to look at Durango. "Another reason I'm here is to rescue Walker." Her gaze returned to Walker. "He's probably tired of your company about now, but is too nice to say so. So I'm here to rescue him."

Walker saw twelve pairs of eyes shift from their cards to him, but instead of seeing even a speck of curiosity, he saw pity as if they were thinking, *We're glad it's you and not us.* Their gazes then returned to their cards.

"We're not stupid, Bay," Zane Westmoreland said, grinning and throwing a card out. "You think you can pump Walker for information about our plans for Aidan's bachelor party. But we've told Walker the rules. What we say in this room stays in this room."

"Whatever," she said, rolling her eyes. "Well, Walker, do you want to be rescued?"

He didn't have to think twice about it, although he was wondering about her motive. "Why not," he said, sliding back his chair. "But it's not because I haven't enjoyed the company," he said, standing and placing his cards down. "It's because I refuse to lose any more money to you guys. All of you are professional gamblers whether you admit it or not."

Dillon chuckled. "Ian is the only true gambler in the family. We're just wannabes. If he was here you wouldn't be walking out with your shirt on, trust me."

Walker smiled. "Can't wait to meet him." He moved across the room toward the door where Bailey stood. "I'll see you guys in the morning."

"Not too early, though," Zane cautioned, throwing out a card. "This game will probably be an all-nighter, so chances are we'll all sleep late."

Walker nodded. "I'll remember that."

"Any reason you felt the need to rescue me?"

Bailey glanced over at Walker as they headed toward the stairs. "I thought you might want to go riding."

"Horseback riding? This time of night? In this weather?"

She chuckled. "Not horseback riding. Truck riding. And yes, this time of night or, rather, this time of morning since it's after midnight. And it's a nice night. At least nicer than most. Besides, there's something I need to say to you."

He stopped walking and held her gaze. "Didn't get all your accusations off your chest last night?"

She knew she deserved that. "I was out of line and jumped to conclusions."

He crossed his arms over his chest. "Did you?"

"Yes, and if it's okay with you I'd like to talk to you about it. But not here. So if you're up to riding, I know the perfect place where we can have a private conversation."

From his expression she could tell he was wondering what this private conversation would be about. However, instead of asking he merely nodded and said, "Okay, lead the way."

Bailey nodded, too, and then moved forward. Once they made it downstairs she grabbed her coat and waited while he got his. The house was quiet. Everyone with a lick of sense had gone to bed, which didn't say a lot for herself, Walker, her cousins and brothers. But she had been determined to hang around and talk to Walker.

When they stepped outside she saw the temperature had dropped. It was colder than she'd thought. She glanced over at him. "It won't take long for Kent to warm up."

"Kent?"

She nodded, shoving her hands into the pockets of her coat. "Yes. My truck."

He chuckled. "You gave your truck a name?"

"Yes. He and I go a long way back, so we're best buds. I take care of him and he takes care of me." She smiled. "Let me rephrase that. JoJo helps me take care of him."

"JoJo is Stern's wife, right? The mechanic?"

"Yes," Bailey said, reaching her truck. "The best in Denver. Probably the country. The wor—"

"Okay, I get the picture."

She threw her head back and laughed as she opened her truck door. She climbed inside, buckled up and waited until he did the same. "So where are we headed?" he asked.

She looked over at him. "Bailey's Bay."

Walker had heard about Bailey's Bay and had even covered parts of it yesterday while out horseback riding with Ramsey and Zane. He'd been told by Dillon that Westmoreland Country sat on over eighteen hundred acres. Since Dillon was the eldest, he had inherited the main house along with the three hundred acres it sat on. Everyone else, upon reaching the age of twenty-five, received one hundred acres to call their own. Bailey had decided to name each person's homestead and had come up with names such as Ramsey's Web, Stern's Stronghold, Zane's Hideout, Derringer's Dungeon and Megan's Meadows. She had named hers Bailey's Bay.

"I understand you haven't built on your property yet," he said, looking out the window. Because of the darkness, there wasn't much to see.

"That's right. There's no need. I have too many cousins and siblings with guest rooms at their homes. And then there's Gemma's house that sits empty most of the time since she's living in Australia."

He didn't say anything but figured shifting from guest room to guest room and from house to house would get old. "You do plan to build one day though, right?"

"Yes, eventually. Right now Ramsey uses a lot of my land for sheep grazing, but that won't stop me when I'm ready. I know exactly where I intend to sit my home, and it's far away from the grazing land."

"I bet your place will be a beauty whenever you decide to build." He had seen all the other homes. Each one was breathtaking and said a lot about the owners' personalities. He wondered what design Bailey would choose. Single story that spread out with several wings? Or a two-story mansion erected like a magnificent piece of art? Either one would be a lot of house for one person. But then didn't the same hold true for the house he lived in? All that land and all that house.

"Yes. I plan to make it a masterpiece."

He didn't doubt that and could even visualize the home she would probably build for herself.

"Bailey's Bay was chosen for me and sits next to Zane's and between Ramsey and Dillon's properties." She chuckled. "That was a deliberate move on my brothers' and cousins' parts since they figured Zane would stay in my business, and Dillon and Ramsey were the only two people I would listen to."

"Are they?"

"Pretty much, but sometimes I won't listen to anyone."

He couldn't help but smile. Bailey was definitely a rebel. That was probably some of her appeal. That, along with her sensuality. He doubted she knew just how sensual she was. It would be any man's downfall when she did realize it.

They didn't say anything for a while, until she brought the truck to a stop. "Here we are."

Thanks to the full moon and the stars overhead he could make out the lake. It stretched wide and endless and the waters were calm. From riding out here with Zane and Ramsey he knew the lake ran through most of the Westmoreland land. "Gemma Lake, right?"

"Yes. Raphel named it after my great-grandmother. I never knew them, or my grandparents for that matter. They died before I was born. But I heard they were great people and they left a wonderful legacy for us to be proud of."

Walker thought about the legacy his own parents, grandparents and great-grandparents had left and how he'd almost turned his back on that legacy to go after what hadn't been his dream but had been Kalyn's dream. Never again would he allow any woman to have that much power over him.

So why was he here? He had been in a card game and Bailey had showed up, suggesting they leave, and he had. Why? Was he once again allowing a woman to make decisions for him?

Walker glanced over at her. She stared straight ahead and he wondered what she was thinking. He looked back at the lake. It was peaceful. He liked being here with Bailey, parked, sharing this moment with her.

He was well aware they were attracted to each other, although neither of them had acted on it. But the desire was there nonetheless. Whenever they were alone there was always some sort of sexual aura surrounding them. Like now.

Even when there were others around he was aware of her. Like that first night when everyone had shown up at Dillon's for dinner. Walker had kept looking across the table at her, liking the sexy sound of her laugh. He had to be honest with himself—he had deliberately waited for her last night, outside by the barn, knowing she would eventually drop by Dillon's house since Zane had mentioned she did it every day.

The effect she was having on him bothered him, which was why he'd changed his plans so he could leave Saturday evening after the wedding instead of on Monday. The last thing he needed was to get involved with Bailey Westmoreland. He would never marry again, and all he could ever offer her was an affair that led nowhere. That wouldn't be good for her and could affect the friendships he'd made with her family.

He glanced over at her. "You said you wanted to talk," he prompted. The sooner they finished the sooner they could leave. Being out here alone with her could lead to trouble.

She looked over at him. He could barely see her features in the moonlight but he didn't need a bright light to know she was beautiful. She had rolled down the window a little and the cold air coming in enhanced her scent. It was filling his nostrils with the most luscious aroma.

But her looks and her scent weren't the issue; nor should they be. He had to remember he deserved better than a woman who could be another Kalyn.

"About last night."

That got his attention. "What about it?"

"I owe you an apology."

"Do you?"

"Yes. I made accusations that I should not have."

Yes, she had, but he couldn't help wondering what had made her realize that fact. "What makes you so sure?"

She frowned. "Are you saying that I was right?"

"No, that's not what I'm saying. You need to do something about being quick to jump to conclusions."

She waited a second, tapping her fingers on the steering wheel before saying, "I know. My family warns me about it all the time."

He touched her shoulder for emphasis. "Then, maybe you should listen to them."

He suddenly realized touching her had been a mistake. With her layered clothing he was far from coming into contact with bare skin, but he could still feel sensuous heat swelling his fingertips.

"I try to listen."

The catch in her voice sent a ripple of desire through him. He shifted in his seat when a thrumming dose of heat ripped through his gut. "Maybe you should try harder, Bailey."

What made Walker so different from any other man? His touch on her shoulder affected her in a way no man's touch had ever affected her before. How did he have the ability to reach her inner being and remind her that she was a woman?

Personal relationships weren't her forte. Most of the guys in these parts were too afraid of her brothers and cousins to even think of crossing the line, so she'd only had one lover. For her it had been one and done, and executed more out of curiosity than anything else. She certainly hadn't been driven by the kind of sexual desire she was feeling with Walker.

There was a spike of heat that always rolled in her stomach whenever she was around him, not to mention the warmth that settled in the area between her legs. Even now, just being in the same vehicle with him was making her breasts tingle. Had his face inched a little closer to hers?

Suggesting they go for a late-night ride might not have been a good idea after all. "I'm not perfect," she finally said softly.

"No one is perfect," he responded huskily.

Bailey drew in a sharp breath when he rubbed a finger across her cheek. She fought back the slow moan that threatened to slip past her lips. His hand on her shoulder had caused internal havoc; his fingers on her face were stirring something to life inside her that she'd never felt before.

She needed to bring an end to this madness. The last thing she wanted was for him to misunderstand the reason she'd brought him here. "I didn't bring you out here for this, Walker," she said. "I don't want you getting the wrong idea."

"Okay, what's the right idea?" he asked, leaning in even closer. "Why did you bring me out here?"

Nervously, she licked her lips. He was still rubbing a finger across her cheek. "To apologize."

"Apology accepted." Then he lowered his head and took possession of her mouth.

Chapter 5

Walker deepened the kiss, even while trying to convince himself that he should not be kissing Bailey. No way should his tongue be tangling with hers or hers with his.

But she tasted so damn good. And he didn't want to stop. Truth be told, he'd been anxiously waiting for this minute. He would even admit he'd waited ever since that day at the airport when he'd first thought her lips were a luscious pair. A pair he wanted to taste. Now he was getting his chance.

Her tongue was driving him insane. Her taste was hot, simply addictive. She created a wildness within him, unleashing a sexual beast that wanted to consume every bone-melting inch of her. When had he kissed any woman so thoroughly, with such unapologetic rawness?

He tangled his fingers in her hair, holding her mouth captive as his mouth and tongue sucked, licked and teased every delicious inch of her mouth. This kiss was so incredibly pleasurable his testicles ached. If he didn't end things now, this kiss could very well penetrate his very soul.

He reluctantly broke off the kiss, but made sure his mouth didn't stray far. He could feel the sweet, moist heat of her breath on his lips and he liked it. He liked it so much that he gave in to temptation and used his tongue to trace a path along her lips. Moments later that same tongue tracked a line down her neck and collarbone before returning to her mouth.

She slowly opened her eyes and looked at him. He knew he shouldn't be thinking it, but at that moment he wished the truck had a backseat. All the things he would do to her filled his mind.

"That was some acceptance," she whispered hotly against his lips.

He leaned forward and nibbled around her chin. "Acceptance of what?"

"My apology. Maybe I should apologize more often."

He chuckled lightly, leaning back to meet her gaze. "Do you often do or say things that require an apology?"

"So I'm told. I'm known to put my foot in my mouth more often than not. But do you know what?"

"What?"

"I definitely like your tongue in my mouth a lot better, Walker."

Walker drew in a ragged breath. He was learning there was no telling what would come out of that luscious mouth of hers. "No problem. That can be arranged."

He leaned in and kissed her again; this time was more intense than the last. He figured he needed the memory of this kiss to take back to Kodiak for those long cold nights, when he would sit in front of the fireplace alone and nurse a bottle of beer.

She was shivering in his arms and he knew it had nothing to do with the temperature. She was returning his kiss in a way that ignited every cell in his body, and tasted just as incredibly sexy as she looked. Never had he sampled a woman whose flavor fired his blood to a degree where he actually felt heat rushing through his veins.

He could do a number on her mouth forever, and would have attempted to do so if he hadn't felt her fingers fumbling with the buttons on his shirt. He needed to end this now or else he would be a goner. There was only so much he could take when it came to Bailey.

Walker broke off the kiss, resting his forehead against hers. The needs filtering through him were as raw as raw could get. Primitive. It had been years since a woman had filled him with such need. He was like a starving man who was only hungry for her.

"I didn't bring you out here for this, Walker."

Her words had come out choppy but he understood them. "You said that already." He kept his forehead plastered to hers. There was something so alluring about having his mouth this close to hers. At any time he could use his tongue to swipe a taste of her.

"I'm saying it again. I only wanted to park and talk."

He chuckled against her lips. "That's all?"

Now it was her turn to chuckle. "You are so typically male. Ready to get laid, any time or any place."

"Um, not really. I have very discriminating taste. And speaking of taste," he said, leaning back slightly so he could look into her eyes, "I definitely like yours."

Bailey nervously licked her lips. What was a woman supposed to say to a line like that? In all honestly, there was nothing she could say, especially while gazing into the depths of Walker's dark eyes. He held her gaze hostage and there was nothing she could do about it. Mainly because there was nothing she wanted to do about it. His eyes had her mesmerized, drawing her under his spell.

The same thing had happened earlier when she'd watched his two movies back-to-back. What Chloe had said was true. His performances in both roles had been award-worthy material. Sitting there, watching him on her television screen, was like watching a totally different person. She could see how he'd become a heartthrob in a short period of time. His sexiness had been evident in his clothes, his voice and the roles he'd chosen. And those lovemaking scenes had blazed off the charts. They'd left her wishing she had been the woman in those scenes with him. And tonight, as unbelievable as it seemed, she had lived her own memorable scene with him.

She had to remember the reason she had brought him here. Apologizing for last night was only part of it. "There's something else I need to talk to you about, Walker."

He tipped his head back. "Is there?"

"Yes."

"Can I kiss you again first?" he asked, rubbing his thumb over her bottom lip.

Bailey knew she should say no. Another kiss from him was the last thing she needed. She feared it would detonate her brain. But her brain was halfway gone already, just from the sensuality she heard in his voice. His thumb gently stroking her lip stirred a need that primed her for something she couldn't define but wanted anyway.

He was staring at her, waiting for an answer. She could feel the effects of his spellbinding gaze all over her body. Suddenly she felt bold, empowered, filled with a burning need. Instead of answering him, she pushed in the center console, converting the truck from bucket seats to bench seats. Easing closer to him, she wrapped her arms around his neck and tilted her mouth up to his. "Yes, Walker. You can kiss me again."

And as if that was all he needed to hear, he swooped down and sucked her tongue into his mouth. Bailey couldn't help but moan. He was consuming her. She sensed a degree of hunger within him she hadn't recognized in the other kisses. It was as if he was laying claim to her mouth, branding it in a way no other man had or ever would, and all while his knuckles softly stroked her jaw.

She kissed him back with the same greediness. No matter what costar she'd watched him with earlier, he was with her now. This was real, no acting involved. The only director they were following was their own desire, which seemed to be overtaking them.

Walker's hand reached under her sweater to caress her stomach, and she moaned at the contact. The feel of his fingers on her bare flesh made her shiver, and when he continued to softly rub her skin she closed her eyes as awareness spiked fully into her blood.

The moment he released her mouth, she leaned closer and used her tongue to lick the corners of his lips. His hand inched upward, stroking her ribs, tracing the contours of her bones until he reached her breasts. She drew in a deep breath when his fingertips drew circles on the lace bra covering her nipples. The twin buds hardened and sent a signal to the juncture of her thighs. When he pushed her sweater out of the way, her body automatically arched toward him.

As if he knew what she wanted, what she needed, he undid the front clasp of her bra. As soon as her breasts sprang free, he lowered his mouth to them. Her nipples were hard and ready for him and he devoured them with a greediness that had her moaning deep in her throat.

When she felt the truck's leather touch her back, she realized he had lowered her onto her back. She ran her hands over his shirt and began undoing the buttons, needing to touch his bare skin like he was touching hers. Moments later, her fingers speared into the hair covering his chest.

She heard him growl her name seconds before he captured her wrists, holding her captive while his tongue swirled languorously over her stomach. Her skin sizzled everywhere his mouth touched. And when his mouth reached her navel, he laved it with his tongue. Her stomach muscles flexed beneath his mouth.

Walker was convinced Bailey's body was calling out to him. He was determined to answer the call. She tasted wonderful and when she rocked her body beneath his mouth he couldn't help but groan. His control was eroding. He'd thought all he wanted was a kiss to remember, but he discovered he wanted something more. He wanted her. All of her. He wanted to explode in the heat she was generating. But first, he wanted to fill her with the rapturous satisfaction she needed.

Raising his head, he met her gaze. The fire in her eyes almost burned him. "Lift up your hips, Bailey," he whispered.

When she did as he requested, he unsnapped her jeans and worked the denim down past her thighs. He then grazed his fingers against the scrap of lace covering her femininity. He inhaled deeply, drawing her luscious scent through his nostrils. His heart pounded hard in his chest and every cell in his body needed to please her. To give her a reason to remember him. Why that was important, he wasn't sure. All he knew was that it was.

His erection jerked greedily in anticipation of her feminine taste. When he lowered his head and eased his tongue inside her, he forced himself not to climax just from the delicious flavor of her. She pushed against his shoulders and then, seconds later, gripped him hard, holding his mouth right there as she moaned his name. He delved deep inside, stroking her, lapping up her taste with every inch of his tongue.

She lifted her hips to his mouth and he gripped her thighs tightly, devouring her in a way he'd dreamed of doing every night since he'd met her. Her scent and her taste filled him with emotions and sensations he hadn't felt in years.

He felt her body jerk beneath his mouth in an explosive orgasm. She screamed his name, but he kept his mouth crushed to her, sucking harder and hoping this was one intimate kiss she would never, ever forget.

Moments later, after he felt her body go still, except for the shuddering of her breath, he slowly withdrew his tongue—but not before brushing his lips over her womanly mound. Marking. Branding. Imprinting.

"Walker…"

"Yes, baby. I'm here." He eased over her body and kissed her.

Bailey's breath caught in her throat. When Walker finally released her mouth, she could only lie there enmeshed in a web of sensations that had left her weak but totally fulfilled. Never in her life had she experienced anything like what Walker had done. How he had made her feel. The pleasure had been so sharp she might never recover. He had taken her to rapturous heights she hadn't known existed between a man and a woman.

"I think we better go," Walker said softly as he rezipped her jeans, placing a kiss on her stomach. When she felt the tip of his tongue around her belly button, she whispered his name.

He took his time refastening her bra, cupping her breasts and licking her nipples before doing so. Then he pulled her sweater down before helping her into a sitting position. She was tempted to resist. She wanted to lie there while memories washed over her.

"Your breasts are beautiful, you know, Bailey."

She shook her head. No, she didn't know. No other man had ever complimented her breasts. But then, no other man would have had a reason to do so. She drew in a deep breath, rested her head against the seat and closed her eyes. Had she actually experienced an orgasm from a man going down on her? In a parked truck?

"The lake is beautiful tonight."

How could he talk about how beautiful the lake was after driving her into a sexual frenzy and blowing her mind? And just think, he hadn't even made love to her. What he'd given her was an appetizer. She could only imagine what the full course meal would be like.

She slowly opened her eyes and followed his gaze through the windshield to the lake. She knew he was giving her time to pull herself together, clear her head, finish straightening up her clothes. She took another deep breath. In her mind she could still feel his mouth on her breasts and between her thighs. It took her a while to respond to what he'd said. "Yes, it's beautiful. I love coming here. Day or night. Whenever I need to think."

"I can see this being a good thinking spot."

She decided not to add that he'd just proved it was a good making-out spot, as well. She glanced over at him and saw the buttons of his shirt were still undone, reminding her of when her tongue had licked his skin. Her blood seared at the memory.

"What we did tonight was wrong, Bailey. But I don't regret it."

She didn't regret it, either. The only thing she regretted was not taking things further. They were adults, not kids. Consenting adults. And if they had enjoyed it, then what was the problem? "And why was it wrong?"

"Because you deserve more than a meaningless affair and that's all I can offer you."

She didn't recall asking for more. "What makes you

think I want any more than that, Walker? I'm not into serious relationships, either. They can get messy."

He lifted a brow. "How so?"

"Men have a tendency to get possessive, territorial. Act crazy sometimes. Trust me, I know. I grew up with twelve of them. That's why I have my rules."

"Bailey's Rules, right?"

"Yep. Those are the ones."

"So if you don't do affairs, what do you do? I assume you date."

"When it suits me." No need to tell him she'd never had a steady boyfriend. "I assume you date, too."

"Yes, when it suits me," he said, repeating her words.

"So we understand each other," she said, wondering if they really did.

"Yes, I guess you can say that," he said, buttoning his shirt. "And now is as good a time as any to mention that I've decided to return to Kodiak right after the wedding on Saturday instead of on Monday as planned."

Her jaw dropped in surprise. "You're leaving Saturday?"

"Yes."

"Why?"

He looked over at her. "There's no need to stay here any longer than that. What I have to tell the Outlaws won't change. Your family is good people, and it will be Garth and his brothers' loss if they listen to Bart and decide not to meet all of you."

She didn't say anything while she considered her plans for him to be interviewed by one of her writers. "I need you to stay until Monday…at least."

He glanced over at her with keen, probing eyes. "Why do you need me to stay until Monday?"

Something cautioned her to choose her words carefully. "Remember earlier, I told you there was something else I needed to discuss with you?"

He nodded. "Yes, I remember."

"Well, it was about a favor I need to ask."

"What kind of favor?"

She nervously nibbled at her bottom lip. "Today I found out that you used to be an actor. Ty Reklaw."

He didn't say anything for a minute. "So what of it? And what does that have to do with me staying until Monday?"

She heard a tinge of annoyance in his voice and had a feeling he didn't like being reminded of his past. "I understand you were at the peak of your acting career when you left Hollywood to return to Alaska. I was sorry to hear about you losing your family. Must have been a difficult time for you."

She paused and when he didn't say anything, she pressed on. "It's been almost ten years and you're still alone, living on your island. It just so happens that *Simply Irresistible* will be doing an article about men who are loners and I would love to make you our feature story."

He still didn't say anything. He merely stared at her. She swallowed deeply, hesitating only a second before asking, "So will you do it? Will you let me schedule an interview for you with one of my writers to be our feature story?"

It was then, there in the moonlight, that she saw the stiffening of his jaw and the rage smoldering in his gaze. "No. And you have a lot of damn nerve. Is that what this little truck ride was about, Bailey? How far did you intend to go to get me to say yes?"

Her gaze narrowed. "What are you asking? Are you insinuating I used my body to get my way?"

"Why not? I've been approached in the past by reporters who will do just about anything for a story."

"Well, I'm not one of them. The main reason I asked you here was to apologize for my behavior last night. Then I wanted to ask a favor of you."

"And why do you think I would want to be interviewed? I left Hollywood for a reason and I've never looked back. Why would I want to relive those years?"

"You have it all wrong. The article we plan to publish will have nothing to do with your time in Hollywood. You're a loner and we want to find out why some men prefer that kind of life."

"Have you ever considered the fact that not everyone needs to constantly be around people? It's not as if I'm some damn recluse. I have friends. Real friends. Friends who know how to respect my privacy when I need them to. And they are the ones whose company I seek."

"Yes, however—"

"But you wouldn't understand that. You're dependent on your family for your livelihood, your happiness and your very reason for breathing. That's probably why you've made it one of your rules never to stray too far away from them."

His words fired her up. "And is there anything wrong with that?"

"Not if that's how you choose to live. Which is nobody's business. Just like how I choose to live is nobody's business, either. What makes you think I want to broadcast how I chose to live after losing two of the most important people in my life?"

He wasn't letting her get a word in. "If you just let me finish, I can explain wh—"

"There's nothing to explain. You just got this promotion to features editor and you need a story. Sorry, I refuse to accommodate you. Go find your story someplace else."

An hour or so later, Walker was back in his guest room and still finding it hard to accept the ease with which Bailey had asked that favor of him. Did she not realize the magnitude of the favor she'd asked or did she not care? Was she so into her family that she had no understanding or concept that some people preferred solitude? That not everyone wanted a crowd?

He could only shake his head, since he doubted he could get any angrier than he was at that minute. And he had just warned himself not to let her or any woman who'd shown the same persuasive powers Kalyn had possessed to get close to him. Yet he'd fallen under Bailey's spell after that first kiss. After the second, he'd been a goner.

Even now, memories of those kisses were embedded into the core of his soul. The mere idea of another woman getting that much under his skin stopped him cold with a helplessness he felt in every bone of his body.

He let out a slow, controlled breath. In less than a week he'd allowed Bailey to penetrate an area of his mind he'd thought dead forever. And earlier tonight when he'd reached across the seat and dragged her body against his, it hadn't mattered that they were both fully clothed. Just the idea of her being in his arms had brought out his primitive animal instincts. He'd wanted to mate with her. How he'd found the strength to deny what they'd both wanted was beyond his ability to comprehend, but he had. And for that he was grateful. There was no telling how far she would have gone to get her story. She might have had him eating out of her hands while he spilled his guts.

A part of him wanted to think she was just a woman, easy to forget. But he knew she wasn't just any woman. She wasn't the only person with rules, and somehow Bailey had breached all the rules he'd put in place. At the top of his list was not letting another woman get to him.

Whether it was her making him smile or her making him frown, or her filling him with the degree of anger like he was feeling now—she made him feel too much.

He heard the sound of doors opening and closing downstairs and figured the card game had run its course. Pretty much like he'd run his.

It would be to his advantage to remain true to what he knew. Bailey called it being a loner, but he saw it as surviving.

Bailey glanced at her watch as she got out of her truck once she'd reached Ramsey's Web. Most of her day had been filled with meetings, getting to know her new staff as they got to know her management style. It was important for them to know they were a team.

However, no matter how busy she'd stayed today, thoughts of Walker had filled her mind. He was furious with her, angrier than he'd been two nights ago. Was his anger justified? Had she crossed the line in asking him to do that piece for the magazine?

She was still upset about his insinuation that she would go as far as to use her body to get what she wanted. She didn't play those kinds of games, and for him to assume she did didn't sit well with her. So the way she saw it, they'd both been out of line. They'd both said things they probably regretted today. But she had to remember that Walker was a guest of her family, and the last thing she wanted to be was guilty of offending him. Dillon had placed a lot of confidence in her, and her family would never forgive her if she had offended Walker.

She needed to talk to someone about it before she saw Walker today, and the two people she could always go to for advice were Dillon and Ramsey. There was a chance she would run into Walker at Dillon's place, so she thought it best to seek out Ramsey and ask how she could fix things with Walker before the situation got too out of hand.

She found her eldest brother in his six-car garage with his head stuck under the hood of his Jeep. She loved Ramsey's Web and during her brother's before-Chloe days, she'd spent time here getting deliberately underfoot, knowing he wouldn't have it any other way. The two years when Ramsey had lived in Australia had been hard for her.

The sound of her footsteps must have alerted him to her presence. He lifted his head and smiled at her. "Bay? How are things going?"

"Fine. I would give you a hug but I don't want grease all over me. Why are you changing your oil instead of letting JoJo do it?"

Ramsey chuckled as he wiped his hands. "Because there are some things I'd rather do myself, especially to this baby here. She's been with me since the beginning."

Bailey nodded. She knew the Jeep had been Ramsey's first car and the last gift he'd gotten from their parents. It had been a birthday gift while he'd been in college. "You still keep it looking good."

"Always." He leaned back against the Jeep and studied her curiously. "So what's going on with you, Bailey Joleen Westmoreland?"

This was her eldest brother and he'd always had the ability to read her when others couldn't. "It's Walker."

He lifted a brow. "What about Walker?"

She glanced down at her pointed-toe boots a second before meeting Ramsey's gaze. "I think I might have offended him."

Ramsey crossed his arms over his chest, and she could tell from his expression that he didn't like the sound of that. "How?"

"It's a long story."

"Start from the beginning. I have time."

So she did, not rushing through most of the story and deliberately leaving out some parts. Such as how she'd found Walker utterly attractive from the first, how they'd both tried to ignore the sexual chemistry between them and how they'd made out in her truck last night.

"Well, there you have it, Ram. I apologized to him last night about my wrong assumptions about his feelings on marriage, but I made him mad again when I asked him to do the interview."

Ramsey shook his head. "Let me get this straight.

You found out he used to be a movie star who left Hollywood after the deaths of his wife and child, yet you wanted to interview him about being a loner since that time?"

Ramsey sounded as if he couldn't believe she'd done such a thing. "But that wasn't going to be the angle to the story," she argued. "*Simply Irresistible* isn't a tabloid. I'm not looking for details of his life in Hollywood. Women are curious about men who hang back from the crowd. Not everyone is interested in a life-of-the-party type of male. Women see loners as mysterious and want to know more about them. I thought Walker would be perfect since he's lived by himself for ten years on that ranch in Alaska. I figured he could shed some light on what it's like to be a loner."

"Think about what you were asking him to do, Bay. You were asking to invade his space, pry into his life and make public what he probably prefers to keep private. I bet if you had run your idea by Chloe or Lucia, they would have talked you out of it. Your plan was kind of insensitive, don't you think?"

With Ramsey presenting it that way she guessed it was. She honestly hadn't thought about it that way. She had seen an opportunity and jumped without thinking. "But I would have made the Hollywood part of his life off-limits. It was the loner aspect I wanted to concentrate on. I tried to explain that to him."

"And how were you planning to separate the two? Our pasts shape us into the people we are today. Look at you. Like him, you suffered a double loss. A quadruple one, to be exact. And look how you reacted. Would you want someone to show up and ask to interview you about that? How can you define the Bailey you are today without remembering the old you, and what it took to make you grow from one into the other?"

His question had her thinking.

"And I think you missed the mark on something," he added.

She lifted a brow. "What?"

"Assuming being a loner means being antisocial. You can be a loner and still be close to others. Everybody needs some *me* time. Some people need it more so than others. Case in point, I was a loner before Chloe. Even when I had all of you here with me in Westmoreland Country, I kept to myself. At night, when I came here alone, I didn't need anyone invading my space."

She nodded, realizing something. "But I often invaded it, Ram."

"Yes, you did."

Bailey wondered, for the first time, if he had minded. As if reading her thoughts, he said, "No, Bay. Your impromptu visits never bothered me. All I want you to see is that not everyone needs a crowd. Some people can be their own company, and it's okay."

That was practically what Walker had said. In fact, he had gone even further by saying she was dependent on a crowd. Namely, her large family.

"Looks as if I need to apologize to Walker again. If I keep it up, he's going to think 'I'm sorry' is my middle name. Guess I'll go find him."

"That's going to be pretty difficult."

Her brow furrowed. "Why?"

"Because Walker isn't here. He's left."

"Left?"

"Yes, left. He's on his way back to Alaska. Zane took him to the airport around noon."

"B-but he had planned to stay for the wedding. He hadn't met everyone since some of the cousins won't be coming in until tomorrow."

"Couldn't be helped. He claimed something came up on his ranch that he had to take care of."

What Ramsey didn't say, but what she figured he was thinking, was that Walker's departure had nothing to do with his ranch and everything to do with her. "Fine. He left. But I'm going to apologize to him anyway."

"Um, I probably wouldn't ask Dillon for Walker's phone number if I were you, especially not if you tell him the same story you just told me."

Bailey nibbled her bottom lip. How was she going to get out of the mess she'd gotten herself into?

Chapter 6

"So tell me again why you cut the trip short."

Walker glared across the kitchen at his best friend, who had made himself at home, sitting at Walker's table and greedily devouring a bowl of cereal.

"Why? I've told you once already. The Westmorelands are legit. I didn't have to prolong the visit. Like I said, no matter what Bart believes, I think you and your brothers should take them seriously. They're good people."

Walker turned to the sink with the pretense of rinsing out his coffee cup. What he'd told Garth about the Westmorelands being good people was true—up to a point. As far as he was concerned, the jury was still out on Bailey.

Bailey.

There was no way Walker could have hung around

another day and breathed the same air that she did. He clenched his jaw at the thought that he had allowed her to get under his skin. She was just the type who could get embedded in a man's soul if he was weak enough to let it happen.

On top of everything else, she was as gutsy as the day was long. She'd definitely had a lot of nerve asking him to do that interview. She was used to getting what she wanted, but he wasn't one of her brothers or cousins. He had no reason to give in to her every wish.

"You actually played cards with Thorn Westmoreland?" Garth asked with what sounded like awe.

"Yes," Walker said over his shoulder. "He told us about the bike he's building for some celebrity."

"Really? Did you mention that you used to be an actor and that you know a lot of those folks in Hollywood?"

"No."

"Why not?"

Walker turned around. "I was there to get to know them, not the other way around, Garth. They didn't need to know anything about me other than that I was a friend to the Outlaws who came in good faith to get to know them."

But that hadn't stopped them from finding out about his past anyway. He wasn't sure who all knew, since the only person who'd mentioned anything about his days in Hollywood was Bailey. If the others knew, they'd been considerate enough to respect his privacy. That had been too much to expect of Bailey. All she'd seen was an opportunity to sell magazines.

"I think I'll take your advice and suggest to the others that we pay those Westmorelands a visit. In fact, I'm looking forward to it."

"You won't be disappointed," Walker said, opening the dishwasher to place his cup inside. "How are you going to handle Bart? Do you have any idea why he's so dead set against any of you establishing relationships with your new cousins?"

"No, but it doesn't matter. He'll have to get over it." Garth glanced at his watch. "I hate to run but I have a meeting back in Fairbanks in three hours. That will give Regan just enough time to fly me out of here and get me back to the office."

Regan Fairchild had been Garth's personal pilot for the past two years. She'd taken her father's place as the corporate pilot for the Outlaws after he retired. "I'll see you out."

When they passed through the living room, Garth glanced over at Walker. "When you want to tell me the real reason you left Denver early, let me know. Don't forget I can read you like a book, Walker."

Walker didn't want to hear that. "Don't waste your time. Go read someone else."

They had almost made it across the room when Walker's doorbell sounded. "That's probably Macon. He's supposed to stop by today and check out that tractor he wants to buy from me."

They had reached the door and, without checking to see who was on the other side, Walker opened it. Shocked, his mouth dropped open as his gaze raked over the woman standing there.

"Hello, Walker."

He recovered, although not as quickly as he would have liked. "Bailey! What the hell are you doing here?"

Instead of answering, her gaze shifted to the man standing by his side. "Hey, you look like Riley," she said, as her face broke into a smile.

It was a smile that Garth returned. "And you look like Charm."

She chuckled. "No, Charm looks like me. I understand I'm older."

"Excuse me for breaking up this little chitchat, but what are you doing here, Bailey?" Walker asked in an annoyed tone.

"Evidently she came here to see you, and on that note, I am out of here. I need to make that meeting," Garth said, slipping out the door. He looked over his shoulder at Walker with an expression that clearly said, *You have a lot of explaining to do.*

To Bailey, Garth said, "Welcome to Hemlock Row. I'll let the family know you're here. Hopefully Walker will fly you into Fairbanks."

"Don't hold your breath for that to happen," Walker said. He doubted Garth heard as he quickly darted to his parked car. His best friend had a lot of damn nerve. How dare he welcome anyone to Walker's home?

Walker turned his attention back to Bailey, trying to ignore the flutter in his stomach at seeing just how beautiful she looked. Nor did he want to concentrate on her scent, which had filled his nostrils the moment he'd opened the door.

Walker crossed his arms over his chest. "I've asked you twice already and you've yet to answer," he said in a harsh tone. "What are you doing here?"

Bailey blew out a chilled breath, wrapped her arms around herself and tried not to shiver. "Could you invite me inside first? It's cold out here."

He hesitated, as if he were actually considering doing just the opposite, and then he stepped back. She hurriedly came inside and closed the door behind her. She had dressed in layers, double the amount she would have used in Denver, yet she still felt chilled to the bone.

"You might as well come and stand in front of the fireplace to warm up."

"Thanks," she said, surprised he'd made the offer. After sliding the carry-on bag from her shoulders, she peeled off her coat, then her jacket and gloves.

Instead of renting a car, she had opted for a cab service, even though the ride from the airstrip had cost her a pretty penny. But she hadn't cared. She'd been cold, exhausted and determined to get to Walker's place before nightfall.

The cabbie had been chatty, explaining that Walker seldom got visitors and trying to coax her into telling him why she was there. She'd let him talk, and when he'd figured out she wasn't providing any information, he'd finally lapsed into silence. But only for a little while. Then he'd pointed out a number of evergreen trees and told her they were mountain hemlocks, a tree common to Alaska. He'd told her about the snowstorm headed their way and said she'd made it to the island just in time or she would have been caught in it. Sounded to her as if she would get caught in it anyway since her return flight was forty-eight hours from now. The man had been born and raised on the island and had a lot of history to share.

When the cabbie had driven up to the marker for Hemlock Row, the beautiful two-story ranch house that sat on Walker's property made her breath catch. It was like looking at a gigantic postcard. It had massive windows, multiple stone chimneys and a wraparound porch. It sat on the Shelikof Strait, which served as a backdrop that was simply beautiful, even if it was out in the middle of nowhere and surrounded by snow. The only other house they'd passed had to be at least ten to fifteen miles away.

Walker's home was not as large as Dillon's, but like Dillon's, it had a rustic feel, as if it belonged just where it sat.

"Drink this," Walker said, handing her a mug filled with hot liquid. She hadn't realized he'd left her alone. She'd been busy looking around at the furniture, which seemed warm and welcoming.

"Thanks." She took a sip of what tasted like a mixture of coffee, hot chocolate and a drop of tea. It tasted delicious. As delicious as Walker looked standing directly in front of her, barefoot, with an open-collar sweater and jeans riding low on his hips. What man looked this mouthwatering so early in the day? Had it really been a week since she'd seen him last? A week when she'd thought about him every day, determined to make this trip to Kodiak Island, Alaska, to personally deliver the apology she needed to make.

"Okay, now that you've warmed up, how about telling me what you're doing here."

She lowered the cup and met his gaze. After telling Lucia and Chloe what she'd done and what she planned to do, they had warned her that Walker probably wouldn't be happy to see her. She could tell from the look on his face that they'd been right. "I came to see you. I owe you an apology for what I said. What I suggested doing with that piece for the magazine."

He frowned. "Why are you apologizing? Doing something so inconsiderate and uncaring seems to be so like you."

His words hurt but she couldn't get mad. That was unfortunately the way she'd presented herself since meeting him. "That goes to show how wrong you are about me and how wrong I was for giving you reason to think that way."

"Whatever. You shouldn't have bothered. I don't think there's anything you can do or say to change my opinion of you."

That angered her. "I never realized you were so judgmental."

"I'm as judgmental as you are."

She wondered if all this bitterness and anger were necessary. Possibly, but at the moment she was too exhausted to deal with it. What should have been a fifteen-hour flight had become a twenty-two-hour flight when the delay of one connection had caused her to miss another. On top of everything else, due to the flight chaos, her luggage was heaven knew where. The airline assured her it would be found and delivered to her within twenty-four hours. She hoped that was true because she planned to fly out again in two days.

"Look, Walker. My intentions were good, and regardless of what you think of me I did come here to personally apologize."

"Fine. You've apologized. Now you can leave.'

"Leave? I just got here! Where am I to go?"

He frowned. "How did you get here?"

"I caught a taxi from the airport."

A dark brow lowered beneath a bunched forehead. "Then, call them to come pick you up."

He couldn't be serious. "And go where? My return flight back to Denver isn't for forty-eight hours."

His frown deepened. "Then, I suggest you stay with your cousins in Fairbanks. You've met Garth. He will introduce you to the others."

Her spine stiffened. "Why can't I wait it out here?"

He glared at her. "Because you aren't welcome here, Bailey."

Walker flinched at the harshness of his own words. He regretted saying them the moment they left his lips. He could tell by the look on her face that they'd hurt her. He then remembered how kind her family had been to him, a virtual stranger, and he knew that no matter how he felt about her, she didn't deserve what he'd just said. But then, what had given her the right to come here uninvited?

He watched as she placed the cup on the table and slid back into her jacket. Then she reached for her coat.

"What the hell do you think you're doing?" he asked, noticing how the loud sound of his voice seemed to blast off the walls.

She lifted her chin as she buttoned up her coat. "What does it look like I'm doing? Leaving. You've made it clear you don't want me here, and one thing I don't do is stay where I'm not wanted."

He wanted to chuckle at that. Hadn't her cousins and brothers told him, jokingly, how she used to impose herself on them? Sometimes she'd even done so purposely, to rattle any of their girlfriends she hadn't liked. "Forget what I said. I was mad."

When her coat was buttoned practically to her neck, she glared at him. "And you're still mad. I didn't come all the way here for verbal abuse, Walker. I came to apologize."

"Apology accepted." The memory of what had followed the last time he'd said those words slammed into his mind. He'd kissed her, feasting on her mouth like a hungry man who'd been denied food for years.

He could tell from the look in her eyes that she was remembering, as well. He figured that was the reason she broke eye contact with him to look at the flames blazing in the fireplace. Too late—the wood burning wasn't the only thing crackling in the room. He could feel that stirring of sensual magnetism that always seemed to surround them. It was radiating more heat than the fireplace.

"Now that I think about it, staying here probably isn't a good idea," she said, glancing back at him.

He released a deep breath and leaned back on his heels. She was right. It wasn't a good idea, but it was too late to think about that now. "A storm's headed this way so it doesn't matter if you don't think it's a good idea."

"It matters to me if you don't want me here," she snapped.

He rubbed his hand down his face. "Look, Bailey. I think we can tolerate each other for the next forty-eight hours. Besides, this place is so big I doubt if I'll even see you during that time." To be on the safe side, he would put her in one of the guest rooms on the south wing. That part of the house hadn't been occupied in over fifteen years.

"Where's your luggage?" he asked. The quicker he could get her settled in, the quicker he could ignore her presence.

"The airline lost it, although they say it has just been misplaced. They assured me they will deliver it here within twenty-four hours."

That probably wasn't going to happen, he thought, but figured there was no reason to tell her that. "Just in case they're delayed, I have a couple of T-shirts you can borrow to sleep in."

"Thanks."

"If you're hungry I can fix you something. I hadn't planned on preparing dinner till later, but there are some leftovers I can warm up."

"No, thanks. I'm not hungry. But I would appreciate if I could wash up and lie down for a bit. The flight from Anchorage was sort of choppy."

"Usually it is, unfortunately. I'll show you up to the room you'll be using. Just follow me."

Chapter 7

The sound of a door slamming somewhere in the house jarred Bailey awake and had her scrambling to sit up in bed and try to remember where she was. It all came tumbling back to her. Kodiak Island, Alaska. Walker's ranch.

She settled back down in bed, remembering the decision she had made to come here. She could finally admit it had been a bad one. Hadn't Walker said she wasn't welcome? But she had been determined to come after deciding a phone-call apology wouldn't do. She needed to tell him in person that she was sorry.

And she would even admit that a part of her had wanted to see him face-to-face. Everyone in the family had been surprised he'd left early, and although no one questioned her about it, she knew they suspected she was to blame. And she had been. So no one had seemed surprised when she announced her plans to travel to Kodiak. However, Dillon had pulled her aside to ask if that was something she really wanted to do. She'd assured him that it was, and told him she owed Walker an apology and wanted to deliver it to him personally.

So here she was, in an area as untamed and rugged as the most remote areas of Westmoreland Country. But there were views she had passed in the cab that had been so beautiful they had almost taken her breath away. Part of her couldn't wait to see the rest of it.

Bailey heard the sound of a door slamming again and glanced over at the clock on the nightstand. Had she slept for four hours?

She suddenly sniffed the air. Something smelled good, downright delicious. Walker had been cooking. She hoped he hadn't gone to any trouble just for her. When her stomach growled she knew she needed to get out of bed and go downstairs.

She recalled Walker leading her up to this room and the two flights of stairs they'd taken to get here. The moment she'd followed him inside she'd felt something she hadn't felt in years. Comfort. Somehow this guest room was just as warm and welcoming as the living room had been.

It might have been the sturdy-looking furniture made of dark oak. Or the huge bed that had felt as good as it looked. She couldn't wait to sleep in it tonight. Really sleep in it. Beneath the covers and not on top like she'd done for her nap. Getting out of bed, she headed for the bathroom, glad she at least had her carry-on containing her makeup and toiletries.

A few minutes later, feeling refreshed and less exhausted, she left the guest room to head downstairs. She hoped Walker was in a better mood than he'd been in earlier.

Walker checked the timer on the stove before lifting the lid to stir the stew. He'd cooked more than the usual amount since he had a houseguest. Bailey had been asleep for at least four hours and even so, her presence was disrupting his normal routine. He would have driven around his land by now, checking on the herds and making sure everything was ready for the impending snowstorm. He'd talked to Willie, his ranch foreman, who had assured him everything had been taken care of.

That brought his thoughts back to Bailey, and he uttered an expletive under his breath. He'd figured out the real reason, the only one that made sense, as to why she was here, using an apology as an excuse. She probably thought she could make him change his mind about doing the interview, but she didn't know how wrong she was.

As far as he was concerned, she'd wasted her time coming here. Although he had to admit it had been one hell of a gutsy move. As gutsy as it was crazy. He'd warned her the first day they'd met that winters in Alaska were a lot worse than the coldest day in Denver. Evidently she hadn't believed him and now would find out the truth for herself. She had arrived nearly frozen.

But nearly frozen or not, that didn't stop the male in him from remembering how good she'd looked standing on his porch. Or how she'd looked standing by his fireplace after she'd removed layer after layer of clothing.

He had awakened this morning pretty much prepared for anything. He figured it was only a matter of time before Garth showed up. And a snowstorm blowing in was the norm. What he hadn't counted on was Bailey showing up out of Alaska's cold blue sky. When he'd left Denver, he had assumed their paths wouldn't cross again. There was no reason why they should. Even if the Outlaws kindled a relationship with the Westmorelands, that wouldn't necessarily mean anything to *him*, because he lived here on the island and seldom flew to Fairbanks.

"Sorry I overslept."

He turned around and then wished he hadn't. She was still wearing the clothes she'd had on earlier, since she didn't have any others, but his gaze moved beyond that. From what he could tell, she wasn't wearing any makeup and she had changed her hairstyle. It no longer hung around her shoulders but was pulled back in a ponytail. The style made her features look younger, delicate and sexy enough to make his lower body throb.

"No problem," he said, turning his attention back to the stove.

He'd seen enough of her. Too much for his well-being. Having her standing in the middle of his kitchen, a place he'd never figured she would be, was sending crazy thoughts through his head. Like how good she looked in that particular spot. A spot where Kalyn had never stood. In fact, his wife had refused to come to Kodiak. She hadn't wanted to visit the place where he was born. Had referred to it as untamed wilderness that lacked civilization. She hadn't wanted to visit such a remote area, much less live there. She was a California girl through and through. She'd lived for the beaches, the orange groves and Hollywood. Anything else just didn't compute with her.

"What are you cooking? Smells good."

He inwardly smiled, although he didn't want to. Was that her way of letting him know she was hungry? "Bison stew. My grandmother's recipe," he said over his shoulder.

"No wonder it smells good, then."

Now, aren't you full of compliments, he thought sarcastically, knowing she was probably trying to be nice for a reason. But he wasn't buying it, because he knew her motives. "By the time you wash up I'll have dinner on the table."

"I've washed up and I can help. Thanks to Chloe I'm pretty good in the kitchen. Tell me what you need me to do."

"Why Chloe?"

"In addition to all her other talents, she is a wonderful cook and often prepares breakfast for Ramsey and his men. Remind me to tell you one day how she and Ramsey met."

He came close to saying that he wouldn't be reminding her of anything, and he didn't need her to do anything, unless she could find her way back to the airport. But he reined in his temper and said, "You can set the table. Everything you need is in that drawer over there." He never ate at a set table but figured it would give her something to do so she wouldn't get underfoot. Not that trying to put distance between them really mattered. Her scent had already downplayed the aroma of the stew.

The ringing of his cell phone on the kitchen counter jarred him out of his thoughts. He moved from the stove to pick it up, recognizing his foreman's ringtone.

"Yes, Willie? What is it?"

"It's Marcus, boss," Willie said in a frantic tone. "A big brown's got him pinned in a shack and nothing we can do will scare him off. We've been firing shots, but we haven't managed a hit."

"Damn. I'm on my way."

Walker turned and quickly moved toward the closet where his parkas hung and his boots were stored. "Got to go," he said quickly. "That was Willie Hines, my foreman. A brown bear has one of my men holed up in a shack and I need to get there fast."

"May I go?"

He glanced over his shoulder to tell her no. Then he changed his mind. It probably had something to do with that pleading look on her face. "Yes, but stay out of the way. Grab your coat, hat and scarf. And be quick. My men are waiting."

She moved swiftly and by the time he'd put on his boots she was back. He grabbed one of the rifles off the rack. When she reached up and grabbed a rifle off the rack as well, he stared at her. "What do you think you're doing?"

"I'm not a bad shot. Maybe I can help."

He doubted she could and just hoped she stayed out of the way, but he didn't have time to argue. "Fine, let's go."

"I thought bears normally hibernated in the winter," Bailey said, hanging on in the Jeep. Walker was driving like a madman and the seat belt was barely holding her in place. On top of that, her thick wool coat was nothing against the bone-chilling wind and the icy slivers of snow that had begun to fall.

"It's not officially winter yet. Besides, this particular brown is probably the same one who's been causing problems for the past year. Nothing he does is normal. There's been a bounty on his head for a while now."

Bailey nodded. Although bears were known to reside in the Rockies, they were seldom seen. She'd known of only one incident of a bear in Westmoreland Country. Dillon had called the authorities, who had captured the bear and set him free elsewhere. She then remembered what Walker had told her the first day they'd met. There were more bears than people living on Kodiak Island.

The Jeep came to a sudden stop in front of three men she figured worked for Walker. He was out of the truck in a flash and before she could unbuckle her seat belt, he snapped out an order. "Stay put, Bailey."

She grudgingly did as she was told and watched him race toward the men. They pointed at the scene taking place a hundred or so feet ahead of them. The creature wasn't what she'd expected of a brown bear. He was a huge grizzly tearing away at a small, dilapidated shack, pawing through timber, lumber and planks trying to get to the man trapped inside. Unless someone did something, it wouldn't take long for the bear to succeed. And if anyone tried shooting the bear now, they would place the man inside the shack at risk.

She didn't have to hear what Walker and his men were saying to know they were devising a plan to pull the bear's attention away from the shack. And it didn't take long to figure out that Walker had volunteered to be the bait. Putting his own life at risk.

She watched, horrified, as Walker raced forward to get the bear's attention, coming to a stop at what seemed to be just a few feet from the animal. At first it seemed as if nothing could dissuade the bear. A few more loose timbers and he would get his prey. She could hear the man inside screaming in fright, begging for help before it was too late.

Walker then picked up a tree limb and hit the bear. That got the animal's attention. Bailey held her breath when the bear turned and went charging after Walker. The plan was for Walker to lure the bear away from the shack so his men could get a good shot. It seemed the ploy was working until Walker lost his balance and fell to the ground.

Bailey was out of the Jeep in a flash, her rifle in her hand. She stood beside the men and raised her gun to take a shot.

"There's no way you can hit that bear from here, lady," one of the men said.

She ignored his words, knowing Walker would be mauled to death unless she did something. She pulled the trigger mere seconds before the bear reached Walker. The huge animal fell and it seemed the earth shook under the weight.

"Did you see that?"

"She got that grizzly and her rifle doesn't even have a scope on it."

"How can she shoot like that? Where did she come from?"

Ignoring what the three men were saying, she raced over to Walker. "Are you okay?"

"I'm fine. I just banged my leg against that damn rock when I tripped."

Placing her rifle aside, she leaned down to check him over and saw the red bloodstain on the leg of his jeans. He wasn't fine.

She turned to his men, who were looking at her strangely. "He's injured. I need two of you to lift him and take him to the Jeep. The other one, I need to check on the man in the shack. I think he passed out."

"I said I'm fine, Bailey, and I can walk," Walker insisted.

"Not on that leg." She turned to the men. "Lift him and take him to the truck," she ordered again.

"Don't anyone dare lift me. I said I can walk," Walker snapped at the two men who moved toward him.

"No, you can't walk," she snapped back at him. She then glared at his men, who stood staring, unsure whose orders to follow. "Do it!" she demanded, letting them know she expected her order to be followed regardless of what Walker said.

As if they figured any woman who could shoot that well was a woman whose order should be obeyed, they quickly moved to lift Walker. He spewed expletives, which they all ignored.

"I'll call Doc Witherspoon to come quick," one of the men said after they placed Walker in the Jeep. "And we'll be right behind you to help get him out once you reach the ranch house."

She quickly got in on the driver's side. "Thanks."

She glanced over at Walker, who was now unconscious, and fought to keep her panic at bay. Of all the things she figured she'd have to deal with upon reaching Alaska, killing a grizzly bear hadn't been one of them.

Chapter 8

Walker came awake, then reclosed his eyes when pain shot up his leg. It took him a while before he reopened them. When he did, he noted that he was in his bed and flat on his back. It didn't take him long to recall why. The grizzly.

"Bailey?" he called out softly when he heard a sound from somewhere in the room.

"She's not here, Walker," a deep masculine voice said.

He didn't have to wonder who that voice belonged to. "Doc Witherspoon?"

"Who else? I only get to see you these days when you get banged up."

Walker shook his head, disagreeing. "I never get banged up."

"You did this time. Story has it that bear would have eaten you alive if that little lady hadn't saved you."

The doctor's words suddenly made Walker remember what he'd said earlier. "Bailey's not here? Where is she?"

"She left for the airport."

Airport? Bailey was returning to Denver already? "How long have I been out, Doc?" he asked. A lot of stuff seemed fuzzy in his mind.

"Off and on close to forty-eight hours. Mainly because I gave you enough pain pills to down an elephant. Bailey thought it was best. You needed your rest. On top of all that, you were an unruly patient."

Who cared what Bailey thought when she wasn't there? He then replayed in his mind every detail of that day with the bear. "How's Marcus?"

"I treated him for shock but he's fine now. And since he's a ladies' man, he's had plenty of women parading in and out of his place pretending to be nurses."

Walker nodded, trying to dismiss the miserable feelings flooding through when he thought about Bailey being gone. She'd told him she was returning to Denver within forty-eight hours, so what had he expected? Besides, hadn't he wanted her gone? Hadn't he told her she wasn't welcome? So why was he suddenly feeling so disheartened? Must be the medication messing with his mind.

"You have a nasty cut to the leg, Walker. Went real deep. You lost a lot of blood and I had to put in stitches. You've got several bruised ribs but nothing's broken. If you stay off that leg as much as possible and follow my orders, you'll be as good as new in another week or so. I'll be back to check on you again in a few days."

"Whatever." Walker knew Doc Witherspoon would

ignore his surly attitude; after all, he was the same man who'd brought Walker into the world.

Walker closed his eyes. He wasn't sure how long he slept, but when he opened his eyes some time later, it was a feminine scent that awakened him. Being careful not to move his leg, he shifted his head and saw Bailey sitting in the chair by the bed reading a book. He blinked to make sure he wasn't dreaming. It wouldn't be the first time he'd dreamed of her since leaving Denver. But never had he dreamed of her sitting by the bed. In all his dreams she had been in the bed with him.

He blinked again and when she still sat there, he figured it was the real thing. "Doc said you left for the airport."

She glanced over at him and their gazes held. Ripples of awareness flooded through him. Why was her very presence in his room filling every inch of space within it? And why did he want her out of that chair and closer to the bed? Closer to him?

She broke eye contact to brush off a piece of lint from her shirt. "I did leave for the airport. Their twenty-four hours were up and I hadn't gotten my luggage."

"You went to the airport to get your luggage?"

"Yes."

He couldn't explain the relief that raced through him. At the moment he didn't want to explain it. He felt exhausted and was in too much pain to think clearly. "I thought you were on your way back to Denver."

"Sorry to disappoint you."

He drew in a deep breath. She'd misunderstood and was assuming things again. Instead of telling her how wrong she was, he asked, "Well, did you get your luggage?"

"Yes. They'd found it, but were taking their time bringing it here. I guess I wasn't at the top of their priority list."

He bet they wished they hadn't made that mistake. She'd probably given them hell.

"You want something to eat?" she asked him. "There's plenty of bison stew left."

Walker was glad because he was hungry and remembered he'd been cooking the stew when he'd gotten the call about Marcus. "Yes. Thanks."

"I'll be right back."

He watched Bailey get out of the chair and place the book aside before heading for the door. He couldn't help but appreciate the shape of her backside in sweats. At least his attention to physical details hadn't lessened any. He brought his hand to his jaw and realized he needed to trim his beard.

When Bailey pulled the door shut behind her, Walker closed his eyes and again remembered in full detail everything that had happened down by the shack. The one thing that stuck out in his mind above everything else was the fact that Bailey Westmoreland had saved his life.

"Yes, Walker is fine just bruised and he had to get stiches in his leg," she said to Ramsey on the phone. "I hated killing that bear but it was him or Walker. He was big and a mean one."

"You did what you had to do, Bay. I'm sure Walker appreciated you being there."

"Maybe. Doesn't matter now, though. He's confined to bed and needs help. The doctor wants him to stay off his leg as much as possible. That means I need to tell Chloe and Lucia that I'll need a few more days off. Possibly another week."

"Well, you're in luck because Lucia is here, so I'll let you speak to both her and Chloe. You take care of yourself."

"Thanks, I will. I miss everyone."

"And we miss you. But it's nice to have you gone for a while," he teased.

"Whatever," she said, grinning, knowing he was joking. She was certain every member of her family missed her as much as she missed them.

A short while later she hung up. Chloe and Lucia had understood the situation and told her to take all the time she needed to care for Walker. She appreciated that.

Drawing in a deep breath, she glanced around the kitchen. Over the past three days she had become pretty familiar with it. She knew where all the cooking equipment was located and had found a recipe book that had once belonged to Walker's grandmother. There was a family photo album located in one of the cabinets. She'd smiled at the pictures of Walker's family, people she figured were his parents and grandparents. But nowhere in the album did she find any of his wedding pictures or photographs of his wife and child.

She looked out the window. It was snowing hard outside and had been for the past two days. She had met all the men who worked on Walker's ranch. They had dropped by and introduced themselves and told her they would take care of everything for their boss. News of her encounter with the bear had spread and a lot of the men stared at her in amazement. She found them to be a nice group of guys. A number of them had worked on the ranch when Walker's father was alive. She could tell from the way they'd inquired about Walker's well-being that they were very fond of him and deeply loyal.

She snorted at the thought of that. They evidently knew a different Walker from the one she'd gotten to know. Due to all the medication the doctor had given him, he slept most of the time, which was good. And he refused to let her assist him to the bathroom or in taking his baths. Doctor Witherspoon had warned him about getting the stitches wet and about staying off his leg as much as possible, so at least he was taking that advice. One of his men had dropped off crutches for him to use, and he was using them, as well.

Snow was coming down even worse now and everything was covered with a white blanket. The men had made sure there was plenty of wood for the fireplace and she had checked and found the freezer and pantry well stocked, so there was nothing for her to do but take things one day at a time while waiting for Walker to get better.

Garth had called for Walker and she'd told him what had happened. He'd left his number and told her to call if she needed anything or if Walker continued to give her trouble. Like she'd told Garth, Walker had pretty much slept for the past three days. When he was awake, other than delivering his meals and making sure he took his medication, she mostly left him alone.

But not today. His bedroom was dark and dreary and although the outside was barely any better, she intended to go into his room and open the curtains. And she intended for him to get out of bed and sit in a chair long enough for her to change the linens.

According to Garth, Walker had a housekeeper, an older woman by the name of Lola Albright, who came in each week, no matter how ugly the weather got outside. She had located Ms. Albright's phone number in the kitchen drawer and called to advise her that she need not come this week. Somehow, but not surprisingly, the woman had already heard what happened. After complimenting Bailey for her skill with a gun, she had thanked Bailey for calling and told her if she needed anything to let her know. Ms. Albright and her husband were Walker's closest neighbors and lived on a farm about ten miles away.

Grabbing the tray with the bowl of chicken noodle soup that she'd cooked earlier, Bailey moved up the stairs to Walker's bedroom. She opened the door and stopped, surprised to see him already out of bed and sitting in the chair.

The first thing she noticed was that he'd shaved. She couldn't stop her gaze from roaming over his face while thinking about just how sexy he looked. He was as gorgeous without facial hair as he was with it. He had changed clothes and was looking like his former self. A part of her was grateful he was sitting up, but then another part of her was annoyed that he hadn't asked for her assistance.

"Lunchtime," she said, moving into the room and putting the tray on a table beside his chair. She wanted to believe he said thanks, although it sounded more like a grunt. She moved across the room to open the curtains.

"What do you think you're doing?"

Without turning around, she continued opening the curtains. "I thought you might want to look outside."

"I want the curtains closed."

"Sorry, but now they're open." She turned back around and couldn't help but shiver when she met his stare. His *glare* was more like it, but his bad mood didn't bother her. After five brothers and a slew of male cousins she knew how to deal with a man who couldn't have his way.

"Glad you're up. I need to change the linens," she said, moving toward the bed.

"Lola's my housekeeper. She's coming tomorrow and can do it then."

"I talked to Lola this morning and told her there was no need for her to come out in this weather. I can handle things while I'm here."

He didn't say anything but she could tell by his scowl that he hadn't liked that move. And speaking of moves, she felt his eyes on her with every move she made while changing the sheets. She could actually feel his gaze raking across her. When she finished and turned to look at him, his mouth was set in a hard, tight line.

"You know, if you keep looking all mean and cranky, Walker, you might grow old looking that way."

His frown deepened. "No matter what you do, I won't be changing my mind about the interview. So you're wasting your time."

Drawing in a deep, angry breath, she moved across the room to stand in front of him. She leaned down a little to make sure her eyes were level with his. "You ungrateful bastard!"

That was followed by a few more obscenities she hadn't said since the last time Dillon had washed out her mouth with soap years ago. But Walker's accusations had set her off. "Do you think that's why I'm here? That I only killed that bear, hung around, put up with your crappy attitude just because I want an interview? Well, I've got news for you. I don't want an interview from you. You're no longer a viable candidate. Women are interested in men who are loners but decent, not loners who are angry and couldn't recognize a kind deed if it bit them on the—"

She hadn't expected him to tug on a lock of her hair and capture her mouth. She hadn't expected him to kiss her with a hunger that sent desire raging through her, flooding her with memories of the night they'd parked in her truck at Bailey's Bay.

Convincing herself she was only letting him have his way with her mouth because she didn't want to move and hurt his leg, she found herself returning the kiss, moaning when his tongue began doing all kinds of delicious things to hers.

They were things she had dreamed about, and craved—but only with him. She could admit that at night, in the guest room, in that lonely bed, she had thought of him, although she hadn't wanted to do so. And since all she had were memories, she had recalled how he had licked a slow, wet trail from her mouth to her breasts and then lower.

Her thoughts were snatched back to the present when she felt Walker ease up her skirt and softly skim her inner thighs. His fingers slipped beneath the elastic of her panties before sliding inside her.

She shuddered and his finger moved deeper, pushing her over the edge. She wanted to pull back but couldn't. Instead, she followed his lead and intensified the kiss while his fingers did scandalous things.

Then he released her mouth to whisper against her wet lips, "Come for me again, Bailey."

As if his request was a sensual command her body had to obey, ragged heat rolled in her stomach as her pulse throbbed and her blood roared through her veins. Her body exploded, every nerve ending igniting with an intensity that terrified her. This time was more powerful than the last, and she had no willpower to stop the moan released from her lips. No willpower to stop spreading her thighs wider and arching her mouth closer to once again be taken.

That was when Walker placed his mouth over Bailey's again, kissing her with no restraint. He deepened the kiss, pushing his fingers even farther inside her. He loved the sounds she made when she climaxed; he loved knowing he was the one to make it happen. And he intended to make it happen all over again. Moments later, when she shuddered and groaned into his mouth, he knew he had succeeded.

She grabbed his shoulders, and he didn't flinch when she dug her fingers into his skin. Nor did he flinch when she placed pressure on his tongue. He merely retaliated by sucking harder on hers.

He had been hungry for her taste for days. Each time she had entered his bedroom, he had hated lying flat on his back, not being able to do the one thing he'd wanted to do—kiss her in a way that was as raw as he felt.

Most of the time he'd feigned sleep, but through heavy-lidded eyes he had watched her, studied her and longed for her. He'd known each and every time she had walked around his room, cursing under her breath about his foul mood, using profanity he'd never heard before. He had laid there as his ears burned, pretending to sleep as she called him every nasty name in the book for being so difficult and pigheaded.

He'd also known when she'd calmed down enough to sit quietly in the chair by his bed to read, or softly hum while flipping through one of his wildlife magazines. And he would never forget the day she had worn a sweater and a pair of leggings. She had stretched up to put something away on one of the top shelves in his room and caused his entire body to harden in desire watching her graceful movements. And the outlines of her curves covered by those leggings… His need for her had flowed through him like a potent drug, more intoxicating than the medication Doc Witherspoon had him taking. Knowing she was off-limits, because he had decided it had to be so, had only sharpened his less-than-desirable attitude.

But today had been different. He had awakened with his raging hormones totally out of control. He'd felt better and had wanted to clean himself up, move around and wait for her. He hadn't anticipated kissing her but he was glad he had.

There were multiple layers to Bailey Westmoreland, layers he wanted to unpeel one at a time. The anticipation was almost killing him.

Growling low in his throat, he slowly pulled his mouth away and pulled his fingers from inside her. Then, as she watched, he brought those same fingers to his lips and licked them in slow, greedy movements.

He held her gaze, tempted to take possession of her mouth again. Instead, he whispered, "Thank you for saving my life, Bailey."

He could tell his words of thanks had surprised her.

Little did she know she would be in for a few more surprises before she left his ranch to return to Denver.

"And thank you for letting me savor you," he whispered. "To have such a filthy mouth, you have a very delicious taste."

And he meant it. He loved the taste of her on his fingers. Bailey was a woman any man would want to possess. The good. The bad. And the ugly. And for some reason that he didn't understand or could explain, he wanted that man to be him.

With that thought planted firmly in his mind, he leaned close, captured her mouth with his and kissed her once again.

Chapter 9

"What have you gotten yourself into, Bailey?" she asked herself a few days later while standing outside on Walker's front porch.

This was the first time the weather had improved enough for her to be outside. As far as she could see, snow covered everything. It had seemed to her that it hadn't been snowflakes falling for the past several days but ice chips. The force of them had hit the roof, the windowpanes and blanketed the grounds.

Yesterday, Josette told her a bad snowstorm had hit Denver and threatened to close the airport. Bailey had endured Denver's snowstorms all her life, but what she'd experienced over the past few days here in Alaska was far worse. Even though parts of this place reminded her of Denver, looking out at the Strait from her bedroom window meant she saw huge gla-

ciers instead of mountains. And one of the ponds on
Walker's property had been a solid block of ice since
she'd arrived.

Wrapping her hands around the mug of coffee she
held in her hand, she took a sip. Would her question to
herself ever be answered? Was there even an answer?
All she knew was that she had to leave this place and
return home before…

Before what?

Already Walker had turned her normally structured
mind topsy-turvy. It had started the day he'd kissed
her in his bedroom. Oh, he'd done more than kiss her.
He had inserted his fingers inside her and made her
come. Just like before. But this time he had tasted her
on his fingers, letting her watch. And then he'd kissed
her again, letting her taste herself on his lips.

At least when that kiss had ended she'd had the
good sense to get out of the room. And she had stayed
out until it was time to deliver his dinner. Luckily
when she'd entered the room later that day, he had
been asleep, so she had left the covered tray of food
by his bed. Then Willie had dropped by that evening
to visit with Walker and had returned the tray to the
kitchen. That had meant she didn't have to go up to
his room to get it.

She had checked on him before retiring for the night
and he'd been sitting up again, in that same chair. After
asking him if there was anything he needed before she
went to bed, she had quickly left the room.

That had been three days ago and she'd avoided
going into his room since then. She'd only been in to
deliver his food. Each time she found him dressed and
sitting in that same chair. It was obvious he was im-

proving, so why hadn't she made plans to leave Kodiak Island?

She kept telling herself she wanted to wait until Dr. Witherspoon assured her that Walker could manage on his own. Hopefully, today would be that day. The doctor had arrived an hour ago and was up there with Walker now. It shouldn't be long before Bailey could work her way out of whatever she'd gotten herself into with Walker.

Knowing that if she stayed outside any longer she was liable to turn into a block of ice, she went back inside. She was closing the door behind her as Dr. Witherspoon came down the stairs.

"So how is our patient, Doctor?" she asked the tall, muscular man who reminded her of a lumberjack more than a doctor.

"Walker's fine. The stiches are out and he should be able to maneuver the stairs in a day or so. I'm encouraging him to do so in order to work the stiffness out of his legs."

Bailey nodded as she sat her coffee mug on a side table. "So he's ready to start handling things on his own now?"

"Pretty much, but I still don't want him to overdo it. As you know, Walker has a hard head. I'm glad you're here to make sure he doesn't overexert himself."

Bailey nibbled her bottom lip before saying, "But I can't stay here forever. I have a job back in Denver. Do you have any idea when it will be okay for me to leave?"

"If you have pressing business to attend to back home then you should go now. I'm sure Lola won't mind moving in for a few days until Walker's fully recovered."

Dr. Witherspoon was giving her an out, so why wasn't she taking it? Why was she making herself believe she was needed here?

"Just let me know when you plan to leave so I'll know what to do," the doctor added. "I'm sure you know Walker would prefer to be by himself after you leave, but that's not wise. Personally, I think he needs you."

The doctor didn't know just how wrong he was. Sure, Walker liked kissing her, but that didn't mean he needed her. "I doubt that very seriously. He'll probably be glad to have me gone."

"Um, I don't think so. I've known Walker all his life. I delivered him into the world and looked forward to delivering his son, but his wife wouldn't hear of it. She wanted their son born in California. She wasn't too fond of this place."

Dr. Witherspoon paused, and a strange look appeared on his face, as if he'd said too much. "Anyway, if you decide to leave before the end of the week, let me know so I can notify Lola."

"I will."

Before reaching the door, the doctor turned. "Oh, yes, I almost forgot. Walker wants to see you."

Bailey lifted a brow. "He does?"

"Yes." The doctor then opened the door and left.

Bailey wondered why Walker would ask to see her. He'd seen her earlier when she'd taken him breakfast. She hadn't been able to decipher his mood, mainly because she hadn't hung around long enough. She'd placed the tray on the table and left. But she had seen that he'd opened the curtains and was sitting in what was evidently his favorite chair.

After taking a deep breath, she moved toward the stairs. She might as well go see what Walker wanted. All things considered, he might be summoning her to ask her to leave.

"Dr. Witherspoon said you wanted to see me."

Walker turned around at the sound of Bailey's voice. She stood in the doorway as if ready to sprint away at a moment's notice. Had his mood been as bad as Doc Witherspoon claimed? If so, she had put up with it when any other woman would not have. "Come in, Bailey, I won't bite."

He wouldn't bite, but he wouldn't mind tasting her mouth again.

She hesitated before entering, looking all around his bedroom before looking back at him. That gave him just enough time to check her out, to appreciate how she looked in her sweats, sweater and jacket. She wore her hair pinned back from her face, which showed off her beautiful bone structure. Although he hadn't stuck around to meet her sister Gemma, he had met Megan. There was a slight resemblance between the two but he thought Bailey had a look all her own. Both were beautiful women but there was a radiance about Bailey that gave him pause whenever he saw her.

"Okay, I'm in," she said, coming to stand in front of him. However, he noted she wasn't all in his face like last time. She was keeping what she figured was a safe distance.

"You're standing up," she observed.

"Is there a reason for me not to be?"

She shrugged. "No. But normally you're sitting down in that chair over there."

He followed her gaze to the chair. "Yes. That chair has special meaning for me."

"It does? Why?"

"It once belonged to my mother. I'm told she used to sit in it and rock me to sleep. I don't recall that, but I do remember coming in here at night and sitting right there on the floor while she sat in that chair and read me a story."

"I heard you tell Dillon you're an only child. Your parents didn't want any more children?"

"They wanted plenty, which is why they built such a huge house. But Mom had difficulties with my birth and Doc Witherspoon advised her not to try again."

"Oh."

A moment of silence settled between them before Bailey said, "You didn't say why you wanted to see me."

No, he hadn't. He stared at her, wishing he wasn't so fascinated with her mouth. "I need to apologize. I haven't been the nicest person the past several days." No need to tell her Doc Witherspoon hadn't spared any punches in telling Walker just what an ass he'd been.

"No, you haven't. You have been somewhat of a grouch, but I've dealt with worse. I have five brothers and a slew of male cousins. I've discovered men can be more difficult than sick babies when they are in pain."

"Regardless, that was no reason to take out my mood on you and I apologize."

She shrugged. "Apology acc—" As if remembering another time those words had set off a kiss between them, she quickly modified her words. "Thank you for apologizing." She turned to leave.

"Wait!"

Bailey turned back around. "Yes?"

"Lunch."

She raised a brow. "What about it?"

"I thought we could eat lunch together."

Bailey eyed Walker speculatively before asking, "Why would you want us to eat lunch together?"

He countered with a question of his own. "Any reason we can't? Although I appreciate you being here, helping out and everything, you're still a guest in my home. Besides, I'm doing better and Doc suggested I try the stairs. I figured we could sit and eat in the kitchen. Frankly, I'm tired of looking at these four walls."

She could see why he would be. "Okay, I'll serve you lunch in the kitchen."

"And you will join me?"

Bailey nibbled her lips. How could she explain that just breathing the same air as him was playing havoc on her nervous system?

Even now, just standing this close to him was messing with her mind. Making her remember things she shouldn't. Like what had happened the last time she'd stayed this long in this bedroom. And he wanted them to share lunch? What would they talk about? One thing was for certain—she would let him lead the conversation. She would not give him any reason to think she was interviewing him undercover. He'd already accused her of having underhanded motives.

When she'd walked into this room, she hadn't

counted on him standing in the middle of it. She'd been fully aware of his presence the moment she'd opened the door. He was dressed in a pair of well-worn jeans and a flannel shirt that showed what an impressive body he had. If he'd lost any weight she couldn't tell. He still had a solid chest, broad shoulders and taut thighs. She'd been too taken with all that masculine power to do anything but stand and stare.

Without the beard his jaw looked stronger and his mouth—which should be outlawed—was way too sexy to be real.

Bailey couldn't stop herself from wondering why he wanted to share lunch with her. But then, she didn't want to spend time analyzing his reason. So she convinced herself it was because she would be leaving soon, returning to Denver. Then there would be no reason for their paths to cross again. If things worked out between the Westmorelands and the Outlaws, she could see Walker hanging out with her brothers and cousins every now and then, but she doubted she would be invited to attend any of those gatherings.

Knowing he was waiting for an answer, she said, "Yes, I'll share lunch with you."

Chapter 10

"So, Bailey, who taught you how to shoot?"

She bit into her sandwich and held up her finger to let him know it would be a minute before she could answer because she had food in her mouth. Walker didn't mind watching her anyway.

"The question you should probably ask is who *didn't* teach me to shoot. My brothers and cousins were quick to give me lessons, especially Bane. He's so good that he's a master sniper with the navy SEALs. Bane taught me how to hit a target. I don't want to sound as if I'm bragging, but I'm an excellent shot because of him."

"You're not bragging, just stating a fact. I'm living proof, and note I said *living* proof. There's no doubt in my mind that grizzly would have done me in if you hadn't taken it down."

"Well, I'm glad I was there."

He was glad she'd been there, too. At the sight of a huge grizzly any other woman would have gone into shock. But not Bailey. She had showed true grit by bringing down that bear. She'd made that shot from a distance he doubted even he could have made. His three men had admitted they could not have made it without running the risk of shooting him.

"My men are in awe of you," he added. "You impressed them."

She frowned. "I didn't do it to impress anyone, Walker. I did what I felt I had to do. I wasn't going after accolades."

That, he thought, was what made her different. Most of the women he knew would use anything to score brownie points. Hadn't making a good impression meant everything to Kalyn?

"I think you're the real hero, Walker. You risked your life getting that bear away from the shack before it got to Marcus."

He shrugged. "Like you said, I did what I felt I had to do. I wasn't going after accolades." He blinked over at her and smiled. He was rewarded when she smiled back.

Just what was he doing flirting with her? He was pretty rusty at it. There hadn't been a woman he'd really been attracted to since Kalyn. He'd had meaningless affairs solely for the purpose of quenching raging hormones, but he hadn't been interested in a woman beyond sex…until now.

He bit into his sandwich. "This is good. I hope I didn't get underfoot while you prepared lunch, but I couldn't stay in my bedroom a minute longer."

"Thanks, and no, you didn't get underfoot."

But he had made her nervous, he was sure of it. She'd been leaning over looking into the refrigerator when he'd walked into the kitchen. The sight of her sweats stretched over a curvy bottom had definitely increased his testosterone level. He had been happy just to stand there, leaning against the kitchen counter with an erection, and stare. After closing the refrigerator she'd nearly dropped the jars of mayo and mustard when she'd turned around to find him there. Of course she'd scolded him for coming down the stairs without her assistance, but he'd ignored all that. He wasn't used to a woman fussing over him.

She'd made him sit down at the table and had given him a magazine that had been delivered by the mailman earlier. Instead of flipping through the pages, he'd preferred watching her move around the kitchen. More than once she'd caught him staring and he'd quickly glanced back down at the magazine.

Walker would be the first to admit he'd picked up on a difference in the atmosphere of his home. It now held the scent of a woman. Although the guest room she was using was on the opposite side of the house, the moment he'd walked out of his bedroom, the scent of jasmine had flowed through his nostrils. At first he'd been taken off guard by it but then he decided he preferred it to the woodsy smell he was used to. It was then that he realized someone other than himself occupied the house for the first time since his parents' deaths. His privacy had been invaded, but, surprisingly, he didn't have a problem with it. Bailey had a way of growing on a person.

"Will you be returning to your room after you finish lunch?" she asked.

He glanced over at her. "No. There're a few things I need to do."

"Like what?"

He lifted a brow. Did she think whatever he did was any of her business?

As if she read his mind, she said, "I hope you're not planning to do anything that might cause a setback, Walker."

He heard the concern in her voice and clearly saw it in her eyes. It reminded him of what had been missing in his life for almost ten years. A woman who cared.

A woman he desired.

Although they had never made love, they had come close. It didn't take much to remember a pair of perfectly shaped breasts or the wetness of her femininity. Going down on a woman wasn't part of his regular lovemaking routine, but Bailey's scent had made him want to do it for her, and after that first time he'd found her flavor addictive.

So yes, he desired her. With a passion. Whenever he saw her, his mind filled with all the things he'd love to do to her. It had been a long time since he'd slept with a woman, but that wasn't the issue. He desired Bailey simply because she was a woman worthy of desiring. There had been this attraction between them from the start, and they both knew it. The attraction was still alive and kicking, and they both knew that, as well.

How long were they planning to play the "try to ignore it" game?

"No setbacks for me. I intend to follow Dr. Witherspoon's orders."

"Good."

Did Bailey realize she liked getting in the last word?

"I need to go over my books, replenish my stock and order more branding equipment. I'll be fine."

She nodded before getting up from the table. She reached for his plate and he placed his hand on hers. He immediately felt a sizzle race up his spine and he fought to ignore it. "I can take care of my own plate. I appreciate you being here but I don't want you to feel as if you have to wait on me. I'm doing better."

What he didn't add was that he was doing well enough for her to go back home to Westmoreland Country. However, for reasons he wasn't ready to question, her leaving was not what he wanted.

"Fine," she said, moving away from the table.

He tried concentrating on his cup of coffee, but couldn't. He watched her move around the room, putting stuff away. He enjoyed watching how her body looked in sweats. Whenever she moved, so did his sex as it tingled with need.

"Any reason you're staring?" she asked, turning to meet his gaze.

She looked younger today. Softer. It could be the way the daylight was coming in through the window. "You got eyes in the back of your head, Bailey?"

"No, but I could feel you staring."

In that case there was no need to lie. "Yes, I was staring. You look good in that outfit."

She looked down at herself. "In sweats? You've got to be kidding me. You must have taken an extra pill or two this morning."

He smiled as his gaze raked over her. "No, I didn't take an extra pill or two. Just stating the facts."

He sensed she didn't believe him. She brushed her fingers through her hair as if his comment had given her reason to wonder if she looked just the opposite. Possibly disheveled and unkempt. He found that interesting. How could she not know she looked good no matter what she wore? And she probably had no idea that her hot, lush scent filled the kitchen instead of the scent of what she'd prepared for lunch.

As if dismissing what he'd said, she turned back to the sink. "Are you going to sit there and stare or are you going to work in your office?" she asked over her shoulder a few moments later.

"I think I'll just sit here and stare for a while."

"It's not nice to stare."

"So I've heard."

She swung around and frowned at him. "Then, stare at something else, Walker."

A smile touched the corner of his lips. "There's nothing else in this kitchen I would rather stare at than you." And he meant it.

"Sounds as if you've got a case of cabin fever."

"Possibly, but I doubt it."

She placed the dish towel on the counter. "So what do you think it is?"

He placed his coffee cup down, thinking that was easy enough to answer. "Lust. I'm lusting after you, Bailey."

A drugging urgency slammed into Bailey's chest, making her nipples pucker and fire race through her veins. Now, more than before, she felt the weight of Walker's gaze. She didn't usually feel feminine in sweats, but he had a way of making her feel sexy even when she didn't have a right to feel that way.

And while he sat there, watching her every move,

she was fully aware of what was going through his mind. Because she was pretty certain it was the same thing going through hers. This seductive heat was beginning to affect her everywhere—in her breasts, deep in the juncture of her thighs and in the middle of her stomach. The memories of those two kisses they'd previously shared only intensified the hot, aching sensations overwhelming her common sense.

She heard him slide the chair back and watched as he slowly stood. "You can come here or I'm coming over there," he said matter-of-factly in a deep voice.

She swallowed, knowing he was serious. As serious as she was hot for him. But was she ready for this? A meaningless affair with Walker? Hadn't he told her that night in the truck at Bailey's Bay that all he could offer was a meaningless affair? At the time, she'd responded by saying that kind of relationship didn't bother her. Her future was tied to Westmoreland Country and not to any man. There wasn't that much love in the world.

But there was that much passion. That much desire. To a degree she'd never encountered before. She couldn't understand it, but there was no denying the way her body responded to him. It responded in a way it had never reacted to another man. A part of her believed this was no accident. What was taking place between them was meant to be. Not only was that thought a discovery, it was also an acceptance.

It was that acceptance that pushed her to say, "Meet me halfway."

He nodded and moved toward her. She moved toward him. Bailey drew in a deep breath with every step, keeping her gaze fixed on his face. That strong, square chin, those gorgeous dark eyes, his delicious mouth. He was such a striking figure of a man whose looks alone could make a woman shiver. Toss in her nightly naughty dreams and it made her bold enough to turn those dreams into reality.

When they met in the center of the kitchen, he wrapped his arms around her with a possessiveness that took her breath away.

"Be careful of your leg," she warned softly after managing to breathe again. She liked the feel of his body pressed hard against hers.

"My leg isn't what's aching," he said with a huskiness she heard. "Something else is."

She knew what that something else was. She could feel his erection pressed against the juncture of her thighs. Even while recovering from his injury, his strength amazed her. Although he annoyed her at times by not asking for help, his willpower and independence were admirable. And the thought that this was one particular area where this strong, sexy specimen of a man *did* need her sent her mind and body soaring.

He pulled back slightly to look down at her and she almost melted from the heat in his eyes. The feel of him cupping her bottom to keep their middles connected wasn't helping matters. "Our first time making love should be in a bed, Bailey. But I'm not sure I can make it that far. I need you now," he said in a voice filled with need.

"I'm okay with that, Walker. I need you now, too." She was being honest with him. When it came to sex, she felt honesty was the best policy. She detested the lies and games some couples played.

He pulled her back into his arms when he said, "There's something I need to warn you about."

Now she was the one to pull back slightly to look up at him. "What?"

"It's been a long time since I've been with a woman. A few years. About five."

The information, which he hadn't had to give her, tugged at something deep inside her. "It's been a long time since I've been with a man, as well. More than five years."

He smiled and she knew why. She'd been around the males in her family long enough to know they had no problems with double standards. They could sleep around but didn't want to know their women had done the same.

She wrapped her arms around his neck. "What about your leg? How do you plan for this to work? Got any ideas?"

"I've got plenty and I plan to try out every last one of them."

His words made her heart pound hard against her chest. "Bring it on, Walker Rafferty."

"Baby, I intend to do just that." And then he lowered his mouth down to hers.

Chapter 11

Sensation ripped through Walker the moment their mouths connected. He eased his tongue into her mouth and kissed her with a hunger that had her groaning. In response his erection pressed even harder against his zipper.

He captured her tongue with his and did the kinds of erotic things he'd dreamed of doing. He sucked as if the need to taste her was as essential to him as breathing. He deepened the kiss and tightened his arms around her. She tasted of heat and a wildness that he found delectable.

But then he found everything about her delectable—the way she fit in his arms, the way their bodies melded together like that was the way they were supposed to be.

Walker slowly eased away from her mouth and drew

in a deep satisfying breath, missing the feel of her already. "Take off your clothes," he whispered against her lips.

She raised a brow. "In here?"

He smiled. "Yes. I want to make love to you here. We'll try out all the other rooms later."

She chuckled. "Horny, aren't we?"

He leaned in and licked her lips. "Like I said, it's been five years."

"In that case…"

Moving out of his arms, she took a few steps back and began removing her clothes. He watched her every move, getting more turned on with each stitch she discarded. When she had stripped down to nothing but her panties and bra, he finally released the breath he'd been holding.

He was weak in the knees from looking at her and he leaned against the breakfast bar for support. He needed it when she removed her bra and then slowly peeled her panties down her thighs. He couldn't help growling in pleasure.

It was only then he remembered something very important.

"Damn."

She lifted a concerned brow. "What's wrong?"

"Condoms. I don't have any down here. They're upstairs in my nightstand."

She shook her head. "No need, unless you're concerned about it for health reasons. I'm on the pill to regulate my periods."

He nodded. The thought of spilling inside her sent all kinds of luscious sensations through him. "No concerns. I'm okay with it, if you are."

"I'm okay with it."

He couldn't help but rake his gaze over her naked body. "You are beautiful, Bailey. From the top of your head to your pretty little feet, you are absolutely beautiful."

Bailey had never allowed any man's compliments to go to her head…until now. Walker sounded so serious and the look on his face was so sincere that her heart pounded in appreciation. She wasn't sure why his opinion of how she looked mattered, but it did. And she immediately thought of a way to thank him. Reclaiming the distance separating them, she leaned up on her toes and brushed her lips across his. Then she licked a line from one corner of his mouth to the other in a slow and provocative way.

She smiled in pleasure when she heard his quick intake of breath, glad to know she was getting to him as much as he was getting to her. "Now for your clothes, Walker, and I intend to help you." She intended to do more than that but he would find that out soon enough. He braced against the breakfast bar as she bent down to remove his shoes and socks.

Now for his shirt. She leaned forward and undid the buttons while occasionally leaning up to nip and lick his mouth. The more he moaned the bolder she got as she assisted him out of his shirt and then his T-shirt.

Wow, what a chest. She ran her fingers through the coarse hair covering it. She loved the feel of it beneath her hands. She trailed kisses from his lips, past his jawline to his chest and then used her teeth to nibble on his nipples before devouring them with her tongue and lips.

"Bailey." He breathed out her name in a forced whisper. "I need you."

She needed him, too, but first…

She reached down and unsnapped his jeans before easing down his zipper. Then she inserted her hand into the opening to cup him. She smiled at how thick he felt in her hand. "Um, I think we should get rid of your jeans and briefs, don't you?"

Instead of giving him a chance to answer, she kissed him again, using her tongue to further stir the passion between them. She heard him moan, which was followed by a deep growl when she sucked on his lower lip.

"Don't think I can handle this much longer," he said through clenched teeth.

"Oh, I think you can handle more than you think you can, Walker. Let's see."

She helped him remove his jeans and briefs and then stood back and raked her gaze over him before meeting his eyes. "You are so buff. So gorgeously handsome. So—"

Before she could finish he pulled her to him, capturing her lips in an openmouthed kiss as raw as it was possessive. And when she felt his hand between her legs, she broke off the kiss to ease out of his arms.

"Not so fast. I'm a guest in your home, so today I get to have my way," she whispered.

With that, her fingers gripped his hardness and gently squeezed, loving the feel of his bare flesh in her hands.

"Don't torture me, baby."

Torture? He hadn't endured any torture yet, she thought, as she continued to fondle his thick width, texture and length, loving every minute of it. He was huge, and she intended to sample every single inch.

In a move she knew he was not expecting, she dropped down on her knees and took him into the warmth of her mouth.

"Bailey!"

Walker grabbed her head but instead of pulling her mouth away, he wrapped his fingers in the locks of her hair. He lost all control while watching her head bob up and down. Every muscle in his body trembled and his insides shivered with the impact of her mouth on him. She was pushing him deliciously over the edge. He felt ready to explode.

It was then that he tugged on her hair, using enough force to pull her mouth from him. She looked up at him and smiled, licking her lips. "I need to get inside you now," he said in a guttural growl. He had reached his limit.

In a surprise move, he pulled her up and lifted her to sit on the kitchen table, spreading her legs wide in the process.

Thanks to her, his control was shot to hell. He trailed his fingers through the curls surrounding her feminine folds. She wasn't the only one who wanted a taste. He lowered his head to her wetness.

"Walker!"

He ignored her screaming his name as his tongue devoured her as she'd done to him. And when she wrapped her legs around his neck and bucked her hips against his mouth he knew he was giving her a taste of her own medicine.

When he'd pushed her far enough, he spread her legs

farther, positioned his body between them and thrust until he was fully embedded within her. Then he held tight to her hips as he went deeper with every plunge.

Something inside him snapped, and his body moved with the speed of a jackhammer. When she wrapped her legs around his waist he threw his head back and filled his nostrils with her scent.

They came together, him holding tight to her hips. Why this felt so right, he wasn't sure. All he knew was that it did. He needed this. He needed her. And from the sounds of her moans, she needed him.

They were both getting what they needed.

Bailey came awake and shifted in Walker's arms, recalling how they'd made it out of the kitchen to the sofa in his living room. She eased up and tried to move off him when she remembered his leg.

His arms held tight around her like a band of steel. "Where do you think you're going?"

She looked down at him and remembered why he was down there and she was on top. Upon his encouragement, she had shown him that she wasn't only a good shot. She was a pretty damn good rider, as well.

She glanced at the clock. It was close to eight. They had slept almost through dinner. Okay, she would admit they hadn't slept the entire time. They had slept in between their many rounds of lovemaking.

"Your leg," she reminded him, holding his gaze.

He had a sexy, sluggish look in his eyes.

"My leg is fine."

"It's after eight and you didn't take your medicine at five."

A smile curved his lips. "I had another kind of medicine that I happen to like better."

She shook her head. "Tell that to your leg when it starts hurting later."

"Trust me, I will. Making love to you is better than any medicine Doc Witherspoon could have prescribed for me." And then he pulled her mouth down to his and kissed her in a slow, unhurried fashion that clouded her mind. She was grateful for the ringing of her cell phone until she recognized the ringtone.

She broke off the kiss and quickly scooted off Walker to grab her phone off the coffee table, being careful not to bump his leg. "Dillon! What's going on?"

"Hey, Bay. I was calling to check to see how Walker is doing."

She glanced over at Walker who was stretched out naked on the sofa. She licked her lips and then said to Dillon, "Walker is doing fine. Improving every day. The doctor is pleased with his progress."

"That's good to hear. And how are you doing? Is it cold enough there for you?"

"Yes, I'm doing good," she said, glancing down at her own naked body. It was a good thing Dillon had no idea just how good she was doing. "There was a bad snowstorm here."

"I heard about that. You took plenty of heavy clothing didn't you?"

"Yes, I'm good."

"You most certainly are," Walker whispered.

She gave Walker a scolding glance, hoping Dillon hadn't heard what Walker had said.

"Do you have any idea when you'll be coming back home?" Dillon asked.

She swallowed hard and switched her gaze from Walker to the window when she said, "No, I don't know when I'll be back. I don't want to leave Walker too soon. But when the doctor says Walker can handle things on his own, I'll be back."

"All right. Give Walker my regards and tell him the entire family is wishing him a speedy recovery."

"Okay. I'll tell him. Goodbye, Dillon."

"Goodbye, Bay."

She clicked off the phone and held it in her hand a second before placing it back on the table.

"What did Dillon want you to tell me?"

"That the family is wishing you a speedy recovery."

He nodded and pulled up into a sitting position. "That's nice of them."

She smiled and returned to the sofa to sit beside him. "I have a nice family."

"I'll have to agree with you there. You didn't say how the wedding went."

Her smile widened. "It was wonderful and Jill made a beautiful bride. I don't know who cried the most, Jill, Pam or their other two sisters." She paused and then added, "Ian, Reggie and Quade hated they didn't get the chance to meet you."

"And I hate I didn't get the chance to meet them."

She couldn't help but remember he'd left because of her. She looked at him. "Do you think you'll ever return to Denver to visit?"

Walker captured the back of her neck with his hand and brought her mouth closer to his. He nibbled around her lips before placing an openmouthed kiss on her neck. "Um, will you make it worth my while if I do?"

She closed her eyes, loving the way Walker ravished her with his mouth and tongue. Desire coiled in her stomach. "I can't make any promises, but I'll see what I can do."

He pulled back slightly and she opened her eyes and met his gaze. She saw a serious glint in the dark depths as he said, "Dillon asked when you were coming home."

He'd presented it as a statement and not a question. "Yes. I told him when you got better."

He nodded, holding fast to her gaze. "I'm better."

Bailey drew in a deep breath, wondering if he was telling her that because he was ready for her to leave. "Have I worn out my welcome?"

He gently gripped her wrist and brought it to his lips, placing a light kiss on her skin. "I don't think that's possible."

She decided not to remind him he was a loner. A man who preferred solitude to company. "In that case, I'll stay another week."

He flashed a sexy smile. "Or two?"

She tried not to blink in surprise that he was actually suggesting she hang around for two weeks instead of one. She glided her hand across the firmness of his jaw. "Yes. Or two."

As if he was satisfied with her answer, he leaned in and opened his mouth against hers.

Chapter 12

Walker left his bathroom and glanced across the room at his bed and the woman in it. This was the third night she'd spent with him and it was hard to remember a time when she hadn't. A part of him didn't want to remember it.

He rubbed a hand down his face. Bailey in his bed was something he shouldn't get used to. It was countdown time, and in a little less than two weeks she'd be gone and his life would return to normal.

Normal meant living for himself and nobody else. Garth often teased him about living a miserable life. Misery didn't need company. *He* didn't need company, but Bailey had made him realize that five years had been too long to go without a woman. He was enjoying her in his bed a little too damn much. And that unfortunately wasn't the crux of his problem. The real kicker was that he was enjoying her...even without the sex.

He hadn't gotten around to working until yesterday, and she had found what she claimed was the perfect spot in his office to sit and work on the laptop she had brought with her. That way she was still connected to her job in Denver.

They had worked in amicable silence, although he'd been fully aware of her the entire time. Her presence had made him realize what true loneliness was because he didn't want to think of a time when she wouldn't be there.

Forcing that thought to the back of his mind, he moved across the room to rekindle the flames in the fireplace. While jabbing at the wood with the poker, he glanced back over his shoulder when he heard Bailey shift around. She looked small in his huge bed. She looked good. As if she belonged.

He quickly turned back to the fire, forcing his thoughts off her and onto something else. Like Morris James's visit yesterday. The rancher had wanted to meet Bailey after hearing all about her. Word of how she'd downed that bear had spread quickly, far and wide. Morris wanted to present Bailey with the ten-thousand-dollar bounty she'd earned from killing the animal.

Bailey had refused to take it and instead told Morris she wanted to donate the money to charity, especially if there was one in town that dealt with kids. The surprised look on Morris's face had been priceless. What person in her right mind gives up ten thousand dollars? But both Walker and Morris had watched her sign the paperwork to do just that.

As he continued to jab the poker in the fire another Bailey moment came to mind. He recalled the day he'd stepped out onto his front porch for the first time in a week. While sipping a cup of coffee he'd watched in fascination as Bailey had built a snowman. And when she'd invited him to help her, he had. He hadn't done something like that since he was a kid and he had to admit he'd enjoyed it.

For a man who didn't like having his privacy invaded, not only had she invaded that privacy, but for the time being she was making privacy nonexistent. Like when he'd come downstairs for breakfast this morning to find all four of his men sitting at his table. Somehow she'd discovered it was Willie's birthday and she'd wanted to do something special. At first Walker had been a little annoyed that she'd done such a thing without confiding in him, but then he realized that was Bailey's way—to do as she pleased. He couldn't help but smile at that.

But then he frowned upon realizing it was also Bailey's way to be surrounded by people. Although he was used to loneliness, she was not. She had a big family and was used to having people around all the time. He figured the loneliness of Alaska would eventually drive her crazy. What if she decided to leave before the two weeks?

Why should he give a damn if she did?

He returned the poker to the stand, not wanting to think about that. He was expecting another visit from Doc Witherspoon tomorrow. Hopefully it would be his last for a while. He couldn't wait to take out his plane and fly over his land. And he didn't want to question why he wanted Bailey with him to share in the experience.

"Walker?"

He glanced across the room. Bailey was sitting up in his bed. Her hair was mussed up and she had a soft, sleepy and sexy look on her face. Although she held the covers up to her chest, she looked tempting. Maybe because he knew that beneath all those bedcovers she was naked. "Yes?"

"I'm cold."

"I just finished stoking the fire."

"Not good enough, Alaskan. I'm sure you can do better than that."

Oh, yes, he definitely could. He removed his robe and headed for the bed, feeling a deep ache in his groin. The moment he slid in bed and felt her thigh brush against his, the ache intensified. He pulled her into his arms, needing to hold her. He knew there would come a time when he wouldn't be able to do that. The thought had him drawing in a deep, ragged breath.

She pulled back and ran her gaze over his face. "You okay?"

"Yes."

"Your leg?"

"Is fine. Back to the way it used to be. Only lasting reminder is that little scar."

"Trust me, Walker, no woman will care about that scar when you've got this to back things up," she said, reaching her hand beneath the covers to cup him, then stroke him. Walker drew in another ragged breath. Bailey definitely knew how to get to the heart of the matter. And when he saw the way she licked her lips and how the darkness of her eyes shone with desire, his erection expanded in her hand.

She leaned close to his ear and whispered, "Okay,

Walker, what's it going to be? You ride me or I ride you? Take your pick."

He couldn't stop the smile that curved his lips. It was hard—damn difficult, outright impossible—not to tap into all his sexual fantasies when she was around and being so damn accommodating. And she would be around for eleven more days. He intended to make the most of what he considered the best time of his life.

"Um," he said, pulling her back into his arms. "How about if we do both?"

Over the next several days Walker and Bailey settled into a gratifying and pleasurable routine. Now that Walker was back at 100 percent, he would get up every morning around five o'clock to work alongside his men. Then at nine, instead of hanging around and eating Willie's cooking like he normally did, he high-tailed it back to the ranch house, where Bailey would have breakfast waiting on him. No matter how often he told her that she didn't have to go out of her way, she would wave her hand and brush off his words. After placing the most delectable-looking meal in front of him, she would go on and on about what a beautiful kitchen he had. It was one that would entice someone to cook whether they wanted to or not, she claimed.

He began to see his kitchen through her eyes and finally understood. In all the years he had lived here, he'd never thought of his kitchen, or any kitchen, as beautiful. It was a place to cook meals and eat. But she brought his attention to the space, its rustic look. But what she said she liked most was sitting at the table and looking out at the strait. On a clear day the waters looked breathtaking. Just as breathtaking as Gemma Lake, she'd told him. It was during those conversations that he knew she missed her home. Hadn't one of her rules been to never venture far from Westmoreland Country for too long?

Garth had dropped by twice to check on Walker, and because his best friend had been calling every day to see how he was doing, Garth wasn't surprised to find Bailey still there. Garth didn't seem surprised at how comfortable she'd made herself in Walker's home, either. And Walker had caught Garth staring at them with a silly-looking grin on his face more than once.

Garth had mentioned to Bailey that he'd gotten in touch with her family and had spoken to Dillon and Ramsey, and that he and his brothers would be flying to Denver in a few weeks. Bailey mentioned that she would be back home by then and that she and her family would anxiously await Garth's visit. Her comment only made Walker realize that he didn't have a lot of time left with her.

Lola was back on her regular housekeeping schedule and told him more than once how much she liked Bailey. He figured it was because Bailey was chattier with her than he'd ever been. And he figured since Lola had only one bed in the house to make up, the older woman had pretty much figured out that he and Bailey were sharing it. That had suited Lola since she'd hinted more than once that he needed a woman in his life and that being alone on the ranch wasn't good for him.

Walker took a sip of his coffee while looking out at the strait. He remembered the day Bailey had gone into town with him to pick up supplies. News of her and the bear had spread further than Walker had imagined it would, and she'd become something of a legend. And if that wasn't enough, Morris had spread the word about what she'd done with the bounty money. Her generous contribution had gone to Kodiak Way, the local orphanage. Walker hadn't visited the place in years, not since he'd gone there on a field trip with his high school. But he'd decided on that particular day to stop by with Bailey, so she could see where her money had gone.

It had amazed him how taken she'd been with all the children, but he really should not have been surprised. He recalled how much she adored her nieces, nephews and little cousins back in Denver and just how much they'd adored her. He and Bailey had spent longer at the orphanage than he had planned because Bailey couldn't miss the opportunity to take a group of kids outside to build a snowman.

He then recalled the day he'd taken her up in his single-engine plane, giving her a tour of his land. She had been in awe and had told him how beautiful his property was. When she'd asked him how he'd learned to fly, he'd opened up and told her of his and Garth's time together in the marines. She'd seemed fascinated by everything he told her and he'd gotten caught up in her interest.

It had been a beautiful day for flying. The sky had been blue and the clouds a winter white. From the air he had pointed out his favorite areas—the lakes, small coves, hidden caves and mountaintops. And he'd heard himself promising to one day cover the land with her in his Jeep.

And then there had been the day when she'd pulled

him into his office, shoved him down into the chair at his desk and proceeded to sit in his lap so she could show him what she'd downloaded on his desktop computer. Jillian and Aidan had returned from their three-week honeymoon to France, Italy and Spain, and had uploaded their wedding video. Bailey thought that since he'd missed the wedding, he could watch the video.

As far as weddings went, it had been a nice one. Bailey had pointed out several cousins he hadn't met and their wives and children. He agreed that Jillian had been a beautiful bride and he'd seen the love in Aidan's eyes when she'd walked down the aisle on Dillon's arm.

Watching the video made Walker recall his own wedding. Only thing, his wedding had been nothing more than a circus. His parents and Garth had tried to warn him with no luck. A few nights ago he'd dreamed about Kalyn and Connor. A dream that had turned into a nightmare, with Bailey waking him up.

The next day, even though he'd seen the probing curiosity in her eyes, she hadn't asked him about it and he hadn't felt the need to tell her.

Walker took another sip of his coffee and glanced down at his watch. Bailey should be coming down for breakfast any minute. He had finished his chores with the men earlier than usual and had rushed back to the ranch house. More than once he'd been tempted to go upstairs and wake her but he knew if he did they might end up staying in bed the rest of the day. He then thought about the phone call he'd received an hour ago from Charm. It seemed Charm couldn't wait to meet her look-alike and asked that he fly Bailey to Fairbanks this weekend. He hadn't made any promises, but he'd told her he would talk to Bailey about it.

Moments later, he heard her upstairs and felt his sex stir in anticipation. Only Bailey could put him in such a state, arousing him so easily and completely. And he would admit that her mere presence in his home brought him a kind of joy he hadn't thought he would ever feel again.

But then he also knew it was the kind of joy he couldn't allow himself to get attached to. Just as sure as he knew that when he got up every morning the strait would be filled with water, he knew that when Bailey's days were up, she would be leaving.

Already he'd detected a longing in her and figured she'd become homesick. It was during those times that he was reminded of the first day they'd met. She'd told him about her rules and her love for Westmoreland Country. She'd said she never intended to leave it. And since he never intended to leave Kodiak, that meant any wishful thinking about them spending their lives together was a waste of his time.

Walker's grip on the cup tightened. And hadn't she told him about men getting possessive, becoming territorial and acting crazy sometimes? Sadly, he could now see himself doing all three where she was concerned.

It was nobody's fault but his own that he was now in this state. He'd known her rules and had allowed her to get under his skin anyway. But he could handle it. He had no choice. He would store up memories of the good times, and those memories would get him through the lonely nights after she left.

He heard her moving around upstairs again and sat his coffee cup down. Temptation was ruling his senses now. Desire unlike anything he'd ever felt before took control of him, had him sliding back from the table and standing.

Walker left the kitchen and moved quickly toward the stairs, seeking the object of his craving.

Chapter 13

"What am I going to do, Josette? Of all the stupid, idiotic, crazy things I could have done, why did I fall in love with Walker Rafferty?" Bailey asked. She held her mobile phone to her ear and paced Walker's bedroom. Talk about doing something dumb.

She had woken up that morning and glanced out the window on her way to the bathroom. She'd seen Walker and his men in the distance, knee deep in snow, loading some type of farm equipment onto a truck. She had stared at him, admiring how good he looked even dressed in a heavy coat and boots with a hat on his head. All she could think about was the night before, how he had made love to her, how he'd made her scream a number of times. And how this morning before leaving the bed he had brushed a good-morning kiss across her lips.

Suddenly, while standing at the window and ogling him, it had hit her—hard—that all those emotions she'd been feeling lately weren't lust. They were love.

She had fallen head over heels in love with Walker.

"Damn it, Josette. I should have known better."

"Calm down, Bailey. There's nothing stupid, idiotic or crazy about falling in love."

"It is if the man you love has no intention of ever loving you back. Walker told me all he could ever offer is a meaningless affair. I knew that and fell in love with him anyway."

"What makes you think he hasn't changed his mind? Now that the two of you have spent time together at his ranch, he might have."

"I have no reason to think he won't be ready for me to leave when my two weeks are up. Especially after that stunt I pulled the other day. Inviting his men for breakfast without his permission. Although he didn't say anything, I could tell he didn't like it."

"Are you going to tell him how you feel?"

"Of course not! Do you want me to feel even more stupid?"

"So what are you going to do?"

Bailey paused, not knowing how she intended to answer that. And also knowing there was really only one way to answer it. "Nothing. Just enjoy the time I have with him now and leave with no regrets. I believe the reason he refuses to love anyone else is because he's still carrying a torch for his late wife. There's nothing I can do about that and I don't intend to try."

Moments later, after ending her phone call with Josette, Bailey walked back over to the window. Today the weather appeared clearer than it had been the past couple of days. She missed home, but not as much as she'd figured she would. Skype had helped. She communicated regularly with her nieces and nephews and little cousins and, according to Ramsey, although several wives were expecting new babies in the family, none had been born. Everyone was expecting her home for Thanksgiving and was looking forward to her return.

She had worked out a system with Lucia where she could work remotely from Alaska. Doing so helped fill the long days when Walker was gone. In the evenings she looked forward to his return. Although they had established an amicable routine, she knew it was just temporary. Like she'd told Josette, there was no doubt in her mind Walker would expect her to leave next week. Granted, she knew he enjoyed her as his bedmate, but she also knew that, for men, sex was nothing more than sex. She had found that out while watching her then-single Westmoreland brothers and cousins. For her and Walker, there could never be anything between them other than the physical.

Even so, she could sense there was something bothering Walker. More than once she'd awakened in the night to find him standing at the window or poking the fire. And then there had been the night he'd woken up screaming the words, "No, Kalyn! Don't! Connor! Connor!"

She had snuggled closer and wrapped her arms around him, and pretty soon he had calmed down, holding her as tightly as she held him. The next day over breakfast she had expected him to bring up the incident, but he hadn't. She could only assume he didn't remember it or didn't want to talk about it. But she had been curious enough to check online and she'd found out Kalyn had been his wife and Connor his son.

Bailey turned when she heard the bedroom door opening, and there Walker stood, looking more handsome than any man had a right to look. As she stood there staring, too mesmerized by the heat in his eyes to even speak, he closed the door and removed his jacket, then tossed it across the chair.

She'd seen that look in his eyes before, usually in the evenings after he'd spent the entire day on the range. It wasn't quite nine in the morning. She swallowed. Now he was unbuttoning his shirt. "Good morning, Walker."

"Good morning, Bailey." He pulled the belt from his jeans before sitting in the chair to remove his boots and socks. His eyes never left hers.

"You've finished your chores for the day already?"

"No."

"No?"

"Yes, no. The guys took my tractor over to the Mayeses' place for Conley to look at it. He's the area mechanic. Nothing much to do until they get back, which won't be for hours."

She nodded. "I see."

"I came in for coffee and had a cup before hearing you move around up here, letting me know you were awake." Now he was unzipping his pants.

"And?" she asked, as if she really didn't know.

He slid his pants down muscular thighs. "And—" he crooked his finger "—come here a minute."

He stood there stark naked. She couldn't help licking her lips as her gaze moved from his eyes downward, past his chest to the thatch of dark hair covering his erection. "Before or after I take off my clothes?" she asked.

"Before. I want to undress you."

At that moment she didn't care that she'd just finished putting on her clothes. From the look in his eyes, he was interested in more than just taking off her clothes.

Drawing in a deep breath and trying to ignore the throb between her legs, she crossed the room on wobbly knees. Was she imagining things or was his erection expanding with each step she took? When she stopped in front of him, he placed both hands on her shoulders. She felt the heat of his touch through her blouse.

"You look good in this outfit," he said, holding fast to her shoulders as his gaze raked over her.

"Thanks." It was just a skirt and blouse. Nothing spectacular.

"You're welcome." Then he captured her lips with his.

Her last coherent thought was *But this kiss is spectacular.*

Walker was convinced, and had been for some time, that Bailey was what fantasies were made of. What he'd told her was the truth. She looked good in that outfit. Truth be told, she looked good in any outfit…especially in his shirts. Those were the times he felt most possessive, territorial, crazy with lust…and love. All the things that she'd once stated were total turnoffs for her.

He continued kissing her, moving his mouth over her lips with a hunger he felt all the way to his toes. He had wanted this kiss to arouse her, get her ready for what was to come. He figured she knew his motives because of the way she was responding. Their tongues tangled madly, greedily, as hot and intense as it could get.

His hands left her shoulders and cupped her backside, pressing her body against his. There was no way she didn't feel his erection pressing against the juncture of her thighs.

He'd watched her crossing the room and noticed her gaze shifting from his face to his groin, checking him out. He really didn't know why. Nothing about that part of his body had changed. She had cupped it, taken it into her mouth and fondled it. So what had she found so fascinating about it today?

As if she'd guessed his thoughts, she glanced up to meet his eyes just seconds before reaching him. The tint that darkened her cheeks had been priceless, and instead of stripping her clothes off like he'd intended, he kissed her. He'd overplayed his hand with Bailey. This young woman had done what no other could have done. She was on the verge of making him whole. Making him want to believe in love all over again. Restoring his soul to what it had been before Kalyn had destroyed it.

He slowly broke off the kiss. His hands returned to her shoulders only long enough to remove her blouse and unhook her bra. And then he tugged her skirt and panties down past her hips and legs to pool at her feet. He looked his fill. Now he understood her earlier fascination with him because he was experiencing the same fascination now.

Yes, he'd seen it all before. Had tasted and touched every single inch. But still, looking at her naked body almost took his breath away. She was beautiful. His

body ached for her in a way it had never ached for another woman…including Kalyn.

That realization had him lifting her into his arms,
carrying her to the bed. He placed her on it and joined
her there. He had intended to go slow, to savor each
moment as long as he could. But she had other ideas.

When they stretched out together on the huge bed,
her mouth went for his and kissed him hungrily. The
same way he'd kissed her moments ago. The only difference was that her hands were everywhere, touching, exploring and stroking. He joined in with his own
hands, frenzied with the need to touch her and let his
mouth follow. She squirmed against him, biting his
shoulders a few times and licking his chest, trying
to work her mouth downward. But he beat her to the
punch. She released a gasp when he tightened his hold
on her hips and lowered his head between her legs.

He'd only intended to lick her a few times, but her
taste made that impossible. He wanted more, needed
more, and he was determined to get everything he
wanted.

He heard her moans, felt her nails dig deep into his
shoulders. He knew the moment her pleasure came,
when she was consumed in an orgasm that had her
writhing beneath his mouth.

Lust ripped through him, triggered by her moans.
He had to be inside her now. Easing his body over hers,
their gazes held as he slowly entered her. It took all his
strength not to explode right when she arched her back
and lifted her hips to receive every last inch of him.
She entwined her arms around his neck and then, in
a surprise move, she leaned up slightly and traced his
lips with the tip of her tongue.

Something snapped inside him and he began thrusting in and out of her, going deeper with every downward plunge. Over and over, he fine-tuned the rhythm, whipping up sensation after exquisite sensation.

"Walker!"

When she screamed his name, the same earthshaking orgasm that overtook her did the same to him. A fierce growl escaped his lips when he felt her inner muscles clench him, trying to hold him inside.

This was how it was supposed to be. Giving instead of taking. Sharing instead of just being a recipient.

When their bodies had gone limp, he found the strength to ease off her and pull her into his arms, needing to hold her close to his heart. A part of him wished they could remain like that forever, but he knew they couldn't. Time was not on their side.

He knew her rules, especially the one about staying in Westmoreland Country. And he knew the promise he'd made to his father, about never taking Hemlock Row for granted again. That meant that even if Bailey agreed to a long-term affair, there would be no compromise on either of their parts.

Even so, he was determined to stock up on all the memories he could.

"Charm called."

Bailey's body felt weak as water but somehow she managed to open her eyes and meet Walker's gaze. She was convinced the man had more stamina than a bull. And wasn't she seven years younger? He should be flat on his back barely able to move…like her.

She found the strength to draw in a slow breath. Evidently he was telling her this for a reason and there was only one way to find out what it was. "And?"

"And she asked me to bring you to Fairbanks this weekend. Let me rephrase that. She kind of ordered me to."

Bailey couldn't help but chuckle. "Ordered. I didn't think anyone had the nerve to order you to do anything."

"Charm thinks she can. She considers me one of her brothers and she thinks she can wrap all of us around her finger. Like you do with your brothers and cousins."

That got another chuckle from her. "I don't know about that anymore." When he eased down beside her, she snuggled against him. "So are you going to do it? Are you going to take me to Fairbanks?"

He looked over at her. "I thought you didn't want to have anything to do with the Outlaws."

"I never said that. I just didn't like how they handled their business by sending you to Denver instead of coming themselves." Reaching up, she entwined her arms around his neck. "But I'm over that now. If they hadn't sent you, then we would not have met."

She grimaced at the thought of that, and for the first time since meeting Walker she decided the Outlaws had definitely done her a favor. Even if he didn't love her, she now knew how it felt to fall in love with someone. To give that person your whole heart and soul. To be willing to do things you never thought you would do.

Now she understood her sisters. She'd always thought Megan and Gemma were plumb loco to consider living anywhere other than Westmoreland Country. Megan not so much, since she stayed in West-

moreland Country six months out of the year and spent
the other six months in Rico's hometown of Philly. But
Gemma had made Australia her permanent home and
only returned to Denver to visit on occasion. Megan
and Gemma had chosen love over everything else.
They knew home was where the heart was. Now Bailey did, too.

"You've gotten quiet on me."

She glanced over at Walker and smiled. "Only because you haven't answered my question. So are you
going to take me to Fairbanks?" She knew that was a
big request to make, because he'd mentioned once that
he rarely left his ranch.

She could tell he was considering it and then he
said, "Only if you go somewhere with me tomorrow."

She lifted a brow. "Where?"

He pulled her closer. "You'll know when we get
there."

She stared at him silently, mulling over his request.
She was curious, but she knew she would follow him
to the ends of the earth if he asked her to. "Yes, I will
go with you tomorrow."

Chapter 14

The next morning Walker woke up with a heavy heart, pretty much like he'd done for the past ten years. It was Connor's birthday. In the past he'd spent the day alone. Even Garth knew not to bother him on that anniversary. Yet Bailey was here, and of all things he had asked her to go to Connor's grave with him, although she had no idea where they were headed.

"You're still not going to give me a hint?" Bailey asked when he placed his Stetson on his head and then led her outside. Bundled up in her coat, boots, scarf and a Denver Broncos knitted cap, she smiled over at him. Snow covered the ground but wasn't as deep as yesterday.

He shook his head. "Don't waste your smile. You'll know when we get there." She had tried to get him to tell her last night and again this morning, but he wouldn't share. He had thoroughly enjoyed her seductive efforts, though.

"I didn't know you were so mean, Walker."

"And I've always known you were persistent, Bailey. Come on," he said, taking her gloved hand to lead her toward one of his detached garages. When he raised the door she got a peek of what was inside and almost knocked him down rushing past him.

"Wow! These babies are beauties," she said, checking out the two sleek, black-and-silver snowmobiles parked beside one of his tractors. "Are they yours?"

He nodded, leaning against the tractor. "Yes, mine and Garth's. He likes to keep his here to use whenever he comes to visit. But today, this will be our transportation to get where we're going."

"Really?" she gasped excitedly, nearly jumping up and down.

Walker couldn't ignore the contentment he felt knowing he was the one responsible for her enthusiasm. "Yes. You get to use Garth's. I asked his permission for you to do so. He figures any woman who can shoot a grizzly from one hundred feet away should certainly know how to operate one of these."

Bailey laughed. "It wasn't exactly a hundred feet away and yes, I can operate one of these. Riley has one. He loves going skiing and takes it with him when he does. None of us can understand it, but he loves cold weather. The colder the better."

Walker opened a wooden box and pulled out two visored helmets and handed her one. "Where we're going isn't far from here."

She looked up at him as she placed her helmet on her head. "And you still won't give me a hint?"

"No, not even a little one."

* * *

Of all the places Bailey figured they might end up, a cemetery wasn't even on her list. When they had brought the snowmobiles to a stop by a wooden gate she had to blink to make sure she wasn't imagining things.

Instead of asking Walker why they were there, she followed his lead and got off the machine. She watched as he opened a box connected to his snowmobile and pulled out a small broom. He then took her gloved hand in his. "This way."

Walking through snow, he led her through the opening of the small cemetery containing several headstones. They stopped in front of the first pair. "My grandparents," he said softly, releasing her hand to lean down and brush away the snow that covered the names. *Walker and Lora Rafferty.*

She glanced up at him. "You were named after your grandfather?"

He nodded. "Yes. And my father."

"So you're the third?"

He nodded again. "Yes, I'm the third. My grandfather was in the military, stationed in Fairbanks, and was sent here to the island one summer with other troops to work on a government project for a year. He fell in love with the island. He also fell in love with a young island girl he met here."

"The woman who could trace her family back to Alaska when it was owned by Russia?" Bailey asked, letting him know she remembered what he'd told her about his grandparents that first day they'd met.

A smile touched one corner of his mouth. "Yes, she's the one. They married and he bought over a thousand acres through the government land grant. He and Lora settled here and named their property Hemlock Row, after the rows of trees that are abundant on the island. They only had one child. My father."

They then moved to the second pair of headstones and she guessed this was where his parents were buried. *Walker and Darlene Rafferty.* And the one thing she noticed was that they had died within six months of each other.

She didn't want to ask but had to. "How did they die?"

At first she wasn't sure he would answer, but then his voice caught in the icy wind when he said, "Mom got sick. By the time the doctors found out it was cancer there was nothing that could be done. She loved Hemlock Row and wanted to take her last breath here. So we checked her out of the hospital and brought her home. She died less than a week later."

Bailey studied the date on the headstone. "You were here when she died?"

"Yes."

She did quick calculations in her head. Walker had lost his wife and son three months before he'd lost his mother and subsequently his father. He had fled Hollywood to come here to find peace from his grief only to face even more heartache when he'd arrived home. No wonder he'd shut himself off from the world and become a loner. He had lost the four people he'd loved the most within a year's time.

She noticed his hold on her hand tightened when he said, "Dad basically died of a broken heart. He missed Mom that much. Six months. I'm surprised he lasted without her that long. She was his heart, and I guess he figured that without her he didn't need one."

Bailey swallowed. She remembered Ramsey telling her that at least their parents had died together. He couldn't imagine one living without the other. Like Walker's, her parents had had a very close marriage.

"My father was a good one," Walker said, breaking into her thoughts. "The best. He loved Hemlock Row, and when I was a teenager he made me promise to always take care of it and keep it in the family and never sell it. I made him a promise to honor his wishes."

She nodded and recalled hearing her father and uncle had made their father and grandfathers the same such promises. That was why her family considered Westmoreland Country their home. It had been land passed to them from generation to generation. Land their great-grandfather Raphel had worked hard to own and even harder to maintain.

Walker shifted and they moved toward the next headstone. She knew before he brushed the snow off the marker who it belonged to. His son. *Connor Andrew Rafferty.*

From the dates on the headstone, he'd died four days after his first birthday, which would have been…today. She quickly glanced over at the man standing beside her, still holding her hand as he stood staring at the headstone with a solemn look on his face. Today was his son's birthday. Connor would have been eleven today.

There were no words Bailey could say because at that moment she could actually feel Walker's pain. His grief was still raw and she could tell it hadn't yet healed. So she did the only thing she could do. She leaned into him. Instead of rejecting her gesture, he placed his arms around her waist and gently drew her against his side.

They stood there together, silently gazing at the headstone. She was certain his mind was filled with memories of the son he'd lost. Long minutes passed before Walker finally spoke. "He was a good kid. Learned to walk at ten months. And he loved playing hide-and-seek."

Bailey forced a smile through the tears she tried to hold back. She bet he was a good daddy who played hide-and-seek often with his son. "Was he ever hard to find?"

Walker chuckled. "All the time. But his little giggle would always give him away."

Walker got quiet again, and then he turned her in his arms to face him. He touched her chin with his thumb. "Thanks for coming here with me today."

"Thanks for bringing me. I know today has to be painful for you."

He dropped his hand and broke eye contact to look up at the snow-covered mountains behind her. "Yes, it is every year. There are some things you just can't get over."

Bailey nodded. She then glanced around, expecting to see another headstone, and when she didn't, she gazed at Walker and asked, "Your wife?"

He looked back down at her and took her hand. "What about her?"

"Is she not buried here?"

He hesitated a moment and then said, "No." And then he tightened his hold on her hand. "Come on. Let's head back."

* * *

Later that night as Walker lay in bed holding Bailey in his arms while she slept, he thought about their time together at the cemetery. Today had been the first time he'd allowed anyone in on his emotions, his pain, the first time he'd shared his grief. And in turn, he had shared some of his family's history with her. It was history he hadn't shared with any other woman but Kalyn. The difference in how the two women had received the information had been as different as day and night.

Kalyn hadn't wanted to hear about it. Said he should forget the past and move on. She was adamant about never leaving Hollywood to return here to live. She never even visited during the three years they'd been married. How she had hated a place she'd never seen went beyond him. And she had told him that if his parents died and he inherited the place, he should sell it. She'd listed all the things they could buy with the money.

On the other hand, Bailey had listened to his family's history today and seemed to understand and appreciate everything he'd told her. She had even thanked him for sharing it with her.

He hadn't been able to verbalize his own appreciation so he'd expressed it another way. As soon as they returned to his ranch, he had whisked her into his arms, carried her up the stairs and made love to her in a way he'd never made love to any other woman.

Walker released his hold on Bailey now to ease out of bed and cross the room. He stared into the fire as if the heat actually flickered in his soul. Today, while making love to Bailey, he kept telling himself that it was only lust that made him want her so much. That it was appreciation that drove him. He refused to consider anything else. Anything more. And yet now he was fighting to maintain his resolve where she was concerned.

He didn't want or need anyone else in his life. And although he enjoyed her company now, he preferred solitude. Once she was gone, everything in his life would get back to normal. And she *would* leave, he didn't doubt that. She loved Westmoreland Country as much as he loved Hemlock Row.

He inhaled deeply, wanting to take in the smell of wood and smoke. Instead, he was filled with Bailey's scent. "Damn it, I don't want this," he uttered softly with a growl. "And I don't need her. I don't need anyone."

He released a deep breath, wondering whom he was trying to convince.

He knew the answer to that. He had to convince himself or else he'd end up making the mistake of the century, and one mistake with a woman was enough.

When Bailey had noticed Kalyn wasn't buried there, for a second he'd been tempted to confide in her. To tell her the whole sordid story about his wife and her betrayal. But he couldn't. The only living person who knew the whole story was Garth, and that was the way Walker would keep it. He could never open himself up to someone else—definitely not another woman.

He heard Bailey stirring in bed and his body responded, as usual. He wondered how long this erotic craving for her would last. He had a feeling he would have an addiction long after she was gone. But while she was here he would enjoy her and store up the memories.

"Walker?"

He turned and looked toward the bed. "I'm over here."

"I want you here."

His thoughts were pensive. He wanted to be where she was, as well. He crossed the room and eased back into bed, drawing her into his arms. They only had a few more days together and then she would be gone. She would return to Westmoreland Country without looking back. In the meantime, he would make sure the days they had together were days he could cherish forever.

Chapter 15

"I don't believe it," Charm Outlaw said, caught up in a moment of awe as she stared at Bailey. "We do favor. I didn't believe Garth and Walker, but now I do." She gave Bailey a hug. "Welcome to Fairbanks, cousin."

Bailey couldn't help but smile, deciding she liked Charm right away. Everyone had been right—they did look alike. Charm's five brothers also favored their Westmoreland cousins. "Thanks for the invite. I hadn't expected all of this."

"All of this" was the dinner party Charm had planned. Walker had flown them to Fairbanks and Garth had sent a limo to pick them up from the airport. The limo had taken a route through the city's downtown. Even though a thick blanket of snow covered the grounds, Bailey thought downtown Fairbanks was almost as captivating as downtown Denver.

Walker had given her a bit of Fairbanks's history, telling her that it was a diverse city thanks to the army base there. A lot of ex-military personnel decided they liked the area and remained after their tour of duty ended. He also told her Alaska had the highest ratio of men to women than anywhere else in the United States. Online dating was popular here and a lot of the men actually solicited mail-order brides.

After resting up at the hotel for a couple of hours, another limo had arrived to deliver them to the Outlaw Estates. Bailey couldn't help but chuckle when she remembered the marker at the entrance of the huge gated residence. It said, "Unless you're an outlaw, stay out. Josey Wales welcomed." Walker had told her the sign had been Maverick Outlaw's idea. He was a huge fan of Clint Eastwood. The Outlaw mansion sat on over fifty acres of land.

Already Bailey had met Charm and Garth's brothers—Jess, Sloan, Cash and Maverick. In addition to their resemblance to the Westmorelands, they carried themselves like Westmorelands, as well. All five were single and, according to Charm, the thought of getting married made her brothers break out in hives. Jess, an attorney, seemed like the least rowdy of the four, and she wasn't surprised that he had announced his candidacy for senator of Alaska. He indicated he knew of Senator Reggie Westmoreland and although they hadn't met yet, Jess had been surprised to discover they were related. He looked forward to meeting Reggie personally. He'd been following Reggie's political career for a number of years and admired how he carried himself in Washington. He also knew of Chloe's father, Senator Jamison Burton, and hoped as many others did that he would consider running for president one day.

"Every Outlaw is here and accounted for except Dad. He's not dealing with all this very well and decided to make himself scarce tonight."

Garth cleared his throat, making it apparent that he felt Charm had said too much. Bailey hadn't been bothered by Charm's words since on the flight over Walker had prepared her for the fact that Bart Outlaw still hadn't come around. For the life of her she couldn't understand what the big deal was. Why did Bart Outlaw refuse to acknowledge or accept that his father had been adopted?

Walker had also shared that Garth, his brothers and Charm all had different mothers but the brothers had been adopted by Bart before their second birthdays. Charm hadn't joined the group until she was in her teens. Her mother had sent her to Bart after Charm became too unruly. It sounded as if Bailey and Charm had a lot in common, although Dillon never entertained the thought of sending her anywhere.

One thing Bailey noted was that Walker never left her side. Not that it bothered her, but his solicitous manner made it obvious the two of them were more than friends. Every so often he would ask if she was okay. He'd told her before they'd arrived that if the Outlaws got too overbearing at any time, she and Walker would return to the hotel.

She saw a different Walker around the Outlaws. She knew he and Garth were best friends but it was obvious he had a close relationship with the others, as well. This Walker was more outgoing and not as reserved.

But then he'd acted the same way around her brothers and cousins once he'd gotten to know them.

"How long are you staying in Fairbanks, Bailey?" Charm asked her. "I'm hoping you'll be here for a few days so we can get some shopping in."

Before she could answer, Walker spoke up. "Sorry to disappoint you, Charm, but Bailey's returning to Denver on Monday."

"Oh," Charm said, clearly disappointed.

Bailey didn't say anything, merely took a sip of her wine. It sounded as if Walker was counting the days.

"Well, I guess I'll have to make sure I'm included in that trip to Denver with my brothers later this month."

"Then, you'll be in luck because the women who married into the family, as well as me and my sister Megan, all love to shop," Bailey said, trying to put Walker's words to the back of her mind.

Charm's face broke into an elated grin.

Garth shook his head. "Shopping should be Charm's middle name." He checked his watch. "I hate to break up this conversation, but I think dinner is ready to be served."

Charm hooked Bailey's arm in hers as they headed toward the dining room and whispered, "So tell me, Bailey. Are there any real cute single guys in Denver?"

Walker sat with a tight jaw while he listened to Garth give his father hell. Deservedly so. Although Bart had finally shown up for dinner, he'd practically ignored Bailey. It had been obvious from his expression when he'd walked into the dining room and saw Bailey sitting beside Charm that he'd done a double take. He'd definitely noticed the resemblance between the two women. Yet that seemed to spike his resentment. So, like Garth and his brothers, Walker couldn't help wondering why Bart was so dead set against claiming the Westmorelands as kin. It seemed Garth was determined to find out.

After dinner, even before dessert could be served, Garth had encouraged Charm to show Bailey around while he and his brothers had quickly ushered their father upstairs. Garth had invited Walker to sit in on the proceedings.

"You were outright rude to Bailey, Dad."

Bart frowned. "I didn't invite her here."

"No, we did. And with good reason. She's our cousin."

"No, she's not. We are Outlaws, not Westmorelands."

"You're not blind, Dad. You saw the resemblance between Charm and Bailey with your own eyes. Bailey even remarked on how much you favor her father and uncle."

"That means nothing to me," Bart said stubbornly.

Garth drew in a deep breath, and Walker knew his best friend well enough to know he was getting fed up with his father's refusal to accept the obvious. "Why? Why are you so hostile to the idea that your father was adopted? That does not mean he wasn't an Outlaw. All it means is that he had other family—his biological family—that we can get to know. Why do you want to deprive us of that?"

A brooding Bart was silent as he glanced around the room at his sons and at Walker. It was Walker who received the most intense glare. "You were to take care of this, Walker. Things should not have gotten this far. You were to find a way to discredit them."

"That's enough, Dad! How could you even ask something like that of Walker?" Garth asked angrily.

Instead of answering, Bart jerked to his feet and stormed out of the room.

His sons watched his departure with a mixture of anger and confusion on their faces.

"What the hell is wrong with him?" Jess asked the others.

Garth shook his head sadly. "I honestly don't know. You weren't there that day Hugh first told us about the Westmorelands. Dad was adamant that we not claim them as relatives no matter what. When he found out I sent Walker anyway, he was furious."

Sloan shook his head. "There has to be a reason he is handling things this way."

"I agree," Maverick said, standing. "Something isn't right here."

"I agree with Maverick," Walker said. There was something about Bart's refusal to accept that his father was adopted that didn't make sense. "There has to be a reason Bart is in denial. He might have his ways, but I've never figured him to be an irrational man."

"I agree," Cash said, shaking his head. "And he actually told you to find a way to discredit the Westmorelands?"

Walker nodded slowly. "You heard him for yourself."

"Damn," Sloan said, refilling his glass with his favorite after dinner drink. "I agree with Maverick and Walker. Something isn't right. Since Dad won't level with us and tell us what's going on, I suggest we hire someone to find out."

Cash glanced over at his brother, frowning. "Find out what?"

"Hell, I don't know" was Sloan's frustrated reply.

The room got quiet until Walker said, "Have any of you considered the possibility that there's something that went on years ago within the Outlaw family that you don't know about? Something that makes Bart feel he has to maintain that his father was the blood son of an Outlaw?"

Garth sat down with his drink. "I have to admit that thought has occurred to me."

"In that case," Jess said, "we need to find out what."

"You worried it might cause a scandal that will affect your campaign?" Sloan asked his brother.

"I have no idea," Jess said soberly. "But if there's something I need to worry about, then I want to find out before the media does."

Garth nodded. "Then, we're all in agreement. We look into things further."

Everyone in the room nodded.

"I'm sorry about my father's behavior at dinner, Bailey. I honestly don't know what has gotten into him," Charm said apologetically as she led Bailey back to the center of the house.

"No apology needed," Bailey said. "I was anticipating such an attitude. Walker prepared me on the flight here from Kodiak. He said Bart might not be friendly to me."

"Um," Charm said, smiling. "Speaking of Walker. The two of you look good together. I'm glad he's finally gotten over his wife."

Bailey drew in a deep breath, not sure that was the

case. It was quite obvious to her that he was still grieving the loss of his wife and son. And because of the
magnitude of that grief, he refused to open up his heart
to anyone else. "Looks can be deceiving, Charm."

She raised a brow. "Does that mean you're actually
leaving to return to Denver on Monday?"

"No reason for me to stay. Like I said, looks can
be deceiving."

Charm lifted her chin. "In this case, I think not.
I've noticed the way Walker looks at you. He looks
at you—"

Probably like a horny man, Bailey thought silently.
There was no need to explain to Charm that the only
thing between her and Walker was their enjoyment of
sex with each other.

At that moment, Bailey's cell phone went off. At any
other time she would have ignored it, wishing she'd
remembered to turn off the ringer, but not this time.
This particular ringtone indicated the call was from
her cousin Bane.

"Forgive my rudeness," Bailey said to Charm as she
quickly got the phone out of her purse, clicked it on
and said to the caller, "Hold on a minute."

She then looked at Charm. "Sorry, but I need to
take this call. It's my cousin Bane. He's a navy SEAL
somewhere on assignment, and there's no telling when
he'll have a chance to call me again."

"I understand. And if you need to talk privately you
can use any of the rooms off the hall here. I'll be waiting for you downstairs in the main room."

Bailey gave Charm an appreciative smile. "Thanks."
She quickly stepped inside one of the rooms and turned

on the lights. "Bane? What's going on? Where are you?"

"Can't say. And I can't talk long. But I'm going to need your help."

"My help? For what?"

"I need to find Crystal."

Bailey frowned thoughtfully. "Bane, you know what Dillon asked you to do."

"Yes, Bay. Dil asked that I grow up and accept responsibility for my actions, to make something of myself before thinking about reclaiming Crystal. I promised him that I would and I have. Enough time has passed and I don't intend to wait any longer. In a couple of weeks I'll be on an extended military leave."

"An extended leave? Bane, are you okay?"

"I'll be better after I find Crystal, and I need your help, Bay."

Everyone had left the family room to return to the dining room for dessert except for Garth and Walker. Garth refilled Walker's glass with Scotch before proceeding to fill his own.

"So," Garth said, after taking a sip. "Do you think there's something Dad's not telling us?"

Walker, with his legs stretched out in front of him, sat back on the sofa and looked at Garth before taking a sip of his own drink. "Don't you?"

"Yes, and I'm going to hire a private detective. I don't want Hugh involved. He and Dad go way back, and there might be some loyalty there that I don't want to deal with."

"I agree. What about Regan? Isn't some member of her family a PI?"

Garth nodded, studying the drink in his glass. "Yes, her sister's husband. I met him once. He's an okay guy. I understand he's good at what he does. I might call him tomorrow."

"I think that's a good idea."

They were silent for a spell and then Garth asked, "So what's going on with you and Bailey?"

Walker took another sip of his drink. "What makes you think something is going on?"

Garth rolled his eyes. "I can see, Walker."

Walker met his best friend's stare. "All you see is me interested in a woman who's hot. That's nice to have on those cold nights, especially for a man who's been without a female in his bed for a while. You heard her. She's leaving on Monday. Good riddance."

Bailey paused outside the closed door, not wanting to believe what Walker had just said. She'd been making her way back downstairs when she'd heard voices from one of the rooms. The voices belonged to Garth and Walker and when she'd heard her name she'd stopped.

Backing away from the door now, tears filled her eyes. She quickly turned and bumped right into Charm.

"Bailey, I was downstairs wondering if you'd gotten lost or something and—"

Charm stopped talking when she saw the tears in Bailey's eyes. "Bailey? What's wrong? Are you all right?"

Bailey swiped at her tears. "Yes, I'm fine."

Charm frowned. "No, you're not." She then glanced beyond Bailey to the closed door and the voices she heard. "What's going on? What did you hear? Did someone say something to upset you? Is Dad in that room with Garth and Walker? Did you overhear something Dad said?"

When Bailey didn't say anything, an angry Charm moved past her toward the door, ready to confront whoever was in the room about upsetting Bailey.

Bailey grabbed her hand. "No, please. Don't. It's okay." She swiped again at her eyes. "Thanks for your family's hospitality, Charm, but I need to leave." Bailey wanted to put as much distance between her and Walker as she could. "Will you call me a cab? I need a ride to the airport."

Charm frowned. "The airport? What about Walker? What am I supposed to tell him?"

To go to hell, Bailey thought. But instead she said, "You can tell him I got a call…from a family member…and I need to get back to Denver immediately."

Charm's frown deepened. "Do you really want me to tell him that?"

"Yes."

Charm didn't say anything for a minute, then nodded. "Okay, but I won't call you a cab. I'll take you to the airport myself."

Garth stared hard at Walker. "What you just said is nothing more than bull and you know it."

Walker took another sip of his drink before quirking a brow. "Is it?"

"Yes. You've fallen in love with Bailey, Walker. Admit it."

Walker didn't say anything for a long minute. Garth knew him well. "Doesn't matter if you think it's bull or not."

"It does matter. When are you going to let go of the past, Walker? When are you going to consider that perhaps Bailey is your future?"

Walker shook his head. "No, she's not my future. She has these rules, you see. And one of them is that she will never leave Westmoreland Country. And I, on the other hand, made a deathbed promise to my father never to leave Hemlock Row again."

"But you will admit that you love her?" Garth asked.

Walker closed his eyes as if in pain. "Yes, I love her. I love her so damn much. God knows I tried to fight it, but I couldn't. These past three weeks have been the best I've ever had. I thought I could live my life as a bitter and lonely man, but she's made me want more, Garth. She's made my house a real home. And she likes Hemlock Row."

"Then, what's the problem?"

He met Garth's inquisitive stare. "The problem is that I can't compete with her family. She needs them more than she could ever need me."

"Are you sure of that?"

"Yes. She's been homesick. I honestly didn't expect her to stay in Alaska this long. Already she's broken one of her rules."

"Maybe she had a reason to do so, Walker. Maybe you're that reason."

"I doubt it."

Garth was about to say something else when there was a knock on the door. "Come in."

Sloan entered. "Charm just left with Bailey."

Walker raised a brow. "Left? Where did they go? Don't tell me Charm talked Bailey into hitting some shopping mall tonight."

Sloan shook his head. "No. It seems Bailey got a call from some family member and had to leave. I don't know all the details but Charm is taking her to the airport. Bailey is booking a flight back to Denver. Tonight."

Chapter 16

"Ma'am, please buckle your seat belt. The plane will be taking off in a minute."

Bailey nodded and did what the flight attendant instructed. She'd arrived at the Fairbanks airport with no luggage, just the clothes on her back. Charm had promised to go to the hotel and pack up her things and ship them to her. She would do the same for the clothes Bailey had left behind at Hemlock Row.

Luckily Bailey could change her ticket for a fee. And she didn't care that she had two connecting flights before she reached Denver, one in Seattle and the other in Salt Lake City. All she cared about was that in twelve hours she would be back in Westmoreland Country. She hadn't even called her family to let them know her change in plans. She would get a rental car at the airport and go straight to Gemma's house. She needed to be alone for a while before dealing with her family and their questions.

She drew in a deep breath, not wanting to think about Walker. But all she could remember were the words he'd told Garth. So he would be glad when she was gone, would he? Well, he was getting his wish. She had been a fool to think he was worthy of her love. All he'd thought was that she was a hot body to sleep with.

But then, hadn't he told her up front all he wanted from her was a meaningless affair? Well, tonight he'd proved that what they'd shared had been as meaningless as it could get. Knowing it would take at least two hours before the plane landed in Seattle, she closed her eyes to soothe her tattered mind. At that moment she hoped she never saw Walker again.

"Damn her," Walker growled, taking his clothes out of the drawers and slinging them into the luggage that was opened on his bed. He intended to fly back to Kodiak Island tonight. There was no need to hang around. Bailey was why he'd left Hemlock Row to come here in the first place. And then what did she do? She hauled ass the first time she got a call from home.

However, now he knew that even that was a lie. Thinking she'd had a real family emergency, he'd placed a call to Dillon, who didn't know what he was talking about. As far as Dillon knew, nobody had called Bailey.

So now, on top of everything else, she had lied to him. She couldn't wait until Monday to leave? She had to leave tonight? Hell, she hadn't even taken the time to pack her clothes. What the hell was he supposed to do with them?

But what hurt more than anything was that she hadn't even had the decency to tell him goodbye. He felt like throwing something. Why did falling in love always end in heartache for him?

He continued to throw everything in his luggage when he heard a knock on the door. He hoped it wasn't Garth, trying to talk him out of leaving. There was no way he could stay. He wanted to go home to Hemlock Row, where loneliness was expected. Where he could drown his sorrows in a good stiff drink.

When the knocking continued, he moved to the door and snatched it open. Both Garth and Charm stood there. "I'm leaving tonight, Garth, and there's nothing you can say to stop me."

Garth and Charm walked past him to enter the hotel room. "I agree you should leave tonight, but not for Hemlock Row."

Walker looked at Garth. What he'd said didn't make any sense. "Then, where the hell am I supposed to go?"

"To head off Bailey. Stop her from making it to Denver."

That statement came from Charm. He glared at her. "And why on earth would I do that?"

Charm placed her hand on her hip and glared back at him. "Because you and Garth are the reason she left. I don't know what the two of you said about her while huddled in that room together tonight, but whatever you said, she overheard it and it had her in tears. I thought Dad was in there with you and figured he'd said something rude and gave him hell about it. But he said what Bailey overheard must have been a conversation between the two of you," she said, shifting her furious gaze between him and Garth.

Walker frowned. "For your information, I didn't say a damn thing that would have…"

He stopped speaking, swallowed hard and then glanced over at Garth. "Surely you don't think she heard—"

"All that crap you said?" Garth interrupted to ask, shaking his head. "I hope not. But what if she did?"

Walker rubbed a hand down his face. *Yes, what if she did?* "Damn it, I didn't mean it. In fact, later on in the conversation I admitted to falling in love with her."

"You love her?" Charm asked, smiling.

"Yes."

"Well, I doubt she heard that part. In fact, I'm one hundred percent certain she didn't. She was crying as if her heart was broken."

Walker checked his watch. "I've got to go after her."

"Yes, you do," Garth agreed. He then looked at Charm. "Do you have her flight information? I'm sure she has a connecting flight somewhere."

"She has two," Charm answered. "The first is in Seattle and then another in Salt Lake City."

Garth checked his watch. "I'll contact Regan and have her get the jet ready. If we act fast, you can get to Seattle the same time Bailey does. Maybe a few minutes before. And in case you've forgotten, Ollie is director of Seattle's Transportation Security Administration. Knowing the top dog of the TSA might prove to be helpful."

Walker nodded. He, Garth and Oliver Linton had served in the marines together and the three had remained good friends. "You're right." Walker was already moving, grabbing his coat and hat. Like Bailey, he was about to fly with just the clothes on his back.

* * *

Bailey took a sip of her coffee. She hated layovers, especially lengthy ones. She had another hour before she could board her connecting flight to Salt Lake City. And then she would have to wait two more hours before finally boarding the plane that would take her home to Denver.

Home.

Why didn't she have that excited flutter in her stomach that she usually had whenever she went on a trip and was on her way back to Denver? Why did she feel only hurt and pain? "That's easy enough to answer," she muttered to herself. "The man you love doesn't love you back. Get over it."

She drew in a deep breath, wondering if she ever would get over it. If it had been Monday and she'd been leaving because her time in Kodiak was over, it probably would have been different. But hearing the words Walker had spoken to Garth had cut deep. Not just into her heart but also into her soul. Evidently, her time at Hemlock Row had meant more to her than it had to him. All she'd been to him was a piece of ass during the cold nights. He'd practically said as much to Garth.

After finishing off her coffee, she tightened her coat around herself. For some reason she was still feeling the harsh Alaskan temperatures. She hated admitting it, but she missed Hemlock Row already, although she refused to miss Walker. She wished she could think of his ranch without thinking of him. She would miss Willie, Marcus and the guys, as well as Ms. Albright. She would miss standing at Walker's bedroom window every morning to stare out at Shelikof Strait. And she would definitely miss cooking in his kitchen. When she finally got around to designing her own home on Bailey's Bay, she might steal a few of his kitchen ideas. It would serve him right if she did.

"Excuse me, miss."

She glanced up into the face of an older gentleman wearing a TSA uniform. "Yes?"

"Are you Bailey Westmoreland?"

"Yes, I'm Bailey Westmoreland." She hoped nothing was wrong with her connecting flight. She didn't want the man to tell her it was canceled or delayed. She was ready to put as much distance between herself and Alaska as she could.

He nodded. "Ms. Westmoreland, could you please come with me?"

She stood. "Yes, but why? Is something wrong? What's going on?" She didn't have any luggage so there was no way they could have found anything in it. And her ticket was legit. She had made the proper changes in Fairbanks. As far as she was concerned she was all set.

"I'm unable to answer that. I was advised by my director to bring you to his office."

"Your director?" She swallowed. This sounded serious. She hoped she and some terrorist didn't have the same name or something. *Oh, crap.* "Look, sir," she said, following the man. "There must be some mistake."

She was about to say she'd never had done a bad thing in her life and then snapped her mouth shut. What about all those horrific things she, Bane and the twins had done while growing up? But that had been years ago. The sheriff of Denver, who was a good friend of Dillon's, had assured him that since the four of them had been juveniles their records would be wiped clean, as long as they didn't get into any trouble as adults. She couldn't speak for the twins, and Lord knew she couldn't vouch for Bane, but she could certainly speak for herself.

So she did. "Like I said, there must be a mistake. I am a law-abiding citizen. I work for a well-known magazine. I do own a gun. Several. But I don't have any of them with me."

The man stopped walking and looked over at her with a keen eye. She swallowed, wishing she hadn't said that. "I hunt," she quickly added, not wanting him to get the wrong idea. "I have all the proper permits and licenses."

He merely nodded. He then opened a door. "You can wait in here. It won't be long."

She frowned, about to tell him she didn't want to wait in there, that she was an American with rights. But she was too tired to argue. Too hurt and broken. She would wait for the director and see why she was being detained. If she needed an attorney there were a number of them in the Westmoreland family.

"Fine. I'll wait," she said, entering the room and glancing around. It was definitely warmer in here than it had been at the terminal gate. It was obvious this was some kind of meeting room, she thought, shrugging out of her coat and tossing it across the back of a chair. There were no windows, just a desk, several chairs and a garbage can. A map of Washington State was on one wall and a map of the United States on the other. There was a coffeepot on the table in the corner, and although she'd had enough coffee tonight to last her a lifetime, she crossed to the pot, hoping it was fresh.

That was when she heard the door behind her open. Good, the director had arrived and they could get down to business. The last thing she needed was to miss her connecting flight. She turned to ask the man or woman why she was here and her mouth dropped open.

The man who walked into the room was not the TSA director. It was the last person she figured she would see tonight or ever again.

"Walker!"

Chapter 17

Walker entered the room and closed the door behind him. And then he locked it. Across the room stood the woman he loved more than life itself. She'd overheard things straight from his lips that had all been lies, and now he had to convince her he hadn't meant any of what he'd said.

"Hello, Bailey."

She backed up, shock written all over her face. "Walker, what are you doing here? How did you get here? *Why* are you here?"

He shoved his hands into his pockets. He heard the anger in her voice. He also heard the hurt and regretted more than ever what he'd said. "I thought we had a conversation once about you asking a lot of questions. But since I owe you answers to each and every one of them, here goes. I came here to talk to you. I got here with Garth's company jet. And I'm here because I owe you an apology."

She stiffened her spine. "You should not have bothered. I don't think there's anything you can do or say to make me accept your apology."

He recalled when he'd said something similar to her the day she'd shown up at Hemlock Row. "But I did bother, because I know you heard what I said to Garth."

She crossed her arms over her chest. "Yes, I heard you. Pretty loud and clear. And I understood just what I was to you while I was at Hemlock Row and how you couldn't wait for me to leave."

"I didn't mean what I said."

"Sure you did. If nothing else, I've discovered you're a man who says exactly what he means."

He leaned against the wall, tilted his hat back and inhaled deeply, wishing her scent didn't get to him. And he wished she didn't look so desirable. She was still wearing the outfit she'd worn at the Outlaws'— black slacks and a bronze-colored pullover knit sweater with matching jewelry. She looked good then and she looked good now, four hours and over two thousand miles later.

But he liked Bailey best when she wasn't wearing anything at all. When she lay in his bed naked, with her breasts full and perky, the nipples wet from his tongue, and her feminine mound, hot, moist and ready for—

He sucked in a sharp breath and abruptly put an end to those thoughts. "Can we sit and talk?"

She frowned. "I honestly don't want to hear anything you have to say."

"Please. Both times when you apologized to me, I accepted your apologies."

"Good for you, but I have no intention of accepting yours."

She was being difficult, he knew that. He also knew there was only one way to handle Bailey. And that was by not letting her think she had the upper hand. "We are going to talk whether you want to listen to what I say or not. I locked that door," he said, removing his hat to place on a rack and then crossing the room to sit in one of the chairs. "And I don't intend for it to be opened until I say so. I forgot to mention that the director of the TSA here is an old marine friend of mine."

She glared at him. "You can't hold me here like some kind of hostage. I will sue you both."

"Go ahead and do that, if you desire. In the meantime you and I are staying in here until you agree to listen to what I have to say."

"I won't listen."

"I have the time to wait for you to change your mind," he said, leaning back in the chair so the front legs lifted off the floor. He closed his eyes. He heard her cross the room to the door and try it. It was locked. He didn't reopen his eyes when he heard her banging on it, nor when he heard her kick it a few times.

He knew the exact moment when a frustrated and angry Bailey crossed the room to stand in front of him. "Wake up, you bastard. Wake up and let me out of here."

He ignored her, but it wasn't easy. Especially when she began using profanity the likes of which he'd never heard before. He'd heard from one of her cousins that she used to curse like a sailor—worse than a sailor— as a teen, and Walker had even heard her utter a few choice words that day in his bedroom when he'd pissed her off. But now, tonight, she was definitely on a roll.

He would let her have her say—no matter how vulgar it was—and then he would have his. He would tell her everything. Including the fact that he loved her. He didn't expect her to love him back. It was too late for that, although he doubted it would have happened anyway. Bailey loved Westmoreland Country. She was married to it.

It seemed her filthy mouth wouldn't run out of steam anytime soon, so he decided to put an end to it. He'd gotten the picture, heard loud and clear what she thought of him. He slowly opened his eyes and stared at her. "If you recall, Bailey, I once told you that you had too delicious a mouth to fill it with nasty words. Do I need to test it to make sure it's still as delicious as the last time I tasted it?"

She threw her hair over her shoulder, fiery mad. "I'd like to see you try."

"Okay." He grabbed her around the waist and tumbled her into his lap. And then he kissed her.

She tried pushing him away, but just for a minute. Then, as if she had no control of her own tongue, it began tangling with his, sucking as hard as he was. And then suddenly, as if she realized what she was doing, she snatched her mouth away, but she didn't try getting off his lap.

"I hate you, Walker."

He nodded. "And I love you, Bailey."

She'd opened her mouth, probably to spew more filthy words, but what he'd said had her mouth snapping closed. She stared at him, not saying anything, and then she frowned. "I heard what you told Garth."

"Yes, but if you had hung around, you would have heard him say that I was talking bull because he knew how I felt about you. He's been my friend long enough to know. And then I admitted to having fallen in love with you."

She stared at him, studying his face. How long would it be before she said something? Finally she did. "You can't love me."

He shifted her in his lap, both to keep her there but also to bring some relief to the erection pressing painfully against his zipper. "And why can't I love you?"

"Because you're still in love with your wife. You've been grieving for her for ten years and you want me to believe I came along and changed that in less than a month?"

He knew he had to tell her the truth. All of it. He had to tell her what only he and Garth knew. Doing so would bring back memories. Painful memories. But he loved her. And he owed her the truth.

"Yes, I guess that would be hard to believe if I had been grieving for Kalyn for ten years. But I stopped loving my wife months before she died. I stopped loving her when I found out she was having an affair with another man."

Bailey swallowed. Of all the things she'd expected him to say, that wasn't it. "Your wife was unfaithful?" she asked, making sure she'd heard him correctly.

"Yes, among a number of other things."

She lifted a brow. "What other things?"

Walker drew in a deep breath before lifting her from his lap to place her in the chair beside him. He paced the room a few times before finally leaning against the wall.

"I need to start at the beginning," he said in a low, husky tone. But she'd been around Walker enough to detect the deep pain in his voice. "I was in the marines, stationed at Camp Pendleton. A few of the guys and I took a holiday to LA, preferring to tour the country-side. We came across a film crew making a movie. In-trigued, we stopped and, believe it or not, they asked us to be extras."

He paused before continuing, "One of the women who had a small role caught my eye and I caught hers."

"Kalyn?"

He looked over at Bailey. "Yes. That night she and I met at a restaurant and she told me her dream was to become an actress, that she was born in Los Angeles and loved the area. We slept together that night and a few times after that. I was smitten, but I thought that would be the end of it. It was only a few months be-fore my time in the marines ended and I was looking forward to heading home. Both Garth and I were."

He paused. "Dad had written and I knew the ranch was becoming a handful. He couldn't wait for me to come home to help. I told him I would. Practically promised."

He moved away from the wall to sit in the chair be-side her. "I basically broke that promise. A few days before I was supposed to leave I got a call. Someone had viewed a clip of me as an extra and liked what they saw. They didn't know whether I could act or not but thought I had what they termed 'Hollywood looks.' They called me to try out for a part in some movie. I didn't get the part but they asked me to hang around for a week or two, certain they could find me work."

He leaned back in the chair as he continued. "Kalyn said she was happy for me. She also told me she thought she was pregnant. I never questioned her about it, although Garth suggested I should. I didn't listen to him. Nor did I listen when he tried to get me to leave California and return home, reminding me that my dad needed me. All I could think about was that Kalyn might be pregnant and I should do the honorable thing and marry her. So I did."

"Was she pregnant?" Bailey asked curiously.

"No. She said it was a false alarm, but I was determined to make my marriage work regardless. I loved her. I suggested we leave LA and move to Kodiak Island, but she wouldn't hear of it. She would cry every time I brought up the subject. She told me she hated a place she'd never seen and she never wanted to go there."

Bailey couldn't imagine anyone not liking Hemlock Row, especially before they'd seen it.

"I talked to my dad and he told me to stay with my wife and make my marriage work and that he would hire a couple more men to help out around the ranch," Walker continued. "Although he didn't say it, I knew he was disappointed that I wasn't coming home with my wife.

"A few months later I got the chance at a big role and my career took off from there. Kalyn was happy. She loved being in the spotlight as my wife. But I missed home and when I told her I'd made up my mind to leave and return to Alaska, she told me she was pregnant."

Bailey lifted a brow. "Was she really pregnant this

time?" she asked in a skeptical voice. It sounded to her as though Kalyn's claim that first time had been a trick just to get Walker to marry her.

"Yes, she was this time. I went with her to the doctor to confirm it. Things got better between us. I fell in love with Connor the moment I heard his heartbeat. And months later, when I felt him move in Kalyn's stomach, I think my son and I connected in an unbreakable bond. I couldn't wait for him to be born. When he finally arrived I thought he was perfect. I couldn't wait to take him home for my parents to meet their grandson."

"You took him home to Hemlock Row?"

"Yes, but not until he was almost a year old. Kalyn refused to let me take him any sooner than that. Connor loved it there with his grandparents. I took him everywhere and showed him everything. Kalyn didn't go with us and told me I could only be gone with Connor for a week. I was upset about it but was grateful that my parents got to meet Connor and he got to meet them. A few months after I returned to LA I learned my mom was sick and the doctors couldn't figure out why. I went home a few times and each time I did, Kalyn gave me hell."

Bailey frowned. "She didn't want you to go home to check on your sick mother?" she asked, appalled.

"No, she didn't. Things got pretty bad between us, although we worked hard to pretend otherwise. In public we were the perfect, happily married Hollywood couple, but behind closed doors it was a different story."

He stood again to pace and when he came to a stop in front of where she sat, her heart almost stopped. The look on his face was full of hurt and anguish. "Then one day I came home and she dropped a bombshell. She told me that for the past year and a half she'd been having an affair with a married man and he'd finally decided to leave his wife for her."

He drew in a deep breath and closed his eyes. When he reopened them, he said, "And she also wanted me to know that Connor was not my son."

"No!"

The pain of his words hit Bailey like a ton of bricks, so she could imagine how Kalyn's words must have hit him. The son he'd fallen in love with was not his biological son. She couldn't imagine the pain that must have caused him.

"I told her I didn't care if Connor was my biological son or not. He was the son of my heart and that's all that mattered. I loved him. She only laughed and called me a fool for loving a child that wasn't mine."

There were a lot of words Bailey could think of to describe Walker's deceased wife, and none of them were nice. "What happened after that? Did she move out?"

"No. Her lover must have changed his mind about leaving his wife. When I came home one evening after picking up Connor from day care, she ignored both of us and stayed in her room. I knew something was wrong, I just didn't know what.

"A few days later, on the set, I got a call letting me know there'd been an accident. It seemed Kalyn lost control of the car in the rain. She was killed immediately but Connor fought for his life. I rushed to the hospital in time to give my son blood. He'd lost a lot of it."

"So he *was* your biological son!"

"Yes, Connor was my biological son. She had intentionally lied to me, or she might have been sleeping with both me and her lover and honestly didn't know which one of us was Connor's father. Connor lasted another day and then I lost him. I lost my son."

A tear slipped from Bailey's eye, and when more tears began to fall, she swiped at them. He hadn't deserved what his wife put him through. No man would have deserved that.

"But that wasn't the worst of it," she heard him say as she continued swiping at her tears.

"It wasn't?" She couldn't imagine anything worse than that.

"No. After the funeral, I came home and found a letter Kalyn had written to me. She left it in a place where she figured I would find it."

Bailey's brows bunched. "A letter."

He nodded. "Yes. She wanted me to know the car wreck wasn't an accident. It was intentional."

Bailey's heart stopped. "Are you saying that…" She couldn't finish the question.

"Yes," he said softly with even deeper pain in his voice. "Kalyn committed suicide. Being rejected by her lover was too much for her and she couldn't live another day. She wanted to take her lover's son with her."

She saw the tears misting his eyes. No wonder his son was buried in his family's cemetery but his son's mother was not. The awful things she'd done, and the fact that she'd hated Hemlock Row sight unseen.

"Nobody knows about that letter but Garth. He was with me when I found it. We decided turning it over to the authorities would serve no purpose. It would be better to let everyone continue to believe what happened had been an accident."

Bailey nodded. "Did you ever find out the identity of Kalyn's lover?"

"No, although I had my suspicions. I never knew for certain." He paused. "I told myself that I would never love or trust another woman. And I hadn't. Until you. I didn't want to fall in love with you, Bailey. God knows I fought it tooth and nail. But I couldn't stop what was meant to be. Yes, I said what I said to Garth, but I was in denial, refusing to accept what I knew in my heart was true. I'm sorry for the words I said. But the truth is that I do love you. I love you more than I've ever loved any other woman."

She eased out of the chair and went to him, pulled him to her and held him. He had been through so much. He had lost so much. He had experienced the worst betrayal a man could suffer. Not only had Kalyn intentionally taken her life, she had taken the life of an innocent child.

Walker pulled back and looked at her. "I know there can never be anything between us. You don't love me and I understand that. You're in love with your land, and I accept that, too, because I'm in love with mine. I made Dad another promise, this one I intend to keep. I'll never leave Hemlock Row again."

She stared deep into the dark eyes that had always mesmerized her. "You just said you loved me, yet you're willing to let me go back to Westmoreland Country?"

"Yes, because that's your real love. I know your rules, Bailey."

A smile touched her lips. "And I'm breaking the one I thought I would never break."

He looked at her questionably. "What are you saying?"

She wrapped her arms around his neck. "I'm saying that I love you, too. I realized I loved you weeks ago. I think that's why I came to Kodiak to personally apologize. I missed you, although I would never have admitted that to myself or to you. I do love you, Walker, and more than anything I want to make a home with you at Hemlock Row."

"B-but what about Westmoreland Country?"

She chuckled. "I love my home, but Gemma and Megan were right. Home is where the heart is, and my heart is with you."

He studied her features intently. "Are you sure?"

She chuckled again. "I am positive. I'm officially breaking Bailey's Rules."

And then she slanted her mouth over his, knowing their lives together were just beginning.

A few days later, Walker eased out of the bed. Bailey grabbed his thigh. "And where do you think you're going?"

He smiled. "To stoke the fire. I'll be back."

"Holding you to it, Alaskan."

Walker chuckled. He couldn't believe how great his life was going. Everyone was happy that he'd gotten everything straightened out with Bailey and she had decided to stay. Next week was Thanksgiving and they would leave Kodiak Island to spend the holiday with her family in Westmoreland Country.

After stoking the fire and before he returned to bed,

he went to the drawer and retrieved the package he'd put there earlier that day. Grabbing the box, he went back to the bed.

"Bailey?" She opened her eyes to look at him. "Yes?"

"Will you marry me?"

When she saw the box he held she almost knocked him over struggling to sit up. "You're proposing to me?"

He smiled. "Yes."

"B-but I'm in bed, naked and—"

"Just made love to me. I can't think of any other way to complete things. I want you to know it's never been just sex with us…although I think the sex is off the charts."

She grinned. "So do I."

He opened the box and she gasped at the ring shining back at her in the firelight. "It's beautiful, Walker."

"As beautiful as my future wife," he said, sliding the ring on her finger. Halfway there, he stopped and eyed her expectantly. "You didn't say yes."

"Yes!"

He slid the ring the rest of the way and then pulled her into his arms. "My parents would have loved you," he whispered against her ear.

"And I would have loved them, too. And I would have loved Connor."

He pulled back. "He would have loved you." Walker held her hand up and looked at it. "I thought the timing was right since I'll be taking you home next week. I don't want your family to think I'm taking advantage of you. When they see that ring they will know. I love you and intend to make you my wife. Just set the date. But don't make me wait too long."

"I won't."

He brushed his thumb across her cheek. "Thanks for believing I was worthy of breaking your rules, Bailey."

"And thanks for believing I am worthy of your love and trust, Walker."

Their mouths touched, and she knew tonight was the beginning of how things would be for the rest of their lives.

Epilogue

Thanksgiving Day

Bailey looked around the huge table. This was the first time that every one of her brothers, sisters and cousins—the Denver Westmorelands—had managed to come home for Thanksgiving. Even Bane was here. The family had definitely multiplied with the addition of wives, husbands and children. She and Walker would tie the knot here in Westmoreland Country on Valentine's Day.

Everyone was glad to see Bane. It had been years since he'd been home for Thanksgiving. In fact, they hadn't seen him since that time he'd shown up unannounced at Blue Ridge Land Management, surprising Stern and Adrian.

Bailey wondered if she was the only one who noticed he seemed pensive and preoccupied. And not for the first time she wondered if something had happened on his last covert operation that he wasn't sharing with them.

"You okay, baby?" Walker leaned over to ask her.

She smiled at him. "Yes, I'm fine. You love me and I love you, so I couldn't be better."

The announcement that she was marrying and leaving Westmoreland Country had everyone shocked. But all they had to do was look at her and Walker to see how happy they were together.

Thanks to Lucia and Chloe, Bailey would still work for *Simply Irresistible*, working remotely from Kodiak Island. She'd been doing it for a while now and so far things were working out fine.

The Outlaws, all six of them, had come to visit, and just like Bailey had known, everyone had gotten along beautifully. They were invited to the Denver Westmorelands' annual foundation banquet and said they would return in December to attend. That way they would get to meet their Westmoreland cousins from Atlanta, Montana, North Carolina and Texas. Word was that Bart still hadn't come around. According to Walker, Garth intended to find out why his father was being so difficult.

Since Gemma, Callum and their kids were in town, Bailey and Walker were staying at the bed-and-breakfast inn Jason's wife, Bella, owned. It was perfect, and she and Walker had the entire place to themselves.

Bailey figured she would eventually get around to building her own place so she and Walker could have somewhere private whenever they came to visit, but she wasn't in any hurry.

After clinking on his glass to get everyone's attention, Dillon stood. "It's been years since we've had everyone together on Thanksgiving, and I'm thankful that this year Gemma and Bane were able to come home to join us. And I'm grateful for all the additions to our family, especially one in particular," he said, looking over at Walker and smiling.

"I think Mom, Dad, Uncle Thomas and Aunt Susan would be proud of what we've become and that we're still a family."

Bailey wiped a tear from her eye. Yes, they were still a family and always would be. She reached under the table for Walker's hand. She had everything she could possibly want and more.

"You wanted to see me, Dil?" Bane asked, walking into Dillon's home office. Out the window was a beautiful view of Gemma Lake.

Dillon glanced up as his brother entered. Bane appeared taller, looked harder, more mature than he'd seemed the last time he'd been home. "Yes, come on in, Bane."

Dinner had ended a few hours ago and after a game of snow volleyball the ladies had gathered in the sitting room to watch a holiday movie with the kids, and the men had gathered upstairs for a card game. "I want to know how you're doing," Dillon said, studying his baby brother.

"Fine, although my last assignment took a toll on me. I lost a good friend."

Dillon shook his head sadly. "I'm sorry to hear that."

"Me, too. Laramie Cooper was a good guy. The best. We went through the academy together."

Dillon knew not to ask what happened. Bane had explained a while back that all his assignments were confidential. "Is that why you're taking a military leave?"

Bane eased down in the chair across from Dillon's desk. "No. It's time I find Crystal. If nothing else, Coop's death taught me how fragile life is. You can be here today and gone tomorrow."

Dillon came around and sat on the edge of his desk to face his brother. "Not sure if you knew it, but Carl Newsome passed away a few years ago."

Bane shook his head. "No, I didn't know."

"So you haven't seen Crystal since the Newsomes sent her away?"

"No. You were right. I didn't have anything to offer her at the time. I was a hothead and Trouble was my middle name. She deserved better, and I was willing to make something of myself to give her better."

Dillon nodded. "It's been years, Bane. The last time I talked to Emily Newsome was when I heard Carl had died. I called to offer my condolences. I asked about Crystal and Emily said Crystal was doing fine. She was working on her master's degree at Harvard with plans to get a doctorate."

Bane didn't say anything as he listened to what Dillon was saying. "That doesn't surprise me. Crystal was always smart in school."

Dillon stared at his brother, wondering how Bane had figured that out when most of the time he and Crystal were playing hooky. "I don't want to upset you, Bane. But you don't know what Crystal's feelings are for you. The two of you were teens back then. First love doesn't always mean last love. Although you might still love her, for all you know, she might have moved on. Have you ever considered the possibility that she might be involved with someone else?"

Bane leaned back in his chair. "I don't believe that. Crystal and I had an understanding. We have an unbreakable bond."

"But that was years ago. You just said you haven't seen her since that day Carl sent her away. For all you know, she could be married by now."

Bane shook his head. "Crystal wouldn't marry anyone else."

Dillon lifted a brow. "And how can you be so sure of that?"

Bane held his brother's stare. "Because she's already married, Dil. Crystal is married to me, and I think it's time to go claim my wife."

* * * * *

Reese Ryan writes sexy, emotional love stories served with a heaping side of family drama.

Reese is a native Ohioan with deep Tennessee roots. She endured many long, hot car trips to family reunions in Memphis via a tiny clown car loaded with cousins.

Connect with Reese via Facebook, Twitter, Instagram or reeseryan.com. Join her VIP Readers Lounge at bit.ly/VIPReadersLounge. Check out her YouTube show where she chats with fellow authors at bit.ly/ReeseRyanChannel.

Books by Reese Ryan

Harlequin Desire

The Bourbon Brothers
Savannah's Secret
The Billionaire's Legacy
Engaging the Enemy
A Reunion of Rivals
Waking Up Married

Dynasties: Secrets of the A-List
Seduced by Second Chances

Visit the Author Profile page at
Harlequin.com for more titles.

HIS UNTIL MIDNIGHT

Reese Ryan

To Johnathan Royal, Stephanie Perkins, Jennifer Copeland, Denise Stokes, Sharon Blount, Stephanie Douglas-Quick and all of the amazing readers in the Reese Ryan VIP Readers Lounge on Facebook. Seriously, y'all rock! I appreciate your readership, engagement, enthusiasm and continued support. Thank you to each and every one of you!

To my infinitely patient and ever-insightful editor, Charles Griemsman, thank you for all you do.

Chapter 1

Tessa Noble stared at the configuration of high and low balls scattered on the billiard table.

"I'm completely screwed," she muttered, sizing up her next move. After a particularly bad break and distracted play, she was losing badly.

But how on earth could she be expected to concentrate on billiards when her best friend Ryan Bateman was wearing a fitted performance T-shirt that highlighted every single pectoral muscle and his impressive biceps. He could have, at the very least, worn a shirt that fit, instead of one that was a size too small, as a way to purposely enhance his muscles. And the view when he bent over the table in a pair of broken-in jeans that hugged his firm ass like they were made for it...

How in the hell was she expected to play her best?

"You're not screwed," Ryan said in a deep, husky

voice that was as soothing as a warm bath. Three parts sex-in-a-glass and one part confidence out the wazoo.

Tessa's cheeks heated, inexplicably. Like she was a middle schooler giggling over double entendres and sexual innuendo.

"Maybe not, but you'd sure as hell like to be screwed by your best friend over there," Gail Walker whispered in her ear before taking another sip of her beer.

Tessa elbowed her friend in the ribs, and the woman giggled, nearly shooting beer out of her nose.

Gail, always a little too direct, lacked a filter after a second drink.

Tessa walked around the billiard table, pool cue in hand, assessing her options again while her opponent huffed restlessly. Finally, she shook her head and sighed. "You obviously see something I don't, because I don't see a single makeable shot."

Ryan sidled closer, his movements reminiscent of a powerful jungle cat stalking prey. His green eyes gleamed even in the dim light of the bar.

"You're underestimating yourself, Tess," Ryan murmured. "Just shut out all the noise, all the doubts, and focus."

She studied the table again, tugging her lower lip between her teeth, before turning back to him. "Ryan, I clearly don't have a shot."

"Go for the four ball." He nodded toward the purple ball wedged between two of her opponent's balls.

Tessa sucked in a deep breath and gripped the pool cue with one hand. She pressed her other hand to the table, formed a bridge and positioned the stick between her thumb and forefinger, gliding it back and forth.

But the shot just wasn't there.

"I can't make this shot." She turned to look at him. "Maybe you could, but I can't."

"That's because you're too tight, and your stance is all wrong." Ryan studied her for a moment, then placed his hands on either side of her waist and shifted her a few inches. "Now you're lined up with the ball. That should give you a better sight line."

Tessa's eyes drifted closed momentarily as she tried to focus on the four ball, rather than the lingering heat from Ryan's hands. Or his nearness as he hovered over her.

She opened them again and slid the cue back and forth between her fingers, deliberating the position and pace of her shot.

"Wait." Ryan leaned over beside her. He slipped an arm around her waist and gripped the stick a few inches above where she clenched it. He stared straight ahead at the ball, his face inches from hers. "Loosen your grip on the cue. This is a finesse shot, so don't try to muscle it. Just take it easy and smack the cue ball right in the center, and you've got this. Okay?"

"Okay." Tessa nodded, staring at the center of the white ball. She released a long breath, pulled back the cue and hit the cue ball dead in the center, nice and easy.

The cue ball connected with the four ball with a smack. The purple ball rolled toward the corner pocket and slowed, teetering on the edge. But it had just enough momentum to carry it over into the pocket.

"Yes!" Tessa squealed, smacking Ryan's raised palm to give him a high five. "You're amazing. You actually talked me through it."

"You did all the work. I was just your cheering sec-tion." He winked in that way that made her tummy flutter.

"Well, thank you." She smiled. "I appreciate it."

"What are best friends for?" He shrugged, picking up his beer and taking a sip from the bottle.

"Thought I was playing Tess," Roy Jensen grumbled. "Nobody said anything about y'all tag-teaming me."

"Oh, quit complaining, you old coot." Tessa stared down her opponent. "I always turn a blind eye when you ask for spelling help when we're playing Scrabble."

Roy's cheeks tinged pink, and he mumbled under his breath as Tessa moved around the table, deciding which shot to take next. She moved toward the blue two ball.

"Hey, Ryan." Lana, the way-too-friendly barmaid, sidled up next to him, her chest thrust forward and a smile as wide as the Rio Grande spread across her face. "Thought you might want another beer."

"Why thank you, kindly." Ryan tipped an imaginary hat and returned the grin as he accepted the bottle.

Tessa clenched her jaw, a burning sensation in her chest. She turned to her friend, whispering so neither Lana nor Ryan could hear her.

"Why doesn't she just take his head and smash it between the surgically enhanced boobs her ex-boyfriend gave her as a consolation prize? It'd be a lot easier for both of them."

"Watch it there, girl. You're beginning to sound an awful lot like a jealous girlfriend." Gail could barely contain her grin.

"There's nothing to be jealous of. Ryan and I are just friends. You know that."

"*Best* friends," her friend pointed out, as she studied Ryan flirting with Lana. "But let's face it. You're two insanely attractive people. Are you really going to try and convince me that neither of you has ever considered—"

"We haven't." Tessa took her shot, missing badly. It was a shot she should've hit, even without Ryan's help. But she was too busy eavesdropping on his conversation with Lana.

"Well, for a person who doesn't have any romantic interest in her best friend, you seem particularly interested in whether or not he's flirting with the big-boobed barmaid." Gail shrugged when Tessa gave her the stink eye. "What? You know it's true."

Tessa scowled at her friend's words and the fact that Roy was taking advantage of her distraction. He easily sank one ball, then another. With no more striped balls left on the table, Roy had a clear shot at the eight ball.

He should be able to make that shot blindfolded.

"Well?" Gail prodded her.

"I'm not jealous of Lana. I just think Ryan could do better. That he *should* do better than to fall for the calculated ploy of a woman who has dollar signs in her eyes. Probably angling for butt implants this time."

Gail giggled. "And why would he want a fake ass when he was mere inches from the real deal?" She nodded toward Tessa's behind, a smirk on her face.

Tessa was fully aware that she'd inherited her generous curves from her mother. She was just as clear about Ryan Bateman's obliviousness to them. To him, she was simply one of the guys. But then again, the comfy jeans and plaid button-down shirts that filled her closet didn't do much to highlight her assets.

Hadn't that been the reason she'd chosen such a utilitarian wardrobe in the first place?

"Dammit!" Roy banged his pool cue on the wooden floor, drawing their attention to him. He'd scratched on the eight ball.

Tessa grinned. "I won."

"Because I scratched." Roy's tone made it clear that he felt winning by default was nothing to be proud of.

"A win's a win, Jensen." She wriggled her fingers, her palm open. "Pay up."

"You won? Way to go, Tess. I told you that you had this game in the bag." Ryan, suddenly beside her, wrapped a big, muscular arm around her shoulder and pulled her into a half hug.

"Well, at least one of us believed in me." Tessa counted the four wrinkled five-dollar bills Roy stuffed in her palm begrudgingly.

"Always have, always will." He beamed at her and took another swig of his beer.

Tessa tried to ignore the warmth in her chest that filtered down her spine and fanned into areas she didn't want to acknowledge.

Because they were friends. And friends didn't get all…whatever it was she was feeling…over one another. Not even when they looked and smelled good enough to eat.

Tessa Noble always smelled like citrus and sunshine. Reminded him of warm summer picnics at the lake. Ryan couldn't peel an orange or slice a lemon without thinking of her and smiling.

There was no reason for his arm to still be wrapped

around her shoulder other than the sense of comfort he derived from being this close to her.

"Take your hands off my sister, Bateman." Tessa's brother Tripp's expression was stony as he entered the bar. As if he was about five minutes away from kicking Ryan's ass.

"Tessa just beat your man, Roy, here." Ryan didn't move. Nor did he acknowledge Tripp's veiled threat.

The three of them had been friends forever, though it was Tessa who was his best friend. According to their parents, their friendship was born the moment they first met. Their bond had only gotten stronger over the years. Still, he'd had to assure Tripp on more than one occasion that his relationship with Tess was purely platonic.

Relationships weren't his gift. He'd made peace with that, particularly since the dissolution of his engagement to Sabrina Calhoun little more than a year ago. Tripp had made it clear, in a joking-not-joking manner, that despite their longtime friendship, he'd punch his lights out if Ryan ever hurt his sister.

He couldn't blame the guy. Tess definitely deserved better.

"Way to go, Tess." A wide grin spread across Tripp's face. He gave his sister a fist bump, followed by a simulated explosion.

The Nobles' signature celebratory handshake.

"Thanks, Tripp." Tessa casually stepped away from him.

Ryan drank his beer, captivated by her delectable scent which still lingered in the air around him.

"You look particularly proud of yourself today, big brother." Tessa raised an eyebrow, her arms folded.

The move inadvertently framed and lifted Tessa's rather impressive breasts. Another feature he tried hard, as her best friend, to not notice. But then again, he was a guy, with guy parts and a guy brain.

Ryan quickly shifted his gaze to Tripp's. "You still pumped about being a bachelor in the Texas Cattleman's Club charity auction?"

Tripp grinned like a prize hog in the county fair, his light brown eyes—identical to his sister's—twinkling merrily. "Alexis Slade says I'll fetch a mint."

"Hmm…" Ryan grinned. "Tess, what do you think your brother here will command on the auction block?"

"Oh, I'd say four maybe even five…dollars." Tessa, Ryan, Gail and Roy laughed hysterically, much to Tripp's chagrin.

Tripp folded his arms over his chest. "I see you all have jokes tonight."

"You know we're just kidding." Ryan, who had called next, picked up a pool cue as Roy gathered the balls and racked them. "After all, I'm the one who suggested you to Alexis."

"And I may never forgive you for creating this monster." Tessa scowled at Ryan playfully.

"My bad, I wasn't thinking." He chuckled.

"What I want to know is why on earth you didn't volunteer yourself?" Gail asked. "You're a moderately good-looking guy, if you like that sort of thing." She laughed.

She was teasing him, not flirting. Though with Gail it was often hard to tell.

Ryan shrugged. "I'm not interested in parading across the stage for a bunch of desperate women to bid on, like I'm a side of beef." He glanced apologetically at his friend, Tripp. "No offense, man."

"None taken." Tripp grinned proudly, poking a thumb into his chest. "This 'side of beef' is chomping at the bit to be taken for a spin by one of the lovely ladies."

Tessa elbowed Ryan in the gut, and an involuntary "oomph" sound escaped. "Watch it, Bateman. We aren't *desperate*. We're civic-minded women whose only interest is the betterment of our community."

There was silence for a beat before Tessa and Gail dissolved into laughter.

Tessa was utterly adorable, giggling like a schoolgirl. The sound—rooted in his earliest memories of her—instantly conjured a smile that began deep down in his gut.

He studied her briefly. Her curly, dark brown hair was pulled into a low ponytail and her smooth, golden brown skin practically glowed. She was wearing her typical winter attire: a long-sleeved plaid shirt, jeans which hid her curvy frame rather than highlighting it, and the newest addition to her ever-growing sneaker collection.

"You're a brave man." Ryan shifted his attention to Tripp as he leaned down and lined his stick up with the cue ball. He drew it back and forth between his forefinger and thumb. "If these two are any indication—" he nodded toward Tess and Gail "—those women at the auction are gonna eat you alive."

"One can only hope." Tripp wriggled his brows and held up his beer, one corner of his mouth curled in a smirk.

Ryan shook his head, then struck the white cue ball

hard. He relished the loud cracking sound that indicated a solid break. The cue ball smashed through the triangular formation of colorful balls, and they rolled or spun across the table. A high and a low ball dropped into the pockets.

"Your choice." Ryan nodded toward Tessa.

"Low." Hardly a surprise. Tessa always chose low balls whenever she had first choice. She walked around the table, her sneakers squeaking against the floor, as she sized up her first shot.

"You know I'm only teasing you, Tripp. I think it's pretty brave of you to put yourself out there like that. I'd be mortified by the thought of anyone bidding on me." She leaned over the table, her sights on the blue two ball before glancing up at her brother momentarily. "In fact, I'm proud of you. The money you'll help raise for the Pancreatic Cancer Research Foundation will do a world of good."

She made her shot and sank the ball before lining up for the next one.

"Would you bid on a bachelor?" Ryan leaned against his stick, awaiting his turn.

He realized that Tess was attending the bachelor auction, but the possibility that she'd be bidding on one of them hadn't occurred to him until just now. And the prospect of his best friend going on a date with some guy whose company she'd paid for didn't sit well with him.

The protective instinct that had his hackles up was perfectly natural. He, Tripp and Tessa had had each others' backs since they were kids. They weren't just friends, they were family. Though Tess was less like a little sister and more like a really hot distant cousin, three times removed.

"Of course, I'm bidding on a bachelor." She sank another ball, then paced around the table and shrugged. "That's kind of the point of the entire evening."

"Doesn't mean you have to. After all, not every woman attending will be bidding on a bachelor," Ryan reminded her.

"They will be if they aren't married or engaged," Gail said resolutely, folding her arms and cocking an eyebrow his way. "Why, Ryan Bateman, sounds to me like you're jealous."

"Don't be ridiculous." His cheeks heated as he returned his gaze to the table. "I'm just looking out for my best friend. She shouldn't be pressured to participate in something that makes her feel uncomfortable."

Tessa was sweet, smart, funny, and a hell of a lot of fun to hang out with. But she wasn't the kind of woman he envisioned with a paddle in her hand, bidding on men as if she were purchasing steers at auction.

"Doesn't sound like Tess, to me. That's all I'm saying." He realized he sounded defensive.

"*Good.* It's about time I do something unexpected. I'm too predictable…too boring." Tessa cursed under her breath when she missed her shot.

"Also known as consistent and reliable," Ryan interjected.

Things were good the way they were. He liked that Tessa followed a routine he could count on. His best friend's need for order balanced out his spontaneity.

"I know, but lately I've been feeling… I don't know…stifled. Like I need to take some risks in my personal life. Stop playing it so safe all the time." She sighed in response to his wide-eyed, slack-jawed stare. "Relax, Rye. It's not like I'm paying for a male escort."

"I believe they prefer the term *gigolo*," Gail, always helpful, interjected, then took another sip of her drink.

Ryan narrowed his gaze at Gail, which only made the woman laugh hysterically. He shifted his attention back to Tessa, who'd just missed her shot.

"Who will you be bidding on?"

Tessa shrugged. "I don't know. No one in particular in mind, just yet. The programs go out in a few days. Maybe I'll decide then. Or… I don't know…maybe I'll wait and see who tickles my fancy when I get there."

"Who *tickles your fancy*?" Ryan repeated the words incredulously. His grip on the pool cue tightened.

He didn't like the sound of that at all.

Chapter 2

Tessa followed the sound of moaning down the hall and around the corner to her brother's room.

"Tripp? Are you all right?" She tapped lightly on his partially opened bedroom door.

"No!" The word was punctuated by another moan, followed by, "I feel like I'm dying."

Tessa hurried inside his room, her senses quickly assailed by a pungent scent which she followed to his bathroom. He was hugging the porcelain throne and looking a little green.

"Did you go out drinking last night?"

"No. I think it's the tuna sandwich I got from the gas station late last night on my way back in from Dallas."

"How many times have I told you? Gas station food after midnight? No *bueno*." She stood with her hands on her hips, looking down at her brother who looked like he might erupt again at any minute.

Austin Charles Noble III loved food almost as much as he loved his family. And usually he had a stomach like a tank. Impervious to just about anything. So whatever he'd eaten had to have been pretty bad.

"I'm taking you to Urgent Care."

"No, I just want to go to bed. If I can sleep it off for a few hours, I'm sure I'll be fine." He forced a smile, then immediately clutched his belly and cringed. "I'll be good as new for the bachelor auction."

"Shit. The bachelor auction." Tess repeated the words. It was the next night. And as green at the gills as Tripp looked, there was little chance he'd be ready to be paraded on stage in front of a crowd of eager women by then. The way he looked now, he probably wouldn't fetch more than five dollars and a bottle of ipecac at auction.

"Here, let me help you back to bed." She leaned down, allowing her brother to drape his arm around her and get enough leverage to climb to his feet on unsteady legs. Once he was safely in bed again, she gathered the remains of the tainted tuna sandwich, an empty bottle of beer, and a few other items.

She set an empty garbage can with a squirt of soap and about an inch of water beside his bed.

"Use this, if you need to." She indicated the garbage can. "I'm going to get you some ginger ale and some Gatorade. But if you get worse, I'm taking you to the doctor. Mom and Dad wouldn't be too happy with me if I let their baby boy die of food poisoning while they were away on vacation."

"Well, I am Mom's favorite, so…" He offered a weak smile as he invoked the argument they often teased each other about. "And don't worry about the auction,

I'll be fine. I'm a warrior, sis. Nothing is going to come between me and—" Suddenly he bolted out of bed, ran to the bathroom and slammed the door behind him.

Tessa shook her head. "You're staying right here in bed today and tomorrow, 'warrior.' I'll get Roy and the guys to take care of the projects that were on your list today. And I'll find a replacement for you in the auction. Alexis will understand."

Tripp mumbled his thanks through the bathroom door, and she set off to take care of everything she had promised him.

Tessa had been nursing her brother back to health and handling her duties at the ranch, as well as some of his. And she'd been trying all day to get in touch with Ryan.

Despite his reluctance to get involved in the auction, he was the most logical choice as Tripp's replacement. She was sure she could convince him it was a worthy cause. Maybe stroke his ego and tell him there would be a feeding frenzy for a hot stud like him.

A statement she planned to make in jest, but that she feared also had a bit of truth to it. Tessa gritted her teeth imagining Lana, and a whole host of other women in town who often flirted with Ryan, bidding on him like he was a prize steer.

Maybe getting Ryan to step in as Tripp's replacement in the auction wasn't such a good idea after all. She paced the floor, scrolling through a list of names of other possible options in her head.

Most of the eligible men that came to mind were already participating, or they'd already turned Alexis and Rachel down, from what Tessa had heard.

She stopped abruptly mid-stride, an idea brewing in her head that made her both excited and feel like she was going to toss her lunch at the same time.

"Do something that scares you every single day." She repeated the words under her breath that she'd recently posted on the wall of her office. It was a quote from Eleanor Roosevelt. Advice she'd promised herself that she would take to heart from here on out.

Tessa glanced at herself in the mirror. Her thick hair was divided into two plaits, and a Stetson was pushed down on her head, her eyes barely visible. She was the textbook definition of Plain Jane. Not because she wasn't attractive, but because she put zero effort into looking like a desirable woman rather than one of the ranch hands.

She sighed, her fingers trembling slightly. There was a good chance that Alexis and Rachel would veto her idea for Tripp's replacement. But at least she would ask.

Tessa pulled her cell phone out of her back pocket and scrolled through her contacts for Alexis Slade's number. Her palms were damp as she initiated the call. Pressing the phone to her ear, she counted the rings, a small part of her hoping that Alexis didn't answer. That would give her time to rethink her rash decision. Maybe save herself some embarrassment when Alexis rejected the idea.

"Hey, Tess. How are you?" Alexis's warm, cheerful voice rang through the line.

"I'm good. Tripp? Not so much. I think he has food poisoning." The words stumbled out of her mouth.

"Oh my God! That's terrible. Poor Tripp. Is he going to be okay?"

"I'm keeping an eye on him, but I'm sure he'll be

fine in a few days. I just don't think he's going to recover in time to do the bachelor auction."

"We'll miss having him in the lineup, but of course
we understand. His health is the most important thing."
The concern was evident in Alexis's voice. "Tell him
that we hope he's feeling better soon. And if the auction goes well, maybe we'll do this again next year. I'll
save a spot in the lineup for him then."

"Do you have anyone in mind for a replacement?"
Tessa paced the floor.

"Not really. We've pretty much tapped out our list
of possibilities. Unless you can get Ryan to change his
mind?" She sounded hopeful.

"I considered that, and I've been trying to reach him
all day. But just now, I came up with another idea." She
paused, hoping that Alexis would stop her. Tell her that
they didn't need anyone else. When the woman didn't
respond, she continued. "I was thinking that I might
replace my brother in the lineup." She rushed the words
out before she could chicken out. "I know that this is a
bachelor auction, not a bachelorette—"

"Yes!" Alexis squealed, as if it were the best idea
she'd heard all day. "OMG, I think that's an absolutely
fabulous idea. We'll provide something for the fellas,
too. Oh, Tessa, this is brilliant. I love it."

"Are you sure? I mean, I like the idea of doing something completely unexpected, but maybe we should see
what Rachel thinks." Her heart hammered in her chest.

She'd done something bold, something different, by
offering to take Tripp's place. But now, the thought of
actually walking that stage and praying to God that
someone…anyone…would bid on her was giving her
heart palpitations.

"That's a good idea, but I know she's going to agree with me. Hold on."

"Oh, you're calling her now?" Tessa said to the empty room as she paced the floor.

Rachel Kincaid was a marketing genius and an old college friend of Alexis's. She'd come to Royal as a young widow and the mother to an adorable little girl named Ellie. And she'd fallen in love with one of the most eligible bachelors in all of Texas, oil tycoon Matt Galloway.

"Okay, Rachel's on the line," Alexis announced a moment later. "And I brought her up to speed."

"You weren't kidding about doing something unexpected." There was a hint of awe in Rachel's voice. "Good for you, Tess."

"Thanks, Rachel." She swallowed hard. "But do you think it's a good idea? I mean, the programs have already been printed, and no one knows that there's going to be a bachelorette in the auction. What if no one bids on me? I don't want to cause any embarrassment to the club or create negative publicity for the event."

"Honey, the bachelors who aren't in the auction are going to go crazy when they discover there's a beautiful lady to bid on," Rachel said confidently.

"We'll put the word out that there's going to be a big surprise, just for the fellas. I can email everyone on our mailing list. It will only take me a few minutes to put the email together and send it out," Alexis said.

"Y'all are sure we can pull this off?" Tess asked one last time. "I swear I won't be offended if you think we can't. I rather you tell me now than to let me get up there and make a fool of myself."

"It's going to be awesome," Alexis reassured her.

"But I'm sensing hesitation. Are you second-guessing your decision? Because you shouldn't. It's a good one."

Tessa grabbed a spoon and the pint of her favorite Neapolitan ice cream hidden in the back of the freezer. She sat at the kitchen island and sighed, rubbing her palm on her jeans again. She shook her head, casting another glance in the mirror. "It's just that... I'm not the glamorous type, that's for sure."

"You're gorgeous, girl. And if you're concerned... hey, why don't we give you a whole beauty makeover for the event?" Rachel said excitedly. "It'll be fun and it gives me another excuse to buy makeup."

"That's a fantastic idea, Rachel!" Alexis chimed in. "Not that you need it," she added. "But maybe it'll make you feel more comfortable."

"Okay, yeah. That sounds great. I'd like that." Tessa nodded, feeling slightly better. "I was gonna take tomorrow off anyway. Give myself plenty of time to get ready. But I'm sure you both have a million things to do. I don't want to distract you from preparing for the auction, just to babysit me."

"Alexis is the queen of organization. She's got everything under control. Plus, we have a terrific crew of volunteers," Rachel piped in. "They won't miss us for a few hours. I promise, everything will be fine."

"Have you considered what date you're offering?"

"Date?" Tessa hadn't thought that far in advance. "I'm not sure. I guess...let me think about that. I'll have an answer for you by tomorrow. Is that all right?"

"That's fine. Just let me know first thing in the morning," Alexis said.

"I'll make a few appointments for the makeover

and I'll text you both all the details." Rachel's voice brimmed with excitement.

"Then I guess that's everything," Tessa said, more to herself than her friends. "I'll see you both tomorrow."

She hung up the phone, took a deep breath, and shoveled a spoonful of Neapolitan ice cream into her mouth.

There was no turning back now.

Chapter 3

Ryan patted the warm neck of his horse, Phantom, and dismounted, handing the majestic animal off to Ned, one of his ranch hands. He gave the horse's haunches one final pat as the older man led him away to a stall.

Ryan wiped his sweaty forehead with the back of his hand. He was tired, dirty and in desperate need of a shower.

He'd been out on the ranch and the surrounding area since the crack of dawn, looking for several steer that had made their great escape through a break in the fence. While his men repaired the fence, he and another hand tracked down the cattle and drove them back to the ranch.

He'd been in such a hurry to get after the cattle, he'd left his phone at home. Hopefully, his parents hadn't called, worried that he wasn't answering because he'd burned down the whole damn place.

He grumbled to himself, "You nearly burn the barn down as a kid, and they never let you forget it."

Then again, his parents and Tess and Tripp's seemed to be enjoying themselves on their cruise. Their calls had become far less frequent.

Who knows? Maybe both couples would decide it was finally time to retire, give up ranch life, and pass the torch to the next generation. Something he, Tessa and Tripp had been advocating for the past few years. They were ready to take on the responsibility.

When he'd been engaged to Sabrina, his parents had planned to retire to their beach house in Galveston and leave management of the ranch to him. Despite the fact that they hadn't much liked his intended. Not because Sabrina was a bad person. But he and Sabrina were like fire and ice. The moments that were good could be really good. But the moments that weren't had resulted in tense arguments and angry sex.

His mother, in particular, hadn't been convinced Sabrina was the girl for him. She'd been right.

A few months before their wedding, Sabrina had called it off. She just couldn't see herself as a ranch wife. Nor was she willing to sacrifice her well-earned figure to start "popping out babies" to carry on the Bateman name.

He appreciated that she'd had the decency to tell him to his face, well in advance, rather than abandoning him at the altar as Shelby Arthur had done when she'd decided she couldn't marry Jared Goodman.

At least she'd spared him *that* humiliation.

Besides, there was a part of him that realized the truth of what she'd said. Maybe some part of him had always understood that he'd asked her to marry him because it felt like the right thing to do.

He'd been with Sabrina longer than he'd stayed in any relationship. For over a year. So when she'd hinted that she didn't want to waste her time in a relationship that wasn't going anywhere, he'd popped the question.

Neither he nor Sabrina were the type who bought into the fairy tale of romance. They understood that relationships were an exchange. A series of transactions, sustained over time. Which was why he believed they were a good fit. But they'd both ignored an essential point. They were just too different.

He loved everything about ranch life, and Sabrina was a city girl, through and through.

The truth was that he'd been relieved when Sabrina had canceled the wedding. As if he could breathe, nice, deep, easy breaths, for the first time in months. Still, his parents called off their plans to retire.

Maybe this trip would convince them that he and the Bateman Ranch would be just fine without them.

Ryan stretched and groaned. His muscles, taut from riding in the saddle a good portion of the day, protested as he made his way across the yard toward the house.

Helene Dennis, their longtime house manager, threw open the door and greeted him. "There you are. You look an unholy mess. Take off those boots and don't get my kitchen floor all dirty. I just mopped."

Sometimes he wondered if Helene worked for him or if he worked for her. Still, he loved the older woman. She was family.

"All right, all right." He toed off his boots and kicked them in the corner, patting his arms and legs to dislodge any dust from his clothing before entering the house. "Just don't shoot."

Helene playfully punched his arm. "Were you able to round up all of the animals that got loose?"

"Every one of them." Yawning, he kneaded a stubborn kink in his back. "Fence is fixed, too."

"Good. Dinner will be ready in about a half an hour. Go ahead and hop in the shower. Oh, and call Tess when you get the chance."

"Why?" His chest tightened. "Everything okay over at the Noble Spur?"

"Don't worry." She gave him a knowing smile that made his cheeks fill with heat. "She's fine, but her brother is ill. Tess is pretty sure it's food poisoning. She's been trying to reach you all day."

"I was in such a hurry to get out of here this morning, I forgot my phone."

"I know." She chuckled softly "I found it in the covers when I made your bed this morning. It's on your nightstand."

Managing a tired smile for the woman he loved almost as much as his own mother, he leaned in and kissed her cheek. "Thanks, Helene. I'll be down for dinner as soon as I can."

Ryan dried his hair from the shower and wrapped the towel around his waist. The hot water had felt good sluicing over his tired, aching muscles. So he'd taken a longer shower than he'd intended. And though he was hungry, he was tempted to collapse into bed and forgo dinner.

Sighing wearily, he sat on the bed and picked up his phone to call Tess.

She answered in a couple of rings. "Hey, Rye. How'd it go? Were you able to find all the steer you lost?"

Helene had evidently told her where he was and why he hadn't been answering his cell phone.

"Yes, we got them all back and the fence is fixed." He groaned as he reached out to pick up his watch and put it back on. "How's Tripp? Helene said he got food poisoning."

"Wow, you sound like you've been ridden hard and put away wet." She laughed. "And yes, my brother's penchant for late night snacks from suspect eateries finally caught up with him. He looks and feels like hell, but otherwise he's recovering."

"Will he be okay for the auction tomorrow?"

"No." She said the word a little too quickly, then paused a little too long. "He thinks he'll be fine to go through with it, but I'm chalking that up to illness-induced delusion."

"Did you tell Alexis she's a man down?"

"I did." There was another unusual pause. Like there was something she wanted to say but was hesitant.

Ryan thought for a moment as he rummaged through his drawers for something to put on.

"Ahh…" He dragged his fingers through his damp hair. "Of course. She wants to know if I'll take Tripp's place."

Tessa didn't respond right away. "Actually, that's why I was trying so hard to reach you. I thought I might be able to convince you to take Tripp's place…since it's for such a good cause. But when I couldn't reach you, I came up with another option."

"Which is?" It was like pulling teeth to get Tess to just spit it out. He couldn't imagine why that would be…unless he wasn't going to like what she had to say. Uneasiness tightened his gut. "So this other option… are you going to tell me, or should I come over and you can act it out in charades?"

"Smart-ass." She huffed. "No charades necessary. *I'm* the other option. I decided to take Tripp's place in the auction."

"You do know that it's women who will be bidding in this auction, right?" Ryan switched to speakerphone, tossed his phone on the bed, then stepped into his briefs. "Anything you need to tell me, Tess?"

"I'm going to give you a pass because I know you're tired," she groused. "And we've already considered that. If you check your in-box, you'll see that Alexis sent out an email informing all attendees and everyone else on the mailing list that there is going to be a surprise at the end of the auction, just for the gents."

"Oh."

It was the only thing that Ryan could think to say as the realization struck him in the gut like a bull running at full speed. A few days ago, he'd been discomfited by the idea of his friend bidding on one man. Now, there would be who knows how many guys angling for a night with her.

"You sure about this?" He stepped into a pair of well-worn jeans and zipped and buttoned them. "This just doesn't seem much like you."

"That's exactly why I'm doing it." Her voice was shaky. "It'll be good for me to venture outside of my comfort zone."

He donned a long-sleeved T-shirt, neither of them speaking for a moment.

Ryan rubbed his chin and sank on to his mattress.

He slipped on a pair of socks. "Look, I know I said I didn't want to do it, but with Tripp being sick and all, how about I make an exception?"

"You think this is a really bad idea, don't you?" She choked out the words, her feelings obviously hurt.

"No, that's not what I'm saying at all." The last thing he wanted to do was upset his best friend. He ran a hand through his hair. "I'm just saying that it's really last minute. And because of that, it might take people by surprise, that's all."

"I thought of that, too. Alexis and Rachel are positive they can drum up enough interest. But I thought that…just to be safe…it'd be good to have an ace up my sleeve."

"What kind of an ace?"

"I'm going to give you the money to bid on me, in case no one else does. I know it'll still look pretty pathetic if my best friend is the only person who bids on me, but that's a hell of a lot better than hearing crickets when they call my name."

"You want me to bid on you?" He repeated the words. Not that he hadn't heard or understood her the first time. He was just processing the idea. Him bidding on his best friend. The two of them going out on a date…

"Yes, but it'll be my money. And there's no need for us to actually go on the date. I mean, we can just hang out like usual or something, but it doesn't have to be a big deal."

"Sure, I'll do it. But you don't need to put up the money. I'm happy to make the donation myself."

His leg bounced. Despite what his friend believed,

Ryan doubted that he'd be the only man there willing to bid on Tessa Noble during her bachelorette auction.

"Thanks, Ryan. I appreciate this." She sounded relieved. "And remember, you'll only need to bid on me if no one else does. If nothing else, your bid might prompt someone else to get into the spirit."

"Got it," he said gruffly. "You can count on me."

"I know. Thanks again, Rye." He could hear the smile in her sweet voice.

"Hey, since Tripp won't be able to make it...why don't we ride in together?"

"Actually, I'm going straight to the auction from... somewhere else. But I'll catch a ride with a friend, so we can ride home together. How's that?"

"Sounds good." He couldn't help the twinge of disappointment he felt at only getting to ride home with her. "I guess I'll see you there."

"I'll be the one with the price tag on her head." Tessa forced a laugh. "Get some rest, Rye. And take some pain meds. Otherwise, your arm'll be too sore to lift the auction paddle."

Her soft laughter was the last thing he heard before the line went dead. Before he could say good-night.

Ryan released a long sigh and slid his feet into his slippers. He didn't like the idea of Tess putting herself on the auction block for every letch in town to leer at. But she was a grown woman who was capable of making her own decisions.

Regardless of how much he disagreed with them.

Besides, he wasn't quite sure what it was that made him feel more uneasy. Tess being bid on by other men, or the idea that he might be the man who won her at the end of the night.

Chapter 4

Tessa had never been plucked, primped and prodded this much in her entire life.

She'd been waxed in places she didn't even want to think about and had some kind of wrap that promised to tighten her curves. And the thick head of curls she adored had been straightened and hung in tousled waves around her shoulders. Now Milan Valez, a professional makeup artist, was applying her makeup.

"I thought we were going with a natural look," Tess objected when the woman opened yet another product and started to apply what had to be a third or fourth layer of goop to her face.

"This *is* the natural look." The woman rolled her eyes. "If I had a dime for every client who doesn't realize that what they're calling the natural look is actually a full face." The woman sighed, but her expression softened as she directed Tess to turn her head. "You're a beautiful woman with gorgeous skin. If you're not a makeup wearer, I know it feels like a lot. But I'm just using a few tricks to enhance your natural beauty. We'll make those beautiful eyes pop, bring a little drama to these pouty lips, and highlight your incredible cheekbones. I promise you won't look too heavily made up. Just trust me."

Tessa released a quiet sigh and nodded. "I trust you."

"Good. Now just sit back and relax. Your friends should be here shortly. They're going to be very pleased, and I think you will, too." The woman smiled. "Now look up."

Tessa complied as Milan applied liner beneath her eyes. "You sure I can't have a little peek?"

"Your friends made me promise. No peeking. And you agreed." She lifted Tess's chin. "Don't worry, honey, you won't have to wait much longer."

"Tessa? Oh my God, you look...incredible." Rachel entered the salon a few minutes later and clapped a hand over her mouth. "I can hardly believe it's you."

Alexis nearly slammed into the back of Rachel, who'd made an abrupt stop. She started to complain, but when she saw Tessa, her mouth gaped open, too.

"Tess, you look...stunning. Not that you aren't always beautiful, but...wow. Just wow."

"You two are making me seriously self-conscious right now." Tessa kept her focus on Milan.

"Don't be," the woman said emphatically. "Remember what we talked about. I've only enhanced what was already there."

Tessa inhaled deeply and nodded. She ignored the butterflies in her stomach in response to the broad grins and looks of amazement on Alexis's and Rachel's faces.

"There, all done." Milan sat back proudly and grinned. "Honey, you look absolutely beautiful. Ready to see for yourself?"

"Please." Even as Tessa said it, her hands were trembling, and a knot tightened in her stomach. How could something as simple as looking in the mirror be so fraught with anxiety? It only proved she wasn't cut out for this whole glamour-girl thing.

Milan slowly turned the chair around and Alexis and Rachel came over to stand closer, both of them bouncing excitedly.

Tessa closed her eyes, took a deep breath and then opened them.

"Oh my God." She leaned closer to the mirror. "I can hardly believe that's me." She sifted her fingers through the dark, silky waves with toffee-colored highlights. "I mean, it looks like me, just…more glamourous."

"I know, isn't it incredible? You're going to be the star of the evening. We need to keep you hidden until you walk across the stage. Really take everyone by surprise." Rachel grinned in the mirror from behind her.

"Oh, that's a brilliant idea, Rachel," Alexis agreed. "It'll have more impact."

"This is only the beginning." Rachel's grin widened. "Just wait until they get a load of your outfit tonight. Every man in that room's jaw will hit the floor."

Tessa took another deep breath, then exhaled as she stared at herself in the mirror. Between her makeover and the daring outfit she'd chosen, there was no way Ryan, or anyone else, would take her for one of the boys.

Her heart raced and her belly fluttered as she anticipated his reaction. She couldn't wait to see the look of
surprise on Ryan's face.

Ryan entered the beautiful gardens where The Great
Royal Bachelor Auction was being held. Alexis Slade,
James Harris and the rest of the committee had gone
out of their way to create a festive and beautiful setting
for the event. Fragrant wreaths and sprigs of greenery
were strung from the pergolas. Two towering trees decorated with gorgeous ornaments dominated the area.
Poinsettias, elegant red bows and white lights decorated the space, giving it a glowing, ethereal feel. The
garden managed to be both romantic and festive. The
kind of setting that almost made you regret not having
someone to share the night with.

He sipped his Jack and Coke and glanced around the
vicinity. Everyone who was anyone was in attendance.
He made his way through the room, mingling with
Carter Mackenzie and Shelby Arthur, Matt Galloway
and Rachel Kincaid, Austin and Brooke Bradshaw, and
all of the other members of the club who'd turned out
for the event. Several of the bachelors moved around
the space, drumming up anticipation for the auction
and doing their best to encourage a bidding frenzy.

But Tessa was nowhere to be found. Had she
changed her mind? He was looking forward to hanging out with her tonight, but he'd understand if she'd
gotten cold feet. Hell, there was a part of him that was
relieved to think that maybe she'd bailed.

Then again, Tess had said she'd be coming from
somewhere else. So maybe she was just running late.

He resisted the urge to pull out his cell phone and

find out exactly where she was. For once in his life, he'd be patient. Even if it killed him.

"Ryan, it's good to see you." James Harris, president of the Texas Cattleman's Club, shook his hand. "I hate that we couldn't convince you to be one of our bachelor's tonight, but I'm glad you joined us just the same."

"Didn't see your name on the list of bachelors either." Ryan smirked, and both men laughed.

"Touché." James took a gulp of his drink and Ryan did the same.

"Looks like y'all are doing just fine without me." Ryan gestured to the space. "I wouldn't have ever imagined this place could look this good."

"Alexis Slade outdid herself with this whole romantic winter wonderland vibe." James's eyes trailed around the space. "To be honest, I wasn't sure exactly how her vision would come together, but she's delivered in spades. I'm glad we gave her free rein to execute it as she saw fit."

"Judging from everyone here's reaction, you've got a hit on your hands." Ryan raised his glass before finishing the last of his drink.

"Let's just hope it motivates everyone to dig deep in their pockets tonight." James patted Ryan on the back. "I'd better go chat with Rose Clayton." He nodded toward the older woman, who looked stunning in her gown. The touch of gray hair at her temples gleamed in the light. "But I'll see you around."

"You bet." Ryan nodded toward the man as he traversed the space and greeted Rose.

"Ryan, how are you?" Gail Walker took a sip of her drink and grinned. "You look particularly handsome tonight. But I see Alexis still wasn't able to talk you into joining the list of eligible bachelors."

"Not my thing, but looks like they've got plenty of studs on the schedule for you to choose from." Ryan sat his empty glass on a nearby tray. "And you clean up pretty well yourself."

"Thanks." She smoothed a hand over the skirt of her jewel-tone green dress. "But I've got my eye on one bachelor in particular." Her eyes shone with mischief. "And I'm prepared to do whatever it takes to get him."

"Well, I certainly wouldn't want to be the woman who has to run up against you." Ryan chuckled. "Good luck."

"Thanks, Ryan. See you around." Gail made her way through the crowd, mingling with other guests.

Ryan accepted a napkin and a few petite quiches from a server passing by. Ignoring the anticipation that made his heart beat a little faster as he considered the prospect of bidding on his friend.

Tessa paced the space that served as the bachelors' green room. Everyone else had spent most of the night mingling. They came to the green room once the start of the auction drew closer. But she'd been stuck here the entire evening, biding her time until she was scheduled to make her grand entrance.

"Tessa Noble? God, you look…incredible." Daniel Clayton shoved a hand in his pocket. "But what are you doing here? Wait…are you the surprise?"

"Guilty." Her cheeks warmed as she bit into another quiche.

She tried her best not to ruin the makeup that Milan had so painstakingly applied. The woman had assured her that she could eat and drink without the lipstick fading or feathering. But Tess still found herself being extra careful.

"Everyone will definitely be surprised," he said, then added, "Not that you don't look good normally."

"It's okay, Daniel. I get it." She mumbled around a mouth full of quiche. "It was a surprise to me, too."

He chuckled, running a hand through his jet-black hair. "You must be tired of people telling you how different you look. How did Tripp and Ryan react?"

"Neither of them has seen me yet." She balled up her napkin and tossed it in the trash. "I'm a little nervous about their reaction."

"Don't be," Daniel said assuredly. "I can't imagine a man alive could find fault with the way you look tonight." He smiled, then scrubbed a hand across his forehead. "Or any night...of course."

They both laughed.

"Well, thank you." She relaxed a little. "You already know why I feel like a fish out of water. But why do you look so out of sorts tonight?"

He exhaled heavily, the frown returning to his face. "For one thing, I'd rather not be in the lineup. I'm doing this at my grandmother's insistence."

"Ms. Rose seems like a perfectly reasonable woman to me. And she loves you like crazy. I'm pretty sure if you'd turned her down she would've gotten over it fairly quickly."

"Maybe." He shrugged. "But the truth is that I owe my grandmother so much. Don't know where I would've ended up if it wasn't for her. Makes it hard to say no." A shadow of sadness passed over his handsome face, tugging at Tessa's heart.

Daniel had been raised by Rose Clayton after his own mother dumped him on her. It made Tessa's heart ache for him. She couldn't imagine the pain Daniel must feel at being abandoned by a woman who preferred drugs and booze to her own son.

"Of course." Tess nodded, regretting her earlier flippant words. She hadn't considered the special relationship that Daniel had with his grandmother and how grateful he must be to her. "I wasn't thinking."

They were both quiet for a moment, when she remembered his earlier words.

"You said 'for one thing.' What's the other reason you didn't want to do this?"

The pained look on Daniel's face carved deep lines in his forehead and between his brows. He drained the glass of whiskey in his hand.

"It's nothing," he said in a dismissive tone that made it clear that they wouldn't be discussing it any further.

She was digging herself deeper into a hole with every question she asked of Daniel tonight. Better for her to move on. She wished him luck and made her way over to the buffet table.

"Hey, Tessa." Lloyd Richardson put another slider on his small plate. "Wow, you look pretty amazing."

"Thanks, Lloyd." She decided against the slider and put some carrots and a cherry tomato on her plate instead.

There wasn't much room to spare in her fitted pantsuit. She wore a jacket over the sleeveless garment to hide the large cutout that revealed most of her back. That had been one idea of Rachel's for which she'd been grateful.

"Hey, you must be plum sick of people saying that

to you by now." Lloyd seemed to recognize the discomfort she felt at all of the additional attention she'd been getting.

Tess gave him a grateful smile. No wonder her friend Gail Walker had a crush on Lloyd. He was handsome, sweet and almost a little shy. Which was probably why he hadn't made a move on Gail, since he certainly seemed interested in her.

"Okay, bachelors and bachelorette." Alexis acknowledged Tess with a slight smile. "The proceedings will begin in about ten minutes. So finish eating, take a quick bathroom break, whatever you need to do so you'll be ready to go on when your number is called."

Alexis had her serious, drill sergeant face on. Something Tessa knew firsthand that a woman needed to adopt when she was responsible for managing a crew of men—be they ranchers or ranch hands.

Still, there was something in her eyes. Had she been crying?

Before she could approach Alexis and ask if she was all right, she noticed the look Alexis and Daniel Clayton exchanged. It was brief, but meaningful. Chock full of pain.

Could Alexis be the other reason Daniel hadn't wanted to be in the bachelor auction? But from the look of things, whatever was going on between them certainly wasn't sunshine and roses.

Tessa caught up with Alexis as she grabbed the door handle.

"Alexis." Tessa lowered her voice as she studied her friend's face. "Is everything okay? You look like you've been—"

"I'm fine." Alexis swiped at the corner of one eye,

her gaze cast downward. "I just… I'm fine." She forced a smile, finally raising her eyes to meet Tessa's. "You're going to kill them tonight. Just wait until you come out of that jacket. We're going to have to scrape everyone's jaws off the floor." She patted Tess's shoulder. "I'd tell you good luck, but something tells me that you aren't going to need it tonight."

With that, Alexis dipped out of the green room and was gone.

When Tess turned around, Daniel was standing there, staring after the other woman. He quickly turned away, busying himself with grabbing a bottle of water from the table.

There was definitely something going on with the two of them. And if there was, Tessa could understand why they wouldn't want to make their relationship public. Daniel's grandmother, Rose Clayton, and Alexis's grandfather, Gus Slade, once an item, had been feuding for years.

In recent months, they seemed to at least have found the civility to be decent toward one another. Most likely for the sake of everyone around them. Still, there was no love lost between those two families.

"Looks like Royal has its very own Romeo and Juliet," she muttered under her breath.

Tess took her seat, her hands trembling slightly and butterflies fluttering in her stomach. She closed her eyes, imagining how Ryan would react to seeing her out there on that stage.

Chapter 5

Ryan hung back at the bar as the bachelor auction wound down. There were just a couple more bachelors on the list, then Tess would be up.

He gulped the glass of water with lemon he was drinking. He'd talked to just about everyone here. But with neither Tripp nor Tess to hang out with, he'd been ready to leave nearly an hour ago.

Then again, his discomfort had little to do with him going stag for the night and everything to do with the fact that his best friend would be trotted out onto the stage and bid on. His gaze shifted around the garden at the unattached men in attendance. Most of them were members of the Texas Cattleman's Club. Some of them second, third or even fourth generation. All of them were good people, as far as he knew. So why was he assessing them all suspiciously? Wondering which of them would bid on his best friend.

The next bachelor, Lloyd Richardson, was called onto the stage and Alexis read his bio. Women were chomping at the bit to bid on the guy. Including Gail Walker. She'd started with a low, reasonable bid. But four or five other women were countering her bids as quickly as she was making them.

First the bid was in the hundreds, then the thousands. Suddenly, Steena Goodman, a wealthy older woman whose husband had been active in the club for many years before his death, stood and placed her final bid. Fifty-thousand dollars.

Ryan nearly coughed. What was it about this guy that had everyone up in arms?

Steena's bid was much higher than the previous bid of nine thousand dollars. The competing bidders pouted, acknowledging their defeat.

But not Gail. She looked angry and hurt. She stared Steena down, her arms folded and breathing heavily.

Alexis glanced back and forth at the two women for a moment. When Rachel nudged her, she cleared her throat and resumed her duties as auctioneer. "Going once, going twice—"

"One hundred thousand dollars." Gail stared at Steena, as if daring her to outbid her.

The older woman huffed and put her paddle down on the table, conceding the bid.

"Oh my God! One hundred thousand dollars." Alexis began the sentence nearly shrieking but ended with an implied question mark.

Probably because she was wondering the same thing he was.

Where in the hell did Gail Walker get that kind of cash?

Alexis declared Gail the winner of the bid at one hundred thousand dollars.

The woman squealed and ran up on stage. She wrapped her arms around Lloyd's neck and pulled him down for a hot, steamy kiss. Then she grabbed his hand and dragged him off the stage and through the doors that led from the garden back into the main building.

Ryan leaned against the bar, still shocked by Gail's outrageous bid. He sighed. Just one more bachelor, Daniel Clayton. Then Tess was up.

"That was certainly unexpected." Gus Slade ordered a beer from the bar. "Had no idea she was sitting on that kind of disposable cash."

"Neither did I, but I guess we all have our little secrets."

The older man grimaced, as if he'd taken exception to Ryan's words. Which only made Ryan wonder what secrets the old man might be hiding.

"Yes, well, I s'pose that's true." Gus nodded, then walked away.

Ryan turned his attention back to the stage just in time to see Daniel Clayton being whisked away excitedly by an overeager bidder.

There was a noticeable lull as Alexis watched the woman escort Daniel away. Rachel placed a hand on her cohost's back as she took the microphone from Alexis and thanked her for putting on a great event and being an incredible auctioneer.

Alexis seemed to recover from the momentarily stunned look she'd had seconds earlier. She nodded toward Rachel and then to the crowd which clapped appreciatively.

"This has been an amazing night, and thanks to your generosity, ladies, and to the generosity of our bachelors, we've already exceeded our fund-raising goal for tonight. So thank you all for that. Give yourselves a big hand."

Rachel clapped a hand against the inside of her wrist as the rest of the audience clapped, hooted and shouted.

"But we're not done yet. It's time for the surprise you gents have been waiting for this evening. Fellas, please welcome our lone bachelorette, Miss Tessa Noble."

Ryan pulled out his phone. He'd promised Tripp that he'd record his sister's big debut.

There was a collective gasp in the room as Tessa stepped out onto the stage. Ryan moved away from the bar, so he could get a better view of his friend.

His jaw dropped, and his phone nearly clattered to the ground.

"Tess?" Ryan choked out the word, then silently cursed himself, realizing his stunned reaction would end up on the video. He snapped his gaping mouth shut as he watched her strut across the stage in a glamorous red pantsuit that seemed to be designed for the express purpose of highlighting her killer curves.

Damn, she's fine.

He wasn't an idiot. Nor was he blind. So he wasn't oblivious to the fact that his best friend also happened to be an extremely beautiful woman. And despite her tomboy wardrobe, he was fully aware of the hot body buried beneath relaxed fit clothing. But today…those curves had come out to play.

As if she was a professional runway model, Tess pranced to the end of the stage in strappy, glittery heels, put one hand on her hip and cocked it to the side. She seemed buoyed by the crowd's raucous reaction.

First there was the collective gasp, followed by a chorus of Oh my Gods. Now the crowd was whooping and shouting.

A slow grin spread across her lips, painted a deep, flirtatious shade of red that made him desperate to taste them. She turned and walked back toward where Rachel stood, revealing a large, heart-shaped cutout that exposed the warm brown skin of her open back. A large bow was tied behind her graceful neck.

Tessa Noble was one gift he'd give just about anything to unwrap.

She was incredibly sexy with a fiercely confident demeanor that only made him hunger for her more.

Ryan surveyed the crowd. He obviously wasn't the only man in the room drooling over Tessa 2.0. He stared at the large group of men who were wide-eyed, slack-jawed and obviously titillated by the woman on stage.

Tessa's concerns that no one would bid on her were obviously misplaced. There were even a couple of women who seemed to be drooling over her.

Ryan's heart thudded. Suddenly, there wasn't enough air in the tented, outdoor space. He grabbed his auction paddle and crept closer to the stage.

Rachel read Tessa's bio aloud, as Alexis had done with the bachelors who'd gone before her. Tessa stood tall with her back arched and one hand on her hip. She held her head high as she scanned the room.

Was she looking for him?

Ryan's cheeks flushed with heat. A dozen emotions percolated in his chest, like some strange, volatile mixture, as he studied his friend on stage. Initially, he wanted to rush the stage and drape his jacket over her shoulders. Block the other men's lurid stares. Then there was his own guttural reaction to seeing Tess this way. He wanted to devour her. Kiss every inch of the warm, brown skin on her back. Glide his hands over her luscious bottom. Taste those pouty lips.

He swallowed hard, conscious of his rapid breathing. He hoped the video wasn't picking that up, too.

Rachel had moved on from Tessa's bio to describing her date. "For the lucky gentleman with the winning bid, your very special outing with this most lovely lady will be every man's fantasy come true. Your football-themed date will begin with seats on the fifty-yard line to watch America's team play football against their division rivals. Plus, you'll enjoy a special tailgating meal before the game at a restaurant right there in the stadium. Afterward, you'll share an elegant steak dinner at a premium steak house."

"Shit." Ryan cringed, realizing that, too, would be captured on the video.

There was already a stampede of overly eager men ready to take Tessa up on her offer. Now she'd gone and raised the stakes.

Just great.

Ryan huffed, his free hand clenched in a fist at his side, as her words reverberated through him.

You're only supposed to bid if no one else does.

Suddenly, Tessa's gaze met his, and her entire face lit up in a broad smile that made her even more beautiful. A feat he wouldn't have thought possible.

His heart expanded in his chest as he returned her smile and gave her a little nod.

Tess stood taller. As if his smile had lifted her. Made her even more confident.

And why shouldn't she be? She'd commanded the attention of every man in the room, single or not. Had all the women in the crowd enviously whispering among themselves.

"All right, gentlemen, get your paddles ready, because it's your turn to bid on our lovely bachelorette." Rachel grinned proudly.

He'd bet anything she was behind Tessa's incredible makeover. Ryan didn't know if he wanted to thank her or blame her for messing up a good thing. Back when no one else in town realized what a diamond his Tess was.

He shook his head. *Get it together, Bateman. She doesn't belong to you.*

"Shall we open the bidding at five-hundred dollars?" Rachel asked the crowd.

"A thousand dollars." Clem Davidson, a man his father's age, said.

"Fifteen hundred," Bo Davis countered. He was younger than Clem, but still much older than Tess.

Ryan clenched the paddle in his hand so tightly he thought it might snap in two as several of the men bid furiously for Tess. His heart thumped. Beads of sweat formed over his brow and trickled down his back as his gaze and the camera's shifted from the crowd of enthusiastic bidders to Tessa's shocked expression and then back again.

"Ten thousand bucks." Clem held his paddle high and looked around the room, as if daring anyone else to bid against him. He'd bid fifteen hundred dollars more than Bo's last bid.

Bo grimaced, but then nodded to Clem in concession.

"Twelve thousand dollars." It nearly came as a surprise to Ryan that the voice was his own.

Clem scowled. "Thirteen thousand."

"Fifteen thousand." Now Ryan's voice was the one that was indignant as he stared the older man down.

Clem narrowed his gaze at Ryan, his jaw clenched. He started to raise his paddle, but then his expression softened. Head cocked to the side, he furrowed his brows for a moment. Suddenly, he nodded to Ryan and put his paddle back down at his side.

"Fifteen thousand dollars going once. Fifteen thousand dollars going twice." Rachel looked around the room, excitedly. "Sold! Ryan Bateman, you may claim your bachelorette."

Ryan froze for a moment as everyone in the room looked at him, clapping and cheering. Many of them with knowing smiles. He cleared his throat, ended the recording and slowly made his way toward the stage and toward his friend who regarded him with utter confusion.

He stuffed his phone into his pocket, gave Tess an awkward hug and pressed a gentle kiss to her cheek for the sake of the crowd.

They all cheered, and he escorted Tess off the stage. Then Rachel and Alexis wrapped up the auction.

"Oh my God, what did you just do?" Tessa whispered loudly enough for him to hear her over all the noise.

"Can't rightly say I know," he responded, not looking at her, but fully aware of his hand on her waist, his thumb resting on the soft skin of her back. Electricity sparked in his fingertips. Trailed up his arm.

"I appreciate what you did, Rye. It was a very generous donation. But I thought we agreed you would only bid if no one else did." Tessa folded her arms as she stared at him, searching his face for an answer.

"I know, and I was following the plan, I was. But I just couldn't let you go home with a guy like Clem."

Tessa stared up into his green eyes, her own eyes widening in response. Ryan Bateman was her oldest and closest friend. She knew just about everything there was to know about him. But the man standing before her was a mystery.

He'd gone beyond his usual protectiveness of her and had landed squarely into possessive territory. To be honest, it was kind of a turn-on. Which was problematic. Because Rye was her best friend. Emphasis on *friend*.

She folded her arms over her chest, suddenly self-conscious about whether the tightening of her nipples was visible through the thin material.

"And what, exactly, is it that you have against Clem?"

Ryan shook his head. "Nothing really." He seemed dazed, maybe even a little confused himself. "I just didn't want you to go out with him. He's too old for you."

"That's ageist." She narrowed her gaze.

It was true that she'd certainly never considered Clem Davidson as anything other than a nice older man. Still, it wasn't right for Ryan to single him out because of his age. It was a football date. Plain and simple. There would be no sex. With anyone.

"Clem isn't that much older than us, you know. Ten or fifteen years, tops." She relaxed her arms and ran her fingers through the silky waves that she still hadn't gotten accustomed to.

Ryan seemed to tense at the movement. He clenched his hand at his side, then nodded. "You're right on both counts. But what's done is done." He shrugged.

"What if it had been Bo instead? Would you have outbid him, too?"

"Yes." He seemed to regret his response, or at least the conviction with which he'd uttered the word. "I mean…yes," he said again.

"You just laid down fifteen grand for me," Tess said as they approached the bar. "The least I can do is buy you a drink."

She patted her hips, then remembered that her money and credit cards were in her purse backstage.

"Never mind. I've got it. Besides, I'm already running a tab." Ryan ordered a Jack and Coke for himself and one for her, which she turned down, requesting club soda with lime instead. "You…uh…you look pretty incredible."

"Thanks." She tried to sound grateful for the compliment, but when everyone fawned over how good she looked tonight, all she heard was the implication that her everyday look was a hot mess.

Her tomboy wardrobe had been a conscious choice, beginning back in grade school. She'd developed early. Saw how it had changed the other kids' perception of her. With the exception of Ryan, the boys she'd been friends with were suddenly more fascinated with her budding breasts than anything she had to say. And they'd come up with countless ways to cop an "accidental" feel.

Several of the girls were jealous of her newfound figure and the resulting attention from the boys. They'd said hateful things to her and started blatantly false rumors about her, which only brought more unwanted attention from the boys.

Tess had recognized, even then, that the problem was theirs, not hers. That they were immature and stupid. Still, it didn't stop the things they'd said from hurting.

She'd been too embarrassed to tell Tripp or Ryan, who were a few grades ahead of her. And she was worried that Ryan's temper would get him in serious trouble. She hadn't told her parents, either. They would've come to her school, caused a scene and made her even more of a social pariah.

So she'd worn bulky sweaters, loose jeans and flannel shirts that masked her curves and made her feel invisible.

After a while, she'd gotten comfortable in her wardrobe. Made it her own. Until it felt like her daily armor.

Wearing a seductive red pantsuit, with her entire back exposed and every curve she owned on display, made her feel as vulnerable as if she'd traipsed across the stage naked.

But she was glad she'd done it. That she'd reclaimed a little of herself.

The bartender brought their drinks and Ryan stuffed a few dollars into the tip jar before taking a generous gulp of his drink.

"So, is this your new look?" An awkward smile lit Ryan's eyes. "'Cause it's gonna be mighty hard for you to rope a steer in that getup."

"Shut it, Rye." She pointed a finger at him, and they both laughed.

When they finally recovered from their laughter, she took his glass from his hand and took a sip of his drink. His eyes darkened as he watched her, his jaw tensing again.

"Not bad. Maybe I will have one." She handed it back to him.

Without taking his eyes off of her, Ryan signaled for the bartender to bring a Jack and Coke for her, too. There was something in his stare. A hunger she hadn't seen before.

She often longed for Ryan to see her as more than just "one of the boys." Now that it seemed he was finally seeing her that way, it was unsettling. His heated stare made her skin prickle with awareness.

The prospect of Ryan being as attracted to her as she was to him quickened her pulse and sent a shock of warmth through her body. But just as quickly, she thought of how her relationship with the boys in school had changed once they saw her differently.

That wasn't something she ever wanted to happen between her and Ryan. She could deal with her eternal, unrequited crush, but she couldn't deal with losing his friendship.

She cleared her throat, and it seemed to break them both from the spell they'd both fallen under.

They were just caught up in emotions induced by the incredibly romantic setting, the fact that she looked like someone wholly different than her everyday self, and the adrenaline they'd both felt during the auction. Assigning it meaning…that would be a grave mistake. One that would leave one or both of them sorely disappointed once the bubble of illusion burst.

"So…since it's just us, we don't need to go out on a date. Because that would be…you know…weird. But, I'm totally down for hanging out. And seats on the fifty-yard line…so…yay."

"That's what I was really after." Ryan smirked, sipping his drink. "You could've been wearing a brown potato sack, and I still would've bid on those tickets. It's like the whole damned date had my name written all over it." His eyes widened with realization. "Wait… you did tailor it just for me, didn't you?"

Tessa's cheeks heated. She took a deep sip of her drink and returned it to the bar, waving a hand dismissively.

"Don't get ahead of yourself, partner. I simply used your tastes as a point of reference. After all, you, Tripp and my dad are the only men that I've been spending any significant time with these days. I figured if you'd like it, the bidders would, too."

"Hmm…" Ryan took another sip of his drink, almost sounding disappointed. "Makes sense, I guess."

"I'm glad you get it. Alexis and Rachel thought it was the least romantic thing they could imagine. They tried to talk me into something else. Something grander and more flowery."

"Which neither of us would've enjoyed." Ryan nodded. "And the makeover… I assume that was Rachel's idea, too."

"Both Alexis and Rachel came up with that one.

Alexis got PURE to donate a spa day and the make-over, so it didn't cost me anything." Tessa tucked her hair behind her ear and studied her friend's face. "You don't like it?"

"No, of course I do. I love it. You look...incredible. You really do. Your parents are going to flip when they see this." He patted the phone in his pocket.

"You recorded it? Oh no." Part of her was eager to see the video. Another part of her cringed at the idea of watching herself prance across that stage using the catwalk techniques she'd studied online.

But no matter how silly she might feel right now, she was glad she'd successfully worked her magic on the crowd.

The opening chords of one of her favorite old boy band songs drew her attention to the stage where the band was playing.

"Oh my God, I love that song." Tessa laughed, sipping the last of her drink and then setting the glass on the bar. "Do you remember what a crush I had on these guys?"

Rye chuckled, regarding her warmly over the rim of his glass as he finished off his drink, too. "I remember you playing this song on repeat incessantly."

"That CD was my favorite possession. I still can't believe I lost it."

Ryan lowered his gaze, his chin dipping. He tapped a finger on the bar before raising his eyes to hers again and taking her hand. "I need to make a little confession."

"You rat!" She poked him in the chest. "You did something to my CD, didn't you?"

A guilty smirk curled the edges of his mouth. "Tripp

and I couldn't take it anymore. We might've trampled the thing with a horse or two, then dumped it."

"You two are awful." She realized that she'd gone a little overboard in her obsession with the group. But trampling the album with a horse? That was harsh.

"If I'm being honest, I've always felt incredibly guilty about my role in the whole sordid affair." Ryan placed his large, warm hand on her shoulder. The tiny white lights that decorated the space were reflected in his green eyes. "Let me make it up to you."

"And just how do you plan to do that?" Tessa folded her arms, cocking a brow.

He pulled out his phone, swiped through a few screens. "First of all, I just ordered you another copy of that album—CD and digital."

She laughed. "You didn't need to do that, Rye."

"I did, and I feel much better now. Not just because it was wrong of us to take away something you loved so much. Because I hated having that secret between us all these years. You're the one person in the world I can tell just about anything. So it feels pretty damn good to finally clear my conscience." He dropped his hand from her shoulder.

"All right." She forced a smile, trying her best to hide her disappointment at the loss of his touch. "And what's the second thing?"

He held his large, open palm out to her. "It seems I've bought myself a date for the night. Care to dance?"

"You want to dance to this sappy, boy band song that you've always hated?"

He grabbed her hand and led her to the dance floor. "Then I guess there's one more confession I need to make… I've always kind of liked this song. I just didn't want your brother to think I'd gone soft."

Tessa laughed as she joined her best friend on the dance floor.

Chapter 6

Gus Slade watched as Tessa Noble and Ryan Bateman entered the dance floor, both of them laughing merrily. Gus shook his head. Ryan was one of the prospects he'd considered as a good match for his granddaughter Alexis. Only it was clear that Ryan and Tess were hung up on each other, even if the self-proclaimed "best friends" weren't prepared to admit it to themselves.

It was no wonder Ryan's brief engagement to that wannabe supermodel he'd met in the city didn't last long enough for the two of them to make it to the altar.

Encouraging Alexis to start something with the Bateman boy would only result in heartache for his granddaughter once Ryan and Tess finally recognized the attraction flickering between them.

He'd experienced that kind of hurt and pain in his life when the woman he'd once loved, whom he thought truly loved him, had suddenly turned against him, shutting him out of her life.

It was something he'd never truly gotten over. Despite a long and happy marriage that lasted until the death of his dear wife.

Gus glanced over at Rose Clayton, his chest tightening. Even after all these years, the woman was still gorgeous. Just a hint of gray was visible at her temples. The rest of her hair was the same dark brown it was when she was a girl. She wore it in a stylish, modern cut that befit a mature woman. Yet, anyone who didn't know her could easily mistake her for a much younger woman.

And after all these years, Rose Clayton still turned heads, including his. The woman managed to stay as slim now as she had been back when she was a young girl. Yet, there was nothing weak or frail about Rose Clayton.

Her every move, her every expression, exuded a quiet confidence that folks around Royal had always respected. And tonight, he had to admit that she looked simply magnificent.

Gus glanced around the tented garden area again. The space looked glorious. Better than he could ever have imagined when the club first decided to undertake a major renovation of this space and a few other areas of the club, which had been in operation since the 1920s.

Alexis had headed up the committee that put on the auction. And his granddaughter had truly outdone herself.

Gus searched the crowd for Alexis. Her duties as

Mistress of Ceremony appeared to be over for the night. Still, he couldn't locate her anywhere.

Gus walked toward the main building. Perhaps she was in the office or one of the other interior spaces. But as he looked through the glass pane, he could see Alexis inside, hemmed up by Daniel Clayton. From the looks of it, they were arguing.

Fists clenched at his sides, Gus willed himself to stay where he was rather than rushing inside and demanding that Daniel leave his granddaughter alone. If he did that, then Alexis would defend the boy.

That would defeat the purpose of the elaborate plan he and Rose Clayton had concocted to keep their grandkids apart.

So he'd wait there. Monitor the situation without interfering. He didn't want his granddaughter marrying any kin to Rose Clayton. Especially a boy with a mother like Stephanie Clayton. A heavy drinker who'd been in and out of trouble her whole life. A woman who couldn't be bothered to raise her own boy. Instead, she'd dumped him off on Rose who'd raised Daniel as if he was her own son.

From where he stood, it appeared that Daniel was pleading with Alexis. But she shoved his hand away when he tried to touch her arm.

Gus smirked, glad to see that someone besides him was getting the sharp end of that fierce stubborn streak she'd inherited from him.

Suddenly, his granddaughter threw her arms up and said something to Daniel that he obviously didn't like. Then she turned and headed his way.

Gus moved away from the door and around the corner to the bar as quickly and quietly as he could. He waited for her to pass by.

"Alexis!" Gus grabbed hold of her elbow as she hurried past him. He chuckled good-naturedly. "Where's the fire, darlin'?"

She didn't laugh. In fact, the poor thing looked dazed, like a wounded bird that had fallen out of the nest before it was time.

"Sorry, I didn't see you, Grandad." Her eyes didn't meet his. Instead, she looked toward the office where she was headed. "I'm sorry I don't have time to talk right now. I need to deal with a major problem."

"Alexis, honey, what is it? Is everything all right?"

"It will be, I'm sure. I just really need to take care of this now, okay?" Her voice trembled, seemed close to breaking.

"I wanted to tell you how proud I am of you. Tonight was magnificent and you've raised so much money for pancreatic cancer research. Your grandmother would be so very proud of you."

Alexis suddenly raised her gaze to his, the corners of her eyes wet with tears. Rather than the intended effect of comforting her, his words seemed to cause her distress.

"Alexis, what's wrong?" Gus pleaded with his darling girl. The pain in her blue eyes, rimmed with tears, tore at his heart. "Whatever it is, you can talk to me."

Before she could answer, Daniel Clayton passed by. He and Alexis exchanged a long, painful look. Then Daniel dropped his gaze and continued to the other side of the room.

"Alexis, darlin', what's going on?"

The tears spilled from her eyes. Alexis sucked in a deep breath and sniffled.

"It's nothing I can't handle, Grandad." She wiped away the tears with brusque swipes of her hand and shook her head. "Thank you for everything you said. I appreciate it. Really. But I need to take care of this issue. I'll see you back at home later, okay?"

Alexis pressed a soft kiss to his whiskered cheek. Then she hurried off toward the clubhouse offices.

Gus sighed, leaning against the bar. He dropped on to the stool, tapped the bar to get the bartender's attention, and ordered a glass of whiskey, neat. He gripped the hard, cold glass without moving it to his lips.

Their little plan was a partial success. Neither he nor Rose had been able to match their grandchildren up with an eligible mate. Yet, they'd done exactly what they'd set out to do. They'd driven a wedge between Daniel and Alexis.

So why didn't he feel good about what they'd done?

Because their grandkids were absolutely miserable.

What kind of grandfather could rejoice in the heartbreak of a beautiful girl like Alexis?

"Hello, Gus." Rose had sidled up beside him, and ordered a white wine spritzer. "The kids didn't look too happy with each other just now."

"That's an understatement, if ever I've heard one." He gripped his glass and gulped from it. "They're in downright misery."

"Is it that bad?" She glanced over at him momentarily, studying his pained look, before accepting her glass of wine and taking a sip.

"Honestly? I think it's even worse." He scrubbed a hand down his jaw. "I feel like a heel for causing baby girl so much pain. And despite all our machinations, neither of us has found a suitable mate for our respective grandchildren."

She nodded sagely. Pain dimmed the light in her gray eyes. And for a moment, the shadow that passed over her lovely face made her look closer to her actual years.

"I'm sorry that they're both hurting. But it's better that they have their hearts broken now than to have it happen down the road, when they're both more invested in the relationship." She glanced at him squarely. "We've both known that pain. It's a feeling that never leaves you. We're both living proof of that."

"I guess we are." Gus nodded, taking another sip of his whiskey. "But maybe there's something we hadn't considered." He turned around, his back to the bar.

"And what's that?" She turned on her bar stool, too, studying the crowd.

"Daniel and Alexis share our last names, but that doesn't make them us. And it doesn't mean they're doomed to our fates."

Rose didn't respond as she watched her grandson Daniel being fawned over by the woman who'd bought him at auction. He looked about as pleased by the woman's attentions as a man getting a root canal without anesthesia.

"We did what was in their best interests. The right thing isn't always the easiest thing. I know they're hurting now, but when they each find the person they were meant to be with, they'll be thankful this happened."

Rose paid for her drink and turned to walk away.

"Rose."

She halted, glancing over her shoulder without looking directly at him.

"What if the two of them were meant to be together? Will they be grateful we interfered then?"

A heavy sigh escaped her red lips, and she gathered her shawl around her before leaving.

His eyes trailed the woman as she walked away in a glimmering green dress. The dress was long, but form-fitting. And despite her age, Rose was as tantalizing in that dress as a cool drink of water on a hot summer day.

After all these years he still had a thing for Rose Clayton. What if it was the same for Daniel and Alexis?

He ordered another whiskey, neat, hoping to God that he and Rose hadn't made a grave mistake they'd both regret.

Chapter 7

Ryan twirled Tessa on the dance floor and then drew her back into his arms as they danced to one of his favorite upbeat country songs. Everyone around them seemed to be singing along with the lyrics which were both funny and slightly irreverent.

Tessa turned her back to him, threw her hands up, and wiggled her full hips as she sang loudly.

His attention was drawn to the sway of those sexy hips keeping time to the music. Fortunately, her dancing was much more impressive than her singing. Something his anatomy responded to, even if he didn't want it to. Particularly not while they were in the middle of a crowded dance floor.

Ryan swallowed hard and tried to shove away the rogue thoughts trying to commandeer his good sense. He and Tessa were just two friends enjoying their night together. Having a good time.

Nothing to see here, folks.

"Everything okay?" Tessa had turned around, her beautiful brown eyes focused on him and a frown tugging down the corners of her mouth.

"Yeah, of course." He forced a smile. "I was just… thinking…that's all." He started to dance again, his movements forced and rigid.

Tessa regarded him strangely, but before she could probe further, Alexis appeared beside them looking flustered. Her eyes were red, and it looked like she'd been crying.

"Alexis, is something wrong?" Tessa turned to her friend and squeezed her hand.

"I'm afraid so. I've been looking everywhere for you two. Would you mind meeting with James and me in the office as soon as possible?" Alexis leaned in, so they could both hear her over the blaring music.

"Of course, we will." Tessa gave the woman's hand another assuring squeeze. "Just lead the way."

Alexis made her way through the crowd with Tessa and Ryan following closely behind.

Ryan bit back his disappointment at the interruption. If the distress Alexis appeared to be experiencing was any indication, the situation was one level below the barn being on fire. Which triggered a burning in his gut.

Whatever Alexis and James wanted with the two of them, he was pretty sure neither of them was going to like it.

"Tessa, Ryan, please, have a seat." James Harris, president of the Texas Cattleman's Club, gestured to the chairs on the other side of the large mahogany desk in his office.

After such a successful night, he and Alexis looked incredibly grim. The knot that had already formed in her gut tightened.

She and Ryan sat in the chairs James indicated while Alexis sat on the sofa along one wall.

"Something is obviously wrong." Ryan crossed one ankle over his knee. "What is it, James?"

The other man hesitated a moment before speaking. When he did, the words he uttered came out in an anguished growl.

"There was a problem with one of the bids. A *big* problem."

"Gail." Tessa and Ryan said her name simultaneously.

"How does something like this happen?" Ryan asked after James had filled them both in. "Can anyone just walk in off the street and bid a bogus hundred K?"

James grimaced.

Tessa felt badly for him. James hadn't been president of the Texas Cattleman's Club for very long. She could only imagine how he must be feeling. He'd been riding high after putting on what was likely the most successful fund-raiser in the club's history. But now he was saddled with one of the biggest faux pas in the club's history.

"It's a charity auction. We take folks at their word when they make a bid," James replied calmly, then sighed. "Still, I don't like that this happened on my watch, and I'll do everything I can to remedy the situation."

Tessa's heart broke for the man. She didn't know

James particularly well, but she'd heard the tragic story about what had happened to his brother and his sister-in-law. They'd died in an accident, leaving behind their orphaned son, who was little more than a year old, to be raised by James.

He was a nice enough guy, but he didn't seem the daddy type. Still, he was obviously doing the best he could to juggle all the balls he had in the air.

Tessa groaned, her hand pressed to her forehead. "I knew Gail had a thing for Lloyd Richardson, but I honestly never imagined she'd do something so reckless and impulsive."

"No one thinks you knew anything about it, Tess. That's not why we asked you here," Alexis assured her.

"Then why are we here?" Ryan's voice was cautious as he studied the other man.

"Because we have another dilemma that could compound the first problem." James heaved a sigh as he sat back in his chair, his hands steepled over his abdomen. "And we could really use your help to head it off."

"Was there another bid that someone can't make good on?" Ryan asked.

"No, but there is a reporter here, whom I invited." Alexis cringed as she stood. "He's intrigued by that one-hundred thousand dollar bid, and he wants to interview Gail and Lloyd."

"Damn. I see your dilemma." Ryan groaned sympathetically. "Instead of getting good press about all of the money the club did raise, all anyone will be talking about is Gail and her bogus bid."

"It gets even worse," Alexis said. She blew out a frustrated breath as she shook her head, her blond locks flipping over her shoulder. "We can't find hide nor hair of either Gail or Lloyd. It's like the two of them simply vanished."

Ryan shook his head. "Wow. That's pretty messed up."

"What is it that you want Ryan and me to do?" Tessa looked at James and then Alexis.

"The reporter was also very intrigued by everyone's reaction to you and all the drama of how Ryan beat out Clem and Bo's bids." A faint smile flickered on Alexis's mouth. "So we suggested that he follow the two of you on your little date."

"What?"

Panic suddenly seized Tessa's chest. It was one thing to play dress up and strut on the stage here at the club. Surrounded mostly by people she'd known her entire life. It was another to be followed by a reporter who was going to put the information out there for the entire world to see.

"We hadn't really intended to go on a date," Tessa said. "Ryan and I were just going to hang out together and have fun at the game. Grab a bite to eat at his favorite restaurant. Nothing worthy of reporting on."

"I know." There was an apology in Alexis's voice. "Which is why I need to ask another big favor…"

"You want us to go on a real date after all." Ryan looked from Alexis to James.

"Going out with a beautiful woman like Tess here, who also just happens to be your best friend…not the worst thing in the world that could happen to a guy." James forced a smile.

"Only…well, I know that the date you'd planned is the perfect kind of day for hanging with the guys." Alexis directed her attention toward Tess. "But this needs to feel like a big, romantic gesture. Something worthy of a big write-up for the event and for our club."

"I d-don't know, Alexis," Tessa stuttered, her heart racing. "I'm not sure how comfortable either of us would feel having a reporter follow us around all day."

"We'll do it," Ryan said suddenly. Decisively. "For the club, of course." He cleared his throat and gave Tess a reassuring nod. "And don't worry, I know exactly what to do. I'll make sure we give him the big, romantic fantasy he's looking for."

"I'm supposed to be the one who takes you out on a date," Tess objected. "That's how this whole thing works."

"Then it'll make for an even grander gesture when I surprise you by sweeping you off your feet."

He gave her that mischievous half smile that had enticed her into countless adventures. From searching for frogs when they were kids to parasailing in Mexico as an adult. After all these years, she still hadn't grown immune to its charm.

"Fine." Tessa sighed. "We'll do it. Just tell him we'll need a day or two to finalize the arrangements."

"Thank you!" Alexis hugged them both. "We're so grateful to you both for doing this."

"You're saving our asses here and the club's reputation." James looked noticeably relieved, though his eyebrows were still furrowed. "I can't thank you enough. And you won't be the only ones on the hot seat. Rose Clayton persuaded her grandson Daniel to give the reporter an additional positive feature related to the auction."

Alexis frowned at the mention of Daniel's name, but then she quickly recovered.

"And about that bid of Gail's...no one outside this room, besides Gail and Lloyd, of course, knows the situation." James frowned again. "We'd like to keep it that way until we figure out how we're going to resolve this. So please, don't whisper a word of this to anyone."

"Least of all the reporter," Alexis added, emphatically.

Tessa and Ryan agreed. Then Alexis introduced them to the reporter, Greg Halstead. After Greg gathered some preliminary information for the piece, Ryan insisted that he be the one to exchange contact information with Greg so they could coordinate him accompanying them on their date.

Every time Greg repeated the word *date*, shivers ran down Tessa's spine.

The only thing worse than having a thing for her best friend was being shanghaied into going on a fake date with him. But she was doing this for the club that meant so much to her, her family and the community of Royal.

Alexis had worked so hard to garner positive publicity for the club. And she'd raised awareness of the need to fund research for a cure for pancreatic cancer—the disease that had killed Alexis Slade's dear grandmother. Tess wouldn't allow all of her friend's hard work to be squandered because of Gail's selfish decision. Not if she could do something to prevent it.

Maybe she hadn't been aware of what Gail had planned to do tonight. But she'd been the one who'd invited Gail to tonight's affair. Tess couldn't help feeling obligated to do what she could to rectify the matter.

Even if it meant torturing herself by going on a pretend date that would feel very real to her. No matter how much she tried to deny it.

Chapter 8

Ryan and Tessa finally headed home in his truck after what felt like an incredibly long night.

He couldn't remember the last time he and Tessa had danced together or laughed as much as they had that evening. But that was *before* James and Alexis had asked them to go on an actual date. Since then, things felt…different.

First, they'd politely endured the awkward interview with that reporter, Greg Halstead. Then they'd gone about the rest of the evening dancing and mingling with fellow club members and their guests. But there was a strange vibe between them. Obviously, Tessa felt it, too.

Why else would she be rambling on, as she often did when she was nervous.

Then again, lost in his own thoughts, he hadn't been

very good company. Ryan drummed his fingers on the steering wheel during an awkward moment of silence.

"This date…it isn't going to make things weird between us, is it?" Tess asked finally, as if she'd been inside his head all along.

One of the hazards of a friendship with someone who knew him too well.

He forced a chuckle. "C'mon, Tess. We've been best buds too long to let a fake date shake us." His eyes searched hers briefly before returning to the road. "Our friendship could withstand anything."

Anything except getting romantically involved. Which is why they hadn't and wouldn't.

"Promise?" She seemed desperate for reassurance on the matter. Not surprising. A part of him needed it, too.

"On my life." This time, there was no hesitation. There were a lot of things in this world he could do without. Tessa Noble's friendship wasn't one of them.

Tessa nodded, releasing an audible sigh of relief. She turned to look out the window at the beautiful ranches that marked the road home.

His emphatic statement seemed to alleviate the anxiety they'd both been feeling. Still, his thoughts kept returning to their date the following weekend. The contemplative look on Tess's face, indicated that hers did, too.

He changed the subject, eager to talk about anything else. "What's up with your girl bidding a hundred K she didn't have?"

"I don't know." Tess seemed genuinely baffled by Gail's behavior.

Tessa and Gail certainly weren't as close as he and

Tess were. But lately, at her mother's urging, Tessa had tried to build stronger friendships with other women in town.

She and Gail had met when Tessa had used the woman's fledgling grocery delivery business. They'd hit it off and started hanging out occasionally.

He understood why Tess liked Gail. She was bold and a little irreverent. All of the things that Tess was not. But Ryan hadn't cared much for her. There was something about that woman he didn't quite trust. But now wasn't the time for I told you so's. Tessa obviously felt badly enough about being the person who'd invited Gail to the charity auction.

"I knew she had a lightweight crush on Lloyd Richardson," Tessa continued. "Who doesn't? But I certainly didn't think her capable of doing something this crazy and impulsive."

"Seems there was a lot of that going around," Ryan muttered under his breath.

"Speaking of that impulsiveness that seemed to be going around…" Tessa laughed, and Ryan chuckled, too.

He'd obviously uttered the words more to himself than to her. Still, she'd heard them, and they provided the perfect opening for what she'd been struggling to say all night.

"Thank you again for doing this, Rye. You made a very generous donation. And though you did the complete opposite of what I asked you to do—" they both laughed again "—I was a little…no, I was a *lot* nervous about going out with either Clem or Bo in such a high pressure situation, so thank you."

"Anything for you, Tess Noble." His voice was deep and warm. The emotion behind his words genuine. Something she knew from their history, not just as theory.

When they were in college, Ryan had climbed into his battered truck, and driven nearly two thousand miles to her campus in Sacramento after a particularly bad breakup with a guy who'd been an all-around dick. He'd dumped her for someone else a few days before Valentine's Day, so Ryan made a point of taking her to the Valentine's Day party. Then he kissed her in front of everyone—including her ex.

The kiss had taken her breath away. And left her wanting another taste ever since.

Tessa shook off the memory and focused on the here and now. Ryan had been uncharacteristically quiet during the ride home. He'd let her chatter on, offering a grunt of agreement or dissension here or there. Otherwise, he seemed deep in thought.

"And you're sure I can't pay you back at least some of what you bid on me?" Tessa asked as he slowed down before turning into the driveway of the Noble Spur, her family's ranch. "Especially since you're commandeering the planning of our date."

"Oh, we're still gonna use those tickets on the fifty-yard line, for sure," he clarified. "And there's no way I'm leaving Dallas without my favorite steak dinner. I'm just going to add some flourishes here and there. Nothing too fancy. But you'll enjoy the night. I promise." He winked.

Why did that small gesture send waves of electricity down her spine and make her acutely aware of her nipples prickling with heat beneath the jacket she'd put on to ward against the chilly night air?

"Well, thank you again," she said as he shifted his tricked out Ford Super Duty F-350 Platinum into Park. Ryan was a simple guy who didn't sweat the details—except when it came to his truck.

"You're welcome." Ryan lightly gripped her elbow when she reached for the door. "Allow me. Wouldn't want you to ruin that fancy outfit of yours."

He hopped out of the truck and came around to her side. He opened the door and took her hand.

It wasn't the first time Ryan had helped her out of his vehicle. But something about this time felt different. There was something in his intense green eyes. Something he wouldn't allow himself to say. Rare for a man who normally said just about anything that popped into his head.

When she stepped down onto the truck's side rail, Ryan released her hand. He gripped her waist and lifted her to the ground in a single deft move.

Tessa gasped in surprise, bracing her hands on his strong shoulders. His eyes scanned her once more. As if he still couldn't believe it was really her in the sexiest, most feminine item of clothing she'd ever owned.

Heat radiated off his large body, shielding her from the chilliness of the night air and making her aware of how little space there was between them.

For a moment, the vision of Ryan's lips crashing down on hers as he pinned her body against the truck flashed through her brain. It wasn't an unfamiliar image. But, given their positions and the way he was looking at her right now, it felt a little too real.

Tessa took short, shallow breaths, her chest heaving.

She needed to get away from Ryan Bateman before she did something stupid. Like lift on to her toes and press a hot, wet kiss to those sensual lips.

She needed to get inside and go to her room. The proper place to have ridiculously inappropriate thoughts about her best friend. With her battery-operated boyfriend buried in the nightstand drawer on standby, just in case she needed to take the edge off.

But walking away was a difficult thing to do when his mouth was mere inches from hers. And she trembled with the desire to touch him. To taste his mouth again. To trace the ridge behind the fly of his black dress pants.

"Good night." She tossed the words over her shoulder as she turned and headed toward the house as quickly as her feet would carry her in those high-heeled silver sandals.

"Tessa." His unusually gruff voice stopped her dead in her tracks.

She didn't turn back to look at him. Instead, she glanced just over her shoulder. A sign that he had her full attention, even if her eyes didn't meet his. "Yes?"

"I'm calling an audible on our date this weekend." Ryan invoked one of his favorite football terms.

"A last-minute change?" Tessa turned slightly, her curiosity piqued.

She'd planned the perfect weekend for Ryan Bateman. What could she possibly have missed?

"I'll pick you up on Friday afternoon, around 3:00 p.m. Pack a bag for the weekend. And don't forget that jumpsuit."

"We're spending the entire weekend in Dallas?" She turned to face him fully, stunned by the hungry look on his face. When he nodded his confirmation, Tessa focused on slowing her breath as she watched the cloud her warm breath made in the air. "Why? And since when do you care what I wear?"

"Because I promised Alexis I'd make this date a big, grand gesture that would keep the reporter preoccupied and off the topic of our missing bachelor and his hundred-thousand-dollar bidder." His words were matter of fact, signaling none of the raw, primal heat she'd seen in his eyes a moment ago.

He shut the passenger door and walked around to the driver's side. "It doesn't have to be that same outfit. It's just that you looked mighty pretty tonight. Neither of us gets much of a chance to dress up. Thought it'd be nice if we took advantage of this weekend to do that." He shrugged, as if it were the most normal request in the world.

This coming from a man who'd once stripped out of his tuxedo in the car on the way home from a mutual friend's out-of-town wedding. He'd insisted he couldn't stand to be in that tuxedo a moment longer.

"Fine." Tessa shrugged, too. If it was no big deal to Ryan, then it was no big deal to her either. "I'll pack a couple of dresses and skirts. Maybe I'll wear the dress I'd originally picked out for tonight. Before I volunteered to be in the auction."

After all that waxing, she should show her baby smooth legs off every chance she got. Who knew when she'd put herself through that kind of torture again?

"Sounds like you got some packing to do." A restrained smirk lit Ryan's eyes. He nodded toward the house. "Better get inside before you freeze out here."

"'Night, Ryan." Tessa turned up the path to the

house, without waiting for his response, and let herself in, closing the door behind her. The slam of the heavy truck door, followed by the crunch of gravel, indicated that Ryan was turning his vehicle around in the drive and heading home to the Bateman Ranch next door.

Tessa released a long sigh, her back pressed to the door.

She'd just agreed to spend the weekend in Dallas with her best friend. Seventy-two hours of pretending she didn't secretly lust after Ryan Bateman. Several of which would be documented by a reporter known for going after gossip.

Piece of cake. Piece of pie.

Chapter 9

"Tessa, your chariot is here," Tripp called to her up-stairs. "Hurry up, you're not gonna believe this."

Tripp was definitely back to his old self. It was both a blessing and a curse, because he hadn't stopped needling her and Ryan about their date ever since.

She inhaled deeply, then slowly released the breath as she stared at herself in the mirror one last time.

It's just a weekend trip with a friend. Ryan and I have done this at least a dozen times before. No big deal.

Tessa lifted her bag on to her shoulder, then made her way downstairs and out front where Tripp was handing her overnight suitcase off to Ryan.

Her eyes widened as she walked closer, studying the sleek black sedan with expensive black rims.

"Is that a black on black Maybach?"

"It is." Ryan took the bag from her and loaded it into the trunk of the Mercedes Maybach before closing it and opening the passenger door. He gestured for her to get inside. "You've always said you wanted to know what it was like to ride in one of these things, so—"

"You didn't go out and buy this, did you?" Panic filled her chest. Ryan wasn't extravagant or impulsive. And he'd already laid out a substantial chunk of change as a favor to her.

"No, of course not. You know a mud-caked pickup truck is more my style." He leaned in and lowered his voice, so only she could hear his next words. "But I'm supposed to be going for the entire illusion here, remember? And Tess…"

"Yes?" She inhaled his clean, fresh scent, her heart racing slightly from his nearness and the intimacy of his tone.

"Smile for the camera." Ryan nodded toward Greg Halstead who waved and snapped photographs of the two of them in front of the vehicle.

Tess deepened her smile, and she and Ryan stood together, his arm wrapped around her as the man clicked photos for the paper.

When Greg had gotten enough images, he shook their hands and said he'd meet them at the hotel later and at the restaurant tomorrow night to get a few more photos.

"Which hotel? And which restaurant?" Tessa turned to Ryan.

A genuine smile lit his green eyes and they sparkled in the afternoon sunlight. "If I tell you, it won't be a surprise, now will it?"

"Smart-ass." She folded her arms and shook her

head. Ryan knew she liked surprises about as much as she liked diamondback rattlesnakes. Maybe even a little less.

"There anything I should know about you two?" Tripp stepped closer after the reporter was gone. Arms folded over his chest, his gaze shifted from Ryan to her and then back again.

"You can take the protective big brother shtick down a notch," she teased. "I already explained everything to you. We're doing this for the club, and for Alexis."

She flashed her I'm-your-little-sister-and-you-love-me-no-matter-what smile. It broke him. As it had for as long as she could remember.

The edge of his mouth tugged upward in a reluctant grin. He opened his arms and hugged her goodbye before giving Ryan a one-arm bro hug and whispering something to him that she couldn't hear.

Ryan's expression remained neutral, but he nodded and patted her brother on the shoulder.

"We'd better get going." Ryan helped her into the buttery, black leather seat that seemed to give her a warm hug. Then he closed her door and climbed into the driver's seat.

"God, this car is beautiful," she said as he pulled away from the house. "If you didn't buy it, whose is it?

"Borrowed it from a friend." He pulled on to the street more carefully than he did when he was driving his truck. "The guy collects cars the way other folks collect stamps or Depression-era glass. Most of the cars he wouldn't let anyone breathe on, let alone touch. But he owed me a favor."

Tessa sank back against the seat and ran her hand along the smooth, soft leather.

"Manners would dictate that I tell you that you shouldn't have, but if I'm being honest, all I can think is, Where have you been all my life?" They both chuckled. "You think I can have a saddle made out of this leather?"

"For the right price, you can get just about anything." A wide smile lit his face.

Tessa sighed. She was content. Relaxed. And Ryan seemed to be, too. There was no reason this weekend needed to be tense and awkward.

"So, what did my brother say to you when he gave you that weird bro hug goodbye?"

The muscles in Ryan's jaw tensed and his brows furrowed. He kept his gaze on the road ahead. "This thing has an incredible sound system. I already synced it to my phone. Go ahead and play something. Your choice. Just no more '80s boy bands. I heard enough of those at the charity auction last week."

Tessa smirked. "You could've just told me it was none of my business what Tripp said."

His wide smile returned, though he didn't look at her. "I thought I just did."

They both laughed, and Tessa smiled to herself. Their weekend was going to be fun. Just like every other road trip they'd ever taken together. Things would only be uncomfortable between them if she made them that way.

Ryan, Tessa and Greg Halstead headed up the stone stairs that led to the bungalow of a fancy, art-themed boutique hotel that he'd reserved. The place was an easy drive from the football stadium.

Tessa had marveled at the hotel's main building and

mused about the expense. But she was as excited as a little kid in a candy store, eager to see what was on the other side of that door. Greg requested to go in first, so he could set up his shot of Tessa stepping inside the room.

When he signaled that he was ready, Ryan inserted the key card into the lock and removed it quickly. Once the green light flashed, he opened the door for her.

Tessa's jaw dropped, and she covered her mouth with both hands, genuinely stunned by the elegant beauty of the contemporary bungalow.

"So...what do you think?" He couldn't shake the nervousness he felt. The genuine need to impress her was not his typical MO. So what was going on? Maybe it was the fact that her impression would be recorded for posterity.

"It's incredible, Ryan. I don't know what to say." Her voice trembled with emotion. When she glanced up at him, her eyes were shiny. She wiped quickly at the corners of her eyes. "I'm being silly, I know."

"No, you're not." He kissed her cheek. "That's exactly the reaction I was hoping for."

Ryan stepped closer and lowered his voice. "I want this to be a special weekend for you, Tess. What you did last week at the charity auction was brave, and I'm proud of you. I want this weekend to be everything the fearless woman who strutted across that stage last Saturday night deserves."

His eyes met hers for a moment and his chest filled with warmth.

"Thanks, Rye. This place is amazing. I really appreciate everything you've done." A soft smile curled the edges of her mouth, filling him with the overwhelming desire to lean down and kiss her the way he had at that Valentine's Day party in college.

He stepped back and cleared his throat, indicating that she should step inside.

Tessa went from room to room of the two-bedroom, two-bath hotel suite, complete with two balconies. One connected to each bedroom. There was even a small kitchen island, a full-size refrigerator and a stove. The open living room boasted a ridiculously large television mounted to the wall and a fireplace in both that space and the master bedroom, which he insisted that she take. But Tessa, who could be just as stubborn as he was, wouldn't hear of it. She directed the bellman to take her things to the slightly smaller bedroom, which was just as beautiful as its counterpart.

"I think I have all the pictures I need." Greg gathered up his camera bag and his laptop. "I'll work on the article tonight and select the best photos among the ones I've taken so far. I'll meet you guys at the restaurant tomorrow at six-thirty to capture a few more shots."

"Sounds good." Ryan said goodbye to Greg and closed the door behind him, glad the man was finally gone. Something about a reporter hanging around, angling for a juicy story, felt like a million ants crawling all over his skin.

He sank on to the sofa, shrugged his boots off, and put his feet up on the coffee table. It'd been a short drive from Royal to Dallas, but mentally, he was exhausted.

Partly from making last-minute arrangements for their trip. Partly from the effort of reminding himself that no matter how much it felt like it, this wasn't a real date. They were both just playing their parts. Making the TCC look good and diverting attention from the debacle of Gail's bid.

"Hey." Tess emerged from her bedroom where she'd gone to put her things away. "Is Greg gone?"

"He left a few minutes ago. Said to tell you good-bye."

"Thank goodness." She heaved a sigh and plopped down on the sofa beside him. "I mean, he's a nice guy and everything. It just feels so... I don't know..."

"Creepy? Invasive? Weird?" he offered. "Take your pick."

"All of the above." Tessa laughed, then leaned forward, her gaze locked on to the large bouquet of flowers in a glass vase on the table beside his feet.

"I thought these were just part of the room." She removed the small envelope with her name on it and slid her finger beneath the flap, prying it open. "These are for me?"

"I hope you like them. They're—"

"Peonies. My favorite flower." She leaned forward and inhaled the flowers that resembled clouds dyed shades of light and dark pink. "They're beautiful, Ryan. Thank you. You thought of everything, didn't you?" Her voice trailed and her gaze softened.

"I meant it when I said you deserve a really special weekend. I even asked them to stock the freezer with your favorite brand of Neapolitan ice cream."

"Seriously?" She was only wearing a hint of lip gloss in a nude shade of pink and a little eyeshadow and mascara. But she was as beautiful as he'd ever seen her. Even more so than the night of the auction when she'd worn a heavy layer of makeup that had covered her creamy brown skin. Sunlight filtered into the room, making her light brown eyes appear almost golden. "What more could I possibly ask for?"

His eyes were locked on her sensual lips. When he finally tore his gaze away from them, Tess seemed disappointed. As if she'd expected him to lean in and kiss her.

"I like the dress, by the way."

"Really?" She stood, looking down at the heather-gray dress and the tan calf-high boots topped by knee socks. The cuff of the socks hovered just above the top of the boot, drawing his eye there and leading it up the side of her thigh where her smooth skin disappeared beneath the hem of her dress.

His body stiffened in response to her curvy silhouette and her summery citrus scent.

Fucking knee socks. *Seriously*? Tess was *killing* him.

For a moment he wondered if she was teasing him on purpose. Reminding him of the things he couldn't have with her. The red-hot desires that would never be satisfied.

Tess seemed completely oblivious to her effect on him as she regarded the little gray dress.

Yet, all he could think of was how much he'd like to see that gray fabric pooled on the floor beside his bed.

Ryan groaned inside. This was going to be the longest seventy-two hours of his life.

Chapter 10

"Is that a bottle of champagne?" Tessa pointed to a bottle chilling in an ice bucket on the sideboard along the wall.

She could use something cold to tamp down the heat rising in her belly under Ryan's intense stare. It also wouldn't be a bad idea to create some space between them. Enough to get her head together and stop fantasizing about what it would feel like to kiss her best friend again.

"Even better." Ryan flashed a sexy, half grin. "It's imported Italian Moscato d'Asti. I asked them to chill a bottle for us."

Her favorite. Too bad this wasn't a real date, because Ryan had ticked every box of what her fantasy date would look like.

"Saving it for something special?"

"Just you." He winked, climbing to his feet. "Why don't we make a toast to kick our weekend off?"

Tessa relaxed a little as she followed him over to the ice bucket, still maintaining some distance between them.

Ryan opened the bottle with a loud pop and poured each of them a glass of the sparkling white wine. He handed her one.

She accepted, gratefully, and joined him in holding up her glass.

"To an unforgettable weekend." A soft smile curved the edges of his mouth.

"Cheers." Tessa ignored the beading of her nipples and the tingling that trailed down her spine and sparked a fire low in her belly. She took a deep sip.

"Very good." Tessa fought back her speculation about how much better it would taste on Ryan's lips.

Ryan returned to the sofa. He finished his glass of moscato in short order and set it on the table beside the sofa.

Tessa sat beside him, finishing the remainder of her drink and contemplating another. She decided against it, setting it on the table in front of them.

She turned to her friend. God, he was handsome. His green eyes brooding and intense. His shaggy brown hair living in that space between perfectly groomed and purposely messy. The ever-present five o'clock shadow crawling over his clenched jaw.

"Thanks, Rye." She needed to quell the thoughts in her head. "This is all so amazing and incredibly thoughtful. I know this fantasy date isn't real, but you went out of your way to make it feel that way, and I appreciate it."

Tessa leaned in to kiss his stubbled cheek. Something she'd done a dozen times before. But Ryan turned his head, likely surprised by her sudden approach, and her lips met his.

She'd been right. The moscato did taste better enmeshed with the flavor of Ryan's firm, sensual lips.

It was an accidental kiss. So why had she leaned in and continued to kiss him, rather than withdrawing and apologizing? And why hadn't Ryan pulled back either?

Tessa's eyes slowly drifted closed, and she slipped her fingers into the short hair at the nape of Ryan's neck. Pulled his face closer to hers.

She parted her lips, and Ryan accepted the unspoken invitation, sliding his tongue between her lips and taking control. The kiss had gradually moved from a sweet, inadvertent, closed-mouth affair to an intense meshing of lips, teeth and tongues. Ryan moved his hands to her back, tugging her closer.

Tessa sighed softly in response to the hot, demanding kiss that obliterated the memory of that unexpected one nearly a decade ago. Truly kissing Ryan Bateman was everything she'd imagined it to be.

And she wanted more.

They'd gone this far. Had let down the invisible wall between them. There was nothing holding them back now.

Tessa inhaled deeply before shifting to her knees and straddling Ryan's lap. He groaned. A sexy sound that was an undeniable mixture of pain and pleasure. Of intense wanting. Evident from the ridge beneath his zipper.

As he deepened their kiss, his large hand splayed against her low back, his hardness met the soft, warm space between her thighs, sending a shiver up her spine. Her nipples ached with an intensity she hadn't experienced before. She wanted his hands and lips on her naked flesh. She wanted to shed the clothing that prevented skin-to-skin contact.

She wanted…sex. With Ryan. Right now.

Sex.

It wasn't as if she'd forgotten how the whole process worked. Obviously. But it'd been a while since she'd been with anyone. More than a few years. One of the hazards of living in a town small enough that there was three degrees or less of separation between any man she met and her father or brother.

Would Ryan be disappointed?

Tessa suddenly went stiff, her eyes blinking.

"Don't," he whispered between hungry kisses along her jaw and throat that left her wanting and breathless, despite the insecurities that had taken over her brain.

Tess frowned. "Don't do what?"

Maybe she didn't have Ryan Bateman's vast sexual experience, but she was pretty sure she knew how to kiss. At least she hadn't had any complaints.

Until now.

"Have you changed your mind about this?"

"No." She forced her eyes to meet his, regardless of how unnerved she was by his intense stare and his determination to make her own up to what she wanted. "Not even a little."

The edge of his mouth curved in a criminally sexy smirk. "Then for once in your life, Tess, stop overthinking everything. Stop compiling a list in your head of all the reasons we shouldn't do this." He kissed her again, his warm lips pressed to hers and his large hands gliding down her back and gripping her bottom as he pulled her firmly against him.

A soft gasp escaped her mouth at the sensation of his hard length pressed against her sensitive flesh. Ryan swept his tongue between her parted lips, tangling it with hers as he wrapped his arms around her.

Their kiss grew increasingly urgent. Hungry. Desperate. His kiss made her question whether she'd ever *really* been kissed before. Made her skin tingle with a desire so intense she physically ached with a need for him.

A need for Ryan's kiss. His touch. The warmth of his naked skin pressed against hers. The feel of him inside her.

Hands shaking and the sound of her own heartbeat filling her ears, Tessa pulled her mouth from his. She grabbed the hem of her dress and raised it. His eyes were locked with hers, both of them breathing heavily, as she lifted the fabric.

Ryan helped her tug the dress over her head and he tossed it on to the floor. He studied her lacy, gray bra and the cleavage spilling out of it.

Her cheeks flamed, and her heart raced. Ryan leaned in and planted slow, warm kisses on her shoulder. He swept her hair aside and trailed kisses up her neck.

"God, you're beautiful, Tess." His voice was a low growl that sent tremors through her. He glided a callused hand down her back and rested it on her hip. "I think it's pretty obvious how much I want you. But I need to know that you're sure about this."

"I am." She traced his rough jaw with her palm. Glided a thumb across his lips, naturally a deep shade of red that made them even more enticing. Then she crashed her lips against his as she held his face in her hands.

He claimed her mouth with a greedy, primal kiss that strung her body tight as a bow, desperate for the release that only he could provide.

She wanted him. More than she could ever remember wanting anything. The steely rod pressed against the slick, aching spot between her thighs indicated his genuine desire for her. Yet, he seemed hesitant. As if he were holding back. Something Ryan Bateman, one of the most confident men she'd ever known, wasn't prone to do.

Tess reached behind her and did the thing Ryan seemed reluctant to. She released the hooks on her bra, slid the straps down her shoulders and tossed it away.

He splayed one hand against her back. The other glided up and down her side before his thumb grazed the side of her breast. Once, twice, then again. As if testing her.

Finally, he grazed her hardened nipple with his open palm, and she sucked in a sharp breath.

His eyes met hers with a look that fell somewhere between asking and pleading.

Tessa swallowed hard, her cheeks and chest flushed with heat. She nodded, her hands trembling as she braced them on his wide shoulders.

When Ryan's lips met her skin again, she didn't fight the overwhelming feelings that flooded her senses, like a long, hard rain causing the creek to exceed its banks. She leaned into them. Allowed them to wash over her. Enjoyed the thing she'd fantasized about for so long.

Tessa gasped as Ryan cupped her bottom and pulled her against his hardened length. As if he was as desperate for her as she was for him. He kissed her neck, her shoulders, her collarbone. Then he dropped tender, delicate kisses on her breasts.

Tessa ran her fingers through his soft hair. When he raised his eyes to hers, she leaned down, whispering in his ear.

"Ryan, take me to bed. Now."

Before she lost her nerve. Before he lost his.

Ryan carried her to his bed, laid her down and settled between her thighs. He trailed slow, hot kisses down her neck and chest as he palmed her breast with his large, work-roughened hand. He sucked the beaded tip into his warm mouth. Grazed it with his teeth. Lathed it with his tongue.

She shuddered in response to the tantalizing sensation that shot from her nipple straight to her sex. Her skin flamed beneath Ryan's touch, and her breath came in quick little bursts. He nuzzled her neck, one large hand skimming down her thigh and hooking behind her knee. As he rocked against the space between her thighs, Tessa whimpered at the delicious torture of his steely length grinding against her needy clit.

"That's it, Tess." Ryan trailed kisses along her jaw. "Relax. Let go. You know I'd never do anything to hurt you." His stubble scraped the sensitive skin of her cheek as he whispered roughly in her ear.

She did know that. She trusted Ryan with her life. With her deepest secrets. With her body. Ryan was sweet and charming and well-meaning, but her friend could sometimes be a bull in the china shop.

Would he ride roughshod over her heart, even if he didn't mean to?

Tessa gazed up at him, her lips parting as she took

in his incredibly handsome form. She yanked his shirt from the back of his pants and slid her hands against his warm skin. Gently grazed his back with her nails. She had the fleeting desire to mark him as hers. So that any other woman who saw him would know he belonged to her and no one else.

Ryan moved beside her, and she immediately missed his weight and the feel of him pressed against her most sensitive flesh. He kissed her harder as he slid a hand up her thigh and then cupped the space between her legs that throbbed in anticipation of his touch.

Tessa tensed, sucking in a deep breath as he glided his fingertips back and forth over the drenched panel of fabric shielding her sex. He tugged the material aside and plunged two fingers inside her.

"God, you're wet, Tess." The words vibrated against her throat, where he branded her skin with scorching hot kisses that made her weak with want. He kissed his way down her chest and gently scraped her sensitive nipple with his teeth before swirling his tongue around the sensitive flesh.

Tessa quivered as the space between her thighs ached with need. She wanted to feel him inside her. To be with Ryan in the way she'd always imagined.

But this wasn't a dream; it was real. And their actions would have real-world consequences.

"You're doing it again. That head thing," he muttered in between little nips and licks. His eyes glinted in the light filtering through the bedroom window. "Cut it out."

God, he knew her too well. And after tonight, he would know every single inch of her body. If she had her way.

Chapter 11

Ryan couldn't get over how beautiful Tessa was as she lay beside him whimpering with pleasure. Lips parted, back arched and her eyelashes fluttering, she was everything he'd imagined and more.

He halted his action just long enough to encourage her to lift her hips, allowing him to drag the lacy material down her legs, over her boots, and off. Returning his attention to her full breasts, he sucked and licked one of the pebbled, brown peaks he'd occasionally glimpsed the outline of through the thin, tank tops she sometimes wore during summer. He'd spent more time than he dared admit speculating about what her breasts looked like and how her skin would taste.

Now he knew. And he desperately wanted to know everything about her body. What turned her on? What would send her spiraling over the edge, his name on her lips?

He eagerly anticipated solving those mysteries, too.

Ryan inserted his fingers inside her again, adding a third finger to her tight, slick channel. Allowed her body to stretch and accommodate the additional digit.

He and Tess had made it a point not to delve too deeply into each other's sex lives. Still, they'd shared enough for him to know he wouldn't be her first or even her second. She was just a little tense, and perhaps a lot nervous. And she needed to relax.

Her channel stretched and relaxed around his fingers as he moved to her other nipple and gave it the same treatment he'd given the first. He resumed the movement of his hand, his fingers gliding in and out of her. Then he stroked the slick bundle of nerves with his thumb.

Tessa's undeniable gasp of pleasure indicated her approval.

The slow, small circles he made with his thumb got wider, eliciting a growing chorus of curses and moans. Her grip on his hair tightened, and she moved her hips in rhythm with his hand.

She was slowly coming undone, and he was grateful to be the reason for it. Ryan wet his lips with a sweep of his tongue, eager to taste her there. But he wanted to take his time. Make this last for both of them.

He kissed Tessa's belly and slipped his other hand between her legs, massaging her clit as he curved the fingers inside her.

"Oh god, oh god, oh god, Ryan. Right there, right there," Tess pleaded when he hit the right spot.

He gladly obliged her request, both hands moving with precision until he'd taken Tess to the edge. She'd

called his name, again and again, as she dug the heels
of her boots into the mattress and her body stiffened.

Watching his best friend tumble into bliss was a
thing of beauty. Being the one who'd brought her such
intense ecstasy was an incredible gift. It was easily the
most meaningful sexual experience he'd ever had, and
he was still fully clothed.

Ryan lay down, gathering Tess to him and wrapping her in his arms, her head tucked under his chin.
He flipped the cover over her, so she'd stay warm.

They were both silent. Tessa's chest heaved as she
slowly came down from the orgasm he'd given her.

When the silence lingered on for seconds that turned
to minutes, but felt like hours, Ryan couldn't take it.

"Tess, look, I—"

"You're still dressed." She raised her head, her eyes
meeting his. Her playful smile eased the tension they'd
both been feeling. "And I'm not quite sure why."

The laugh they shared felt good. A bit of normalcy
in a situation that was anything but normal between
them.

He planted a lingering kiss on her sweet lips.

"I can fix that." He sat up and tugged his shirt over
his head and tossed it on to the floor unceremoniously.

"Keep going." She indicated his pants with a wave
of her hand.

"Bold and bossy." He laughed. "Who is this woman
and what did she do with my best friend?"

She frowned slightly, as if what he'd said had hurt
her feelings.

"Hey." He cradled her face in one hand. "You know
that's not a criticism, right? I like seeing this side of
you."

"Usually when a man calls a woman bossy, it's code for bitchy." Her eyes didn't quite meet his.

Ryan wanted to kick himself. He'd only been teasing when he'd used the word bossy, but he hadn't been thinking. He understood how loaded that term was to Tess. She'd hated that her mother and grandmother had constantly warned her that no ranch man would want a bossy bride.

"I should've said assertive," he clarified. "Which is what I've always encouraged you to be."

She nodded, seemingly satisfied with his explanation. A warm smile slid across her gorgeous face and lit her light brown eyes. "Then I'd like to assert that you're still clothed, and I don't appreciate it, seeing as I'm not."

"Yes, ma'am." He winked as he stood and removed his pants.

Tessa gently sank her teeth into her lower lip as she studied the bulge in his boxer briefs. Which only made him harder.

He rubbed the back of his neck and chuckled. "Now I guess I know how the fellas felt on stage at the auction."

"Hmm…" The humming sound Tess made seemed to vibrate in his chest and other parts of his body. Specifically, the part she was staring at right now.

Tess removed her boots and kneeled on the bed in front of him, her brown eyes studying him. The levity had faded from her expression, replaced by a heated gaze that made his cock twitch.

She looped her arms around his neck and pulled his mouth down toward hers. Angling her head, she kissed him hard, her fingers slipping into his hair and her naked breasts smashed against his hard chest.

If this was a dream, he didn't want to wake up.

Ryan wrapped his arms around Tess, needing her body pressed firmly against his. He splayed one hand against the smooth, soft skin of her back. The other squeezed the generous bottom he'd always quietly admired. Hauling her tight against him, he grew painfully hard with the need to be inside her.

He claimed her mouth, his tongue gliding against hers, his anticipation rising. He'd fantasized about making love to Tess long before that kiss they'd shared in college.

He'd wanted to make love to her that night. Or at the very least make out with her in his truck. But he'd promised Tripp he wouldn't ever look at Tess that way.

A promise he'd broken long before tonight, despite his best efforts.

Ryan pushed thoughts of his ill-advised pledge to Tripp and the consequences of breaking it from his mind.

Right now, it was just him and Tess. The only thing that mattered in this moment was what the two of them wanted. What they needed from each other.

Ryan pulled away, just long enough to rummage in his luggage for the condoms he kept in his bag.

He said a silent prayer, thankful there was one full strip left. He tossed it on the nightstand and stripped out of his underwear.

Suddenly she seemed shy again as his eyes roved every inch of her gorgeous body.

He placed his hands on her hips, pulling her close to him and pressing his forehead to hers.

"God, you're beautiful, Tess." He knew he sounded like a broken record. But he was struck by how breathtaking she was and by the fact that she'd trusted him with something as precious as her body.

"You're making me feel self-conscious." A deep blush stained Tess's cheeks and spread through her chest.

"Don't be." He cradled her cheek, hoping to put her at ease. "That's not my intention. I just…" He sighed, giving up on trying to articulate what he was feeling.

One-night stands, even the occasional relationship… those were easy. But with Tess, everything felt weightier. More significant. Definitely more complicated. He couldn't afford to fuck this up. Because not having Tess as his friend wasn't an option. Still, he wanted her.

"Ryan, it's okay." She wrapped her arms around him. "I'm nervous about this, too. But I know that I want to be with you tonight. It's what I've wanted for a long time, and I don't want to fight it anymore."

He shifted his gaze to hers. A small sigh of relief escaped his mouth.

Tess understood exactly what he was feeling. They could do this. Be together like this. Satisfy their craving for each other without ruining their friendship.

He captured her mouth in a bruising kiss, and they both tumbled on to the mattress. Hands groping. Tongues searching. Hearts racing.

He grabbed one of the foil packets and ripped it open, sheathing himself as quickly as he could.

He guided himself to her slick entrance, circling his hips so his pelvis rubbed against her hardened clit. Tessa gasped, then whimpered with pleasure each time he ground his hips against her again. She writhed against him, increasing the delicious friction against the tight bundle of nerves.

Ryan gripped the base of his cock and pressed its head to her entrance. He inched inside, and Tess whimpered softly. She dug her fingers into his hips, her eyes meeting his as he slid the rest of the way home. Until he was nestled as deeply inside her as the laws of physics would allow.

When he was fully seated, her slick, heated flesh surrounding him, an involuntary growl escaped his mouth at the delicious feel of this woman who was all softness and curves. Sweetness and beauty. His friend and his lover.

His gaze met hers as he hovered above her and moved inside her. His voice rasping, he whispered to her. Told her how incredible she made him feel.

Then, lifting her legs, he hooked them over his shoulders as he leaned over her, his weight on his hands as he moved.

She gasped, her eyes widening at the sensation of him going deep and hitting bottom due to the sudden shift in position.

"Ryan… I…oh… God." Tessa squeezed her eyes shut.

"C'mon, Tess." He arched his back as he shifted his hips forward, beads of sweat forming on his brow and trickling down his back. "Just let go. Don't think. Just feel."

Her breath came in quick pants, and she dug her nails in his biceps. Suddenly, her mouth formed a little *O* and her eyes opened wide. The unmistakable expression of pure satisfaction that overtook her as she called his name was one of the most beautiful things he'd ever seen. Something he wanted to see again and again.

Her flesh throbbed and pulsed around him, bringing him to his peak. He tensed, shuddering as he cursed and called her name.

Ryan collapsed on to the bed beside her, both of them breathing hard and staring at the ceiling overhead for a few moments.

Finally, she draped an arm over his abdomen and rested her head on his shoulder.

He kissed the top of her head, pulled the covers over them, and slipped an arm around her. He lay there, still and quiet, fighting his natural tendency to slip out into the night. His usual MO after a one-night stand. Only he couldn't do that. Partly because it was Tess. Partly because what he'd felt between them was something he couldn't quite name, and he wanted to feel it again.

Ryan propped an arm beneath his head and stared at the ceiling as Tessa's soft breathing indicated she'd fallen asleep.

Intimacy.

That was the elusive word he'd been searching for all night. The thing he'd felt when his eyes had met hers as he'd roared, buried deep inside her. He'd sounded ridiculous. Like a wounded animal, in pain. Needing someone to save him.

Ryan scrubbed a hand down his face, one arm still wrapped around his best friend. Whom he'd made love to. The woman who knew him better than anyone in the world.

And now they knew each other in a way they'd never

allowed themselves to before. A way that made him feel raw and exposed, like a live wire.

While making love to Tess, he'd felt a surge of power as he'd teased her gorgeous body and coaxed her over the edge. Watched her free-fall into ecstasy, her body trembling.

But as her inner walls pulsed, pulling him over the cliff after her, he'd felt something completely foreign and yet vaguely familiar. It was a thing he couldn't name. Or maybe he hadn't wanted to.

Then when he'd startled awake, his arm slightly numb from being wedged beneath her, the answer was on his tongue.

Intimacy.

How was it that he'd managed to have gratifying sex with women without ever experiencing this heightened level of intimacy? Not even with his ex—the woman he'd planned to marry.

He and Sabrina had known each other. What the other wanted for breakfast. Each other's preferred drinks. They'd even known each other's bodies. *Well.* And yet he'd never experienced this depth of connection. Of truly being known by someone who could practically finish his sentences. Not because Tessa was so like him, but because she understood him in a way no one else did.

Ryan swallowed the hard lump clogging his throat and swiped the backs of his fingers over his damp brow.

Why is it suddenly so goddamned hot in here?

He blew out a long, slow breath. Tried to slow the rhythm of his heart, suddenly beating like a drum.

What the hell had he just done?

He'd satisfied the curiosity that had been simmering just below the surface of his friendship with Tessa. The desire to know her intimately. To know how it would feel to have her soft curves pressed against him as he'd surged inside her.

Now he knew what it was like for their bodies to move together. As if they were a single being. How it made his pulse race like a freight train as she called his name in a sweet, husky voice he'd never heard her use before. The delicious burn of her nails gently scraping his back as she wrapped her legs around him and pulled him in deeper.

And how it felt as she'd throbbed and pulsed around his heated flesh until he could no longer hold back his release.

Now, all he could think about was feeling all of those things again. Watching her shed the inhibitions that had held her back at first. Taking her a little further.

But Tessa was his best friend, and a very good friend's sister. He'd crossed the line. Broken a promise and taken them to a place they could never venture back from. After last night, he couldn't see her and not want her. Would never forget the taste and feel of her.

So what now?

Tess was sweet and sensitive. Warm and thoughtful. She deserved more than being friends with benefits. She deserved a man as kind and loving as she was.

Was he even capable of being that kind of man?

His family was nothing like the Nobles. Hank and Loretta Bateman weren't the doting parents that kissed injured knees and cheered effort. They believed in tough love, hard lessons and that failure wasn't to be tolerated by anyone with the last name Bateman.

Ryan knew unequivocally that his parents loved him, but he was twenty-nine years old and could never recall hearing either of them say the words explicitly.

He'd taken the same approach in his relationships. It was how he was built, all he'd ever known. But Tess could never be happy in a relationship like that.

Ryan sucked in another deep breath and released it quietly. He gently kissed the top of her head and screwed his eyes shut. Allowed himself to surrender to the sleep that had eluded him until now.

They'd figure it all out in the morning. After he'd gotten some much-needed sleep. He always thought better with a clear head and a full stomach.

Chapter 12

Tessa's eyes fluttered opened. She blinked against the rays of light peeking through the hotel room curtain and rubbed the sleep from her eyes with her fist. Her leg was entwined with Ryan's, and one of her arms was buried beneath him.

She groaned, pressing a hand to her mouth to prevent a curse from erupting from her lips. She'd made love with her best friend. Had fallen asleep with him. She peeked beneath the covers, her mouth falling open.

Naked. Both of them.

Tessa snapped her mouth shut and eased the cover back down. Though it didn't exactly lie flat. Not with Ryan Bateman sporting a textbook definition of morning wood.

She sank her teeth into her lower lip and groaned internally. Her nipples hardened, and the space between her thighs grew incredibly wet. Heat filled her cheeks.

She'd been with Ryan in the most intimate way imaginable. And it had been…incredible. Better than anything she'd imagined. And she'd imagined it more than she cared to admit.

Ryan had been intense, passionate and completely unselfish. He seemed to get off on pleasing her. Had evoked reactions from her body she hadn't believed it capable of. And the higher he'd taken her, the more desperate she became to shatter the mask of control that gripped his handsome face.

Tessa drew her knees to her chest and took slow, deep breaths. Willed her hands to stop shaking. Tried to tap into the brain cells that had taken a siesta the moment she'd pressed her lips to Ryan's.

Yes, sex between them had been phenomenal. But the friendship they shared for more than two decades— that was something she honestly couldn't do without.

She needed some space, so she could clear her head and make better decisions than she had last night. Last night she'd allowed her stupid crush on her best friend to run wild. She'd bought into the Cinderella fantasy. Lock, stock and barrel.

What did she think would happen next? That he'd suddenly realize she was in love with him? Maybe even realize he was in love with her, too?

Not in this lifetime or the next.

She simply wasn't that lucky. Ryan had always considered her a friend. His best friend, but nothing more. A few hours together naked between the sheets wouldn't change that.

Besides, as her mother often reminded her, tigers don't change their stripes.

How many times had Ryan said it? *Sex is just sex.*

A way to have a little fun and let off a little steam. Why would she expect him to feel differently just because it was her?

Her pent-up feelings for Ryan were her issue, not his.

Tessa's face burned with an intense heat, as if she was standing too close to a fire. Waking up naked with her best friend was awkward, but they could laugh it off. Blame it on the alcohol, like Jamie Foxx. Chalk it up to them both getting too carried away in the moment. But if she told him how she really felt about him, and he rejected her...

Tessa sighed. The only thing worse than secretly lusting after her best friend was having had him, knowing just how good things could be, and then being patently rejected. She'd never recover from that. Would never be able to look him in the face and pretend everything was okay.

And if, by some chance, Ryan was open to trying to turn this into something more, he'd eventually get bored with their relationship. As he had with every relationship he'd been in before. They'd risk destroying their friendship.

It wasn't worth the risk.

Tessa wiped away tears that stung the corners of her eyes. She quietly climbed out of bed, in search of her clothing.

She cursed under her breath as she retrieved her panties—the only clothing she'd been wearing when they entered the bedroom. Tessa pulled them on and grabbed Ryan's shirt from the floor. She slipped it on and buttoned a few of the middle buttons. She glanced back at his handsome form as he slept soundly, hoping everything between them would be all right.

Tessa slowly turned the doorknob and the door creaked open.

Damn.

Wasn't oiling door hinges part of the planned maintenance for a place like this? Did they not realize the necessity of silent hinges in the event a hotel guest needed a quiet escape after making a questionable decision with her best friend the night before?

Still, as soundly as Ryan was sleeping, odds were, he hadn't heard it.

"Tess?" Ryan called from behind her in that sexy, sleep-roughened voice that made her squirm.

Every. Damn. Time.

She sucked in a deep breath, forced a nonchalant smile and turned around. "Yes?"

"Where are you going?"

He'd propped himself up in bed on one elbow as he rubbed his eyes and squinted against the light. His brown hair stood all over his head in the hottest damn case of bed head she'd ever witnessed. And his bottle-green eyes glinted in the sunlight.

Trying to escape before you woke up. Isn't it obvious?

Tessa jerked a thumb over her shoulder. "I was about to hop into the shower, and I didn't want to wake you."

"Perfect." He sat up and threw off the covers. "We can shower together." A devilish smile curled his red lips. "I know how you feel about conserving water."

"You want to shower…together? The two of us?" She pointed to herself and then to him.

"Why? Were you thinking of inviting someone else?"

"Smart-ass." Her cheeks burned with heat. Ryan was in rare form. "You know what I meant."

"Yes, I do." He stalked toward her naked, at more than half-mast now. Looking like walking, talking sex-on-a-stick promising unicorn orgasms.

Ryan looped his arms around her waist and pressed her back against the wall. He leaned down and nuzzled her neck.

Tessa's beaded nipples rubbed against his chest through the fabric of the shirt she was wearing. Her belly fluttered, and her knees trembled. Her chest rose and fell with heavy, labored breaths. As if Ryan was sucking all the oxygen from the room, making it harder for her to breathe.

"C'mon, Tess." He trailed kisses along her shoulder as he slipped the shirt from it. "Don't make this weird. It's just us."

She raised her eyes to his, her heart racing. "It's already weird *because* it's just us."

"Good point." He gave her a cocky half smile and a micro nod. "Then we definitely need to do something to alleviate the weirdness."

"And *how* exactly are we going to do—" Tess squealed as Ryan suddenly lifted her and heaved her over his shoulder. He carried her, kicking and wiggling, into the master bathroom and turned on the water.

"Ryan Bateman, don't you dare even think about it," Tessa called over her shoulder, kicking her feet and holding on to Ryan's back for dear life.

He wouldn't drop her. She had every confidence of that. Still…

"You're going to ruin my hair."

"I like your curls better. In fact, I felt a little cheated that I didn't get to run my fingers through them. I always wanted to do that."

Something about his statement stopped her objections cold. Made visions dance in her head of them together in the shower with Ryan doing just that.

"Okay. Just put me down."

Ryan smacked her bottom lightly before setting her down, her body sliding down his. Seeming to rev them both up as steam surrounded them.

She slowly undid the three buttons of Ryan's shirt and made a show of sliding the fabric down one shoulder, then the other.

His green eyes darkened. His chest rose and fell heavily as his gaze met hers again after he'd followed the garment's descent to the floor.

Ryan hooked his thumbs into the sides of her panties and tugged her closer, dropping another kiss on her neck. He gently sank his teeth into her delicate flesh, nibbling the skin there as he glided her underwear over the swell of her bottom and down her hips.

She stepped out of them and into the shower. Pressed her back against the cool tiles. A striking contrast to the warm water. Ryan stepped into the shower, too, closing the glass door behind him and covering her mouth with his.

Tessa lay on her back, her hair wound in one of Ryan's clean, cotton T-shirts. He'd washed her hair and taken great delight in running a soapy loofah over every inch of her body.

Then he'd set her on the shower bench and dropped

to his knees. He'd used the removable shower head as a makeshift sex toy. Had used it to bring her to climax twice. Then showed her just how amazing he could be with his tongue.

When he'd pressed the front of her body to the wall, lifted one of her legs, and taken her from behind, Tessa honestly hadn't thought it would be possible for her to get there again.

She was wrong.

She came hard, her body tightening and convulsing, and his did the same soon afterward.

They'd gone through their morning routines, brushing their teeth side by side, wrapped in towels from their shower together. Ryan ordered room service, and they ate breakfast in bed, catching the last half of a holiday comedy that was admittedly a pretty crappy movie overall. Still, it never failed to make the two of them laugh hysterically.

When the movie ended, Ryan had clicked off the television and kissed her. A kiss that slowly stoked the fire low in her belly all over again. Made her nipples tingle and the space between her thighs ache for him.

She lay staring up at Ryan, his hair still damp from the shower. Clearly hell-bent on using every single condom in that strip before the morning ended, he'd sheathed himself and entered her again.

Her eyes had fluttered closed at the delicious fullness as Ryan eased inside her. His movements were slow, deliberate, controlled.

None of those words described the Ryan Bateman she knew. The man she'd been best friends with since they were both still in possession of their baby teeth.

Ryan was impatient. Tenacious. Persistent. He

wanted everything five minutes ago. But the man who hovered over her now, his piercing green eyes boring into her soul and grasping her heart, was in no hurry. He seemed to relish the torturously delicious pleasure he was giving her with his slow, languid movements.

He was laser-focused. His brows furrowed, and his forehead beaded with sweat. The sudden swivel of his hips took her by surprise, and she whimpered with pleasure, her lips parting.

Ryan leaned down and pressed his mouth to hers, slipping his tongue inside and caressing her tongue.

Tessa got lost in his kiss. Let him rock them both into a sweet bliss that left her feeling like she was floating on a cloud.

She held on to him as he arched his back, his muscles straining as his own orgasm overtook him. Allowed herself to savor the warmth that encircled her sated body.

Then, gathering her to his chest, he removed her makeshift T-shirt turban and ran his fingers through her damp, curly hair.

She'd never felt more cherished or been more satisfied in her life. Yet, when the weekend ended, it would be the equivalent of the clock striking twelve for Cinderella. The dream would be over, her carriage would turn back into a pumpkin, and she'd be the same old Tessa Noble whom Ryan only considered a friend.

She inhaled his scent. Leather and cedar with a hint of patchouli. A scent she'd bought him for Christmas three years ago. Ryan had been wearing it ever since. Tess was never sure if he wore it because he truly liked it or because he'd wanted to make her happy.

Now she wondered the same thing about what'd

happened between them this weekend. He'd tailored
the entire weekend to her. Had seemed determined to
see to it that she felt special, pampered.

Had she been the recipient of a pity fuck?

The possibility of Ryan sleeping with her out of a
sense of charity made her heart ache.

She tried not to think of what would happen when
the weekend ended. To simply enjoy the moment between them here and now.

Tessa was his until "midnight." Then the magic of
their weekend together would be over, and it would be
time for them to return to the real world.

Chapter 13

Ryan studied Tessa as she gathered her beauty products and stowed them back into her travel bag in preparation for checkout. They'd had an incredible weekend together. With the exception of the time they spent politely posing for the reporter at dinner and waxing poetic about their friendship, they'd spent most of the weekend just a few feet away in Ryan's bed.

But this morning Tessa had seemed withdrawn. Before he'd even awakened, she'd gotten out of bed, packed her luggage, laid out what she planned to wear to the football game, and showered.

Tessa opened a tube of makeup.

"You're wearing makeup to the game?" He stepped behind her in the mirror.

"Photos before the game." She gave his reflection a cursory glance. "Otherwise, I'd just keep it simple. Lip gloss, a little eye shadow. Mascara."

She went back to silently pulling items out of her makeup bag and lining them up on the counter.

"Tess, did I do something wrong? You seem really... I don't know...distant this morning."

A pained look crimped her features, and she sank her teeth into her lower lip before turning to face him. She heaved a sigh, and though she looked in his direction, she was clearly looking past him.

"Look, Rye, this weekend has been amazing. But I think it's in the best interest of our friendship if we go back to the way things were. Forget this weekend ever happened." She shifted her gaze to his. "I honestly feel that it's the only way our friendship survives this."

"Why?"

His question reeked of quiet desperation, but he could care less. The past two days had been the best days of his life. He thought they had been for her, too. So her request hit him like a sucker punch to the gut, knocking the wind out of him.

She took the shower cap off her head, releasing the long, silky hair she'd straightened with a blow-dryer attachment before they'd met Greg at the restaurant for dinner the night before.

"Because the girl you were attracted to on that stage isn't who I am. I can't maintain all of this." She indicated the makeup on the counter and her straightened hair. "It's exhausting. More importantly, it isn't me. Not really."

"You think all of this is what I'm attracted to? That I can't see...that I haven't always seen you?"

"You never kissed me before, not seriously," she added before he could mention that kiss in college. "And we certainly never..." She gestured toward the bed, as if she was unable to bring herself to say the words or look at the place where he'd laid her bare and tasted every inch of her warm brown skin.

"To be fair, you kissed me." Ryan stepped closer.

She tensed, but then lifted her chin defiantly, meeting his gaze again. The rapid rise and fall of her chest, indicated that she was taking shallow breaths. But she didn't step away from him. For which he was grateful.

"You know what I mean," she said through a frustrated little pout. "You never showed any romantic interest in me before the auction. So why are you interested now? Is it because someone else showed interest in me?"

"Why would you think that?" His voice was low and gruff. Pained.

Her accusation struck him like an openhanded slap to the face. It was something his mother had often said to him as a child. That he was only interested in his old toys when she wanted to give them to someone else.

Was that what he was doing with Tess?

"Because if I had a relationship…a life of my own, then I wouldn't be a phone call away whenever you needed me." Her voice broke slightly, and she swiped at the corners of her eyes. "Or maybe it's a competitive thing. I don't know. All I know is that you haven't made a move before now. So what changed?"

The hurt in her eyes and in the tremor of her voice felt like a jagged knife piercing his chest.

She was right. He was a selfish bastard. Too much of a coward to explore his attraction to her. Too afraid of how it might change their relationship.

"I… I…" His throat tightened, and his mouth felt dry as he sought the right words. But Tessa was his best friend, and they'd always shot straight with each other. "Sex, I could get anywhere." He forced his gaze to meet hers. Gauged her reaction. "But what we have... I don't have that with anyone else, Tess. I didn't want to take a chance on losing you. Couldn't risk screwing up our friendship like I've screwed up every relationship I've ever been in."

She dropped her gaze, absently dragging her fingers through her hair and tugging it over one shoulder. Tess was obviously processing his words. Weighing them on her internal bullshit meter.

"So why risk it now? What's changed?" She wrapped her arms around her middle. Something she did to comfort herself.

"I don't know." He whispered the words, his eyes not meeting hers.

It was a lie.

Tess was right. He'd been prompted to action by his fear of losing her. He'd been desperate to stake his claim on Tess. Wipe thoughts of any other man from her brain.

In the past, she had flirted with the occasional guy. Even dated a few. But none of them seemed to pose any real threat to what they shared. But when she'd stood on that stage as the sexiest goddamn woman in the entire room with men falling all over themselves to spend a few hours with her...suddenly everything was different. For the first time in his life, the threat of losing his best friend to someone else suddenly became very real. And he couldn't imagine his life without her in it.

Brain on autopilot, he'd gone into caveman mode. Determined to win the bid, short of putting up the whole damn ranch in order to win her.

Tessa stared at him, her pointed gaze demanding further explanation.

"It felt like the time was right. Like Fate stepped in and gave us a nudge."

"You're full of shit, Ryan Bateman." She smacked her lips and narrowed her gaze. Arms folded over her chest, she shifted to a defensive stance. "You don't believe in Fate. 'Our lives are what we make of them.' That's what you've always said."

"I'm man enough to admit when I'm wrong. Or at least open-minded enough to explore the possibility."

She turned to walk away, but he grasped her fingertips with his. A move that was more of a plea than a demand. Still, she halted and glanced over her shoulder in his direction.

"Tess, why are you so dead set against giving this a chance?"

"Because I'm afraid of losing you, too." Her voice was a guttural whisper.

He tightened his grip on her hand and tugged her closer, forcing her eyes to meet his. "You're not going to lose me, Tess. I swear, I'm not going anywhere."

"Maybe not, but we both know your MO when it comes to relationships. You rush into them, feverish and excited. But after a while you get bored, and you're ready to move on." She frowned, a pained look furrowing her brow. "What happens then, Ryan? What happens once you've pulled me in deep and then you decide you just want to go back to being friends?" She shook her head vehemently. "I honestly don't think I could handle that."

Ryan's jaw clenched. He wanted to object. Promise to never hurt her. But hadn't he hurt every woman he'd ever been with except the one woman who'd walked away from him?

It was the reason Tripp had made him promise to leave his sister alone. Because, though they were friends, he didn't deem him good enough for his sister. Didn't trust that he wouldn't hurt her.

Tessa obviously shared Tripp's concern.

Ryan wished he could promise Tess he wouldn't break her heart. But their polar opposite approaches to relationships made it seem inevitable.

He kept his relationships casual. A means of mutual satisfaction. Because he believed in fairy-tale love and romance about as much as he believed in Big Foot and the Loch Ness Monster.

Tess, on the other hand, was holding out for the man who would sweep her off her feet. For a relationship like the one her parents shared. She didn't understand that Chuck and Tina Noble were the exception, rather than the rule.

Yet, despite knowing all the reasons he and Tess should walk away from this, he couldn't let her go.

Tessa's frown deepened as his silent response to her objection echoed off the walls in the elegant, tiled bathroom.

"This weekend has been amazing. You made me feel like Cinderella at the ball. But we've got the game this afternoon, then we're heading back home. The clock is about to strike midnight, and it's time for me to turn back into a pumpkin."

"You realize that you've just taken the place of the Maybach in this scenario." He couldn't help the smirk that tightened the edges of his mouth.

Some of the tension drained from his shoulders as

her sensual lips quirked in a rueful smile. She shook her head and playfully punched him in the gut.

"You know what I mean. It's time for me to go back to being me. Trade my glass slippers in for a pair of Chuck Taylors."

He caught her wrist before she could walk away. Pulling her closer, he wrapped his arms around her and stared deep into those gorgeous brown eyes that had laid claim on him ever since he'd first gazed into them.

"Okay, Cinderella. If you insist that things go back to the way they were, there's not much I can do about that. But if you're mine until midnight, I won't be cheated. Let's forget the game, stay here and make love."

"But I've already got the tickets."

"I don't care." He slowly lowered his mouth toward hers. "I'll reimburse you."

"But they're on the fifty-yard line. At the stadium that's your absolute favorite place in the world."

"Not today it isn't." He feathered a gentle kiss along the edge of her mouth, then trailed his lips down her neck.

"Ryan, we can't just blow off the—" She dug her fingers into his bare back and a low moan escaped her lips as he kissed her collarbone. The sound drifted below his waist and made him painfully hard.

"We can do anything we damn well please." He pressed a kiss to her ear. One of the many erogenous zones he'd discovered on her body during their weekend together. Tessa's knees softened, and her head lolled slightly, giving him better access to her neck.

"But the article…they're expecting us to go to the game, and if we don't…well, everyone will think—"

"Doesn't matter what they think." He lifted her chin and studied her eyes, illuminated by the morning sunlight spilling through the windows. He dragged a thumb across her lower lip. "It only matters what you and I want."

He pressed another kiss to her lips, lingering for a moment before reluctantly pulling himself away again so he could meet her gaze. He waited for her to open her eyes again. "What do you want, Tess?"

She swallowed hard, her gaze on his lips. "I want both. To go to the game, as expected, and to spend the day in bed making love to you."

"Hmm...intriguing proposition." He kissed her again. Tess really was a woman after his own heart. "One that would require us to spend one more night here. Then we'll head back tomorrow. And if you still insist—"

"I will." There was no hesitation in her voice, only apology. She moved a hand to cradle his cheek, her gaze meeting his. "Because it's what's best for our friendship."

Ryan forced a smile and released an uneasy breath. Tried to pretend that his chest didn't feel like it was caving in. He gripped her tighter against him, lifting her as she wrapped her legs around him.

If he couldn't have her like this always, he'd take every opportunity to have her now. In the way he'd always imagined. Even if that meant they'd be a little late for the game.

Chapter 14

They'd eaten breakfast, their first meal in the kitchen since they'd arrived, neither of them speaking much. The only part of their conversation that felt normal was their recap of some of the highlights during their team's win the day before. But then the conversation had returned to the stilted awkwardness they'd felt before then.

Ryan had loaded their luggage into the Maybach, and they were on the road, headed back to Royal, barely two words spoken between them before Tessa finally broke their silence.

"This is for the best, Rye. After all, you were afraid to tell my brother about that fake kiss we had on Valentine's Day in college." Tessa grinned, her voice teasing.

Ryan practically snorted, poking out his thumb and holding it up. "A… I am *not* afraid of your brother."

Not physically, at least. Ryan was a good head taller than Tripp and easily outweighed him by twenty-five pounds of what was mostly muscle. But, in all honesty, he *was* afraid of how the weekend with Tessa would affect his friendship with Tripp. It could disrupt the connection between their families.

The Batemans and Nobles were as thick as thieves now. Had been since their fathers were young boys. But in the decades prior, the families had feuded over land boundaries, water rights and countless other ugly disputes. Some of which made Ryan ashamed of his ancestors. But everything had changed the day Tessa's grandfather had saved Ryan's father's life when he'd fallen into a well.

That fateful day, the two families had bonded. A bond which had grown more intricate over the years, creating a delicate ecosystem he dared not disturb.

Ryan continued, adding his index finger for effect. "B… Yes, I think it might be damaging to our friendship if Tripp tries to beat my ass and I'm forced to defend myself." He added a third finger, hesitant to make his final point. An admission that made him feel more vulnerable than he was comfortable being, even with Tess. "And C…it wasn't a fake kiss. It was a little too real. Which is why I've tried hard to never repeat it."

Ryan's pulse raced, and his throat suddenly felt dry. He returned his other hand to the steering wheel and stared at the road ahead. He didn't need to turn his head to know Tessa was staring at him. The heat of her stare seared his skin and penetrated his chest.

"Are you saying that since that kiss—" Her voice was trembling, tentative.

"Since that kiss, I've recognized that the attraction

between us went both ways." He rushed the words out, desperate to stop her from asking what he suspected she might.

Why hadn't he said anything all those years ago? Or in the years since that night?

He'd never allowed himself to entertain either question. Doing so was a recipe for disaster.

Why court disaster when they enjoyed an incomparable friendship? Shouldn't that be good enough?

"Oh." The disappointment in her voice stirred heaviness in his chest, rather than the ease and lightness he usually felt when they were together.

When Ryan finally glanced over at his friend, she was staring at him blankly, as if there was a question she was afraid to ask.

"Why haven't you ever said anything?"

Because he hadn't been ready to get serious about anyone back then. And Tessa Noble wasn't the kind of girl you passed the time with. She was the genuine deal. The kind of girl you took home to mama. And someone whose friendship meant everything to him.

"Bottom line? I promised your brother I'd treat you like an honorary little sister. That I'd never lay a hand on you." A knot tightened in his belly. "A promise I've obviously broken."

"Wait, you two just decided, without consulting me? Like I'm a little child and you two are my misfit parents? What kind of caveman behavior is that?"

Ryan winced. Tessa was angry, and he didn't blame her. "To be fair, we had this conversation when he and I were about fourteen. Long before you enlightened us on the error of our anti-feminist tendencies. Still, it's a promise I've always taken seriously. Especially since, at the time, I did see you as a little sister. Obviously, things have changed since then."

"When?" Her tone was soft, but demanding. As if she needed to know.

It wasn't a conversation he wanted to have, but if they were going to have it, she deserved his complete honesty.

"I first started to feel some attraction toward you when you were around sixteen." He cleared his throat, his eyes steadily on the road. "But when I left for college I realized how deep that attraction ran. I was miserable without you that first semester in college."

"You seemed to adapt pretty quickly by sleeping your way across campus," she huffed. She turned toward the window and sighed. "I shouldn't have said that. I'm sorry. I…" She didn't finish her statement.

"Forget it." Ryan released a long, slow breath. "This is uncharted territory for us. We'll learn to deal with it. Everything'll be fine."

But even as he said the words, he couldn't convince himself of their truth.

After Ryan's revelations, the ride home was awkward and unusually quiet, even as they both tried much too hard to behave as if everything was fine.

Everything most certainly was *not* fine.

Strained and uncomfortable? *Yes*. Their forced conversation, feeble smiles and weak laughter were proof they'd both prefer to be anywhere else.

And it confirmed they'd made the right decision by not pursuing a relationship. It would only destroy their friendship in the end once Ryan had tired of her and was ready to move on to someone polished and gorgeous, like his ex.

This was all her fault. She'd kissed Ryan. Tessa clenched her hands in her lap, willing them to stop trembling.

She only hoped their relationship could survive this phase of awkwardness, so things could go back to the way they were.

Tessa's phone buzzed, and she checked her text messages.

Tripp had sent a message to say that he'd landed a meeting with a prospect that had the potential to become one of their largest customers. His flight to Iowa would leave in a few days, and she would be in charge at the Noble Spur.

She scrolled to the next text and read Bo's message reminding her that she'd agreed to attend a showing of *A Christmas Carol* with him at the town's outdoor, holiday theater.

Tessa gripped her phone and turned it over in her lap, looking over guiltily at Ryan. After what had happened between them this weekend, the thought of going out with someone else turned her stomach, but she'd already promised Bo.

And even though she and Bo were going to a movie together, it could hardly be considered a date. Half the town of Royal would be there.

Would it be so wrong for them to go on a friendly outing to the movies?

Besides, maybe seeing other people was just the thing to alleviate the awkwardness between them and prompt them to forget about the past three days.

Tessa worried her lower lip with her teeth. Deep

down, she knew the truth. Things would never be the same between them.

Because she wanted Ryan now more than ever.

No matter how hard she tried, Tessa would never forget their weekend together and how he'd made her feel.

Chapter 15

Gus sat in his favorite recliner and put his feet up to watch a little evening television. Reruns of some of his favorite old shows. Only he held the remote in his hand without ever actually turning the television on.

The house was quiet. Too quiet.

Alexis was in Houston on business, and her brother Justin was staying in Dallas overnight with a friend.

Normally, he appreciated the solitude. Enjoyed being able to watch whatever the hell he wanted on television without one of the kids scoffing about him watching an old black-and-white movie or an episode of one of his favorite shows that he'd seen half a dozen times before. But lately, it had been harder to cheerfully bear his solitude.

During the months he and Rose had worked together to split up Daniel and Alexis, he'd found himself enjoying her company. So much so that he preferred it mightily to being alone in this big old house.

Gus put down the remote and paced the floor. He hadn't seen Rose since the night of the bachelor auction at the Texas Cattleman's Club. They'd spoken by phone twice, but just to confirm that their plan had worked.

As far as they could tell, Alexis and Daniel were no longer seeing each other. And both of them seemed to be in complete misery.

Gus had done everything he could to try and cheer Alexis up. But the pain in her eyes persisted. As did the evidence that she'd still been crying from time to time.

He'd tried to get his granddaughter to talk about it, but she'd insisted that it wasn't anything she couldn't handle. And she said he wouldn't understand anyway.

That probably hurt the most. Especially since he really did understand how she was feeling. And worse, he and Rose had been the root cause of that pain.

The guilt gnawed at his gut and broke his heart.

Rose had reminded him of why they'd first hatched the plan to break up Daniel and Alexis. Their families had been mortal enemies for decades. Gus and Rose had hated each other so much they were willing to work together in order to prevent their grandchildren from being involved with each other. Only, Gus hadn't reckoned on coming to enjoy the time he spent with Rose Clayton. And he most surely hadn't anticipated that he'd find himself getting sweet on her again after all these years.

He was still angry at Rose for how she'd treated him all those years ago, when he'd been so very in love with her. But now he understood that because of her cruel father, holding the welfare of her ill mother over

Rose's head, she'd felt she had no choice but to break it off with him and marry someone Jedediah Clayton had deemed worthy.

He regretted not recognizing the distress Rose was in back then. That her actions had been a cry for help. Signs he and his late wife, Sarah, who had once been Rose's best friend, had missed.

Gus heaved a sigh and glanced over his shoulder at the television. His reruns could wait.

Gus left the Lone Wolf Ranch and headed over to Rose's place, The Silver C, one last time to say goodbye. Maybe share a toast to the success of their plan to look out for Alexis and Daniel in the long run, even if the separation was hurting them both now.

The property had once been much vaster than his. But over the years, he'd bought quite a bit of it. Rose had begrudgingly sold it to him in order to pay off the gambling debts of her late husband, Ed.

Rose's father must be rolling over in his grave because the ranch hand he'd judged unworthy of his daughter was now in possession of much of the precious land the man had sought to keep out of his hands. Gus didn't normally think ill of the dead. But in Jedediah's case, he was willing to make an exception.

When Gus arrived at The Silver C, all decked out in its holiday finest, Rose seemed as thrilled to see him as he was to see her.

"Gus, what on earth are you doing here?" A smile lighting her eyes, she pulled the pretty red sweater she was wearing around her more tightly as cold air rushed in from outside.

"After all these months working together, I thought

it was only right that we had a proper goodbye." He held up a bottle of his favorite top-shelf whiskey.

Rose laughed, a joyful sound he still had fond memories of. "Well, by all means, come on in."

She stepped aside and let Gus inside. The place smelled of pine from the two fresh Christmas trees Rose had put up. One in the entry hall and another in the formal living room. And there was the unmistakable scent of fresh apple pie.

Rose directed Gus to have a seat on the sofa in the den where she'd been watching television. Then she brought two glasses and two slices of warm apple pie on a little silver tray.

"That homemade pie?" Gus inquired as she set the tray on the table.

"Wouldn't have it any other way." She grinned, handing him a slice and a fork. She opened the bottle of whiskey and poured each of them a glass, neat.

She sat beside him and watched him with interest as he took his first bite of pie.

"Hmm, hmm, hmm. Now that's a little slice of heaven right there." He grinned.

"I'm glad you like it. And since we're celebrating our successful plot to save the kids from a disastrous future, pie seems fitting." She smiled, but it seemed hollow. She took a sip of the whiskey and sighed. "Smooth."

"That's one of the reasons I like it so much." He nodded, shoveling another bite of pie into his mouth and chewing thoughtfully. He surveyed the space and leaned closer, lowering his voice. "Daniel around today?"

"No, he's gone to Austin to handle some ranch business." She raised an eyebrow, her head tilted. "Why?"

"No reason in particular." Gus shrugged, putting down his pie plate and sipping his whiskey. "Just wanted to ask how the boy is doing. He still as miserable as my Alexis?"

Pain and sadness were etched in Rose's face as she lowered her gaze and nodded. "I'm afraid so. He's trying not to show how hurt he is, but I honestly don't think I've ever seen him like this. He's already been through so much with his mother." She sighed, taking another sip of whiskey. Her hands were trembling slightly as she shook her head. "I hope we've done the right thing here. I guess I didn't realize how much they meant to each other." She sniffled and pulled a tissue out of her pocket, dabbing at her eyes.

Rose forced a laugh. "I'm sorry. You must think me so ridiculous sitting here all teary-eyed over having gotten the very thing we both wanted."

Gus put down his glass and took Rose's hand between his. It was delicate and much smaller than his own. Yet, they were the hands of a woman who had worked a ranch her entire life.

"I understand just what you're feeling." He stroked her wrist with his thumb. "Been feeling pretty guilty, too. And second-guessing our decision."

"Oh, Gus, we spent so many years heartbroken and angry. It changed us, and not for the better." Tears leaked from Rose's eyes, and her voice broke. "I just hope we haven't doomed Alexis and Daniel to the same pain and bitterness."

"It's going to be okay, Rose." He took her in his arms and hugged her to his chest. Tucked her head beneath his chin as he swayed slowly and stroked her hair. "We won't allow that to happen to Alexis and Daniel. I promise."

"God, I hope you're right. They deserve so much more than that. Both of them." She held on to him. One arm wrapped around him and the other was pressed to his chest.

He should be focused on Daniel and Alexis and the dilemma that he and Rose had created. Gus realized that. Yet, an awareness of Rose slowly spread throughout his body. Sparks of electricity danced along his spine.

He rubbed her back and laid a kiss atop her head. All of the feelings he'd once experienced when he'd held Rose in his arms as a wet-behind-the-ears ranch hand came flooding back to him. Overwhelmed his senses, making his heart race in a way he'd forgotten that it could.

After all these years, he still had a thing for Rose Clayton. Still wanted her.

Neither of them had moved or spoken for a while. They just held each other in silence, enjoying each other's comfort and warmth.

Finally, Rose pulled away a little and tipped her head, her gaze meeting his. She leaned in closer, her mouth hovering just below his, her eyes drifting closed.

Gus closed the space between them, his lips meeting hers in a kiss that was soft and sweet. Almost chaste.

He slipped his hands on either side of her face, angling it to give him better access to her mouth. Ran his tongue along her lips that tasted of smooth whiskey and homemade apple pie.

Rose sighed with satisfaction, parting her lips. She

clutched at his shirt, pulling him as close as their position on the sofa would allow.

She murmured with pleasure when he slipped his tongue between her lips.

Time seemed to slow as they sat there, their mouths seeking each other's out in a kiss that grew hotter. Greedier. More intense.

There was a fire in his belly that he hadn't felt in ages. One that made him want things with Rose he hadn't wanted in so long.

Gus forced himself to pull away from Rose. He gripped her shoulders, his eyes searching hers for permission.

Rose stood up. She switched off the television with the remote, picked up their two empty whiskey glasses, then walked toward the stairs that led to the upper floor of The Silver C. Looking back at him, she flashed a wicked smile that did things to him.

"Are you coming or not?"

Gus nearly knocked over the silver tray on the table in front of him in his desperation to climb to his feet. He hurried toward her but was halted by her next words.

"Don't forget the bottle."

"Yes, ma'am." Grinning, he snatched it off the table before grabbing her hand and following her up the stairs.

Chapter 16

When he heard his name called, Ryan looked up from where Andy, his farrier, was shoeing one of the horses.

It was Tripp.

The muscles in Ryan's back tensed. He hadn't talked to Tess or Tripp in the three days since they'd been back from their trip to Dallas. He could tell by his friend's expression that Tripp was concerned about something.

Maybe he had come to deliver a much-deserved ass-whipping. After all, Ryan had broken his promise by sleeping with Tess.

"What's up, Tripp?" Ryan walked over to his friend, still gauging the man's mood.

"I'm headed to the airport shortly, but I need to ask a favor."

"Sure. Anything."

"Keep an eye on Tess, will you?"

Ryan hadn't expected that. "Why, is something wrong?"

"Not exactly." Tripp removed his Stetson and adjusted it before placing it back on his head. "It's just that Mom and Dad are still gone, and I'm staying in Des Moines overnight. She'll be kicking around that big old house by herself mostly. We let a few hands off for the holidays. Plus… I don't like that Bo and Clem have been sniffing around the last few days. I'm beginning to think that letting Tessa participate in that bachelor auction was a mistake."

Ryan tugged his baseball cap down on his head, unsettled by the news of Bo and Clem coming around. He'd paid a hefty sum at the auction to ward those two off. Apparently, they hadn't gotten the hint.

"First, if you think you *let* your sister participate in that bachelor's auction, you don't know your sister very well. Tess has got a mind of her own. Always has. Always will."

"Guess you're right about that." Tripp rubbed the back of his neck. "And I'm not saying that Bo or Clem are bad guys. They're nice enough, I guess."

"Just not when they come calling on your sister." Ryan chuckled. He knew exactly how Tripp felt.

"Yeah, pretty much."

"Got a feeling the man you'll think is good enough for your little sister ain't been born yet."

"And probably never will be." Tripp chuckled. "But as her big brother, it's my job to give any guy who comes around a hard time. Make him prove he's worthy."

"Well, just hold your horses there, buddy. It's not like she's considering either of them." Ryan tried to appear nonchalant about the whole ordeal. Though on the inside he felt like David Banner in the midst of turning into the Incredible Hulk. He wanted to smash both Bo and Clem upside the head and tell them to go sniffing around someone else. "I think you're getting a little ahead of yourself."

"You haven't been around since you guys got back." The statement almost sounded accusatory. "Looks like the flower show threw up in our entry hall."

"Clem and Bo have been sending Tessa flowers?" Ryan tried to keep his tone and his facial expression neutral. He counted backward from ten in his head.

"Clem's apparently determined to empty out the local florist. Bo, on the other hand, has taken Tessa out to some play and this afternoon they're out riding."

Ryan hoped like hell that Tripp didn't notice the tick in his jaw or the way his fists clenched at his sides.

Tripp flipped his wrist, checking his watch. "Look, I'd better get going. I'll be back tomorrow afternoon, but call me if you need anything."

"Will do." Ryan tipped the brim of his baseball hat. "Safe travels."

He watched his friend climb back into his truck and head toward the airport in Dallas.

Jaw clenched, Ryan uncurled his fists and reminded himself to calm down. Then he saddled up Phantom, his black quarter horse stallion, and went for a ride.

For the past few days, he hadn't been able to stop thinking about his weekend with Tess. The moments they'd shared replayed again and again in his head. Distracted him from his work. Kept him up staring at the ceiling in the middle of the night.

He knew Tess well. Knew she'd been as affected by

their weekend together as he had. So how could she dismiss what they'd shared so easily and go out with Bo, or for God's sake, Clem?

Phantom's hooves thundered underneath him as the cold, brisk air slapped him in the face. He'd hoped that his ride would calm him down and help him arrive at the same conclusion Tess had. That it would be better for everyone if they remained friends.

But no matter how hard and fast he'd ridden, it didn't drive away his desire for Tess. Nor did it ease the fury that rose in his chest at the thought of another man touching her the way he had. The way he wanted to again.

He recognized the validity of Tessa's concerns that he wasn't serious and that he'd be chasing after some other skirt in a few months. He couldn't blame her for feeling that way. After all, as Helene was fond of saying, the proof was in the pudding.

He wouldn't apologize for his past. Because he'd never lied to or misled any of the women he'd dated. So he certainly wouldn't give his best friend any sense of false hope that he'd suddenly convert to the romantic suitor he'd been over the course of the weekend, for the sake of the Texas Cattleman's Club.

Ryan wasn't that guy any more than Tessa was the kind of woman who preferred a pair of expensive, red-bottomed heels to a hot new pair of sneakers.

So why couldn't he let go of the idea of the two of them being together?

He'd asked himself that question over and over the past few days, and the same answer kept rising above all the bullshit excuses he'd manufactured.

He craved the intimacy that they shared.

It was the thing that made his heart swell every time he thought of their weekend together. The thing that made it about so much more than just the sex.

He'd even enjoyed planning their weekend. And he'd derived a warm sense of satisfaction from seeing her reaction to each of his little surprises.

Ryan had always believed that people who made a big show of their relationships were desperate to make other people believe they were happy. But despite his romantic gestures being part of a ruse to keep the club from being mired in scandal, they had brought him and Tess closer. Shown her just how much he valued her.

Maybe he didn't believe that love was rainbows and sugarplums. Or that another person was the key to his happiness. But he knew unquestionably that he would be miserable if Tess got involved with someone else.

He couldn't promise her that he'd suddenly sweep her off her feet like some counterfeit Prince Charming. But he sure as hell wanted to try, before she walked into the arms of someone else.

Ryan and Phantom returned to the stables, and he handed him off to Andy. Then he hurried into the house to take a shower. He needed to see Tess right away.

Chapter 17

Tessa checked her phone. The only messages were from Tripp, letting her know that his plane had landed safely, and from Clem asking if she'd received his flowers ahead of their casual dinner date later that night.

She tossed the phone on the counter. No messages from Ryan. They'd maintained radio silence since he'd set her luggage in the entry hall, said goodbye, and driven off.

Tessa realized that the blame wasn't all his. After all, the phone worked both ways. On a typical day, she would've called her best friend a couple of times by now. She was clearly avoiding him, as much as he was avoiding her.

She was still angry that Ryan and Tripp had made a pact about her. As if she were incapable of making her own decisions. Mostly, she was hurt that Ryan hadn't countered her accusation that he'd eventually tire of her and move on to someone else.

She wanted him to deny it. To fight for her. But Ryan hadn't raised the slightest objection. Which meant what he really wanted was a no-strings fuck buddy until something better came along.

For her, that would never be enough with Ryan. She was already in way too deep. But the truth was, she would probably never be enough for him. She was nothing like the lithe, glamorous women who usually caught Ryan's eye. Women like Sabrina Calhoun who was probably born wearing a pair of Louboutins and carrying an Hermès bag. Or women like Lana, the overly friendly barmaid. Women who exuded sex and femininity rather than looking like they shopped at Ranchers R Us.

Headlights shone in the kitchen window. Someone was in the driveway. As soon as the vehicle pulled up far enough, Tess could see it clearly.

It was Ryan's truck.

Her belly fluttered, and her muscles tensed. She waited for him to come to the kitchen door, but he didn't. Instead, he made a beeline for the stables.

Ryan had likely come to check on the stables at Tripp's request. He was obviously still avoiding her, and she was over it.

Nervousness coiled through her and knotted in her belly. They both needed to be mature about this whole thing. Starting right now.

She wouldn't allow the fissure between them to crack open any wider. If that meant she had to be the one to break the ice, she would.

Tessa's hair, piled on top of her head in a curly bun, was still damp from the shower. She'd thrown on an old graphic T-shirt and a pair of jeans, so she could run out and double-check the stables.

Not her best look.

Tess slipped on a jacket and her boots and trudged out to the stables.

"Hey." She approached him quietly, her arms folded across her body.

"Hey." Ryan leaned against the wall. "Sorry, I haven't called. Been playing catch-up since we returned."

"I've been busy, too." She pulled the jacket tighter around her.

"I heard. Word is you've got a date tonight." The resentment in his voice was unmistakable. "You spent the weekend in my bed. A few days later and suddenly you and Bo are a thing and Clem is sending you a houseful of flowers?"

"Bo and I aren't *a thing*. We've just gone out a couple times. As friends." Her cheeks were hot. "And despite what happened this weekend, you and I *aren't* a thing. So you don't get a say in who I do or don't spend time with." The pitch of her voice was high, and the words were spilling out of her mouth. Tessa sucked in a deep breath, then continued. "Besides, are you going to tell me you've never done the same?"

Crimson spread across his cheeks. He stuffed his hands in his pockets. "That was different."

"Why? Because you're a guy?"

"Because it was casual, and neither of us had expectations for anything more."

"How is that different from what happened between us?"

Ryan was playing mind games with her, and she didn't appreciate it.

"Because I *do* expect more. That is, I want more. With you." He crept closer.

Tessa hadn't expected that. She shifted her weight from one foot to the other, her heart beating faster. "What are you saying?"

"I'm saying I want more of what we had this past weekend. That I want it to be me and you. No one else. And I'm willing to do whatever you need in order to make it happen."

"Whatever *I* need?" The joy that had been building in her chest suddenly slammed into a brick wall. "As in, you'd be doing it strictly for my benefit, not because it's what you want?"

"You make it sound as if I'm wrong for wanting you to be happy." His brows furrowed, and his mouth twisted in confusion. "How does that make me the bad guy?"

"It doesn't make you a bad person, Ryan. But I'm not looking for a fuck buddy. Not even one who happens to be my best friend." She pressed a hand to her forehead and sighed.

"I wouldn't refer to it that way, but if it makes us happy, why not?" Ryan's voice was low, his gaze sincere. He took her hand in his. "Who cares what anyone else thinks as long as it's what we want?"

"But it isn't what *I* want." Tears stung Tessa's eyes, and her voice wavered.

Ryan lifted her chin, his green eyes pinning her in place. "What *do* you want, Tess?"

"I want the entire package, Ryan. Marriage. Kids, eventually." She pulled away, her back turned to him for a moment before turning to face him again. "And

I'll never get any of that if I settle for being friends with benefits."

"How can you be so sure it wouldn't work between us?" he demanded.

"Because you can't even be honest about what you want in bed with me." She huffed, her hands shaking.

There, she'd said it.

"What the hell are you talking about, Tess?"

Her face and chest were suddenly hot, and the vast barn seemed too small a space for the two of them. She slipped off her jacket and hung it on a hook.

Though the remaining ranch staff had left for the day and Tripp was gone, she still lowered her voice. As if the horses would spread gossip to the folks in town.

"I know you like it…rough. You weren't like that with me."

"Really? You're complaining about my performance?" He folded his arms, his jaw clenched.

"No, of course not. It was amazing. *You* were amazing. But I overheard Sabrina talking to a friend of hers on the phone when you two were still together. She was saying that she liked rough sex, and there was no one better at it than you."

Tessa's heart thumped. Her pulse, thundering in her ears, seemed to echo throughout the space.

"You overheard her say that on the phone?"

Tessa nodded.

"You know that wasn't an accident, right? She got a kick out of rattling your cage."

Tess suspected as much. Sabrina had never much liked her.

"You didn't answer my question." She looked in his

direction, but her eyes didn't quite meet his. "No judgment. I just want to know if it's true."

"Sometimes." He shrugged. "Depends on my mood, who I'm with. And we're not talking whips and chains, if that's what you're imagining." He was clearly uncomfortable having this discussion with her. Not that she was finding it to be a walk in the park either. "Why does it matter?"

"Because if that's what you like, but with me you were…"

"Not rough," he offered tersely. "And you're angry about that?"

"Not angry. Just realistic. If you can't be yourself with me in bed, you're not going to be happy. You'll get bored and you'll want out."

Ryan stared down at her, stepping closer. "I responded to you. Gave you what I thought you wanted."

"And you did." She took a step backward, her back hitting the wall. She swallowed hard. "But did it ever occur to you that I would've liked the chance to do the same for you?"

Sighing heavily, Ryan placed one hand on the wall behind her and cradled her cheek with the other. "It's not like that's the only way I like it, Tess. I don't regret anything about my weekend with you."

"But the point was you felt you *couldn't*. Because of our friendship or maybe because of your promise to Tripp. I don't know. All I know for sure is that pretending that everything will be okay is a fool's game." She forced herself to stand taller. Chin tipped, she met his gaze.

"So that's it? Just like that, you decide that's reason enough for us to not be together?" His face was red, and anger vibrated beneath his words, though his expression remained placid.

"Isn't that reason enough for you?"

"Sex isn't everything, Tess."

"For you, it always has been. Sex is just sex, right? It's not about love or a deeper connection." The knot in Tessa's stomach tightened when Ryan dropped his gaze and didn't respond. She sighed. "Tigers can't change their stripes, Ryan. No matter how hard they might try."

She turned to dip under his arm, but he lowered it, blocking her escape from the heated look in his eyes. His closeness. His scent. Leather. Cedar. Patchouli.

Damn that patchouli.

"Ryan, what else is there for us to say?"

"Nothing." He lowered his hands to her waist and stepped closer, his body pinning hers to the wall.

Time seemed to move in slow motion as Ryan dipped his head, his lips hovering just above hers. His gaze bored into hers. She didn't dare move an inch. Didn't dare blink.

When she didn't object, his lips crushed hers in a bruising, hungry kiss that made her heart race. He tasted of Helene's famous Irish stew—one of Ryan's favorite meals—and an Irish ale.

His hands were on her hips, pinning her in place against the wall behind her. Not with enough force to hurt her, but he'd asserted himself in such a way that it was crystal clear that he wanted her there, and that she shouldn't move.

She had no plans to.

As much as she'd enjoyed seeing a gentler side of Ryan during their weekend together, the commanding look in his eye and the assertiveness of his tone revved her up in a way she would never have imagined.

He trailed his hands up her sides so damned slowly she was sure she could count the milliseconds that passed. The backs of his hands grazed her hips, her waist, the undersides of her breasts.

The apex of her thighs pulsed and throbbed with such power she felt like he might bring her over the edge just from his kiss and his demanding touch.

Her knees quivered, and her breaths were quick and shallow. His kisses grew harder, hungrier as he placed his large hands around her throat. Not squeezing or applying pressure of any real measure. But conveying a heightened sense of control.

Ryan pulled back, his body still pinning hers, but his kiss gone. After a few seconds, her eyes shot open. He was staring at her with an intensity that she might have found scary in any other situation. But she knew Ryan. Knew that he'd never do anything to hurt her.

"You still with me, Tess?"

She couldn't pry her lips open to speak, so she did the only thing she could. Her impression of a bobble-head doll.

His eyes glinted, and he smirked. Ryan leaned in and sucked her bottom lip. Gently sank his teeth into it. Then he pushed his tongue between her lips and swept it inside the cavern of her mouth. Tipped her head back so that he could deepen the kiss. Claimed her mouth as if he owned every single inch of her body and could do with it as he pleased.

Her pebbled nipples throbbed in response, and she made a small gasp as his hard chest grazed the painfully hard peaks.

His scorching, spine-tingling kiss coaxed her body into doing his bidding, and his strong hands felt as if they were everywhere at once.

Tessa sucked in a deep breath when Ryan squeezed her bottom hard, ramping up the steady throb between her thighs.

When she'd gasped, he sucked her tongue into his mouth. He lifted her higher on the wall, pinning her there with his body as he settled between her thighs.

She whimpered as his rock-hard shaft pressed against the junction of her thighs. He seemed to enjoy eliciting her soft moans as she strained her hips forward, desperate for more of the delicious friction that made her belly flutter and sent a shudder up her spine.

"Shirt and bra off," he muttered against her lips, giving her barely enough room to comply with his urgent request. But she managed eagerly enough and dropped the garments to the floor.

He lifted her higher against the wall until her breasts were level with his lips. She locked her legs around his waist, anchoring herself to the wall.

Ryan took one heavy mound in his large hand. Squeezed it, then savagely sucked at her beaded tip, upping the pain/pleasure quotient. He gently grazed the pebbled tip with his teeth, then swirled his tongue around the flesh, soothing it.

Then he moved to the other breast and did the same. This time his green eyes were locked with hers. Gauging her reaction. A wicked grin curved the edge of his mouth as he tugged her down, so her lips crashed against his again.

Could he feel the pooling between her thighs through her soaked underwear and jeans? Her cheeks heated, momentarily, at the possibility. But her embarrassment was quickly forgotten as he nuzzled her ear and whispered his next command.

"When I set you down again I want you out of every single stitch of clothing you're wearing."

"Out here? In the stable? Where anyone could see us?" she stuttered, her heart thudding wildly in her chest.

"There's no one but us here," he said matter-of-factly. "But if you want me to stop…"

"No, don't." Tess was shocked by how quickly she'd objected to ending this little game. The equivalent of begging for more of him. For more of this.

At least he hadn't made her undress alone. Ryan tugged the beige plaid shirt over his head and on to the floor, giving her a prize view of his hard abdomen. She wanted to run the tip of her tongue along the chiseled lines that outlined the rippled muscles he'd earned by working as hard on the ranch as any of his hands. To kiss and suck her way along the deep V at his hips that disappeared below his waist. Trace the ridge on the underside of his shaft with her tongue.

Ryan toed off his work boots, unzipped his jeans and shoved them and his boxers down his muscular thighs, stepping out of them.

Tess bit into her lower lip, unable to tear her gaze from the gentle bob of his shaft as he stalked toward her and lifted her on to the edge of the adjustable, standing desk where she sometimes worked.

He raised the desk, which was in a seated position, until it was at just the right height.

"I knew this table would come in handy one day." She laughed nervously, her hands trembling slightly.

He didn't laugh, didn't smile. "Is this why you came out here, Tess? Why you couldn't be patient and wait until I came to your door?"

Before she could respond, he slid into her and they both groaned at the delicious sensation of him filling her. His back stiffened and he trembled slightly, his eyes squeezed shut.

Then he cursed under his breath and pulled out, retrieving a folded strip of foil packets from the back pocket of his jeans.

They'd both lost control momentarily. Given into the heat raging between them. But he'd come prepared. Maybe he hadn't expected to take her here in the stable or that he'd do so with such ferocity. But he had expected that at some point he'd be inside of her.

And she'd caved. Fallen under the hypnotic spell of those green eyes which negated every objection she'd posed up till then.

Sheathed now, Ryan slid inside her, his jaw tensed. He started to move slowly, but then he pulled out again.

"On your knees," he growled, before she could object.

Tessa shifted onto all fours, despite her self-consciousness about the view from behind as she arched her back and widened her stance, at his request.

Ryan adjusted the table again until it was at the perfect height. He grabbed his jeans and folded them, putting them under her knees to provide cushion.

Then suddenly he slammed into her, the sound of his skin slapping against hers filling the big, empty space. He pulled back slowly and rammed into her again. Then he slowly built a rhythm of rough and gentle strokes. Each time the head of his erection met the perfect spot deep inside her she whimpered at the pleasure building.

When he'd eased up on his movement, stopping just short of that spot, she'd slammed her hips back against him, desperate for the pleasure that the impact delivered.

Ryan reached up and slipped the tie from her hair, releasing the damp ringlets so that they fell to her shoulders and formed a curtain around her face.

He gathered her hair, winding it around his fist and tugging gently as he moved inside her. His rhythm was controlled and deliberate, even as his momentum slowly accelerated.

Suddenly, she was on her back again. Ryan had pulled out, leaned forward, and adjusted the table as high as it would go.

"Tell me what you want, Tess," he growled, his gaze locked with hers and his eyes glinted.

"I... I..." She couldn't fix her mouth to say the words, especially here under the harsh, bright lights in the stable. She averted her gaze from his.

He leaned in closer. His nostrils flared and a subtle smirk barely turned one corner of his mouth. "Would it help if I told you I already know *exactly* what you want. I just need to hear you say it. For you to beg for it."

His eyes didn't leave hers.

"I want..." Tessa swallowed hard, her entire body trembling slightly. "Your tongue."

He leaned in closer, the smirk deepening. "Where?"

God, he was really going to make her say it.

"Here." She spread her thighs and guided his free hand between her legs, shuddering at his touch. Tess hoped that show-and-tell would do, because she was teetering on the edge, nearly ready to explode. "Please."

"That wasn't so hard, now, was it?" He leaned down and lapped at her slick flesh with his tongue.

She quivered from the pleasure that rippled through her with each stroke. He gripped her hips, holding her in place to keep her bottom at the edge of the table, so she couldn't squirm away. Despite the pleasure building to a crescendo.

Tess slid her fingers in his hair and tugged him closer. Wanting more, even as she felt she couldn't possibly take another lash of his tongue against her sensitive flesh.

Ryan sucked on the little bundle of nerves and her body stiffened. She cursed and called his name, her inner walls pulsing.

Trailing kisses up her body, he kissed her neck. Then he guided her to her feet and turned her around, so her hands were pressed to the table and her bottom was nestled against his length.

He made another adjustment of the table, then lifted one of her knees on to it. He pressed her back down so her chest was against the table and her bottom was propped in the air.

He slid inside her with a groan of satisfaction, his hips moving against hers until finally he'd reached his own explosive release. As he gathered his breath, each pant whispered against her skin.

"Tess, I didn't mean to…" He sighed heavily. "Are you all right?"

She gave him a shaky nod, glancing back at him over her shoulder. "I'm fine."

He heaved a long sigh and placed a tender kiss on

her shoulder. "Don't give up on this so easily, Tess. Or do something we'll both regret."

Ryan excused himself to find a trash can where he could discreetly discard the condom.

Tessa still hadn't moved. Her limbs quivered, and her heart raced. Slowly, she gathered her bra, her jeans and her underwear. Her legs wobbled, as if she were slightly dazed.

She put on the clothing she'd managed to gather, despite her trembling hands.

When he returned, Ryan stooped to pick up her discarded shirt. Glaring, he handed it to her.

She muttered her thanks, slipping the shirt on. "You're upset. Why? Because I brought up your sex life with Sabrina?"

"Maybe it never occurred to you that the reason Sabrina and I tended to have rough, angry sex is because we spent so much of our relationship pissed off with each other.

He put his own shirt on and buttoned it, still staring her down.

Tessa felt about two inches tall. "I hadn't considered that."

She retrieved the hair tie from the standing desk, that she'd never be able to look at again without blushing. She pulled her hair into a low ponytail, stepped into her boots, and slipped her jacket back on.

"It can be fun. Maybe even adventurous. But in the moments when you're not actually having sex, it makes for a pretty fucked-up relationship. That's not what I want for you, Tess. For us." He shook his head, his jaw still clenched. "And there's something else you failed to take into account."

"What?"

"Rough sex is what got Sabrina off. It was her thing, not mine. What gets me off is getting you there. But I guess you were too busy making your little comparisons to notice." He stalked away, then turned back, pointing a finger at her for emphasis. "I want something more with you, Tess, because we're good together. We always have been. The sex is only a small component of what makes us fit so well together. I would think that our twenty plus years of friendship should be evidence enough of that."

Tessa wished she could take back everything she'd said. That she could turn back time and get a do-over.

"Rye, I'm sorry. I didn't mean to—"

"If you don't want to be with me, Tess, that's fine. But just be honest about it. Don't make up a bunch of bullshit excuses." He tucked his plaid shirt into his well-worn jeans, then pulled on his boots before heading toward the door. "Enjoy your date with Clem."

"It's not a date," she yelled after him, her eyes stinging with tears.

He didn't respond. Just left her standing there shaking. Feeling like a fool.

And she deserved it. Every angry stare. Every word uttered in resentment.

She'd been inventing reasons for them not to be together. Because she was terrified of the truth. That she wanted to be with Ryan more than anything. She honestly did want it all—marriage, a house of her own, kids. And she wanted them with her best friend. But she wouldn't settle for being in a relationship where she was the only one in love.

And she was in love with Ryan.

But as much as she loved him, she was terrified of the deafening silence she'd face if she confessed the truth to him. Because Ryan didn't believe in messy, emotional commitments.

He'd never admitted to being in love with a single one of his girlfriends. In fact, he'd never even said that he loved Sabrina. Just that there was a spark with her that kept things exciting between them. Something he hadn't felt with anyone else.

Tessa's sight blurred with tears and she sniffled, angrily swiping a finger beneath each eye. She'd done this, and she could fix it. Because she needed Ryan in her life. And he needed her, too. Even if all they'd ever be was friends.

Tessa's phone buzzed. She pulled it from her pocket. *Clem.*

She squeezed her eyes shut, her jaw clenched. Tess hated to bail on him, but after what had happened between her and Ryan, the thought of going out with someone else made her physically ill.

She answered the phone, her fingers pressed to her throbbing temple.

"Hey, Clem, I was just about to call you. Suddenly, I'm not feeling very well."

Chapter 18

Ryan hopped into his truck and pulled out of the Noble Spur like a bat out of hell. He was furious with Tess and even madder that he'd been so turned on by her when she was being completely unreasonable.

He pulled into the drive of the Bateman Ranch and parked beside an unfamiliar car. A shiny red BMW.

As Ryan approached the big house, Helene hurried to the door to meet him. By the way she was wringing that dish towel in her hand, he wasn't going to like what she had to say one bit.

He glanced at the car again, studying the license plate. Texas plates, but it could be a rental car. And only one person he knew would insist on renting a red BMW.

Hell.

This was the last thing he needed.

"Ryan, I am so sorry. I told her that you weren't home, but she insisted on waiting for you. No matter how long you were gone." She folded her arms, frowning.

"It's okay, Helene." Ryan patted the woman's shoulder and forced a smile.

"Well, well, well. Look who finally decided to come home." His ex-fiancée, Sabrina Calhoun, sashayed to the front door. "Surprised to see me, baby?"

The expression on Helene's face let him know she was fit to be tied. Never a fan of the woman, his house manager would probably sooner quit than be forced to deal with his ex's condescending attitude again.

Ryan gave Helene a low hand signal, begging her to be civil and assuring her that everything would be all right.

Sabrina was the kind of mistake he wouldn't make twice. No matter how slick and polished she looked. Outrageously expensive clothes and purse. A haircut that cost more than most folks around here made in a week. A heavy French perfume that costed a small mint.

His former fiancée could be the dictionary illustration for high maintenance. He groaned internally, still kicking himself for ever thinking the two of them could make a life together.

Sabrina wasn't a villain. They just weren't right for each other. A reality that became apparent once she'd moved to Texas and they'd actually lived together.

Suddenly, her cute little quirks weren't so cute anymore.

"What brings you to Royal, Sabrina?" Ryan folded

his arms and reared back on his heels. He asked the question as politely as he could manage.

"I happened to be in Dallas visiting a friend, and I thought it would be rude not to come by and at least say hello." She slid her expensive sunglasses from her face and batted her eyelashes. "You think we can chat for a minute? Alone?"

She glanced briefly at Helene who looked as if she was ready to claw the woman's face off.

"Do you mind, Helene?" He squeezed her arm and gave her the same smile he'd been using to charm her out of an extra slice of pie since he was a kid.

She turned and hurried back into the house, her path littered with a string of not-so-complimentary Greek terms for Sabrina.

Ryan extended an arm toward the front door and followed Sabrina inside.

Whatever she was here for, it was better that he just let her get it out, so she could be on her merry way.

They sat down in the living room, a formal space she was well aware that his family rarely used. An indication that he didn't expect her visit to last long. And that he didn't consider her visit to be a friendly one.

"The place looks great." Sabrina glanced around.

He crossed his ankle over his knee and waited a beat before responding. "I don't mean to be rude, Brie, but we both know you're not the kind of person who'd drop by unannounced without a specific purpose in mind. I'm pressed for time today. So, it'd be great if we could just skip to the part where you ask whatever it is you came to ask."

"You know me well. Probably better than anyone."

Sabrina moved from the sofa where she was seated to the opposite end of the sofa where he was situated.

Ryan watched her movement with the same suspicion with which he'd regard a rattlesnake sidling up to him. Turning slightly in his seat, so that he was facing her, he pressed a finger to his temple and waited.

He knew from experience that his silence would drive Sabrina nuts. She'd spill her guts just to fill the empty void.

"I have a little confession to make. I visited my friend in Dallas because she emailed that article about you."

He'd nearly forgotten about that article on the bachelor's auction featuring him and Tess. Helene had picked up a few copies for his parents, but he hadn't gotten around to reading the piece. Between issues on the ranch and everything that had been going on with Tess, the article hadn't seemed important.

"And that prompted you to come to Royal because…?"

Sabrina stood, walking over to the fireplace, her back to him for a moment. She turned to face him again.

"It made me think about you. About us. I know we didn't always get along, but when we did, things were really great between us. I miss that." She tucked her blond hair behind her ears as she stepped closer. "I miss you. And I wondered if maybe you missed me, too."

Ryan sighed heavily. Today obviously wasn't his day. The woman he wanted insisted they should just be friends, and the woman he didn't want had traveled halfway across the country hoping to pick up where they'd left off.

He couldn't catch a break.

Ryan leaned forward, both feet firmly on the floor. "Sabrina, we've been through all this. You and I, we're just too different."

"You know what they say." She forced a smile after her initial frown in response to his rejection. "Opposites attract."

"True." He had been intrigued by their differences and because she'd been such a challenge. It had made the chase more exciting. "But in our case, it wasn't enough to maintain a relationship that made either of us happy. In fact, in the end, we were both miserable. Why would you want to go back to that?"

"I'm a different person now. More mature." She joined him on the sofa. "It seems you are, too. The time we've spent away from each other has made me realize what we threw away."

"Sabrina, you're a beautiful woman and there are many things about you that I admire." Ryan sighed. "But you just can't force a square peg into a round hole. This ranch is my life. Always has been, always will be. That hasn't changed. And I doubt that you've suddenly acquired a taste for country living."

"They do build ranches outside of Texas, you know." She flashed her million-dollar smile. "Like in Upstate New York."

"This ranch has been in my family for generations. I have no interest in leaving it behind and starting over in Upstate New York." He inhaled deeply, released his breath slowly, then turned to face her. "And I'm certainly not looking to get involved."

"With me, you mean." Sabrina pushed to her feet and crossed her arms, the phony smile gone. She peered up at him angrily. "You sure seemed eager to 'get in-volved' with your precious Tess. You went all out for her."

"It was a charity thing. Something we did on behalf of the Texas Cattleman's Club."

"And I suppose you two are still *just* friends?" The question was accusatory, but she didn't pause long enough for him to respond either way. "Suddenly you're a romantic who rents her fantasy car, knows exactly which flowers she likes, and which wine she drinks?" She laughed bitterly. "I always suspected you two were an item. She's the real reason our relation-ship died. Not because we're so different or that we want different things."

"Wait. What do you mean Tess is the reason we broke up?"

Sabrina flopped down on the sofa and sighed, shak-ing her head. "It became painfully obvious that I was the third wheel in the relationship. That I'd never mean as much to you as she does. I deserve better."

Ryan frowned, thinking of his time with Sabrina. Especially the year they'd lived together in Royal be-fore their planned wedding.

He hadn't considered how his relationship with Tessa might have contributed to Sabrina's feelings of isolation. At the time, he'd thought her jealousy of Tess was unwarranted. There certainly hadn't been any-thing going on between him and Tess back then. Still, in retrospect, he realized the validity of her feelings.

He sat beside Sabrina again. "Maybe I did allow my relationship with Tess to overshadow ours in some ways. For that, I'm sorry. But regardless of the reason for our breakup, the bottom line is, we're just not right for each other. In my book, finding that out before we got married is a good thing."

"What if I don't believe it. What if I believe…" She inhaled deeply, her stormy blue eyes rimmed with tears. "What if I think it was the biggest mistake I ever made, walking away from us?"

"We never could have made each other happy, Brie." He placed his hand over hers and squeezed it. "You would've been miserable living in Royal, even if we had been a perfect match. And God knows I'd be miserable anywhere else. Because this is where my family and friends are. Where my future lies."

"Your future with Tessa?" She pulled her hand from beneath his and used the back of her wrist to wipe away tears.

"My future with Tessa is the same now as it was back then." Regardless of what he wanted. "We're friends."

Sabrina's bitter laugh had turned caustic. She stalked across the floor again. "The sad thing is, I think you two actually believe that."

"What do you mean?"

"You've been in love with each other for as long as I've known you. From what I can tell, probably since the day you two met in diapers. What I don't understand is why, for the love of God, you two don't just admit it. If not to everyone else, at least to yourselves. Then maybe you'd stop hurting those of us insane enough to think we could ever be enough for either of you."

Ryan sat back against the sofa and dragged a hand across his forehead. He'd tried to curtail his feelings for Tess because of his promise to Tripp and because he hadn't wanted to ruin their friendship. But what lay at the root of his denial was his fear that he couldn't be the man Tess deserved. A man as strong as he was loving and unafraid to show his affection for the people he loved.

A man like her father.

In his family, affection was closely aligned with weakness and neediness. In hers, it was just the opposite. With their opposing philosophies on the matter, it was amazing that their parents had managed to become such good friends.

He'd been afraid that he could never measure up to her father and be the man she deserved. But what he hadn't realized was the time he'd spent with Tessa and her family had taught him little by little how to let go of his family's hang-ups and love a woman like Tess.

Sabrina was right. He *was* in love with Tess. Always had been. And he loved her as much more than just a friend. Tessa Noble was the one woman he couldn't imagine not having in his life. And now, he truly understood the depth of his feelings. He needed her to be his friend, his lover, his confidante. He wanted to make love to her every night and wake up to her gorgeous face every morning.

He'd asked Tess to give their relationship a chance, but he hadn't been honest with her or himself about *why* he wanted a relationship with her.

He loved and needed her. Without her in his life, he felt incomplete.

"It wasn't intentional, but I was unfair to you, Sabrina. Our relationship was doomed from the start, because I do love Tess that way. I'm sorry you've come all this way for nothing, but I need to thank you, too.

For helping me to realize what I guess I've known on some level all along. That I love Tess, and I want to be with her."

"As long as one of us is happy, right?" Her bangs fluttered when she blew out an exasperated breath.

Ryan stood, offering her an apologetic smile. "C'mon, it's getting late. I'll walk you to your car."

Ryan gave Sabrina a final hug, grateful to her. He'd ask Tess again to give them a chance.

This time, he wouldn't screw it up.

Chapter 19

Tessa had been going crazy, pacing in that big old house all alone. She hadn't been able to stop thinking about Ryan. Not just what had happened in the stables, but she'd replayed everything he'd said to her.

She hadn't been fair to him, and she needed to apologize for her part in this whole mess. But first, she thought it best to let him cool off.

Tessa got into her truck and drove into town to have breakfast at the Royal Diner. It was a popular spot in town, so at least she wouldn't be alone.

She ordered coffee and a short stack of pancakes, intending to eat at the counter of the retro diner owned by Sheriff Battle's wife, Amanda. The quaint establishment was frozen in the 1950s with its red, faux-leather booths and black-and-white checkerboard flooring. But Amanda made sure that every surface in the space was gleaming.

"Tessa?"

She turned on her stool toward the booth where someone had called her name.

It was the makeup artist from PURE. Milan Valez.

"Milan. Hey, it's good to see you. How are you this morning?"

"Great. I always pass by this place. Today, I thought I'd stop in and give it a try." Milan's dark eyes shone, and her pecan brown skin was flawless at barely eight in the morning. "I just ordered breakfast. Why don't you join me?"

Tessa let the waitress know she'd be moving, then she slid across from Milan in the corner booth where the woman sat, sipping a glass of orange juice.

When the waitress brought Milan's plate, she indicated that she'd be paying for Tess's meal, too.

"That's kind of you, really, but you're the one who is new in town. I should be treating you," Tess objected.

"I insist." Milan waved a hand. "It's the least I can do after you've brought me so much business. I'm booked up for weeks, thanks to you and that article on the frenzy you caused at the charity auction. Good for you." Milan pointed a finger at her. "I told you that you were a beautiful woman."

"I'm glad everything worked out for at least one of us." Tess muttered the words under her breath, but they were loud enough for the other woman to hear.

"Speaking of which, how is it that you ended up going on this ultra-romantic weekend with your best friend?" Milan tilted her head and assessed Tessa. "And if you two are really 'just friends'—" she used air quotes "—why is it that you look like you are nursing a broken heart?"

Tessa's cheeks burned, and she stammered a bit before taking a long sip of her coffee.

"Don't worry, hon. I don't know enough folks in town to be part of the gossip chain." Milan smiled warmly. "But I've been doing this long enough to recognize a woman having some serious man troubles."

Tessa didn't bother denying it. She took another gulp of her coffee and set her cup on the table. She shook her head and sighed. "I really screwed up."

"By thinking you and your best friend could go on a romantic weekend and still remain just friends?" Milan asked before taking another sip of her orange juice.

"How did you—"

"I told you, been doing this a long time. Makeup artists are like bartenders or hairdressers. Folks sit there in that chair and use it as a confessional." Milan set her glass on the table and smiled. "Besides, I saw those pictures in the paper. That giddy look on your face? That's the look of a woman in love, if ever I've seen it."

"That obvious, huh?"

"Word around town is there's a pool on when you two finally get a clue." Milan laughed.

Tessa buried her face in her hands and moaned. "It's all my fault. He was being a perfect gentleman. I kissed him and then things kind of took off from there."

"And how do you feel about the shift in your relationship with…?"

"Ryan," Tess supplied. She thanked the waitress for her pancakes, poured a generous amount of maple syrup on the stack and cut into them. "I'm not quite sure how to feel about it."

"I'm pretty sure you are." Milan's voice was firm, but kind. "But whatever you're feeling right now, it scares the hell out of you. That's not necessarily a bad thing."

Milan was two for two.

"It's just that we've been best friends for so long. Now everything has changed, and yeah, it is scary. Part of me wants to explore what this could be. Another part of me is terrified of what will happen if everything falls apart. Besides, I'm worried that…" Tessa let the words die on her lips, taking a bite of her pancakes.

"You're worried that…what?" One of Milan's perfectly arched brows lifted.

"That he'll get bored with a Plain Jane like me. That eventually he'll want someone prettier or more glamorous than I could ever be." She shrugged.

"First, glammed up or not, you're nobody's Plain Jane," Milan said pointedly, then offered Tess a warm smile. "Second, that look of love that I saw…it wasn't just in your eyes. It was there in his, too."

Tessa paused momentarily, contemplating Milan's observation. She was a makeup artist, not a mind reader, for goodness' sake. So it was best not to put too much stock in the woman's words. Still, it made her hopeful. Besides, there was so much more to the friendship she and Rye had built over the years.

They'd supported one another. Confided in each other. Been there for each other through the best and worst of times. She recalled Ryan's words when he'd stormed out of the stables the previous night.

They *were* good together. Compatible in all the ways that mattered. And she couldn't imagine her life without him.

"Only you can determine whether it's worth the risk to lean into your feelings for your friend, or if you're better off running as fast as you can in the opposite direction." Milan's words broke into her thoughts. The woman took a bite of her scrambled eggs. "What's your gut telling you?"

"To go for the safest option. But that's always been my approach to my love life, which is why I haven't had much of one." Tessa chewed another bite of her pancakes. "In a perfect world, sure I'd take a chance. See where this relationship might lead. But—"

"There's no such thing as a perfect world, darlin'." A smile lit Milan's eyes. "As my mama always said, nothing ventured, nothing gained. You can either allow fear to prevent you from going for what you really want, or you can grow a set of lady *cojones*, throw caution to the wind, and confess your feelings to your friend. You might discover that he feels the same way about you. Maybe he's afraid of risking his heart, too."

Milan pointed her fork at Tessa. "The question you have to ask yourself is—is what you two could have together worth risking any embarrassment or hurt feelings?"

"Yes." The word burst from her lips without a second of thought. Still, its implication left her stunned, her hands shaking.

A wide smile lit the other woman's face. "Then why are you still sitting here with me? Girl, you need to go and get your man, before someone else does. Someone who isn't afraid."

Tess grabbed two pieces of bacon and climbed to her feet, adrenaline pumping through her veins. "I'm sorry, Milan. Rain check?"

"You know where to find me." She nodded toward the door. "Now go, before you lose your nerve."

Tessa gave the woman an awkward hug, then she hurried out of the diner, determined to tell Ryan the truth.

She was in love with him.

Ryan was evidently even angrier with Tessa than she'd thought. She'd called him repeatedly with no answer. She'd even gone over to the Bateman Ranch, but Helene said he'd left first thing in the morning and she didn't expect him until evening. Then she mentioned that his ex, Sabrina, had been at the house the day before.

Tess's heart sank. Had her rejection driven Ryan back into the arms of his ex?

She asked Helene to give her a call the second Ryan's truck pulled into the driveway, and she begged her not to let Ryan know.

The woman smiled and promised she would, giving Tess a huge hug before she left.

Tessa tried to go about her day as normally as possible. She started by calling Bo and Clem and apologizing for any misunderstanding. Both men were disappointed, but gracious about it.

When Tripp arrived back home from the airport, he brought her up to speed on the potential client. He'd landed the account. She hugged her brother and congratulated him, standing with him when he video conferenced their parents and told them the good news.

Tripp wanted to celebrate, but she wasn't in the mood to go out, and he couldn't get a hold of Ryan, either. So he called up Lana, since it was her day off.

Tessa had done every ranch chore she could think of

to keep her mind preoccupied, until finally Roy Jensen ran her off, tired of her being underfoot.

When Roy and the other stragglers had gone, she was left with nothing but her thoughts about what she'd say to Ryan once she saw him.

Finally, when she'd stepped out of the shower, Helene called, whispering into the phone that Ryan had just pulled into the drive of the Bateman Ranch.

Tessa hung up the phone, dug out her makeup bag and got ready for the scariest moment of her life.

Ryan hopped out of the shower, threw on a clean shirt and a pair of jeans. He picked up the gray box and stuck it in his pocket, not caring that his hair was still wet. He needed to see Tess.

He hurried downstairs. The entire first floor of the ranch smelled like the brisket Helene had been slow-cooking all day. But as tempted as he was by Helene's heavenly cooking, his stomach wasn't his priority. It would have to wait a bit longer.

"I was beginning to think you'd dozed off up there. And this brisket smells so good. It took every ounce of my willpower not to nab a piece." Tessa stood in the kitchen wearing a burgundy, cowl-neck sweater dress that hit her mid-thigh. "I mean, it would be pretty rude to start eating your dinner before you've had any."

"Tessa." He'd been desperate to see her, but now that she was here, standing in front of him, his pulse raced and his heart hammered against his ribs. "What are you doing here?"

She frowned, wringing her hands before forcing a smile. "I really needed to talk to you. Helene let me in before she left. Please don't be mad at her."

"No, of course I'm not mad at Helene."

"But you are still angry with me?" She stepped closer, peering up at him intensely.

"I'm not angry with you, Tess. I…" He sighed, running a hand through his wet hair.

He'd planned a perfect evening for them. Had gone over the words he wanted to say again and again. But seeing her now, none of that mattered. "But I do need to talk to you. And, despite the grand plans that I'd made, I just need to get this out."

"What is it, Rye?" Tessa worried her lower lip with her teeth. "What is it you need to tell me?" When he didn't answer right away, she added, "I know Sabrina was here yesterday. Did you two…are you back together?"

"Sabrina and me? God, no. What happened with us was for the best. She may not see it now, but one day she will."

Tessa heaved a sigh of relief. "Okay, so what do you need to tell me?"

Ryan reached for her hand and led her to the sofa in the family room just off the kitchen. Seated beside her, he turned his body toward hers and swallowed the huge lump in his throat.

"Tess, you've been my best friend since we were both knee-high to a grasshopper. The best moments of my life always involve you. You're always there with that big, bright smile and those warm, brown eyes, making me believe I can do anything. That I deserve everything. And I'm grateful that you've been my best friend all these years."

Tess cradled his cheek with her free hand. The corners of her eyes were wet with tears. She nodded. "Me, too. You've always been there for me, Ryan. I guess we've both been pretty lucky, huh?"

"We have been. But I've also been pretty foolish. Selfish even. Because I wanted you all to myself. Was jealous of any man who dared infringe on your time, or God forbid, command your attention. But I was afraid to step up and be the man you deserved."

"*Was* afraid?'" Now the tears flowed down her face more rapidly. She wiped them away with the hand that had cradled his face a moment ago. "As in past tense?"

"*Am* terrified would be more accurate." He forced a smile as he gently wiped the tears from her cheek with his thumb. "But just brave enough to tell you that I love you, Tessa Noble, and not just as a friend. I love you with all my heart. You're everything to me, and I couldn't imagine my life without you."

"I love you, too, Rye." Tessa beamed. "I mean, I'm in love with you. I have been for so long, I'm not really even sure when it shifted from you being my best friend to you being the guy I was head over heels in love with."

"Tess." He kissed her, then pulled her into his arms. "You have no idea how happy I am right now."

Relief flooded his chest and his heart felt full, as if it might burst. He loved this woman, who also happened to be his best friend. He loved her more than anything in the world. And he wanted to be with her.

Always.

For the first time in his life, the thought of spending the rest of his days with the same woman didn't give him a moment's pause. Because Tessa Noble had laid claim to his heart long ago. She was the one woman whose absence from his life would make him feel incomplete. Like a man functioning with only half of his heart.

"Tessa, would you…" He froze for a moment. His tongue sticking to the roof of his mouth. Not because he was afraid. Nor was he having second thoughts. There were a few things he needed to do first.

"What is it, Ryan?" She looked up at him, her warm, brown eyes full of love and light. The same eyes he'd been enamored with for as long as he could remember.

"I'd planned to take you out to dinner. Maybe catch a movie. But since Helene has already made such an amazing meal…"

"It'd be a shame to waste it." A wicked smile lit her beautiful face. "So why don't we eat dinner here, and then afterward…" She kissed him, her delicate hands framing his face. "Let's just say that dinner isn't the only thing I'm hungry for."

"That makes two of us." He pulled her into the kitchen and made them plates of Helene's delicious meal before they ended up naked and starving.

After their quick meal, Ryan swept Tessa into his arms and kissed her. Then he took her up to his bedroom where he made love to his best friend.

This time there was no uncertainty. No hesitation. No regrets. His heart and his body belonged to Tessa Noble. Now and always.

Ryan woke at nearly two in the morning and patted the space beside him. The space where Tess had lain, her bottom cuddled against his length. Her spot was still warm.

He raised up on his elbows and looked around. She

was in the corner of the room, wiggling back into her dress.

"Hey, beautiful." He scrubbed the sleep from his eye. "Where are you going?"

"Sorry, I didn't mean to wake you." She turned a lamp on beside the chair.

"You're leaving?" He sat up fully, drawing his knees up and resting his arms on them when she nodded in response. "Why?"

"Because until we talk to our families about this, I thought it best we be discreet."

"But it's not like you haven't spent the night here before," he groused, already missing the warmth of her soft body cuddled against his. It was something he'd missed every night since their return from Dallas.

"I know, but things are different now. I'm not just sleeping in the guest room." She gave him a knowing look.

"You've slept in here before, too."

"When we fell asleep binge-watching all the Marvel movies. And we both fell asleep fully dressed." She slipped on one of her boots and zipped it. "Not when I can't stop smiling because we had the most amazing night together. Tripp would see through that in two seconds."

He was as elated by her statement as he was disappointed by her leaving. What she was saying made sense. Of course, it did. But he wanted her in his bed, in his life. Full stop.

Tessa deserved better than the two of them sneaking around. Besides, with that came the implication that the two of them were doing something wrong. They weren't. And he honestly couldn't wait to tell everyone in town just how much he loved Tessa Noble.

"I'll miss you, too, babe." She sat on the edge of the bed beside him and planted a soft kiss on his lips.

Perhaps she'd only intended for the kiss to placate him. But he'd slipped his hands beneath her skirt and glided them up to the scrap of fabric covering her sex.

She murmured her objection, but Ryan had swallowed it with his hungry kiss. Lips searching and tongues clashing. His needy groans countered her small whimpers of pleasure.

"Rye... I really need to go." Tess pulled away momentarily.

He resumed their kiss as he led her hand to his growing length.

"Guess it would be a shame to waste something that impressive." A wicked smile flashed across Tess's beautiful face. She encircled his warm flesh in her soft hand as she glided it up and down his straining shaft. "Maybe I could stay a little longer. Just let me turn off the light."

"No," he whispered against the soft, sweet lips he found irresistible. "Leave it on. I want to see you. All of you."

He pulled the dress over her head and tossed it aside. Then he showed Tess just how much he appreciated her staying a little while longer.

Chapter 20

Ryan waved Tripp to the booth he'd secured at the back of the Daily Grind.

Tripp was an uncomplicated guy who always ordered the same thing. At the Royal Diner, a stack of pancakes, two eggs over easy, crispy bacon and black coffee. Here at the Daily Grind, a bear claw that rivaled the size of one's head and a cup of black coffee, two sugars.

Ryan had placed their order as soon as he'd arrived, wanting to get right down to their conversation.

His friend slid into the booth and looked at the plate on the table and his cup of coffee. "You already ordered for me?"

"Don't worry. It's still hot. I picked up our order two minutes ago."

Tripp sipped his coffee. "Why do I have the feeling that I'm about to get some really bad news?"

"Depends on your point of view, I guess." Ryan shoved the still warm cinnamon bun aside, his hands pressed to the table.

"It must be really bad. Did something happen to our parents on the cruise?"

"It's nothing like that." Ryan swallowed hard, tapping the table lightly. He looked up squarely at his friend. "I just… I need to tell you that I broke my promise to you…about Tess." Ryan sat back in the booth. "Tripp, I love her. I think I always have."

"I see." Tripp's gaze hardened. "Since you're coming to me with this, it's probably safe to assume you're already sleeping with my little sister."

Ryan didn't respond either way. He owed Tripp this, but the details of their relationship, that was between him and Tess. They didn't owe anyone else an explanation.

"Of course." Tripp nodded, his fists clenched on the table in front of him. "That damn auction. The gift that keeps on giving."

Ryan half expected his friend to try to slug him, as he had when they were teenagers and the kids at school had started a rumor that Ryan was Tess's boyfriend. It was the last time the two of them had an honest-to-goodness fight.

That was when Tripp had made him promise he'd never lay a hand on Tess.

"Look, Tripp, I know you didn't think I was good enough for your sister. Deep down, I think I believed that, too. But more than anything I was afraid to ruin my friendship with her or you. You and Tess…you're more than just friends to me. You're family."

"If you were so worried about wrecking our friendships, what's changed? Why are you suddenly willing to risk it?" Tripp folded his arms as he leaned on the table.

"I've changed. Or at least, my perspective has. I can't imagine watching your sister live a life with someone else. Marrying some other guy and raising their children. Wishing they were ours." Ryan shook his head. "That's a regret I can't take to my grave. And if it turns out I'm wrong, I honestly believe my friendship with you and Tess is strong enough to recover. But the thing is… I don't think I am wrong about us. I love her, Tripp, and I'm gonna ask her to marry me. But I wanted to come to you first and explain why I could no longer keep my promise."

"You're planning to propose? Already? God, what the hell happened with you guys in Dallas?" Tripp shut his eyes and shook his head. "Never mind. On second thought, don't *ever* tell me what happened in Dallas."

"Now that's a promise I'm pretty sure I can keep." Ryan chuckled.

"I guess it could be worse. She could be marrying some dude I hate instead of one of my best friends."

It was as close to a blessing as he was likely to get from Tripp. He'd gladly take it.

"Thanks, man. That means a lot. I promise, I won't let you or Tess down."

"You'd better not." Tripp picked up his bear claw and took a huge bite.

It was another promise he had every intention of keeping.

Ryan, Tessa, Tripp and both sets of their parents, had dinner at the Glass House restaurant at the exclu-

sive five-star Bellamy resort to celebrate their parents'
return and Tripp landing the Noble Spur's biggest cus-
tomer account to date.

The restaurant was decked out in festive holiday
decor. Two beautiful Douglas firs. Twinkling lights
everywhere. Red velvet bows and poinsettias. Then
there were gifts wrapped in shiny red, green, gold and
silver foil wrapping paper.

Tessa couldn't be happier. She was surrounded by
the people who meant the most to her. And both her
parents and Ryan's had been thrilled that she and Ryan
had finally acknowledged what both their mothers
claimed to have known all along. That she and Ryan
were hopelessly in love.

Ryan had surprised her with an early Christmas
gift—the Maybach saddle she'd mused about on their
drive to Dallas.

Even Tripp was impressed.

The food at the Glass House was amazing, as always. And a live act, consisting of a vocalist and an
acoustic guitar player, set the mood by serenading the
patrons with soft ballads.

When they started to play Christina Perri's "A
Thousand Years," Ryan asked her to dance. Next, the
duo performed Train's song, "Marry Me."

"I love that song. It's so perfect." Tessa swayed happily to the music as the vocalist sang the romantic lyrics.

"It is." He grinned. "And so are you. I'm so lucky
that the woman I love is also my best friend. You, Tess,
are the best Christmas gift I could ever hope for."

"That's so sweet of you to say, babe." Her cheeks

flushed and her eyes shone with tears. She smiled. "Who says you're not romantic?"

"You make me want to be. Because you deserve it all. Romance, passion, friendship. A home of our own, marriage, kids. You deserve all of that and more. And I want to be the man who gives that to you."

Tessa blinked back tears. "Ryan, it sounds a lot like you're asking me to marry you."

"Guess that means I ain't doing it quite right." Ryan winked and pulled a gray velvet box from his pocket. He opened it and Tessa gasped, covering her mouth with both hands as he got down on one knee and took her left hand in his.

"Tessa Marie Noble, you're my best friend, my lover, my confidante. You've always been there for me, Tess. And I always want to be there for you, making an incredible life together right here in the town we both love. Would you please do me the great honor of being my wife?"

"Yes." Tessa nodded, tears rolling down her cheeks. "Nothing would make me happier than marrying my best friend."

Ryan slipped on the ring and kissed her hand.

He'd known the moment he'd seen the ring that it was the one for Tess. As unique and beautiful as the woman he loved. A chocolate diamond solitaire set in a strawberry gold band of intertwined ribbons sprinkled with vanilla and chocolate diamonds.

Tessa extended her hand and studied the ring, a wide grin spreading across her gorgeous face. "It's my Neapolitan engagement ring!"

"Anything for you, babe." Ryan took her in his arms

and kissed her with their families and fellow diners cheering them on.

But for a few moments, everyone else disappeared, and there was only Tessa Noble. The woman who meant everything to him, and always would.

* * * * *

**IF YOU ENJOYED THIS BOOK
WE THINK YOU WILL ALSO LOVE**

◆ HARLEQUIN
DESIRE

*Luxury, scandal, desire—welcome to
the lives of the American elite.*

Be transported to the worlds of oil barons, family dynasties,
moguls and celebrities. Get ready for juicy plot twists,
delicious sensuality and intriguing scandal.

6 NEW BOOKS AVAILABLE EVERY MONTH!

"I'm grateful you're considering my offer," Riley said. "But could we accelerate the timeline? I was hoping we could elope to Vegas maybe. And soon."

"I appreciate your dilemma," Travis said coolly. "But surely you can appreciate mine. I'm not spending a year of my life tied to someone I can't stand being in the same room with. So before I'll agree to this little deal, I need to know that we're compatible enough to make a long-term *nonsexual* relationship work." He stressed the word and her heart deflated a little.

Was he not attracted to her? Riley was sure she'd seen him checking her out on more than one occasion. At Henri's. At the lake. And just now, she was sure that there'd been heat in his dark eyes as they'd taken her in. She'd offered a bona fide consummated marriage.

So why was he insistent that sex was off the table?

"Just take a breath and—"

Travis was midsentence when Riley stepped forward, clutched the soft fabric of his button-down shirt and lifted onto her toes. She pressed her mouth to his and he stiffened.

She cradled his whiskered chin, kissing him again. And again.

After the third kiss, Travis's arms slipped around her waist. He backed her against the wall and tilted his head, his lips gliding over hers. Travis angled her head, deepening their kiss as his warm tongue slipped between her lips.

Riley sighed softly, her eyes closed as her fingertips drifted to his back. "Ahem."

They were both startled as they turned toward the petite woman who stood there smiling.

"Sorry to interrupt your…reunion," Giada said. "But your father needs to eat, and we wouldn't think of starting without you."

"Of course. We're sorry." Riley's face flamed with heat as she stepped away from Travis and straightened her shirt.

Giada looked at Travis, then circled her mouth, indicating the colored gloss all over his.

He nodded his thanks, then stepped inside the bathroom.

"See you two in a sec. Then after dinner…have at it." Giada grinned before heading back up the hall.

Riley sighed, her heart still racing from the kiss that had set her entire body on fire and left her wanting much more from the man she'd asked to be her fake husband.

Travis washed and dried his hands before stepping into the hall and looking around.

"Giada went back to the dining room," Riley assured him as she leaned against the wall.

The sensation of how it had felt to be pinned between Travis's hard body and the wall sent a fresh wave of electricity up her spine.

"Looks like the plan is in motion." Travis ran a hand over his head.

"Excellent. I'll have my lawyer draw up the agreement and get it to your lawyer by the end of next week."

"Fine." Travis nodded stiffly, then held out his open palm to her. "Showtime?"

"Showtime." Riley slipped her hand in his and they walked into dining room, greeted by wide, knowing grins from Jameson and Giada.

Let the games begin.

Don't miss what happens next in…
Just a Little Married
by Reese Ryan,
the final book in the Moonlight Ridge series!

Available October 2021 wherever
Harlequin Desire books and ebooks are sold.

Harlequin.com

HDEXP73519

Love Harlequin romance?

DISCOVER.

Be the first to find out about promotions, news and exclusive content!

f Facebook.com/HarlequinBooks

y Twitter.com/HarlequinBooks

⊙ Instagram.com/HarlequinBooks

℗ Pinterest.com/HarlequinBooks

You Tube YouTube.com/HarlequinBooks

ReaderService.com

EXPLORE.

Sign up for the Harlequin e-newsletter and download a free book from any series at
TryHarlequin.com

CONNECT.

Join our Harlequin community to share your thoughts and connect with other romance readers!
Facebook.com/groups/HarlequinConnection